I0658805

Pharma Con

Peg Herring

Pharma Con © Peg Herring, 2019

Pharma Con is a work of fiction. The names, characters, and incidents are entirely the work of the author's imagination. Any resemblance to actual persons, living or dead, or events, is entirely coincidental.

All rights reserved. No part of this publication may be copied, transmitted, or recorded by any means whatsoever, including printing, photocopying, file transfer, or any form of data storage, mechanical or electronic, without the express written consent of the publisher. In addition, no part of this publication may be lent, re-sold, hired, or otherwise circulated or distributed, in any form whatsoever, without the express written consent of the publisher.

Editor: Elliott Bay Editing
Copy Editor: R. Hodges

Printed in the USA

Chapter One

Eddie Rice left his office heading west, toward his favorite restaurant. Thinking of lunch and not much else, he rounded a corner and spotted something lying on the sidewalk.

A wallet.

Slowing his pace, Rice glanced around. No one seemed to be paying attention to him or the invitingly fat billfold. Casually he stepped forward and kicked it against the side of a building. Taking out his phone, he pretended to answer a call as he covered the prize with one foot. Talking animatedly to no one, he waited for the sidewalk to clear.

A blow to his back sent Rice staggering, and his Italian leather shoe slipped off the wallet. When he regained his balance, he saw a young Asian man in khakis and a shirt embroidered with the logo of a floral delivery service. Irrelevantly, Rice wondered if the boss knew his employee had added a lime-green scarf to the uniform, turning it into a fashion statement.

The young man bent and scooped up the wallet.

"Hey!" Rice kept his voice low. "That's not yours."

"It's not yours either. I saw it from across the street."

"I'm an attorney, friend. You have no legal right to take it."

The guy chuckled. "You can have the wallet. I will take the cash inside."

Rice tried once more. "I got here first."

A shrug. "And I have it in my hot little hands. Possession is nine-tenths of the law, yes?"

Rice told himself he should just walk away. The wallet might be empty, and he shouldn't engage some jerk over a possible nothing. Still, he'd been first to touch it. He deserved what some poor slob had lost.

"I saw it before you did," the flower delivery guy repeated.

"Are you saying you get whatever's in there because your eye happened to fall on it before mine did? That's bull."

"Listen, bro." The younger man glanced around at the people passing, most intent on their cell phones or the music flowing from their ear buds. "This should not become a group project." He opened the wallet to let Rice see inside. It was stuffed with hundred-dollar bills.

Mirroring the man's concern, Rice surveyed the passers-by with a quick glance. If a third party butted in, he might insist on a share or demand they turn the wallet in to the authorities. Rice sensed his rival agreed with him that neither of those things should happen. "Fifty-fifty?"

"My van's over there." He pointed. "We can split the cash in private."

Rice felt a little spring in his step as he followed the guy to a gray vehicle with a large magnetic sign emblazoned with flowers on the slider. He was about to pick up an easy five hundred, maybe more, for doing nothing more strenuous than walking down the street. His companion went to the back of the vehicle. "Front's kind of messy, but there's lots of space here."

Rice's happy mood evaporated when he saw the van's cargo area. There were no flowers inside, not even leftover petals sprinkled across the black carpet. Instead there was darkness, foam padding, and mesh-covered, blacked-out windows.

Before he could back away, the man pushed him inside. He landed on a rubbery surface, and someone punched him hard in the gut before rolling him forward. As Rice struggled to get air into his lungs, someone slid the phone from his jacket pocket. The van rocked as the second person jumped out. The door closed with a slam. In seconds both doors up front closed, and a deep voice yelled, "Go, Clarabell!"

He hollered and pounded, but the padded walls made his efforts useless. There was no handle on the door's interior side. The van was a sound-proofed, escape-proof box, and the box was heading somewhere unknown. Rice was thrown to one side as they took a corner, then rolled to the center again as their path straightened out. There was a stop, then another, probably for red lights. After that they accelerated to what he judged was freeway speed.

He'd been kidnapped. The question was why. Fighting his fears, Rice ran through the list of possibilities. It couldn't be a dissatisfied client. Eddie was too smart to have any of those.

Sometime later, maybe ten minutes, maybe a half hour, the van slowed, turned, and stopped. The doors opened, at first to blackness. Then several bright lights clicked on, momentarily blinding him. Squinting, Rice saw two masked figures, one tall and the other very tall. They were dressed in unrelieved black, including gloves and masks.

"Get out," a robotic voice ordered. He obeyed, stepping into the glow of six cheap trouble lights clipped to metal uprights. Aluminum reflectors focused them on a lawn chair a few feet away. Heavy orange cords snaked to a power strip on a concrete floor. Beyond them he could see nothing, but echoes indicated a small space made of sheet metal. A pole building maybe.

"Sit there."

The mechanical voice was creepy, and Rice suppressed a shiver. "Listen. I'm a reasonable guy, so whatever you're after—"

"Mr. Rice," the smaller figure interrupted, "we'll tell you what kind of guy you are."

That made him blink. "What?"

"You're going to admit to your crimes. Then you're going to start making up for them."

"What?" He puffed himself up like an angry cat. Outraged innocence was often an effective ploy.

His posturing accomplished nothing. "Let's start with your most recent betrayal of client trust, Mary Ann Swenson. Husband is a millionaire who cheated on her for over a decade while she served as his caterer, event planner, bookkeeper, and unofficial secretary. In the divorce she got thirty thousand a year for a period of five years, which you told her was fair." Despite the voice filter, the speaker's sarcasm came through. "One would hope Mr. Swenson will provide her with job references for her years of unpaid service, but that's doubtful, since he's already planning to marry a woman half Mary Ann's age." Before Rice could respond the voice added, "Soon after the divorce decree, one of your bank accounts showed a deposit of $50,000, which we traced back to Mr. Swenson."

Rice found his voice. "I did work for his firm on a different—"

"You charged a woman thousands of dollars," the voice interrupted, "then helped her husband cheat her out of a secure future." Again Rice opened his mouth to argue, but the speaker went on. "Shirley Kenworth, mother of three. Her husband hid most of his assets by transferring them to a friend in England. You told her there was no way to prove it, which was a lie."

Before Rice could frame an argument, the speaker went on to another story. The litany of his crimes was surprisingly complete. Each time a woman accepted a weak settlement, Eddie Rice's bank account had received a fat fee from the man who'd sat on the other side of the courtroom. One or two such cases might be ascribed to bad luck or poor timing, but the sheer numbers were damning.

When the speaker finished, Rice said in a sulky tone, "So now I'm supposed to pay you off or something?"

"You'll pay. But you'll also admit to collusion on video."

"I'm an attorney. I know better than to do something that dumb."

"The recording will remain private, as long as you behave yourself."

Rice tried a different tack. "So I don't always win big. Sue me."

"We don't sue anyone, Mr. Rice. We work outside the system that men like you subvert for their own profit. If you don't do as we demand, tomorrow morning we'll purchase a full-page ad in the *Journal* that lists dates and amounts paid to you by your clients' ex-husbands. When your former clients see the pattern that's gone on for years, they'll be lining up to get at you."

"You can't sue a lawyer just because he doesn't get the ruling you want."

"True. But there will be an investigation, and your good old boy network will dissolve as other law firms wash their hands of you to protect themselves. You'll probably be disbarred, and you'll do prison time if some eager assistant DA gets her teeth into you."

Rice's tone turned whiny. "Why do you people want to ruin me?"

"You're a type of vermin we work to eliminate." Now the voice revealed pride. "We're pretty good at it."

His pout was worthy of a three-year-old. "So what do I have to do?"

"You admit on the record that you colluded to defraud your clients. You'll be assessed a fine we believe is fair, and you'll make restitution to your current clients. Once that's done, you can either agree to deal honestly in the future, or you can retire from the practice of law."

He considered that. "I can keep working?"

"We will monitor your behavior. If at any point we feel you're backsliding, everything becomes public, including the recording."

"A confession made under duress—"

"Isn't admissible in court. If the public knows what you are, that will be good enough for us."

Rice sighed. "If I agree?"

"You get to go on with your life."

"With you looking over my shoulder all the time."

"Think of us as guardian angels," the voice said. "Only we don't protect you; we protect others *from* you."

An hour later, Eddie Rice was deposited on the sidewalk almost exactly where he'd been abducted. He was a little sweaty and disheveled. He was a good deal poorer. And he found he no longer had any desire whatsoever for Asian food.

Chapter Two

When Robin came downstairs, Em was already at the breakfast table, her cane leaned against the table and a cup of coffee before her despite the warmth of the August morning. "How'd the caper go?"

"Good." Robin took a glass from the cupboard, closing the door twice to make it stay. "Everything's okay here?"

Em grinned, and her grumpy old person look turned to smart-aleck octogenarian. "You mean is the freezer still gasping along and did the latest plumbing disaster get resolved? Yes. Our wreck still stands."

A partially-renovated mansion outside Kansas City, Kansas, served as headquarters for KIDNAP, housing five kidnappers and two orphans who considered themselves kidnappers-in-training. All of them acknowledged that work on the place would never be finished in the sense of "everything works and looks good." The residents felt lucky when *almost* everything worked. Beauty, as they say, is in the eye of the beholder.

Hua stood at the gas stove, making omelets that smelled of bacon and cilantro. At his customary place at the knotty-pine table was a glass of tap water, and he took a sip as he set a plate with three fluffy, eggy semicircles on the table center. After pouring herself a glass of orange juice, Robin took the chair that was considered hers, reflecting briefly on how seating quickly became proscribed in group situations. "Her" chair was at the head of the table, with Em on her right.

Having heard the clank of pipes, Robin knew Cam was showering and would soon take his place at her left. Next to Cam's seat was Hua's, and across from him they'd added two mismatched chairs for Kai and Mai. That left Tom Wyman, the newest team member, to fill the chair at the far end of the table. Though it was unplanned, the arrangement unsettled Robin somewhat: she and Tom seated like Mom and Dad in old movies, with the family between them.

Tasting the eggs, Robin gave a little hum of pleasure. "These are wonderful, Hua." He waved in thanks but didn't turn away from the pan as he assembled more helpings. Robin reached for a slice of toast, and the second-hand table teetered a little. Taking her ever-present notebook from her shorts pocket she turned to her to-do list and added *Ask Cam— fix uneven leg*. The entry seemed incongruous below the other items: *Send $$ to ?? charity* and *Remind Hua—Erase evidence Omaha*. Tasks relating to KIDNAP ranged from mundane to technical to death-defying.

Tom came in the back door, his t-shirt damp from a morning run. Before she, Hua, and Cam left for Omaha, Tom had gone to Chicago to be fitted for a prosthesis for his missing left arm, but there was no sign of it this morning. Wiping his forehead with a paper towel, Tom sat, picked up the serving plate, and slid two omelets onto his own. "Looks good, Hua. What time did you guys get in?"

"Around two," Hua replied without turning from his task at the stove. "It went very well, I think."

Robin had to agree, mostly because she'd experienced lighter than usual post-kidnap turbulence. That didn't mean she considered the Rice Caper a total success. All night she'd gone over the rights and wrongs of their demands. Had they gone too far? Far enough? Would Rice go right back to his old tricks, still cheating clients but going about it more carefully?

It's happened before. How hard should we push these people?

Self-doubt being Robin's usual state, no one at the breakfast table commented on her droopy eyes and pillow-squashed hair.

The twins entered the kitchen, eyes downcast in the polite way of Asian youth, and murmured a general greeting. Kai took two glasses from the cupboard, filled them with juice, and handed one to Mai as they took their places. Soon Cam lumbered in, his dark hair wet from the shower and smelling of the ginger shampoo he used these days because Hua said it had an "extremely nice aroma." Going to the fridge, he took out a Pepsi, popped the lid with a hiss, and drank half the contents in one swallow.

Tom surveyed the group. "Now that we're all here, let's hear about Omaha."

Hua brought the last of the omelets, slid one onto his plate, and passed the rest to the twins. Cam started the story, his face lit with enthusiasm. "We did the oldest trick in the book. Isn't that what you said, Robin?"

She merely nodded, letting the partners tell the story between them. Cam, who was gorgeous and built like a hero from *The Iliad*, spoke haltingly due to developmental delays. Hua, half Cam's size but precise in speech, added explanations and color commentary. The way they told it, Robin's plan for kidnapping the crooked lawyer had been a stroke of genius. She didn't share with the others that she'd learned the sting from her own father: conman, megalomaniac, and abuser of women and children. *Dear Old Dad.*

"It's called the Dropped Wallet," Cam explained. "You throw a big, fat billfold on the street just before the target comes by. Our guy went after it like a duck goes after a minnow, but Hua was right there."

"I was the Finder," Hua interjected. "I offered to act as the wheel man, but Robin said it was best if she drove and I helped Cam with the…What do you call it, Ms. Em?"

"The snatch," Em said. "That was the way to go, Hua. You're quicker on your feet."

Everyone but Hua knew that the real reason Robin drove was that Hua tended to look anywhere but at the road when at the wheel. Having spent a decade as a slave, he found the outside world endlessly interesting, so he tended to gawk at cows in a field or crane his neck to watch geese fly overhead. It made riding with him nerve-wracking, sometimes terrifying. Experience was gradually making his driving less dangerous, but they still preferred that someone else drive in stressful situations.

13

Cam went on with the story. "When Rice saw those hundred-dollar bills, his eyes got big as teacups."

"How you know he would not say to take this wallet to the police?" Kai asked.

Em's laugh was more cackle than music. "He's a lawyer. That tells you what kind of person he is."

"That's not fair," Robin objected. "Mink's a lawyer, and he helps us a lot."

Butler Mink of Cedar, Georgia, advised KIDNAP on legal issues, and his objective analysis of proposed capers had several times helped them avoid capture. Mink's expertise came, he said, from years of working for clients who didn't bother to make even the flimsiest of plans before committing a crime.

Em shifted on her chair. "Mink's the exception that proves the rule."

Perhaps to change the subject Tom said, "I assume your brother suggested this guy as a target."

Robin set her fork on her empty plate and pushed it away. "Rice has teaser ads all over the internet: *Need a divorce? For a flat, up-front fee, Eddie takes care of everything.*"

Tom took a second piece of toast. "Some woman desperate for a new start likes the sound of that."

"Right. She pays him several thousand dollars, but. Rice goes straight to the husband's lawyer and makes a deal."

Em raised both hands, palms up. "A guttersnipe like that isn't going to turn a wallet full of cash in to the police."

Tom drank the last of his coffee, and Mai immediately jumped up to get him a refill. "Thanks, Mai," he made eye contact and smiled at the girl before turning back to Robin. "So you did your thing."

Cam was eager to tell it. "I was waiting behind the van, and when he got close, I kinda lifted him inside. He's pretty skinny, so it wasn't even very hard."

"I quickly closed the doors." Hua brought his hands together like a pair of doors slamming. "We were on our way without anyone on the street noticing."

"To a storage unit outside town, no doubt, rented by Robin in her Blond Bimbo outfit." Tom hadn't seen Robin in that particular disguise, but he seemed to like the idea of it.

Robin blushed. "We got Rice to admit to collusion, though he insisted he only does it to ease animosity between the two parties." Her expression said what she thought of that argument.

"And you made him pay, I assume?"

Hua answered, "I've confirmed just under $10,000 from each of his five bank accounts."

"All a person can transfer without the bank alerting the authorities." Tom stirred sugar into his coffee.

"In addition the women Rice currently represents—not that the word actually applies—will receive a 50 percent 'refund' due to a 'clerical error.' And there won't be any deals with their husbands' lawyers." Robin shrugged. "It won't fix everything he did, but it's something."

"Sounds like you guys made the world a better place one more time."

"Rice didn't think so." Cam finished his Pepsi. "I thought lawyers had big vocabularies, but he just kept saying one really bad word, over and over."

"Still, he will be required to treat future clients more fairly," Hua said. "This is very good."

Robin glanced at her to-do list. "What about giving half of what we charged Rice to a women's shelter?"

"Sounds fair to me," Em said. Everyone else nodded, even Mai, who understood none of what had been said. Down syndrome combined with poor English meant Mai smiled a lot, cleaned a lot, and followed her sister's lead in everything.

Kai had an opinion. "This is good, what you did, but I think maybe you should also cut a part off this man."

"Cut a part off?" Robin was confused.

"Nothing he need much—one finger, maybe, or a toe." Kai's smile was as sweet as her suggestion was shocking. "That way he will remember much better to be nice."

When the others went off to their tasks, Tom and Robin took their drinks and went outside to the reclaimed patio. It was Kai and Mai's turn to clean the kitchen, and Kai cast a resentful glance at their backs as she cleared the table. She didn't like that her hero chose to spend time alone with Robin, and like most fifteen year olds, she didn't bother to hide it.

Robin and Tom settled in two Adirondack chairs Hua had found, battered and listing, at a secondhand shop. Between Cam's carpentry skills and Hua's application of paint, the chairs were reborn, now stable and decorated with fanciful flowers. The porch, also repaired by Cam but not yet repainted, overlooked the heavily wooded area behind the house. Busy in their pursuit of their own breakfasts, squirrels and chipmunks paid them little heed, and birds Robin had no names for darted among the leaves above. On their left was the garden Hua and Cam tended lovingly, now with help from Kai and Mai. The quiet settled on Robin's shoulders, banishing the remaining tension from the caper. She'd never dreamed she'd like country living until she moved to this place and felt the peace it bestowed, peace that required nothing of her.

"What'd you bring home from Chicago?" she asked Tom.

"They gave me two prostheses," he replied. "There's a hook the doc said is practical for actually getting work done, and there's what they call a 'social' hand that's more aesthetically pleasing." He grinned. "Makes me look less like a pirate."

"I don't mind having a pirate around. I hear they're fearless and romantic."

Tom paused for a second, as if considering a comment on that, but in the end he said only, "They claim within a year they'll be able to implant sensors that allow me to actually feel the prosthesis."

"You're kidding."

He shrugged. "I'm not. Maybe the doctors are."

"I didn't mean kidding-kidding. I meant that's pretty amazing."

"It could be." Tom's gray eyes, which she'd once thought cold and frightening, turned on her, and she decided gray was in fact a comforting color. "I'm glad the caper went well. Wish I'd been there to help."

"Another time," she promised. "It's getting harder for Em to participate with her hip as bad as it is. Kai has done everything she knows to ease her pain, but—"

"The best thing for an eighty-plus-year-old retired FBI agent is to guard the home front."

Robin laughed. "Don't try to tell Em that. She still wants to be right in the middle."

"So do I," he said. "I get crazy when you're in danger and I'm not there."

She looked down at her hands. "You already saved my life once, Tom."

"You saved mine too, so we're even." Draining the last of his coffee, he set the cup on the floor beside him. "I intend to be part of the Sane Clown Posse again soon. I've even chosen a nickname." During capers they never used their real names. Cam was Bozo; Em was Loonette; Hua went by Bubbles; and Robin was Clarabell. "I want to be Homey." Tom looked at her to see if she got the reference.

"Damon Wayans, right? 'Homey don't play that?'"

"That's the one."

Robin finished her juice, picked up Tom's empty cup, and stood. "You watch way too much vintage television, Wyman, but I think Clarabell and Homey will make a good team."

Finished with their chore, Kai and Mai came outside. Mai went on to the garden, but Kai stopped. "Tom, can you get me a gun like yours?"

Robin was shocked by the question, but Tom answered calmly. "Why do you need a gun, Kai?"

"Is bad people in the world. I could shoot them."

Tom nodded. "Maybe, but it would take a lot of work. You don't want to be a "Yipee-ki-yay Jerk."

Kai frowned. "What is this?"

"There's nothing wrong with having a gun for protection," Tom said, "but like any skill, handling a firearm requires practice. People who just buy a gun and put it in a drawer are less safe than they were before, because they have a false sense of confidence."

"False—"

"They think they can do things they really can't," Robin translated.

"Right." Tom leaned toward Kai, resting his elbow on his knee. "A lot of people buy a gun, visit the shooting range two, three times tops, and then walk around thinking they're safe. Actually they're less safe than a person with no gun, because any bad guy worth his salt can take their gun and use it against them."

"Why is there salt? I want a gun, not spices."

Tom sniffed. "Tell you what. We'll set up some practice sessions, and I'll show you how it's done right. Maybe in a year or so you'll be ready to have your own gun, okay?"

"Hokay." The idea of practice with Tom seemed to please her as much as the promise of her own gun.

When she was gone Robin asked, "Do you think she should have a weapon? She's pretty young."

"Age has nothing to do with it if you've got good training," he replied. A moment later he added grimly, "If you'd been through what Kai has, you'd want a gun too."

Chapter Three

Robin examined the apples in the local market, choosing Red Delicious for Hua, Fujis for Em, McIntosh for herself, and Jonathans for Cam. Mai and Kai preferred plums, and Tom had asked for some kind of melon.

That was just the fruit segment of their diet. The household's meat-eating habits ran the gamut from almost none (Mai and Kai) to fish dishes (Hua's favorite) to beef and lots of it (Em and Cam). Desserts were equally varied, with some favoring a light ending to the meal (Hua again, though he had a fondness for sherbet) and others craving all the richness they could get (Cam's body seemed to run best on fat and sugar). Robin claimed it felt like she shopped for the cast of *The Lord of the Rings*.

"Robin? Robin Parsons, is that you?"

The voice set off all her alarms. Someone knew her real name and had said it out loud. Others nearby might wonder why the woman the town knew as Lynn Taylor was being hailed by a name they'd never heard before. The locals were naturally curious about the couple that had bought the old mansion outside of town for an artists' colony. Lynn Taylor was married to Richard (Cam), whose mother Dee (Em) lived with them. Chan (Hua) was their cook, though Cam joked they should have made it Hop Sing. They hadn't gotten around to explaining Mai and Kai but planned to introduce them as refugees the Taylor family had taken in. The town would have been shocked to know the girls were actually victims of a human trafficking ring, but then, the town would have been shocked by a lot that went on at KIDNAP.

Turning, Robin saw a movie-star-handsome man with a grin that revealed white, even teeth. After a beat her dazed mind supplied a name: Devin Ashford, attorney at law from Cedar, Georgia. He'd done business with the firm Robin Parsons once worked for. He and Robin had dated. That term was imprecise, she realized. Devin was someone she'd imagined herself marrying at one point in time.

Fifteen minutes later, Robin was seated opposite Devin at a small restaurant. She explained that she went by her middle name, Lynn, these days and avoided mentioning a last name at all. "I never liked being a bird," she said lightly. "The move to a new place was the perfect time to change it."

"Lynn," Devin said slowly, as if trying it out. "I'll have to get used to it, but it suits you."

He looked good, not that Devin hadn't always looked good. She remembered her bosses grousing about it, saying he won cases because he was so easy on the eyes. That wasn't fair. The one time she sat in on one of Devin's trials, she'd been impressed with his preparation, his confident speech, and his ability to zero in on a point and make it seem the only possible way to look at things.

She'd been surprised when he asked her out. Devin Ashford, Esquire, seemed like a glittering prince who should hardly have noticed the little drone who ushered him in when business called him to the Green Law Firm. But he'd suggested coffee after work, then a night at the movies, and it had gone on from there. For several months they'd spent most of their free time together.

Robin recalled scouring thrift shops to find clothes that suited the places Devin took her: the opera, her first-ever experience; a swanky party at a mansion centered on enough real estate to support a good-sized zoo; and restaurants she'd only heard about before meeting him, the kind with no prices on the menu, where the sommelier sensed through ESP that she didn't know Cristal from Barefoot Bubbly.

Devin had been great, smiling at her wonder as he showed her his world. After a while she suspected he planned to propose, and she had asked herself more than once what her response would be if he did.

Then one day he'd called to say he was moving to Argentina. "It's an opportunity I can't pass up."

Stunned by the abrupt announcement, she stammered, "I'll miss you." Lame, but she'd been unable to decide how she felt. What would she miss? Glamorous evenings in his company? The knowledge that other women were jealous when Devin stood beside her? If she was honest, Robin didn't know if she was sad about losing the man himself or the lifestyle he'd swept her into.

Shortly after Devin left Georgia, Robin's mom had been killed in an auto accident. Life took more downward turns as she dealt with her mother's substantial debts. With financial worries and the shock of that sudden emotional loss, Robin had no time to moon over a romance that might have been. Nowadays when she remembered times with Devin, she couldn't recall a single conversation of substance. They'd always been going, glowing, and showing themselves to others. There'd been no time to decide exactly what they meant to each other.

Devin's thoughts seemed to travel along the same lines. "I always felt like we'd have been good together if things had gone differently."

"We had fun," she said, unwilling to admit how much it had stung when he left her behind so casually.

"I thought about you a lot, but when I returned to Cedar, no one seemed to know where you'd gone."

She shrugged. "The Greens laid me off, so I decided to make a fresh start." Unwilling to be questioned about what the fresh start entailed, she asked, "What brings you here?"

"My grandparents. They raised me after my parents died, and this is where they live"—he paused—"lived. Gramps died, and Gram agreed, after much persuasion on my part, to move into a nursing facility. I couldn't stand the thought of her alone out there on the farm."

Robin was searching her memory. "I thought you came from Oregon."

He smiled, apparently pleased that she remembered. "That was my aunt's place. I lived with her for a while, but she had three other kids, and"—he raised his hands in a gesture that indicated saying more was unnecessary—"I came here when I was fourteen. Well, not here exactly. The farm's just over the county line." He gestured westward. "I came

22

home for the funeral and soon realized Gram couldn't stay on her own that far out of town." He grimaced. "I want to be sure she's okay."

"There's no one local left?"

He drummed his fingers on the table. "Just me."

"Well, it's great that you're here to help her."

"I wish I could get her to stop worrying about my future." With a rueful grin he went on, "Gram thinks I need a wife to look after me."

"You seem pretty grown up to me: winning cases, rubbing elbows with the rich and famous, brushing your own teeth…"

He chuckled. "Thanks for the vote of confidence, but that's not how Gram looks at things. She fusses all the time about my lack of a 'life partner.' I can tell it bothers her."

"That's too bad."

They sipped their drinks, and then Devin said, "You might be able to help."

"How?"

He seemed embarrassed. "Well, last night I was thinking if I could get a woman to go to the nursing home with me, I could introduce her as my fiancée. It would put Gram's mind at ease, and she'd never know it wasn't real." His head drooped a little. "They figure she won't last long without Gramps."

Robin looked at him in astonishment. "You want me to lie to your grandmother."

Devin spoke quickly. "You wouldn't have to lie. Just smile and let me say what it takes to quiet her mind."

"I don't know, Devin—"

He leaned toward her earnestly. "It won't take more than half an hour. You and I show up at the nursing home, I introduce you, and we visit for ten, fifteen minutes." He smiled. "She'll probably grill you about your 'people' and your skills as a housewife. 'Can you bake a cherry pie?' That sort of thing. She'll be shocked, but I'll say I'm head over heels in love and don't care if you buy pre-made pie crusts."

"Devin, that's weird."

He seemed about to argue but stopped himself, looking down at the table. "You're right. Like they say, 'Not your circus; not your monkey.'"

"I didn't mean that. It's just…"

What was it? It wasn't lying she objected to. She lied every day of her life. She answered to false names. She called her childhood friend Shelly every weekend and made up events and people from her supposedly hum-drum life. If she could lie to everyone else, why couldn't she help an old friend make his grandmother less anxious about her boy's future?

***

Tom opened the back door as Robin approached with an assortment of tote bags. Stepping through, she set her burdens on the table with a soft grunt. Though shaded by trees and built of cooling brick, the house had warmed as summer progressed, and the air felt thick, like she had to push her way through it. She'd never before lived in a place that didn't have A/C, and she wished she didn't have to now, but there was no budget for central air in a house that sprawled east and west like a train station. They kept running into issues like replacing the water pump or fixing a subfloor with rot in one corner.

"Are there more groceries in the car?"

"Lots. We were practically down to tea and crackers."

As they made more trips, he asked, "Anything good in town?" Tom wore the hook he'd been given, and he hung the straps of three bags on it, balancing them on the other side with two bags of canned goods.

"Not much." Robin felt her face warm as she omitted mention of meeting Devin. Tom was more than a friend but less than a lover, and she found herself reluctant to admit that a man from her past, a man who *had* been her lover, had resurfaced. *A man I thought for a while might be the love of my life.*

Glancing at Tom, she felt her blush deepen. She was attracted to him, and Tom admitted he was drawn to her. A licensed private detective, army veteran, and shrewd observer, he'd been hired by their first target, Barney Abrams, to track her down. Instead of reporting her location to his client, Tom had joined KIDNAP. He fit into the group well. Robin just wasn't sure how he fit into her life.

Though still adjusting to the physical and emotional results of his experience with war, Tom was funny, brave, and intelligent. Em treated him like a favored son; Cam and Hua willingly accepted his advice and his presence. Mai and Kai waited on him as if he were the household prince, adding creative touches to his room and fixing his plate each evening at supper though he was perfectly capable of doing it himself. Tom always thanked whichever sister served him with solemn sincerity and ate every morsel.

She and Tom had become close, but they avoided certain topics. No one but her brother knew how hard Robin's childhood had been. They'd made their way together through their father's Jekyll and Hyde personality shifts and his insistence they participate in his cheap confidence games. Robin didn't talk about it with anyone but Chris, and he seldom brought the subject up.

At the same time, Robin sensed gaps in Tom's narrative about his time in the service. Though he spoke easily of people he'd liked, places he'd found interesting, and things he'd learned about other cultures, he never spoke of bombs or bullets, never acknowledged the trauma of war.

What she might dream of for herself wasn't necessarily what the gang needed. If she and Tom let their feelings grow deeper, the group's dynamic would almost certainly change. How would the others react? In six months or a year, if things didn't work out between them, what then?

Would Tom have to leave? Would everything the group had worked for fall apart?

She left the decision on the back burner, which was sometimes cool and sometimes hot. That's how burners are.

"I've got to go back into town tomorrow," she said, keeping her face turned away as she pulled out a green tote that said *I Would Prefer Not To. Bartleby.* "There are a few more things I need to get."

"I could ride along with you." Tom was supposedly a painter in residence at the colony, which he thought was hilarious. "Hope nobody asks me to demonstrate my skills," he'd told them. "I can't even draw water."

Robin bit her lip before answering. "I'm going to be gone a while, I think."

"Why's that?" The question was entirely innocent, and she felt another blush warm her face. Despite the fact that she'd chosen the life of a criminal, Robin found it difficult to tell a direct lie. She could play a part. She could wear a disguise. She could put on a ski mask and make a cheating businessman or civil servant believe she knew everything there was to know about his dirty deeds. But face to face she exhibited obvious symptoms: a blush, a stammer, and an inability to meet the questioner's eyes. Em had once scoffed, "Girl, you might as well scream 'Don't believe a word I say.'"

To avoid looking at Tom, she stacked a half-dozen cereal boxes in the cupboard in descending height, fidgeting until they were exactly straight. "I have an appointment for Bennett to get a haircut."

"Oh."

Now that she'd made the excuse, she'd have to actually take the dog to the groomer. It wasn't a big deal. She could drop Bennett off, go with Devin to see his grandmother, and pick up the dog in an hour.

Pharma Con

The big deal, she realized, wasn't the timing. It was lying to Tom Wyman.

Chapter Four

When Robin arrived at Graystreet Manor Nursing Home, Devin was leaning against the building wall in a flower-and-flag-stone alcove next to the front door. The light summer suit he wore was sharp and fashionable, and his streaky-blond hair ruffled lightly in the breeze. He looked like an actor on a movie set.

Coming forward to meet her, he pressed a light kiss on her cheek. "I can't decide if this is the craziest thing I've ever done or the smartest."

Robin chuckled. "I know what you mean."

He set his shoulders as if heading to battle. "We're here. Let's go find out."

A sign next to the entry said: *Press Red Button Before Opening.* Following the instruction, Devin opened the door and let Robin enter first. In a small lobby tastefully decorated in pastels, an old man in a wheelchair listed to one side like a boat with a hole in it, his face slack. Robin considered helping him sit upright, but Devin walked past, heading into a central court where a large counter circled a staff area. Inside it several workers in scrubs of varying colors and prints entered data on charts, spoke into telephones, or conferred with each other. Outside the circle were several more wheelchairs, each occupied by an elderly person with a blank expression. A janitor mopped the space, bypassing the chairs with practiced ease. When a woman in mismatched clothing entered from a hallway and stopped in confusion, a staffer asked, "Dinah, where are you going?" The woman wouldn't or couldn't answer, and the staffer took her gently by the arm, leading her back the way she'd come.

"This one." Devin turned down a hallway that ran like a spoke off the central hub. As they passed room after room, Robin felt like an interloper spying into the personal lives of the residents. If they made eye contact, should she wave? Say hello? It seemed best to pretend she didn't see them.

"She's in here." A card in a slot beside the door said *Minnie Walter*.

"That's your grandmother—Minnie?"

"Yeah." He hesitated outside the door, and Robin wondered if he was having second thoughts. An aide came out of the room, a wad of dirty clothes in a plastic bag. "How's she doing today?" Devin asked.

"She's in and out." The woman headed down the hallway, leaving the room to them. Devin took Robin's hand, as if he feared she might not follow without a physical connection.

Minnie's last earthly home was the size of Robin's pantry, divided neatly in half by a light blue stripe up one wall and across the floor. Each side held a bed, a night stand, and a rolling tray. In the center of the blank wall was a sink, and beside it a bathroom. In the first bed a white-haired woman watched a TV game show, the volume turned ear-damaging levels. She didn't look away from it as they passed. In the other bed a woman lay motionless, eyes closed. Devin crossed to her and kissed her forehead. "Gram?"

She opened her eyes and smiled, but Robin saw no recognition on her face. He took her hand. "It's me, Devin."

"Devin?"

"That's right." He glanced back at Robin, eyes full of frustration. "I brought someone to meet you." He gestured and she took a step forward. "This is Robin. We're going to be married soon."

"Robin?"

"It's nice to meet you, Mrs. Walter."

Watery eyes shifted from Devin to her. "You're going to marry him?"

Robin hesitated over the lie, though she told herself it was silly. The woman wanted to believe her grandson was on the road to happiness, a common enough wish for people getting ready to leave the world behind. Still, she found it hard to say the words.

Sensing her hesitation, Devin stepped in. "Next month, Gram." Robin threw him a surprised glance. Their romance apparently wasn't

29

dragging its feet. "You need to get stronger so you can be there for our big day, okay?"

"I love weddings," Mrs. Walter said in a dreamy voice. "All brides are beautiful, just like they say."

"Mine certainly is," Devin said. "Don't you think so?"

The old woman smiled, revealing toothless gums. "I love weddings. All brides are beautiful."

As they left the facility, Devin greeted the staff members they met with "Hey, there" or "How are you doing today?" Each one smiled or said something polite in return. A few of the women eyed Devin with obvious interest, which had happened a lot when they'd dated. He was definitely in the eye-candy category of maleness. Outside he took a deep breath, as if relieved. Robin noticed the air seemed fresher now than when she'd gone in, the sunlight more energizing. "That place is...okay, but I wouldn't want to live there."

"I know." He sounded sad. "But there's no way she can stay on the farm without Gramps. I thought about taking her to Georgia, but except for me she wouldn't know a soul there. Here she has friends and people from church who'll visit." He grimaced. "If she remembers who they are."

"You've done the best you can for her."

"I should buy you lunch," he said brightly, and Robin guessed he wanted to banish the topic of his grandmother's future. "It's the least I can do."

Though she knew she shouldn't, it felt good to be with a man who knew her as Robin, not some made up woman with a secret agenda. "I'd like that."

She drove her van, following Devin's rental car to a nearby café, where she chose a table in front of a sunny window, letting its brightness banish the last of the shadows from the nursing home.

Pulling plastic-coated menus from behind the condiment rack Devin said, "I hear in these places you should order whatever's splattered on the front."

"Darn! Mine's clean, so I'll just have the special."

It was a Reuben with fries. They both chose it then settled into a companionable silence. The waitress brought their drinks, a Coke for him and water for her. After she moved away Devin asked, "What brought you to this little burg, Robin—I mean, Lynn? Please don't tell me you relocated for love."

Though she and Cam presented themselves as a couple, it was hard to lie to an old friend. "Not the kind of love you're talking about."

"Good," he said. "Maybe when I come back to visit Gram, we can see each other again."

That couldn't happen, but she guessed once Devin was back in Georgia, he'd forget Lynn as easily as he'd forgotten Robin.

The waitress arrived to set plates before them, which gave her a moment to shift gears. Taking a fry, she dipped it in ketchup. "Looks good."

Devin's answer might have referred to lunch, might have meant something else. "It certainly does."

***

Robin arrived home at two with a dapper Bennett riding shotgun. Hua was painting the back porch, so they entered through the front door. As she passed Tom's room, he stood with his back to her, packing a suitcase.

"Tom?"

He turned briefly and then returned to rolling a dress shirt. "Hey."

"Going somewhere?"

He didn't answer for a while, giving the task more attention than it required. Finally he laid it in the suitcase and looked at her. "Come in, Robin."

His tone set off warning bells, and she pulled the double pocket doors of what had once been the living room closed behind her. She hadn't been in there much since Tom took the space as his own, but she saw little touches of Mai and Kai atop the slightly Spartan "Tom-ness" of the room. She doubted he'd chosen the bird theme on the curtains, pillows, and figurines set in macramé cages in a corner.

"Where are you going?"

He took in a breath and let it out. "Florida. They called to say it's time for me to testify at Luther's trial."

The case that had made Tom a part of their group—their *gang*, Em insisted—now required that he give evidence against the men who'd meant to murder him. They'd known the summons was coming but not the exact date. He'd just returned from Chicago, and Robin found herself wishing he didn't have to leave again so soon.

Tom's testimony would put the traffickers who'd brought Kai and Mai to the U.S. in prison. Butler Mink, the lawyer who advised the group, maintained plausible deniability by pretending to believe he was helping Robin plot suspense novels. Robin believed Mink knew the truth but enjoyed watching as crooks and criminals had a little meet-up with Karma in the form of the KIDNAP gang.

Mink had explained how her fictional witness could tell the truth on the stand without mentioning their group or any of its people. "In stressful situations the memory often becomes fuzzy. When your protagonist was first abducted, he was clearheaded and therefore is perfectly able to identify his captors. Later, after he was beaten, tied up, and threatened with death, it's understandable he can't remember details of his escape."

Tom's posture indicated there was more on his mind than the upcoming trial, and Robin asked, "What's wrong?"

He shrugged, attempting a casual dismissal of the question that didn't quite come off. "I took Em's car into town today. She wanted some yarn."

Dread dropped on her shoulders like a damp towel. "What did you see?"

He tried for a smile. "Well, I saw you kissing a guy, for one thing."

Devin's parting kiss had been more serious than the peck on the cheek he'd given her earlier. He'd apologized afterward, saying he didn't want to press her. Why did Tom have to be around to see that?

"I ran into an old friend," she said.

He apparently had to think about his response. "You don't owe me an explanation."

"But we're all dependent on each other, aren't we? I depend on you not to do things that might get us arrested. You have to depend on me to do the same."

"I know you wouldn't jeopardize—"

"I didn't," she interrupted. "I met Devin by accident, and he asked me to help with something, and then suddenly we were—" She shook her head. "It wasn't how it must have looked."

Tom stepped toward her. "Robin, I'm not accusing you of anything, and I'm not judging you either."

She wrapped her arms around herself, possibly to keep from reaching out to Tom. "Who'd have thought I'd run into an old boyfriend in Lawton?"

"How serious were things between you?"

That was a question she'd been struggling with. "I don't know. We were doing well, I thought, and then he called and said he was leaving the country."

"Just like that?"

"Pretty much."

"But now he's back."

"Not really. I mean he didn't come here looking for me." She grimaced ruefully. "If he hadn't wanted a fresh peach to take to Graystreet Manor, we'd have missed each other entirely."

Tom glanced at the half-full suitcase. "I hate having to leave."

"It's only for a couple of weeks, right?"

"That's what they said. But your brother has a new caper, and"—he fumbled for a word—"with things cropping up from your past, it's bad timing."

"I won't be seeing Devin again." She made her tone definite. "He asked me to meet his grandmother, and I did it. It's over."

Despite his obvious concern, Tom's lips curled with humor. "It didn't look to me like that was all he wanted, but hey, you know the guy better than I do."

Chapter Five

After a day's rest, the group met to choose their next target from among a list of criminals Robin's brother Chris generated, people the law either couldn't catch or wasn't aware of. As in the case of crooked attorney Eddie Rice, their goal would be to force their target to rethink past actions, atone for mistakes, and agree to behave better in the future.

As the others came in and arranged chairs around Hua's large computer monitor, Robin thought to herself that KIDNAP was ninety-eight percent hard work and two percent pure terror. Under the law they were kidnappers, and one might add assault, unlawful detainment, and extortion, just for starters. That was why she stressed over every detail of a caper. No matter what anyone said, she would feel responsible if one or all of them were caught.

Their cases usually came from the work of her brother Chris, who'd lost both legs to an IED he encountered in Afghanistan. Chris had begun a blog about justice, mostly as therapy. With painstaking care he exposed corruption wherever he found it, but to his great disappointment, most Americans couldn't separate his well-researched truths from the cacophony of untruths shouted at them all day, every day. When Robin started her vigilante method of reforming criminals, Chris had at first objected, citing dangers from both their targets and the legal system. Convinced that Robin was determined to continue, he began using the network he'd built to help Robin's group choose targets for their version of rehabilitation.

Diligent research went into every caper. In the weeks before suggesting action, Chris dug up every bit of information he could find about a potential target. First he determined that the person was dishonest enough to deserve what Em referred to as "our friendly little wake-up call." Then he presented the group with the evidence, "enough to convince but not to convict," as he put it. Hua, whose computer skills were almost innate, had set up a website, *KIDNAP.org*, where they could share information, ideas, and warnings when necessary. Em had objected to the name, "You're telling people what we do!"

Hua had raised a finger like a wise elder. "We are hiding in plain sight, Miss Em. Who would expect us to announce our intentions so boldly?" The key to secrecy, Hua said, was never actually launching the website. Each of them had administrator status and could access it, but others who typed in the URL got a message saying the site was "under construction."

The candidate Chris presented that morning was Neil Preston, head of a large pharmaceutical company. Robin had skimmed the material already, and a familiar surge of righteous anger told her Preston was a great choice for their next target. Chris presented the case against Preston, summarizing written information for Kai, who was just starting to learn to read English.

"I got onto Preston and his company when a guy I met at the VA told me he'd been taking a medicine called Merililla for a blood condition. It was in clinical trials at first, and it worked really well for him. Then Preston's company bought the patent from the original owner and raised the price sky high. The vet's insurance company balked at paying for it, so now he's taking a drug that isn't nearly as effective and has significant side effects."

"That's not right," Cam said.

Chris shoved his glasses back into place with a finger. "True, but Preston has the money to get what he wants."

"Who is this guy anyway?" Cam asked. "I never heard of him."

Robin smiled to herself. Cam's only interest in the news was when there was an announcement of a new video game.

"Although he isn't a chemist, Preston made a small fortune with a single successful patent he registered while still in college. Since then his firm, Argent Chemical, has used deception and bribery to get rights to products developed by independent scientists and small biotech firms."

"How do they do that?"

36

"A lot of biotech firms are small, and they operate on a shoestring. Preston looks for one that's found a breakthrough, say a dementia drug or a spray that destroys a MRSA bacterium. He contacts the firm and makes them an offer. For people who are barely paying the bills, it's dazzling."

"So he takes advantage of someone else's idea." Em had pulled her current project from her knitting bag and resumed work on a sweater for Mai, who was always cold. "It stinks, but that's business nowadays."

Chris raised a finger. "But then he sets his lawyers to work, chiseling away at the deal. They claim the scientist misrepresented the product. They refuse to pay further installments. They nickel and dime until the small firm gets half of what they agreed to, maybe less."

"Do they take him to court?"

"Most can't afford to. And Argent has lots of lawyers to cloud the issues."

"With this hip of mine aching like it does today, I'd like to string up every greedy drug company honcho who interferes with decent medical practice," Em said. "But this guy doesn't sound any worse than the rest of the vultures."

"Corruption isn't industry-wide, as you might hear on the internet," Chris said from the monitor. "Yes, there are drug manufacturers who skirt rules and inflate prices when they can. There are also reputable firms who don't. Preston and his people actively develop ways to beat the system."

"Didn't Congress call in a bunch of drug manufacturers and question them about such practices?" Em asked.

"Their answer sounds plausible," Chris replied. "'Prices need to be high on current drugs so we can pay for the research necessary to find and manufacture new ones.' But Argent isn't exactly known for exhaustive research. They just keep buying up other promising patents."

"If the rumors Chris is picking up turn out to be true," Robin added, "they bribe legislators and inspectors to push their products through in record time."

"It sounds like Argent is as crooked as a river bed," Em said, "but it's a corporation. How can we change things with a caper aimed at one person?"

"Technically Argent is a corporation," Chris replied, "but it's styled more like a family business. Preston calls himself CEO, but there's no board that can overrule or fire him."

"I saw a little of his testimony before Congress," Em said. "He struck me as *O-D-D*, all caps."

Hua was scrolling on his tablet. "Preston will be difficult to contact. He greatly fears germs, so the few visitors he sees must practically bathe in bleach before entering." His voice took on a note of disdain as he added, "He's also a great admirer of Stalin."

"I saw that too," Chris said. "Beyond odd if you ask me."

Em's needles clicked a little faster. "I'm ready to vote. I think Preston is exactly the kind of creep we love to target."

"She's right," Cam agreed. "I say we do it."

"I would punch this man in his face," Kai said.

Behind her, Mai repeated, "In his face."

With general agreement to pursue a caper against Neil Preston, they adjourned with the understanding that each member would return the next morning with general suggestions for using their varied and unique talents. Less than two hours later, Robin's phone pulsed in her pocket, and she took it out to find a text from Chris. *Need to tlk to all.* She sent an affirmative answer while Hua once again arranged the chairs so they could all see and hear.

When he appeared on screen, Chris looked serious and shaken. "I made a mistake, guys. This target isn't for us."

"What do you mean?"

He frowned. "I—I changed my mind. I'll find someone else."

"Hey, we know this is a tough one," Robin said. "I've been reading about Preston's estate security and tech-y stuff."

"It's more than that." Chris' frown got deeper as he apparently decided he had to be honest with them. "Preston isn't just greedy. He's dangerous."

In the past Chris had been Robin's protector, often taking blows from their abusive father in her defense. It was easy for her to peg his "keep little sister out of trouble" mode. "What made you change your mind, Big Brother?"

"I started looking for people who spoke out against Argent over the last year or so. I intended to contact a few of them in hopes they'd give us more information."

"Good," Em commented. "First-hand reports are better than hearsay."

"Except they're all dead."

"Murdered?"

The room was silent for a moment. Finally Cam said, "Do you mean this guy shoots people or whatever?"

"I would guess he simply orders it done."

"Are you sure?"

Chris counted on his fingers. "A woman of thirty-five had an unexplained heart attack. A man who'd never been much of a drinker ran his car off the road, his blood alcohol level way off the charts. A chemist who commented he planned to 'make some waves' after he left Argent fell down his basement stairs and broke his neck." His mouth twisted sideways. "There wasn't much of an investigation into any one of the deaths, but I see a disturbing pattern."

"Money means more to this guy than people?" Cam shook his head in disbelief. "Jeez!"

"Some folks just love to take stuff away from others," Em said. "We have to get at them and squeeze 'em until they stop."

"Em's right. We need to make him stop," Cam said.

Chris' voice rose. "Guys, I just told you! Preston is probably killing people who get in his way."

Robin took a step toward Cam. "I agree. We need to stop him."

Chris put up both hands, palms toward them. "This isn't like your other capers. The guy defends his secrets with murder."

"What about the traffickers we stopped in Florida?" Cam asked. "That was dangerous. Robin almost got drowned and shot and—"

Robin elbowed Cam, who stopped talking. She hadn't told her brother everything about that caper, and she guessed he'd have some direct questions for her when next they met. "We get that it won't be easy, Chris."

"If it was easy, it wouldn't take a gang of super-freaks to bring him down, right?" Cam said, and Robin's gaze met Em's in appreciation for his budding sense of humor. It was middle school level, perhaps, but a joke is a joke.

Chris sighed. "Take a look at the stuff I just sent about Green Grove. Maybe that will convince you."

"What's Green Grove?"

"It's Preston's 22,000-square-foot estate outside Tulsa, which he only leaves about twice a year. Green Grove was what Stalin called his favorite dacha. It has some of the same safeguards Stalin had, like tile floors throughout so no one can sneak up on him and the best in surveillance equipment."

"Sounds like he shares Stalin's paranoia."

"It's a big part of why he hides away from the world whenever possible." He sobered. "I'll post the new information on the website. Once you read through it, I think you'll find Preston is more than we're equipped to handle."

Robin opened her mouth to argue, but Em elbowed her to silence. Taking the hint, Hua said, "We will read it very carefully and then discuss future plans. Thank you for this."

The screen went black.

"He's your big brother," Em said to Robin. "He knows he can't stop you if we decide to go ahead with this, and he doesn't want you hurt. But he's stuck in that dumb wheelchair, so he feels like he's not able to really help."

Em was good at assessing people, probably due to her years with the FBI, and Robin saw what she meant. It had to be hard for Chris to watch his little sister take on a dangerous Stalin wannabe while he watched from the sidelines. "Maybe we should let him help with this one," Em suggested.

Robin's first reaction was *No. My brother will not become a criminal.* But he already was part of the group, aware of their crimes, and abetting their efforts. "I guess we could consider it."

"We could," Em agreed. "I think Chris feels like a distant cousin. It's time he became a real member of our gang of super-freaks."

Chapter Six

Cam dumped the last of the gravel from the wheelbarrow, spread it evenly over the area, and laid the shovel in the empty bed. He'd done much of the work of relocating their driveway on his own, and the work pleased him, both as physical exercise and as something he could do to benefit everyone. The original drive was a steep drop from the road with a low point at the bottom that rain or snow melt turned into a small lake. With permission from the county road commission and help from a local contractor, Cam had fashioned a half-circle replacement that would stay drier. Getting onto the road would be safer too, though there wasn't much traffic on Bobby Lane, which dead-ended a half-mile farther down.

"Nice spot you've got here." The voice startled Cam, and he turned to see a man in a suit standing on the road, his hands shoved casually into his pants pockets. Glancing toward the turnoff from the county highway, he saw a car pulled onto the shoulder and resting aslant. A frown knit Cam's brow, and the man apparently read his question.

"I'm looking for blackberries. They said there might be some out here."

Cam almost laughed aloud, but that wouldn't have been polite. The guy was wearing a suit, thin nylon socks, and leather dress shoes. Didn't he know blackberries grow on thick, thorny bushes in out-of-the-way places? Someone in town must have pegged him for a city slicker and sent him out here as a joke.

"I don't think they're ripe yet," he said, keeping his tone polite. "Come back in a week or so."

"Okay." He didn't seem all that disappointed. "I assume your house is back there in the trees?"

They'd agreed to say as little as possible about themselves and their home when talking to strangers, so Cam replied with a nod.

The stranger waited a second, and when Cam didn't say anything, seemed embarrassed. "I wasn't trying to be nosy. I'm new around here, so I was just asking, you know?"

Pharma Con

Cam didn't like being rude when the guy was trying to be friendly, but Em said giving away information in casual conversation was bad. Balancing the politeness his upbringing called for with discretion Cam said, "What do you think of Cryptokitties' new platform using Blockchain?"

***

Hoofing it back to his car was rough on the rutty gravel road, but Devin Ashford was pleased with himself. The big man had to be the one he'd been sent to find, the guy who helped Robin strong-arm a great deal of money from his client. Barney Abrams hadn't been forthcoming about the circumstances of his abduction, but when he'd learned Devin once dated Robin, he'd hired him to locate her. Using bits and pieces picked up in their time together, Devin had done that, starting with her friend Shelly in Wisconsin and tracing Robin to this out-of-the-way place in Kansas.

Seeing Robin again had left him conflicted. In the first place, he suspected that Abrams' intentions toward Robin and her big boyfriend were not kindly. In the second place, he'd forgotten how attractive she was. She'd even improved, he thought, seeming more confident now than the girl he'd dated. Devin had forgotten how he felt when he was with her: better, brighter—cleaner. There was no gray with Robin. Things were right or they were wrong, and if things were wrong, someone had to do something.

They'd attended a party where some drama queen discovered her diamond bracelet was missing. "That guy took it!" she'd accused, pointing to one of the caterers. The young man was the only black person on the crew, and a stuttering problem made it hard for him to defend himself.

"I d-d-didn't!" he protested, but the woman was insistent.

"He bumped into me," she shrilled. "He must have slipped my bracelet off my arm when he pretended to steady me."

43

Their host sided with the guest, calling the caterer into the room and demanding the kid be searched.

To Devin's surprise, Robin stepped forward. "Before you tromp on every civil right this man has, you need to look at all the possibilities." She turned to the woman. "Where have you been in the last half hour?"

Devin recalled being embarrassed when his date started ordering everyone around, but he was also amused and a little admiring. Robin stood up for someone she'd never met before, putting herself between him and a roomful of people who assumed he was guilty because he wasn't one of them.

The incident resolved when someone came out of the bathroom with the bracelet, which the woman had slipped off while she washed her hands. Both the accuser and the host were mortified. Robin hadn't made a big deal of it, but she suggested they leave as soon as it was politely possible. In the car she fumed about people who claim they aren't bigots but blame the only minority person present when there's trouble.

She was something, that Robin. Still, Devin reminded himself, he needed money, and there weren't many ways for him to get it these days. He liked her, but Robin represented a hefty payoff for him. As he unlocked his car he thought, what could it hurt if he waited a while to share what he'd learned with his employer?

***

Skyping with the gang on Saturday, Chris provided the newest information he'd uncovered. "I did some more research, all of which tells me I was right. This one's a no-go."

Robin tried to keep the impatience from her voice. "Tell us everything, Chris. We're a team, so we'll decide together if it's beyond our abilities."

For a few seconds it looked like he'd refuse, but finally he did as she asked. "There are four people Preston deals with personally on a daily

44

basis. Anyone else employed by Argent Chemical only hears from him by email or through one of the Inner Circle."

"Stalin had his four Comrades in Arms," Em muttered, raising a skimpy eyebrow. "Maybe when evil's involved, that's the magic number for stooges."

"Like with Stalin, Preston's 'comrades' do as he says," Chris told them. "Their reward is money, which too often buys all the loyalty creeps like him need." Photos appeared as he talked. "'You might have seen Argent's attorney, Baylor Nixon, on TV, since he appeared with his client before Congress.

I convinced a former PA of Preston's, Linda Castioni, to talk to me a little. She signed a nondisclosure agreement when she went to work for Argent, and she's scared to death Preston will sue her into poverty if anyone finds out she talked about her time at Green Grove. Between my above-average store of charm"—Chris made a hair-smoothing gesture—"and a promise that what she said would never be made public, I got some pretty good dirt."

"What did you learn?"

"She refused to talk about Preston specifically, so I asked about the others on the estate. Linda liked the public relations expert, Bertrand Oliva." The image of a dark-haired man—slim, well-dressed, and smiling—showed up on the screen. "She couldn't tell me much about him, and I can't find anything on him until he came to work for Preston. Linda thought he was Puerto Rican, but since there are tons of Olivas there, that doesn't help much.

"I can see why she liked him," Em said. "The guy is definitely eye candy."

"Oliva is the public face of Argent," Chris said. "Called Bertie by those who know him well, he handles PR and marketing and speaks fluent gobbledygook. Promotional stuff from Argent always contains lots of hype but nothing you can pin a lawsuit to. Oliva's also the go-between on a lot of deals, since Preston is socially incompetent. Oliva meets with patent holders, government officers, anyone who needs to be schmoozed into cooperating."

"A snake-oil salesman," Em said impatiently. "Who's next?"

A photo of a statuesque woman with too much hair and makeup replaced Oliva's. "Joelle Preston is Neil's sister, all that's left of his family. Linda said she's often the only one who can deal with his tantrums. They're different in a lot of ways, which sometimes leads to epic battles."

"They argue?"

"Like Jersey Shore wannabes," Chris said. "Joelle flies off the handle in a crisis, just like Preston does. Linda says it even gets physical, with Joelle slapping at Preston while he ducks and dodges. Eventually she backs off, he accepts her apologies, and they go on as if nothing happened."

"These two brats run a successful company?" Robin asked.

"She stays in the background, claims her role is only as a sounding board, so her genius brother understands how the rest of us lowly beings see things."

Em made a raspberry sound. "She means 'Big brother lets me live on his fancy estate and pays my bills. In return I listen to him when nobody else will.'"

Chris introduced the last member of the household. "Security Chief Monica Covel sees that Preston is insulated from pretty much everyone. Linda told me she seldom interacted with him. Orders were sent via computer, and when she delivered paperwork or notarized documents, she was expected to be swift and silent."

"Little Neil definitely isn't a people person," Em commented.

"He's getting worse. A year ago he decided he shouldn't have to interact with the household staff. Now the yard work is rotated so he doesn't have to see workers from wherever he is, and his meals are served buffet-style."

"What if he wants more ketchup?" Em asked.

"One of the wait staff stands in the hallway, and he calls out orders. If they have to enter the room they're told to keep their eyes directed at the floor and say nothing."

Robin shuddered. "What a strange way to live!"

"Lonely," Cam added.

Chris checked his notes. "The estate is walled, and there are security cameras inside and out and alarms on every door and window. Guards armed with Tasers are on duty all the time."

"No guns?"

"Covel and Belk, the second-in-command for security, carry, but the lesser guards don't. It's apparently better for liability insurance, since armed employees have to pass all kinds of checks."

"And some of them might not pass."

"Exactly. Anyway, one man monitors the surveillance equipment from a guard shack inside the front gate. Another patrols the front half of the estate in a golf cart. At the back entrance are two more guards, one to deal with tradespeople and one to patrol. In the house are two more guards who check the place out every two hours, day and night."

"What, no Dobermans?"

"Preston is afraid of dogs," Chris replied. "In fact, he's afraid of lots of things, notably spiders and swimming pools."

"If he's a scaredy-cat, he might faint when we grab him," Cam said.

"That would be nice, but don't count on it," Chris replied. "Here's a clip of his testimony in D.C."

Video showed a nervous-looking Preston sitting beside his lawyer, Baylor Nixon, as representatives took their turns asking questions, some tough, some almost conciliatory. Robin guessed the latter were members who received large donations from pharmaceutical PACs. Though Nixon spoke for his client at first, a persistent Congresswoman demanded Preston answer for himself. After a whispered conference Preston obeyed, but it was painful to watch. Before beginning, he preened like a spoiled parakeet, patting his tie, touching his brows, and licking his lips. He repeated what his lawyer had said, using the bloated and convoluted sentences of one trying desperately to sound more intelligent than he actually was. "My scientists and myself have continuously striven—" made Robin's teeth clench, and "The efficacy of our efforts has resulted in prodigiously exponential growth in beneficent observances" made Em chuckle, though it wasn't exactly a happy sound.

"His emotional maturity seems to have stalled somewhere in middle school," she observed, and Robin tried to picture Preston at fourteen, an arrogant, misfit kid that only teachers tolerated, and then only because they were required to.

Cam peered at the screen. "He looks really nervous."

"It's a situation he can't control," Chris said. "Over time Preston has become more and more unable to deal with people he can't boss around."

"So he insulates himself from everyone but his chosen sycophants."

Chris chuckled. "There is one thing he enjoys doing face-to-face. Linda said Preston usually fires people—including her—in person."

"'Look how powerful I am!'" Robin muttered.

"If I were this woman, I would have been relieved," Hua remarked.

"Yes," Chris said. "Once we'd talked for a while and Linda felt safe with me, she commented that the atmosphere at Green Grove made her physically sick, all hushed activity interspersed with bouts of Preston screaming. When she got out of there, she says her blood pressure returned to normal levels."

"Why would anybody want to work there?" Cam asked.

"The pay is stellar," Chris replied. "Still, Linda said everyone on Preston's staff hopes the boss never notices them. It's seldom good when he does."

"No one at Green Grove is likely to help with our little enterprise," Em concluded. "Too scared."

They were silent for a few seconds, absorbing the difficulty of the task. "Maybe he'd come to a dinner honoring him for something," Cam suggested.

"He doesn't eat anything that isn't prepared by his own people," Chris said. "And he doesn't do anything he could be honored for. No endowments, no grants, no gifts. To anyone."

"If we wait for him to leave the estate we could stop his car and—"

"He travels by helicopter," Chris interrupted. "And he has no plans to go anywhere for months."

Another silence as they thought it through. "We're never going to get Preston to come out and meet us," Em finally said. "We have to offer him something he wants enough to let us in."

Robin frowned. Being on Preston's home turf would make it harder to intimidate him. Still, Em's analysis was correct. "The security person, Monica Covel. Is she good?"

"Think Rambo with a side of *Fatal Attraction*," Chris replied.

"That means she's really tough but a little crazy," Cam told Hua. One of his areas of expertise was old movies, along with vehicles, video games, and farming small tracts of land.

"Ms. Covel is ex-military," Chris said. "There's nothing wrong with her expertise in security, but she wasn't what you'd call a model soldier. She had trouble re-entering society after her tours."

Em had done her homework. "No self-discipline and mean as Dracula with a bad incisor. I often saw her type wash out at the Bureau. Good potential, but no humanity."

"When Covel first returned to civilian life, she worked for a private security contractor. Every problem she encountered got solved by punching somebody in the face, so after a while no outfit would hire her. She decided to go solo and sent Preston a resume, which he apparently liked, and now she's his chief of security. To his credit, Preston seems to have curtailed Ms. Covel's violent tendencies."

"Or channeled them," Robin said. "If he's having people killed, Covel could be the weapon."

"Arranging murders that look like accidents?" Em asked. "That's a ton of employee loyalty."

Robin stared at a photo of a hard-muscled woman whose glare seemed capable of melting flesh and bone. "If Preston's needs align with her skills, it's a match made in Hades."

"We'll have to find a way around Ms. Covel," Em said. "As Preston's guard dog, she'll stop him from going in any direction she thinks is dangerous."

Chris chewed at his mustache for a moment. "If you did that you'd be dealing with the second-in-command. That might give you a slight advantage."

"Why is that?"

"Lawrence Belk was interim head of security until Covel came along, and he hasn't got much of a following at Green Grove. Preston thinks he's wishy-washy. Belk's rude to Oliva, and he once told Baylor Nixon he's too old for the job and should retire. And the sister, Joelle, absolutely hates him."

"Because?"

"He gets in her way. Joelle is a real man-eater, and from time to time she brings a guest home for an overnight stay. Belk, who's on duty at night, has complained to Covel more than once that it's an unnecessary security risk."

"He probably isn't wrong," Em observed.

"No, but Covel and Joelle are like soul sisters or something. Covel told Belk watching Joelle's guest was his job, and he should keep his mouth shut."

"I would think she'd be concerned about the security lapse too."

"She checks the men out pretty thoroughly before allowing them in."

Em's mind had run ahead. "I'm guessing Covel mentioned Belk's complaint to Joelle."

Chris tilted his head to acknowledge her cleverness. "No matter how valid the concern was, airing it put the guy on Joelle's bad side."

Em nodded. "So if we could remove Covel somehow, we'd be dealing with a security chief nobody likes."

"Their security procedures would still be in place." Chris shook his head. "I have to say it again. This caper is risky."

Robin took up her ever-present notebook and clicked her pen a few times. "Risk is controlled with planning. Let's come back next time with ideas on how to get Ms. Covel out of the way."

The others went off, leaving Chris on the screen and Robin alone at the computer. "Rob?" When he didn't continue, she looked up from her note-taking to meet his gaze. "I want to be in on this one."

Gotta give Em credit. She reads people like nobody else I know.

"I know I can't do much," he went on, "but I'm getting pretty good with my prostheses. I could be the lookout or drive one of the vehicles. Whatever you need. I want to do my part."

"Chris, you haven't actually broken any laws yet. Are you sure you want to change that?"

He gave her a crooked grin. "And be the only non-outlaw in the family? Where's the fun in that?"

It was meant as a joke, so Robin tried to keep her answer light. "I'm the new version of Dad, our generation's liar-in-chief."

He looked at her in amazement. "Is that how you see yourself?"

Tears stung her eyes. "I don't know what I am anymore, Chris."

"Well, you're not like him. You don't hurt innocent women and children. You don't do what you do to make yourself feel powerful or clever or better than other people." He blinked as if a memory had flashed through his mind. "You would never hurt someone just because you like to see them wince."

Her lips quivered. "How long before I start enjoying this?"

"What do you mean?"

"How long before I start needing the adrenaline rush that comes from some guy's terror? Before I become blind to my victims as people?"

Chris leaned toward the screen. "What brought all this on, Sis?"

She hesitated before answering. "I ran into an old friend, an old boyfriend, actually." She brushed hair back from her forehead. "It felt good to be normal and talk and laugh about nothing, you know? But then he got in his car and left, and I was back to being Lynn Taylor, fake wife, fake artist, practiced criminal." She made a sound that was half-laugh, half-sob. "Fake criminal too, if I'm honest. If it weren't for Tom—" She stopped herself. No need for Chris to hear how close she'd come to death in Florida. Tom Wyman's intervention had saved her, but how long could she count on luck and her friends? And how long could she retain a moral edge when she broke the law every single day?

"Sis, you corner criminals and make them face their crimes. You donate half the money to charity and spend the rest supporting your little band. If you're a crook, everyone should be your kind of crook." When she remained silent he added, "And that's what I want to do. Be the kind of kidnapper my little sister is."

***

Focused on making notes for the caper, Robin jumped when her phone pulsed in her pocket. She received few incoming calls, usually only Chris and her friend Shelly, who always chose Sunday for their chats. Since the ringtone was neither Chris nor Shelly's, she ignored the noise until it stopped. A few seconds later she heard the tone that signaled the end of a voicemail. Listening, she smiled and shook her head.

"Robin, it's Devin. When you got up at the restaurant to get ketchup, I stole your number from your phone. Call me."

Hitting the *Call Back* button, she waited until he answered. "That was sneaky." She was laughing, so it didn't come off as an insult.

"Sorry. I don't mean to be a stalker type, but you were a little reticent about your new life. I didn't want to leave without a way to contact you in case...I mean, I'll probably come back to see Gram in a month or so, and if you're still around..." He left the rest unspoken.

"Okay. You have my number, and now I have yours. When you come back, we'll talk."

"That would be great."

She ended the call, telling herself it was harmless to chat with an old friend. When Devin returned to Kansas, she'd tell him she was too busy to meet. The next time she'd say the same. Eventually he'd get the idea and give up on her. Until then, it was nice to remember his gentle touch, that easy laugh, and the admiration she'd seen in his eyes.

It doesn't mean a thing. It's just nice.

Chapter Seven

Robin, Hua, and Em were deep in discussions of the Preston Caper when Chris called. "We really need to rethink this one, guys. Since yesterday I found two more people who meant to speak out against Preston but died unexpectedly before they could."

When a small sound of dismay escaped Robin, Hua and Em turned toward her. Hitting the *FaceTime* button, she set the phone in a stand so Chris could see all three of them. "Two more?"

"Two months ago, a reporter for a local TV station named Ralph Baird was investigating a government employee he thought was taking bribes. On his way to interview the man's coworker, he supposedly got lost in a dangerous area of town, was mugged, and died from a blow to the head."

"You think it was murder."

He nodded. "A while back in my blog, I mentioned Argent Chemical's sleep aid as an example of the outrageous inflation of drug prices. When Baird saw it, he told his wife he suspected the pharmaceutical company was the source of some bribes he was investigating. He hoped to be able to sell his story to a big media outlet like CNN."

"Do the police know that's what he was working on?"

"The wife doesn't think they took the idea her husband had been murdered seriously. The cop in charge said Baird was found in an area where life is cheap. He said crimes there are random and often unsolvable."

"In other words, they're not going to investigate further."

"Baird must have had notes on what he was doing," Em said.

"On his tablet, which is missing. He was a bit paranoid and wouldn't use cloud storage, but the wife says he had quite a case built against Argent. Again, the police think either the mugger or someone who happened by later took the device. They're convinced it was a 'wrong place, wrong time,' incident."

"Which led to the wife contacting you."

"She recalled the name of the drug, Somatella, because to her it sounded more like a new Disney character than a medicine. She Googled it to find the blog he'd mentioned, which is mine, and she contacted me." Chris rubbed a hand through his hair. "She is sure her husband died because he was investigating that drug's path to market."

Having worked at a legal firm, Robin knew family members sometimes blamed a "plot" for the unexpected death of a loved one. Senseless loss made people grasp at straws. Still, she trusted Chris' assessment of Ms. Baird's character, since he'd spoken with her directly. "What's the second case?"

"Two weeks ago Carmen Ostrano, a young technician at one of Preston's labs, told a friend she was being pressured to say a drug was safe when she didn't feel there was enough evidence to be sure. She ended up quitting her job, and the roommate says she told her bosses she intended to report their shoddy research methods. That night she fell from her eight-story balcony."

"I'm guessing her death was ruled an accident?"

"Friends from work had taken her out as a farewell. The theory is she came home tipsy, heard a noise on the street, and went out to see what was happening. She was wearing ridiculously high heels, and they think she might have leaned over the rail to see an accident that had taken place down the street. Between the shoes and the booze, she lost her balance and went over."

"I see one big problem with that theory. The first thing a girl does when she gets home after a day in heels is take them off. Those shoes should have been lying by the door."

"I hadn't thought of that," Chris said. "Her friends say she wasn't much of a drinker, but the friend I spoke with said the police hinted they might be covering for a pal who died due to her own carelessness."

Robin sat back from the computer screen and rubbed the back of her neck with one hand absently, her mind running through the possibilities. "That's quite a body count."

"Which is why you need to drop this." Chris rushed ahead before she could argue. "I won't stop working on it. Eventually I'll find enough evidence to make a legal case against Preston. Then we can leave it to the cops to deal with him and his band of cutthroats."

Robin shook her head, though he couldn't see it. "Chris, if he's killing people who oppose him, we have to stop him now, before someone else dies."

There was a longish pause before Chris said, "Okay," apparently conceding he wouldn't win the argument. "I found the name of someone who might be able to help us understand Preston better, and believe me, there aren't many who can say they know him. The trick will be getting this guy to tell what he knows."

"Why's that?"

"First of all, he's a busy man. Second, he's smarter than all of us put together. Finally, he's known for discretion, a real speak-no-evil type. We won't be the first to ask him about his relationship to Preston, but no one so far has gotten him to talk about it."

"Give me his name and address. We'll see what we can find out."

***

Hua settled himself in a chair opposite the office of Doctor John Rhee. Ridge University, situated outside Baltimore, Maryland, was known for hiring brilliant people like Rhee and then allowing them time to do the work their intelligence and drive compelled them to do. Students

56

participated by helping with research and testing, building the university's reputation as well as the next generation of great minds.

As far as the department secretary knew, Hua was there about a recently discovered isotope of ruthenium. Though he had no idea if that mattered to the world, he liked the sound of it.

"The professor is free now," the woman told Hua when a bespectacled student scuffed his way out the door. "You can go right in."

The office was exactly what Hua had imagined: stacks of books, piles of papers fastened with no-nonsense metal clips, a handsome desk barely visible under open texts, and a legal pad with several sheets folded over the back, the top sheet covered with notes in extremely small handwriting. The place smelled of old ink and yesterday's lunch. Hua had a moment of regret. If he hadn't been abducted and sold into slavery as a child, might he have made his way to academia, done research, and found satisfaction in the pure pursuit of knowledge?

It didn't matter. His life had gone in a different direction.

Hua put out a hand. "Doctor Rhee, it's good of you to see me on such short notice."

John Rhee, professor, researcher, and holder of several PhDs, had probably looked like he was forty when he was twenty and would still look like he was forty when he was sixty. He had a square face, glasses a decade out of fashion, straight, black hair that water-falled over his brow, and a serious expression that changed when he smiled, revealing what Hua suspected was a kind spirit.

"I have a department meeting in twenty minutes, so I haven't much time," Rhee said when he'd cleared a spot for Hua and settled in his slightly ratty office chair. "I'm sorry."

Though the appointment had been made under the pretense of journalism, Hua didn't intend to lie to Rhee himself. Without apology for the deception he said, "I cannot tell you precisely who I am or why I am here, but it is important that I know everything you can tell me about your former college roommate, Neil Preston."

Rhee frowned. "I'm not sure this is—"

Hua, who'd been assessing Rhee and his surroundings from the first moment, had already formed two conclusions. First, although Rhee had received numerous awards for his work, the office walls held only posters of scientists like Einstein, Salk, the Curies, and Neil deGrasse Tyson. He wasn't out to impress visitors with his achievements.

Hua's second conclusion was that Rhee was about to show him the door.

"I represent a group that works outside the law," he said, and Rhee's expression changed from irritation to surprise. "We stop people who use their wealth and power to hurt others and enrich themselves."

Rhee thought about that for a moment. "You're part of some sort of vigilante squad?"

Hua smiled. "I suppose we must accept that term. We do no physical harm to anyone."

"What then? Blackmail?"

"Again I dislike the term, but it is fundamentally correct."

Rhee frowned. "You act illegally to stop others from acting illegally? Not exactly admirable, young man."

"We don't disrupt a person's career for self-serving reasons. We act to protect society from rich and powerful criminals who skirt our laws and profit from the exploitation of others. We believe Mr. Preston has for some time deceived government overseers and the public about the medicines he sells."

There was an odd tone in Rhee's voice as he said, "I see."

"Recently things have gotten worse. We suspect Preston has begun murdering those who seek to uncover his crimes. In order to stop him, we need to understand how he thinks." Hua met Rhee's gaze directly. "You, sir, are one of the few people who can help us and might be willing to."

Rhee examined Hua for a long moment, pulling lightly at his bottom lip. Hua wondered if he should have left off the trailing maroon-and-gold paisley scarf. Still, it went nicely with his navy leggings.

"Murder, you said?"

"I cannot offer proof such as a court would require, but we are convinced it is true."

Rhee rubbed his jaw. "I haven't seen or spoken to Neil for decades."

"We're aware of that. We merely hoped you could give us a sense of how his mind operates."

After some seconds he said again, "Murder?"

"At least five people who stood in his way."

That brought a nod that was probably unconscious but clearly telling. Rhee knew Preston was ruthless. As the clock on the wall ticked the seconds by, Hua waited for him to decide. Would he tell what he knew? Toss Hua out of his office? Call security? Twenty seconds. Thirty. Thirty-eight.

"Neil was unlike anyone else I'd met. I wasn't his first roommate, though I lasted longer than most."

Hua kept his folded hands in his lap, though he wanted to clap for joy. "I'm listening."

"I should say, I was not your run-of-the-mill college freshman." Rhee's eyes sparked briefly with self-deprecating humor. "Sixteen years old and consumed by science, I hardly noticed those around me or what I ate or wore. I suppose since I was odd and so was Neil, someone at university housing thought we might do well together."

"What sort of roommate was he?"

"The most disagreeable sort you can imagine." Leaning back in his chair, Rhee let his mind go back. "Neil disliked human contact, and I learned early on not to touch him or any of his things. He had no friends, in the dorm nor anywhere else, mostly because he was completely unaware that others have feelings. If I did something that upset him, even something completely innocent and not particularly disruptive, he was likely to go into a rage, throwing things—always my things—and shouting insults."

"No self-control."

Rhee rubbed his chin. "I should have moved when I realized what he was like, but I was busy with my work and didn't want the hassle."

"How did you manage to tolerate him?"

"Often I slept on a cot in the lab." A toothy grin appeared briefly. "The gerbils were better company."

Hua set one leg across the other. "What were his parents like?"

"As far as I could tell, they showed little interest in him. Being forced to live in the dorm infuriated Neil, but his father insisted on it."

"Perhaps he thought it would teach him to get along with others."

Rhee shrugged as if to say if that was the elder Preston's thought, he was mistaken. "Neil said it was about money. Once he called home to ask his father for a few dollars for concert tickets. His father refused, and Neil went berserk, tearing down some wall posters and screaming obscenities. When I tried to calm him, he turned on me, calling me a prying weasel."

"He sounds like a great guy to have around."

Rhee waved a hand. "I suppose I irritated him as well, with my constant talk of formulas and laboratory experiments. I was studying with Earnest Maller at the time, testing the idea that T-cells are—" Rhee stopped. "You see? Even now science distracts me. You came to hear about Neil."

Hua touched his own chest. "My friends often nudge me back on track."

Rhee cleared his throat before continuing. "I suppose a psychologist would say Neil is a narcissist who is aware only of his own desires."

"Did you ever meet the sister?"

"Joelle? A real piece of work, as my students say." Rhee pushed his glasses into place with a finger, leaving his hand over his face for a second. "I had to fight my way out of her clutches one night when she visited and Neil was out."

"She was sexually aggressive?"

He pursed his lips. "One assumes she's grown past that over the years."

Though he knew differently, Hua didn't argue. "It sounds like living with Mr. Preston was difficult."

Rhee sighed. "At first I thought I might help him. Neil wanted very much to be...not liked, perhaps, but admired. He often did ridiculous things hoping to impress others, but the more he postured and proclaimed his own brilliance, the more he was disliked." After a moment he added, "I understand he's used his wealth to insulate himself from the world. That seems to fit with tendencies I saw back then. If a man so insecure can't find admiration, he isolates himself so he doesn't see the truth on people's faces."

Hua took up a new topic. "What about the drug Preston discovered while he was here at the university? Did you help with that at all?" Something in Rhee's eyes made Hua say, "You didn't just help with it."

After a long silence, Rhee spoke. "If Neil is guilty of the things you say, he must be stopped. With that in mind, I'll tell you something I've never told anyone else. Near the end of my first year, which was Neil's third, I stumbled on a discovery that promised to ease the pain of diseases like arthritis, lupus, and fibromyalgia. I was so excited to have found a drug beneficial to mankind that I told him about it." Rhee's expression turned rueful. "I was seventeen years old, a scientific whiz kid with the maturity of an adolescent. I was excited." The next words came in a tone of defeat. "I was also stupid. I showed Neil my notes and babbled about the great discovery I'd made." He set his glasses back into place with an index finger. "In my defense, I figured Preston was a business major with no idea what he was looking at. Still, I boasted that the drug could be made easily and cheaply and had virtually no side effects. I said it was hard to believe no one had discovered it before."

Rhee paused, and Hua supplied the conclusion. "He stole your work."

"I didn't know it at first." He ran a hand through his hair. "The morning after I told him about my discovery, Neil was quite friendly. He said he'd been thinking about the new medicine, and he thought I should stay quiet about it a while longer. It would be easy, he said, to get caught up in excitement and miss an important element that might spell disaster later on."

"He made you doubt yourself."

Rhee nodded. "Fearing he was right, I went back to the lab and ran more tests to be sure my findings were correct." He shook his head at his own naiveté. "As I said before, I was stupid."

"You were naïve," Hua corrected, "and your roommate was unscrupulous. People with no conscience often manipulate those who are less experienced."

Rhee nodded, probably more aware of such types after decades of life. "Within a few days, a patent for my formula was applied for by a brand-new company. I was shocked by the news, but when I tried to learn who was behind it, I found only a list of board members I'd never heard of."

"The company was Preston's. A dummy, I believe they call it."

Rhee sighed deeply. "At the time, I concluded I'd come in second on my big discovery. I was even a little relieved that Preston was the only person who knew." He smiled. "When I told Neil the patent had already been applied for, he was sympathetic. He assured me that with my intelligence and work ethic, I'd make a lot of money with my next formula." Rhee spread his hands on the desktop. "He thought that was what it was all about for me, because that's how it was for him."

"How did he steal an idea he didn't even understand?"

Rhee touched some of the items on his desk as if assuring himself the time he spoke of was in the past. "I think he copied my notes while I was attending class. Then he probably took them to someone who understood chemistry. When that person agreed I'd found something worthwhile, Neil set up his company and paid people, possibly other students, to sign the incorporation documents and ask no questions. Later I learned he hired a teaching assistant from the chemistry department to write the patent application."

"Did you ever confront him about it?"

Rhee shrugged. "When I finally got it I said, 'Neil, I know you took my formula.' His response was so quick it made my head spin. 'Rhee,' he said, 'if you say that outside this room, I will sue you for slander. I'll take everything you own and everything your parents own too. They'll be left with nothing. Believe me, I can do it.'" Rhee tapped a pencil on his desk. "I moved out that day, and Neil and I haven't spoken since."

"You believed him when he said he'd ruin your whole family?"

"Neil's father had a reputation for filing lawsuits. It wasn't worth risking my parents' future when I considered it to be my own fault."

Hua shook his head at Preston's gall. "Did the medicine turn out to be as beneficial as you hoped?"

Rhee shrugged. "It works well for certain kinds of pain, so it's profitable. With the money he made from it, Neil began buying other promising patents." He smiled ruefully. "I suppose one could say I started him on the road to wealth."

"You never told anyone what he did?"

"Looking back, it seems obvious I should have done something, but I was stunned at how far he'd gone to get what he wanted." Rhee sighed. "I was naïve to blab about my discovery."

Hua leaned forward. "You told one person, Doctor Rhee. That person betrayed you."

A nod granted Hua the point, but Rhee dismissed the incident with a shrug. "Neil taught me a valuable lesson about discretion. Perhaps it's time he learned a lesson about taking advantage of others."

***

As he waited for his return flight, Hua called to tell the others about his conversation with Rhee, ending with, "He says Mr. Preston wants to believe that everyone admires him, or at least they would if they knew the extent of his genius and his—" Hua stopped and the garbled sound of an announcement bled through the phone. "That's my flight. I'll see you at the airport."

"So the guy has been a crook all his life," Em said. "Egoism, disregard for others—what are his good points?"

Robin thought of the video where Preston adjusted his tie in the classic preening gesture of the self-important businessman. "Certainly not humility."

"But now Bozo says he's killing people," Cam said from the couch. "We need to hurry up and stop him."

Checking the website, Robin noticed new information. "Here's an interesting tidbit. Chris says Preston's secret desire is to be named TIME magazine's Person of the Year."

Em shook her head in wonder. "You have got to be kidding me."

Cam looked up at her, frowning. "Em, Robin doesn't joke around about work stuff."

Em opened her mouth then closed it again, waiting instead for Robin to connect with her brother on Skype. When Chris' face appeared she said, "Person of the Year? We have to hear all about that."

Chris adjusted his body more comfortably in the wheelchair. "Linda's convinced we're buds, and she doesn't mind that I toss in a little financial compensation, so she called me today. After some negotiation, she sent me a copy of a letter left in the copy machine by mistake. Someone at Green Grove was lobbying for Preston to be POTY." He chuckled. "She found it the day Preston fired her, and she was angry, so on her way out she snagged the sheet out of the trash can and stuck it in her bra."

"Why would TIME bother with a scuzzball like him?" Em asked.

"He's going after the only target he might hit," Robin answered. "He's got no hope of an achievement prize like the Nobel, and no chance at an award for humanitarianism, since he helps no one. But businesspeople have been named Person of the Year, like Ted Turner, Mark Zuckerberg, and Jeff Bezos."

"People get recognition just for having money?" Cam said. "That's nuts."

Robin was looking thoughtful. "Didn't Doctor Rhee share a Nobel Prize with some colleagues for their work on a treatment for multiple sclerosis? I think the article was from about two years ago."

"That's about the time Preston began writing TIME to suggest he be Person of the Year," Chris said. "He might still be competing with his genius roommate, at least in his own mind."

"He asked them to choose him?" Em sniffed. "That takes nerve."

Chris shook his head. "It wasn't supposed to look like it came from him, but the syntax and boasting tone are all Preston. I compared it to things I know he wrote, and there's the same distressing tendency to overuse the comma."

"He should read it out loud," Em said pedantically. "You can hear where commas should go."

"Robin can tell him that when she gets him alone." Chris went on in a more serious tone. "If this letter were made public, I'd guess one of Preston's people would confess to writing it out of a misguided but honest sense his boss deserves the honor." He picked up a sheet of paper from his desk. "I'll scan it and post it on the site so you can discuss how it might help us."

When the post appeared, they gathered around the screen to read it.

To the Editors:

I would like to suggest, Neil L. Preston as your Man of the Year. In case you don't know much about him, Mr. Preston is the owner, and CEO, of Argent Pharmaceuticals, a company that has produced multiple, valuable medicines, for the people of the United States, to maintain health, and cure many diseases, that have long plagued our fantastic nation. Mr. Preston, is a tireless seeker of better medicines for Americas' sick and elderly, and he is very deserving of this honor. I strongly urge TIME to consider this great example of American ingenuite.

Sincerely,

Manfred Quinn

PhD, Michigan State University Economics Department

"Is there a Manfred Quinn at Michigan State?" Em asked.

"If there is, I'd hope he knows how to spell *ingenuity*." Robin shook her head. "Do you think there's even a tiny chance he'd be chosen?"

"Only in his own mind." Em's knitting needles clicked as if in agreement with her assessment.

"We should be able to do something with his interest in the award though, don't you think?"

Em smiled. "Chaucer said it: 'Forbid us something, and that thing we desire.' If we dangle a chance at his dream in front of Preston's nose, he'll let down his guard."

"How would we get TIME to consider a nut like him?" Cam asked.

"We wouldn't," Em said. "But don't we lie for a living?"

Robin tried to keep her urge to go full speed ahead under control. "We'd still have to figure out how to make the sister, lawyer, PR man, and security expert let their guard down too, all at the same time."

"Piece of cake," Em said. When they looked at her doubtfully she added, "Okay, it's got nuts in it. We just have to find the right recipe."

Chapter Eight

Once Cam went to Kansas City and brought Hua home from the airport, the gang began planning for the Preston Caper in earnest. During his flight Hua had read everything Chris collected a second time, looking for personality traits that might serve their purpose. "Monica Covel, Preston's head of security, lives for her job," he told the others. "No one enters Green Grove without permission from one of the permanent residents: Neil, his sister Joelle, Bertie Oliva, or Covel herself, and she checks every one of them out beforehand."

Robin looked at the aerial photo Hua had found online. It showed a large, walled estate with various small buildings scattered along the edges. The main building, set at dead center, looked like a gigantic cement block: square, flat-topped, and painted an unrelieved green. There were few windows, none on the ground floor, and they were narrow and unadorned, providing little variation in the blank walls. Trees around the house provided a protective ring but sat far enough back that they offered no easy entry to upper stories. Robin could pick out different species in the rows of color: dark pines, green deciduous, and purple-leafed trees Cam said were Japanese maples. The layout brought to mind *Sleeping Beauty*, and Robin wondered if there was somewhere in all that greenery a wall of thorns.

Em peered over her shoulder. "This guy wanted his house to look like a concrete bunker?"

"Apparently he told the architect to copy Soviet style," Robin replied. "No ornamentation, only function."

"Well, I feel sorry for the architect," Em said, "because the result is Ugly, with a capital *U*."

Robin looked through the photos on a page Chris had posted and Hua had augmented. Preston's clothing often looked slightly military: Mao-style jackets with high collars and gold buttons. Did he imagine himself as Stalin, giving orders that resulted in death? He certainly didn't look like "Uncle Joe" Stalin, who'd been neither spindly nor sulky-looking.

Maybe it was how he *wished* he looked, a great bear of a man with an affable affect that hid an iron will.

They spent a few seconds looking at the photos of the inner circle, trying to guess at their personality traits. Joelle Preston was stocky, with shoulders like a linebacker, but she dressed to conceal her faults. Monica Covel was wiry, with the hips and eyes of a python. Oliva looked like a high-end cabana boy, and Nixon called to mind a '30s movie hero, chin up, eyes bright, and sporting a pencil mustache. "How do we get around this bunch and reach Preston?"

"The same way you eat a plate of nachos," Em replied. "One jalapeno at a time."

"Right. Neutralize each satellite separately then go for the man himself."

"Divide and conquer," Hua said. "This is good." Cam nodded and went on killing aliens.

"I'm glad we agree," Robin said earnestly, "because with four people between us and our target, we'll each be busy. First we need someone inside Green Grove."

"Who's pulling the short straw on that one?" Em asked.

Robin cleared her throat before answering. "Cam."

Em glanced at the big man. "Are you sure you want to do that?"

Instead of answering directly Robin said, "We need to offer Joelle Preston a man she'll want to take home with her. Once Cam's inside, he can isolate her, making sure she's safe and out of our way."

Cam's comment revealed he'd been paying attention. "I can do it, Em. Hua's gonna help me get ready."

Em grimaced but didn't argue. "What about the security woman, Covel?"

"Hua has an idea. I don't like it much because it involves drugging her, but I can't come up with a better plan." She turned her gaze to Em. "That leaves Nixon for you to handle."

Em thought about that for a second then said, "Perfect. I'm in the mood for a road trip, and who doesn't love Tulsa in late August?"

Robin looked out the window, where Mai and Kai knelt on the soft ground of the garden, picking tomatoes as the dog snoozed in the grass along the edge. "The girls and Bennett can mind things here for a week or so, right?"

Em chuckled. "I pity the fool that steps foot on the property when Kai's in charge."

***

"How are things in sunny Florida?" Robin asked when Tom called that evening.

"I think the DA is fairly confident I can testify without making a fool of myself. Now my biggest concern is whether I should wear the hook or the hand when I take the stand."

"One's dashing, one's daring," she said. "Either way, you'll be impressive."

"How goes the caper? Em says it's pretty complicated."

"Where's the challenge in easy?" She wasn't surprised to hear he'd already talked to Em. The two had formed a bond early on, when Robin still thought of Tom as the enemy. "We head out Monday."

"Don't suppose you'd put it on the back burner until I'm done here."

"Tom, he's killing people." When he didn't reply she asked, "Do you think I can't handle this?"

"No." A long pause. "Maybe a little."

"I'm not a damsel who needs to be saved, Tom."

"Of course not."

"Then what is it?"

"Nothing. I'm sorry." After an awkward silence he asked, "Has Mr. Charming shown up again?"

"No." She didn't tell him Devin called almost daily. *Not something he needs to know.*

"He will."

"What is that supposed to mean?"

"Just that...when you realize you missed out on a good thing, you don't throw away a second chance." Robin didn't reply, and after a moment Tom went on.

"So the plans are in place?"

"They're all tentative, so there are a lot of moving parts. I take the first step on Tuesday. If that seems promising, we'll continue."

Whatever doubts he still had, Tom ended the conversation optimistically. "You'll be okay. You've got a great team."

"That's right," she said cheerfully. "If we just stick to the plan, everything will go like clockwork."

***

"Good morning, Boss," Bertie Oliva stopped in the doorway, waiting to be invited in, like the underling his employer kept reminding him he was. He would report while standing, since there were no guest chairs in Preston's office, and he'd become used to surreptitiously shifting his feet to keep them from falling asleep during longer confabs.

"Bertie." Preston looked up, and Oliva tried to judge his mood. *Not terrible,* he thought. *An almost welcoming tone.* "What have you got for me?"

"The patents from HealYou are now ours. It came down to a vote among the three developers, and as you directed, I, um, encouraged the one who was undecided to swing our way." Oliva couldn't count the

71

times he'd slid an envelope of cash across a restaurant table to a greedy inspector or a debt-ridden researcher. He didn't even try.

"It's almost too easy sometimes, isn't it?"

It wasn't really a question, and Oliva didn't answer. "I have some new possibilities for you to look at." Stepping forward, he placed a plastic folder on Preston's desk. "Some good ones in there, I think."

In the two decades since he'd stolen his first patent, Preston had repeated his success many times. Oliva had at first been surprised at how easily Preston wrested valuable formulas from scientists, but he soon learned that many of them lacked any sense of business. Fascinated by science, they had no grasp of real-world practicality. Preston often made fun of them: so intelligent they could barely communicate with ordinary mortals, yet they quailed at production schedules, marketing programs, and governmental red tape.

Bertie Oliva, as the public face of Argent, convinced those brilliant men and women to let his company lift the petty demands of government from their shoulders. If Bertie couldn't convince them with his golden tongue, Preston used other means. Sometimes it was as easy as bribing an employee to copy the promising formula and hand it over.

"Shall I send the HealYou contracts to Nixon one more time to be sure we've dotted the *i*'s and all that?"

"Yes. Then draft the announcement. I'll set up a testing schedule."

Oliva would frame the press release in the best possible terms: Argent Chemical benefiting consumers by facilitating development of new and better medicines. Preston would monitor his scientists, demanding they make their testing seem exhaustive. He'd learned which side effects could be disclosed without losing the chance to put a product on the market. When a device or drug presented risks, officials were encouraged to see them as minimal, and Oliva wrote copy that brilliantly (if he did say so himself) downplayed the perils. He also "informed" doctors of Argent's products, offering incentives, rewards, and propaganda through eager young reps who knew far less about the products than about sales techniques.

Frowning at his notes Oliva said, "Our new drug, Barvasa, has caused some serious allergic reactions."

Preston shrugged. "Strawberries cause allergic reactions. Barvasa's going to be a money-maker for us."

"A third of those tested experienced moderate swelling of their lips, tongues, or throats." Preston scanned his own copy of the report. "Only a few hospitalized, and nobody died. List the chance of a reaction as negligible." He frowned up at Bertie. "Spin it so Barvasa sounds like the best thing ever."

"Well, it does have a slightly better cure rate. The older med cures 80 percent." He thought for a moment. "We could say it's effective for 82 percent of previously untreated patients. A lot of people won't stop to figure out that the risk of side effects isn't worth it for a two percent better chance of a cure."

Preston raised a brow. "Isn't worth it to whom?"

Oliva nodded. "I guess you'll handle the inspectors' objections, as usual."

Neil sat back in his chair. "I'll find a worker bee who'll accept a little reward to help us out." It was a source of pride to Preston that he could shorten testing periods for his products with a dozen little tricks. "And maybe we can find a problem or two with the older med. That would help."

While their patents sailed through the system, Argent often reported its competitors' problems, setting their products back months or years. "Just be sure our promotional material hints at miracles and promises nothing."

"Got it."

"Another winner for Argent Chemical." A cloud appeared in Preston's eyes. "I should be recognized for being a genius at this stuff. Instead I'm called before Congress and grilled like a criminal."

Oliva knew his lines. "It's terrible, boss, I know."

Since Oliva came to work at Green Grove, two events had stirred Preston's resentment to the level of near apoplexy. First, his old roommate Rhee had received a Nobel Prize. When that news came, he'd thrown his phone at the wall, smashing it. He still ranted about it from time to time, listing ways he was better than John Rhee. His house was bigger. His staff was better. His power was greater. "Rhee is nobody!" he would shout. "I am a *success!*"

The other event was the government's investigation of drug pricing. After all the payoffs through lobbyists, after sending Bertie and Nixon to schmooze various Congressmen and women, he'd still suffered the humiliation of being dragged before a group of legislators to justify Argent's practices. Oliva and Nixon had coached him to play the role of a hardworking businessman with the good of the public first in his heart, but Preston was innately unable to appear caring. The media had declared him "arrogant" and "insolent."

Preston's shift of mood gave Oliva the perfect opening. "I've been asked to meet with someone today who has a proposal for you."

Preston snorted disdainfully. "Everybody has a proposal for me."

"Wait till I tell you who she works for." Pleased with himself, Oliva shifted his weight onto his toes. "She tried to keep it a secret, but I managed to find out. Ms. Ronda Talman is employed by TIME magazine."

Preston leaned over his desk like a myopic librarian. "Do you think our letters succeeded?"

"I'll know in a few hours."

Preston's mood turned ebullient. "National recognition would go a long way toward silencing those blowhards in Congress."

"One hopes so." Since the hearings, they'd encountered reluctance on the part of people they'd worked with in the past. Inspectors who once easily succumbed to bribes got all prim-faced at the idea of shortening a timeline or ducking a rule. Preston called them hypocrites and screamed obscenities, but it was clear the investigation had put a chill on the industry, at least for a while.

Because of his public embarrassment, Preston's longtime wish to be named Person of the Year had become an obsession. Now his gaze turned from the magazine cover he no doubt imagined to his second-in-command. "You'd better handle this right, Bertie."

Oliva felt the implied threat but couldn't back away now. "I'll get it done, boss."

***

When Oliva was gone, Preston sat staring at the wall for a while. Was it possible he'd finally get the recognition he deserved? John Rhee had his Nobel, but had his face ever been on a national magazine? Not once.

Thoughts of his old college roommate brought a relaxation of facial muscles that was for Preston a smile. From the moment Rhee showed his precious formula to his roomie back in college, Neil had seen his calling. Not creating cures or designing devices, but bringing those things to market for the millions who needed them—and for the insurance companies who'd pay for them. The moment Rhee went off to class he'd acted, and it had almost been magical how he sensed what to do first and then next and beyond that. Today Neil Preston, business major and *C* student, knew more than anyone else in the world about the development and sale of pharmaceuticals.

His swift action on Rhee's discovery made Preston mildly rich, and he'd built on that until he was worth more than some small countries. He couldn't wave his success under his father's nose—the old man had died of a well-deserved stroke—but he could show America what real success looks like. The kids in school who'd screwed up their faces when he walked by. The women who turned to other men and smiled. And the bastards in Congress who'd frowned when he told them the facts of life in the business world.

Awards were given all the time for philanthropy, intelligence, service, or talent. Why shouldn't he get one? He wasn't dumb enough to give away millions of dollars or serve on some boring charity board to make people like him, and he wasn't interested in funding someone else's education or developing some inner-city kid's self-esteem. He deserved attention—no, *admiration*—from the masses, and it was going to happen, or Bertie Oliva would be sorry.

Chapter Nine

"Hey," Robin said when Shelly answered the phone. They'd arrived in Tulsa, and she'd unpacked her things in the room she shared with Em. While the older woman was napping, Robin had felt a rising urge to reach out to her friend in Green Bay. Though she couldn't tell her the truth about much of anything, Shelly was a link to a time when everything was simpler. Creeping quietly out of the room, she'd found a deserted corner to make a phone call.

Used to Sunday afternoon calls Shelly asked, "Is something wrong?"

"No," she replied quickly. "I just wanted to talk."

After a pause Shelly said, "Okay, talk, girlfriend."

"I ran into Devin Ashford a few days ago."

Shelly, who knew her better than almost anyone on earth, drew a quick conclusion. "Now you're concerned about your relationship with Cam."

To explain her disappearance, Robin let the world think she was living at Shelly's place. Shelly thought Robin was with Cam, doing romantic things. "It's not that. Do you ever miss what you thought your life was going to be like?"

"All the time." Shelly's marriage had dissolved when her husband told her he didn't want to be married anymore, bumping her out of what she'd thought was a good relationship. "But you know what, Rob? Life probably never was the way I imagined it."

"Yeah."

"Do you want to go back to Cedar?"

"No."

"Do you want to be with Devin?"

That answer took more thought. "I don't think so."

"So what exactly are you missing, do you think?"

"Freedom from responsibility, I guess."

Shelly chuckled. "We'd all like to go back to mud pies and Barbie dolls sometimes. You're running a business. You're steering a man around. You're paying bills. Sometimes it all just sucks, but it's called adulting."

She couldn't explain that her brand of adulting meant lying to the world and avoiding the police. "You're right. I need to put on my big girl panties."

"Hey, there's no shame in looking back once in a while," Shelly assured her. "Just remember you can't move forward safely while looking back at what's behind you."

***

"How on God's green earth did you dream up something that ridiculous?" Em said when Hua outlined his idea for dealing with the lawyer, Baylor Nixon.

"I do not think it is ridiculous," Hua replied calmly. "I have read all I can find about this attorney, and two things stand out: his expertise in legal matters, which are mostly without ethical constraints, and a lifelong fascination with western movies, particularly those featuring Marjorie Stanton."

"The name's familiar," Robin said as she entered and sat next to Em, "but I can't place her."

Tapping a few keys, Hua brought up a picture of a young woman with a heart-shaped face, an impossibly small waist, and dark, tousled hair. "Marjorie Stanton," Em said, "often known as 'Our Gal Margy,' played in a string of oaters back in the late fifties."

"What is an *oater*?" Hua asked.

"A western movie," Em and Robin replied together.

"Ah. Mr. Nixon sees himself as a bit of a cowboy," Hua said. "He has a small ranch outside the city where he raises rodeo animals. And with his tailored business suits, he often wears very expensive Stetson hats."

"Matlock meets McCloud," Em muttered, but Hua only frowned. "Don't ask," she told him. "They're both before your time."

Hua went on with his presentation. "Marjorie started out playing the rancher's second or third daughter but ended up co-starring with some of Hollywood's big names in other westerns."

"Robert Ryan was one, if I remember correctly." Em turned a glare on Hua. "I have no idea how anybody thinks I could pretend to be her."

Raising three fingers, Hua counted off his arguments. "You have a similar facial structure. Miss Stanton has not been seen in public for at least ten years. And age, while it adds character, also tends to make us all look more alike."

Em shook her head. "She has brown eyes."

"Colored contacts," Robin said.

"She had the perfect hourglass figure. I'm built like a worm."

"No one would expect her shape to be the same all these years later."

"I walk with a cane."

Hua shrugged. "You'll say there was an accident on the set during your last movie, which was in 1998. It will explain why you don't do public appearances anymore."

"Why does she come out of seclusion now?"

Robin seemed sold on Hua's idea. "We'll think of something."

Em's face pinched as she sought another argument. "Marjorie Stanton was known for ladylike behavior. I'm no lady, and I seldom behave."

"So practice." Robin's voice turned pleading. "Em, you can do this."

"Of course I can," she replied tartly. "The question is if I *will*."

With his usual empathy, Hua saw what was required. "It must be your choice, Ms. Em. Will you do it for the sake of the caper?"

She examined her age-spotted hands for a few seconds. "There's a lot wrong with this old cupboard, but I still have a full set of dishes inside. With a little time to study, I guess I can be Miss Margy for a while."

Once the decision was made, Em read what Hua had found about Stanton and looked at pictures and film online. She'd started her career as an extra in *The King and I*, then moved on to supporting roles in several films. Watching clips to pick out scenes with Marjorie in them, Em observed, "The kid was pretty good."

Though Stanton never reached true star status, she'd found a place in the hearts of audiences who loved westerns. Repeating scenes with the *Rewind* button, Em looked for ways to convey her personality. She picked out a few characteristic gestures: combing her fingers through the hair at the back of her neck and lowering her gaze when someone complimented her. "Can you find an interview?" she asked Hua. "I'd like to see her being herself."

"I found nothing like that," Hua replied. "This is good for us, because Mr. Nixon will not know how the real Miss Stanton behaves."

"Neither will I," Em groused.

Hua was silent for a moment. "Let me search in a different way." In a few seconds he gave a pleased grunt. "No film, but in 1998 Ms. Stanton established a foundation that trains service dogs for brain-damaged individuals. It was done anonymously and continues today."

"Good for you, Hua!" Em said. "That tells us three things: she cares about people, she knows the value animals add to our lives, and she didn't blow her money on drugs and high living." Rubbing her knotty hands together she finished, "Sounds like a woman I won't mind impersonating."

With that decided, they went on to the next facet of the plan.

"Joelle Preston is forty-one years old," Hua reported. "She was married once for about six months. No children. "Her time is mostly spent keeping her brother's anxiety and paranoia under control, pretty much playing the role of Neil's mother, sister, aunt, grandma, and favorite cousin."

Em raised a brow. "Not girlfriend, I hope."

Hua shook his head. "As far as I can tell, the man is completely asexual."

"I'm not sure he's human." Robin had printed off the list of drugs Preston had raised prices on once he got control. "The more people need a medicine, the higher he sets the price."

Cam looked up from his game. "Some of Mom's chemo drugs cost thousands for one shot. That's not right if they can make them cheaper."

Hua brought the conversation back to its intended focus. "Joelle, who returned to using Preston as her surname after her divorce, is definitely interested in the opposite sex."

"Then she's bound to notice Cam."

Hua nodded. "His social unease may actually attract her interest, since she seems to prefer her men inexperienced."

"I'm practicing looking relaxed," Cam said in response to the comment. "If I keep my hands in my pockets, I don't mess with my hair or rub my shirt."

"That's good," Robin said, though she'd seen his new trick and concluded he didn't exactly look relaxed.

"What's the plan?" Em asked.

"First we let Joelle see him," Robin said. "She's attending a science lecture this week, so we'll drop Cam into the crowd and make sure she notices."

Em's brows almost met. "I can't see Cam discussing mitochondrial DNA after some lecture."

Robin tilted her head at him. "Do you think she'll care with such an impressive specimen?"

Hua had a concern. "How will we get Ms. Preston to take Cam back to the estate with her? Often she simply gets a room in a motel, and...um—"

"Makes the beast with two backs," Em supplied. Though obviously puzzled by the idiom, Hua didn't comment.

"We have to work up a story that delays their getting together," Robin said. "Something that requires her to invite him to Green Grove."

Hua seemed doubtful. "I think I should be nearby, to help as needed."

"Fine. You can be his coach."

"Have him put his hands behind his back," Em suggested. "That way it won't look like two hamsters are chasing each other under his jeans."

Chapter Ten

Robin was already seated in a quiet corner of the trendy Chassé Restaurant when Bertie Oliva arrived. As the waiter pointed her out, Oliva's face lit like a roadside flare, but Robin knew better than to be flattered by the apparent admiration. In the first place, Oliva was gay. In the second place, her father had perfected that same appreciative look as a starting point for many of his cons.

Oliva approached the table with a hand outstretched, and like the salesman he was, held the handshake a few seconds longer than Robin would have liked. "Ms. Talman, so nice to meet you." He sat and made himself comfortable, never taking his eyes from hers.

The quintessential metrosexual, Bertrand Oliva ("Please call me Bertie") had perfectly cut black hair and brows shaped to matching arcs. His blue shirt had a white collar, and the jacket over it fit perfectly. He had a good face, not gorgeous but balanced, and an easy manner that suggested he'd fit in anywhere he happened to be.

From reading Oliva's press releases and watching him on video, Robin guessed her lunch partner was a natural conman, the kind of person who believes everyone is as crooked as he is. To the Bertie Olivas of the world, success in life boiled down to who conned whom first.

Bring it on, Flim-flam Man. I was trained by one of the best.

"It was nice of you to meet me, Mr. Oliva."

"Bertie, please!" He repeated. "Mr. Oliva sounds like my dad." Oliva had scrubbed any trace of an accent from his speech. He might have been born in Chicago.

"Bertie. I apologize for the mysterious call and the hurried timeline, but my schedule is demanding and there are things I can't discuss without your assurance they'll remain private."

"I have no problem with secrecy," he said smoothly. "And I can assume the schedule you mention was set by your employer, TIME magazine?"

She tried to appear both surprised and rueful. "I might have known you'd check me out." Hua had based the character Robin was playing on an actual employee, temporarily replacing the real Ronda Talman's file photo on the magazine's site with one of Robin wearing a blond wig, blue contacts, and cheek and jaw pads that rounded her face.

Oliva seemed pleased with his cleverness. "I work for a busy man. I want to assure my time isn't wasted."

"Understood." She swallowed. Nerves and the cheek pads made her mouth dry, and her words tended to come out muffled if she didn't enunciate carefully. "Since you already know who my employer is, I can get right to the reason for my visit to Tulsa."

"Honestly, Ms. Talman— May I call you Ronda?" He didn't wait for her nod but went on, "Ronda, neither Mr. Preston nor I can figure out what a national magazine wants with us." His eyes betrayed the lie and the hope her phone call had kindled.

Robin paused while the waiter set a glass of wine before her and a martini before her companion. When he was gone she said, "We understand Mr. Preston would like to be named our Person of the Year."

"Might I ask how you learned that?"

She huffed a laugh. "How about a series of supposedly objective letters from an array of fake readers who couldn't recommend him highly enough?" Lowering her face slightly, she looked at him through her lashes. "Did he really think we wouldn't figure out where they came from?"

"I told him it was too obvious." There was no trace of embarrassment. "Neil thought it was worth a try."

"He wasn't completely wrong. His attempts, though really clumsy, got our attention." Robin glanced around the room as if wondering how honest she should be. "For decades, Person of the Year has been chosen in great secrecy and good faith attempts to find people representative of the conditions of the time, whether their influence is good or bad." She paused for effect. "Recently one prominent person at the magazine came to the conclusion that the current climate makes that sort of soul-searching outdated."

"Things don't happen the way they used to," Oliva agreed. "It's a reality of modern life."

She put her hands out, palms up. "Everything is up for sale. The interest generated by our choice for Person of the Year is still high, so my employer has decided to secure the future by using that interest."

Oliva sipped at his drink, obviously thinking it over. "The person who sent you can influence the choice?"

"Without question. We know it's not, um, the usual way of operating, but..." She let the statement trail off, affecting embarrassment.

Oliva smiled. "Everyone does that, Ms. Talman, from the Halls of Congress to the streets of Podunkville to the website of your favorite mega-pastor."

Robin sighed as if reluctant to take the next step. "I'm glad you agree, because I was sent to begin negotiations that might get Preston named POTY."

Oliva stroked his martini glass. "We're open to hearing the possibilities."

"Good." Adjusting her black-framed, non-prescription eyeglasses, Robin said, "First, you should be aware that there are several candidates for the honor."

"It's an auction then." After a few seconds he added, "I'll need an idea of where the bidding starts."

She met his gaze. "We think nationwide attention is worth a million."

He whistled softly. "That's quite a price tag."

"My employer believes the magazine won't last much longer in the digital age. S—this person—would prefer not to ever have to look for work again."

"We're aware of the struggles of print media. We're also aware that up to this point, Mr. Preston has had very few friends in that world."

"That's exactly where we can help each other." She raised her brows. "First I need to know if he wants to be in the running at the price quoted."

Oliva's smile reminded her of a pleasant crocodile. "I'll present your proposal to Mr. Preston today."

"Here's a number where you can reach me." She wrote on a business card and slid both the pen and the card across to Oliva. "Keep the pen. I think you'll appreciate the sentiment."

Taking it up, he read the phrase printed on the barrel and chuckled. *"TIME is money.* Cute."

The fake Ronda Talman stood. "I'll be staying in Tulsa until the choice is finalized. If Preston is chosen, I'll do an initial interview so we can get started on the layout."

Oliva put a finger to his lips. "You are assuring me things will go our way?"

"Trust me. My boss knows how things work at TIME."

Robin saw him trying to figure out who at the magazine had the power to do what she'd proposed. Finally he gave her a friendly salute. "Then I'll be in touch."

When Robin returned to the car, Cam was playing games on his phone. "How did it go?"

"He's definitely interested."

"So we're going to go ahead with my part?"

She sighed. "We have to. Tonight's our only chance for at least a week."

"Okay."

She smiled at his casual attitude. Cam lived in the moment, seldom considering the future and what might go wrong. Robin was the one who worried, before, during, and after every single caper.

She started the car. "Next stop, downtown. We need to find a babysitter for the weekend."

Cam made another middle school joke. "For a really big baby."

They used GPS units for getting around, since unlike phones and car guidance systems, they weren't easily trackable by outsiders. Setting the unit for an area of the city where crime statistics showed the most prostitution arrests, Robin followed the commands and parked on the street. Cam fed the meter, and they began people-watching.

"There's a girl over there," he said helpfully after a few minutes. "She looks like a hooker to me."

Robin was beginning to understand that what had sounded doable in the planning session was more difficult in real life. "Cam, we can't just go up to some woman and say, 'Excuse me, are you willing to engage in a criminal conspiracy?'"

"Oh, yeah."

"We need someone who won't mind breaking the law but isn't messed up on booze or drugs. And she needs—I don't know. I guess I'd call it a sense of humor."

Cam gave her a look. "You're looking for a woman who breaks the law and tells jokes too?"

She sighed. "I'll know the right person when I see her. I hope."

The women waiting hopefully on the street were by and large a sad lot, with smiles as fake as their hair colors. When they witnessed an argument between two women and their pimp, Robin had to order Cam not to get out of the car and confront the man. They saw tough women and broken women, but no one who fit the image Robin had in mind for their temporary employee.

In the end, the right woman found them. When someone tapped on the window next to her head, Robin jumped in surprise. Turning she saw, very close up, a woman with skin the color of her mother's old piano. She was slightly overweight, not very tall, and dressed in a blue sateen mini-skirt and a sequined tube top. On her feet were black Skechers, a sensible choice for standing around on concrete, and a jaunty little turquoise beret perched precariously at the side of her head. With a glance at Cam to bolster her courage, Robin rolled down the car window. "Um, hi."

"Y'all writin' a book or something?"

"We're just, um, looking."

"Y'all entertained by less fortunate types that do they own nails?"

"Of course not."

One side of her mouth turned down. "You tellin' me you want action?"

"In a way. We, um, need a certain type of woman."

Dark eyes rolled under pencil-thin brows, and she tossed her dreadlocks over her shoulder. "Lotta people sayin' that 'round here." She leaned in to get a better look at Cam. "He cute. Can't he get his own girls?"

"No—I mean, he could if he wanted to, but that's not why we're here. We—" Robin stopped, embarrassed. "We hoped someone here might help us."

The woman's anger dissipated somewhat. "Girlfriend, just tell me. Diane over there does threesomes, and if one of you just watches, that's okay too."

As Cam slid down in his seat as if he wanted to disappear, Robin said, "We aren't...um, it isn't sex."

The woman smacked her lips in disgust. "You gotta say what you want, honey. I ain't no mind-reader."

As she stuttered to explain, Robin sounded like Cam at his worst. "We, uh, want to h-hire an African-American woman for the weekend. It's not k-kinky or dangerous, but when it's over, she needs to forget it ever happened."

Humor shone in her dark eyes. "Girl, y'all think we study on remembering how crazy white people is?"

"I told you, this isn't about sex. We'd hire you to do some...acting."

"Acting like what?"

"Like a nurse."

She set a fist on one wide hip. "We gonna play doctor?"

"No. I mean, yes. You'd pretend to be a nurse at a real hospital." Hopefully she asked, "Have you ever done any caregiving?"

"I tended to my daddy till he died, did stuff I never wanted to." She brought herself back to the moment. "What that gots to do with anything?"

"This acting job is worth $2,000 if you can pull it off."

The woman's expressive face pinched. "You gonna pay me $2,000?"

"For three days' work."

As she considered it, she rolled her eyes under lashes too long to be real. She glanced at another woman on the street, but she was busy talking to a man in a car. Finally she sighed. "Show me the cash, darlin'. Then we'll talk."

Robin took out five hundred-dollar bills she'd stashed in her pocket. "I'll pay you this much right now if you promise to come back here Friday. You'll get five hundred more on Saturday, again on Sunday, and the final five on Monday when it's done." Remembering the pimp they'd seen earlier, Robin asked, "Is there anyone you have to answer to if you leave for a few days?"

Scarlet lips formed a firm line. "Daddy was the last man had any hold on me. These days ain't nobody tell me where I got to be and what I got to do."

Did she mean her father was the one who—? Robin pushed the thought away. She hadn't come to learn anyone's life story. "All right then. You can call me Clarabell, and this is Bozo. What's your name?"

"Lucastrina, after my daddy Lucas and my momma Trina." She smiled. "Most people calls me Luca."

"All right, Luca. Meet us here Friday at three. If we don't show up, you can keep the money and forget we ever talked. If we show up, we'll explain your role more fully and take you to where you'll spend the weekend. We'll bring you back Monday afternoon. Is that okay?"

Luca was looking at the money. "Sure."

"Tell your friends you have a job for the weekend, no more than that." Robin waited while Luca stuffed the money into her bra. "Can you keep all this to yourself?"

She frowned. "Nobody's gonna get killed or nothin', right?"

"No one will be hurt at all."

Luca shrugged. "Then it ain't no thang to me what y'all is up to."

As Robin drove away, she started worrying. Though Luca didn't seem a bad sort, only time would tell if they'd chosen wisely. The hooker might tell her friends about the odd encounter she'd had. She might show up drunk or high on Friday. She might call the police to report there was a plot afoot. Had she been present, Em would no doubt have added, *Or she might not show up at all now that she has $500 of our money.*

When they got back to the hotel, Hua had connected his phone to his tablet. "I am downloading Mr. Oliva's conversations so we can learn Mr. Preston's response to your proposal."

Cam bent to look. "I can't believe you can spy on people with a pen."

"Inside the barrel is a very small wireless transmitter," Hua told him. "We have about seven hours to listen to what Mr. Oliva says and hears."

"Great," Robin said, "if he went directly to Preston with our offer and if he didn't lose our very expensive toy between the restaurant and the estate." As she spoke, she laid clothes on the bed: a suit for Cam, and for Hua the white tuxedo shirt/black trouser outfit commonly worn by waiters at catered events.

"If all goes well tonight, we will have a better listening device in place," Hua said. "One that does not depend on batteries and won't get lost or left on a desk somewhere."

"It isn't polite to listen to people talking," Cam objected, and Robin hid a smile. Fine with kidnapping and extortion, he apparently drew the line at eavesdropping.

Hua explained the lapse in manners in a way Cam could accept. "We need to be certain Mr. Preston is a criminal before we go in there and talk to him."

The big man bit his lip as he considered. "I guess you're right. We don't want to scare an innocent guy."

While Hua and Cam dressed for the evening, Robin listened to the downloaded files. At first there was little of interest: Oliva grunting as he got into his car, swearing at a driver who cut him off, and belching freely, as one who is alone tends to do.

His arrival at Green Grove was marked with comments to the guards, some bells and rumbles Robin interpreted as the operation of an elevator, and humming as he rattled around in what was apparently a bathroom. When the sound of streaming water stopped (Robin tried to ignore what was happening), she pictured him checking his hair and washing his hands. He sang "Happy Birthday" twice as the water ran, which she hoped meant he was on his way to see his germ-phobic boss.

A few seconds later, the conversation they'd hoped for began. After a few preliminaries, Oliva explained what he'd learned in his meeting with the supposed representative from TIME magazine. His voice came through clearly, though odd noises punctuated his comments. "He's playing with the pen," Hua explained, buttoning his shirt as he listened. Robin, who had a tendency to do the same thing, pictured his movements: tapping, twirling, and what might have been teeth chomping on the barrel.

"You think this woman is legitimate, Bertie?" She recognized Preston's reedy voice from video clips.

They'd made finding that "Ronda" was a TIME employee only difficult enough to convince Oliva she was the real thing, and his reply signaled success. "Ms. Talman is a peon, but whoever sent her to nose out a bribe is clever. If you report the contact, the woman's supervisor can claim the employee acted on her own. If you agree, there's a nice payoff for him."

Preston snorted like an angry donkey. "Everything's for sale, Bertie. You've heard me say that."

"You're absolutely right, boss. The question is whether we pay up or negotiate. She said a million, but I bet they'd take half that."

After a pause Preston said, "Offer the full million. Tell them we'll pay half now and half when the spread with me as Person of the Year is released."

"You aren't going to bargain? That doesn't sound like you."

"First we knock out the competition and get a deal in place. Once the issue is published, who says we have to pay the other half?"

Oliva made a sound of understanding. "They can't come after it without admitting they accepted a bribe."

"Can you get this Talman woman to agree to it?"

Oliva chuckled. "She's pretty green. So nervous I thought she might faint."

Robin blinked at the comment, but Hua offered comfort. "That is exactly how we wanted Ronda Talman to appear. These people believe she is easily fooled, so now they will be less suspicious."

"Yes," she agreed. *Ronda needs to seem green as grass, but Robin needs to hold onto the reins.*

Chapter Eleven

Dressed in his waiter disguise, Hua passed Cam, who begged, "Don't go very far away, okay?" The big man hugged the back wall of a theater lobby where well-dressed people drank wine and nibbled delicacies. Over his shoulder a large poster showed a popular physicist with the words "Scherzer, Son of Science." Scherzer appeared to hold the universe in one hand.

"I won't."

Joelle Preston hunted men like an alley cat in heat, and Chris reported that Neil had finally threatened to cut off funds if she continued trolling bars and clubs for her "dates." These days she instead went to lectures, concerts, and seminars, places where the men were slightly geeky and therefore, her brother believed, less predatory. If she wanted to bring a man home, Covel had to vet him. Joelle seemed to like intelligent but impractical types, men she could impress with what Chris deemed "glamour over style and wealth over worth."

As they waited for Joelle to arrive, Hua stopped as if to offer Cam his choice of items from a silver tray. "You must appear to be alone," he said quietly. "And choose a spot where she will see you right away."

Cam's hand moved toward his hair, but he stopped himself. "Where?"

Hua led the way to a tall table, directing Cam to lean one elbow on it and loosely interlace his fingers. When Cam tried for the enigmatic smile Robin had coached, it came off more like an attack of gas.

As he moved around the room, Hua kept an eye on Cam, who shifted his feet every few seconds both from nerves and the discomfort of wearing shoes not made by Nike. Hua worried that Cam would decide he couldn't go through with the night's business, but he stayed calm, doing his best to look like a man eager to hear a famous scientist speak. Most of the women in the crowd looked him over, and one man with very thin eyebrows passed several times, clearly trying to catch Cam's eye. When he got no response the first two times, he walked so slowly and passed so close that Cam took a step back. "Sorry."

"Completely my fault." He gave Cam an admiring look. "Are you meeting someone?"

"Um, no. But I'm kinda busy."

The man's voice turned irritated. "Doing what? Practicing mental telepathy?"

"What?"

Hua hurried over. "The doors will open soon, gentlemen. If you'd like a good seat, I suggest you move in that direction."

Watching the man walk away Cam said, "That guy was weird."

"Keep to the plan," Hua urged. "I will try to keep the weird guys away."

Just then a woman entered and stopped in the doorway, striking a pose that clearly indicated she intended to make an impression. Heads turned toward her, and a little hum vibrated through the crowd. In a sea of muted clothing tones and graying heads, Joelle Preston was an anomaly. Taller than most women, a fact she emphasized with spiked heels, she wore an expensive dress in cobalt blue that clung to her lush form. Her hair was a shade of red that could only have come from a bottle, and her makeup, though artfully applied, was enough for more than one woman. No one would call her beautiful, but Joelle knew how to make an entrance.

As she surveyed the room, Joelle's gaze stopped on the spot where the two men stood. Tiny muscles around her eyes twitched. She was clearly interested in Cam.

"I will be nearby." Hua melted into the crowd, ignoring his friend's silent plea for support.

Apparently not one to waste time, Joelle approached Cam directly. Hua heard the conversation through his earwig. "I haven't seen you here before."

Cam replied as he'd been coached. "I'm, I'm from Enid, but I wanted to h-hear Scherzer speak."

At her next comment, Hua almost knocked over the glasses he was filling. "It looked like you knew that cute waiter. I wonder if you'd introduce us."

Hua quickly retreated to the prep room, a closet-sized space stacked with boxes and coolers. In only a few seconds Cam stuck his head in, his face concerned. "She wants to meet the cute waiter. I think she means you."

"She's supposed to be interested in you!"

"Well, she isn't." Cam glanced to where Joelle waited. "I told her I'd bring you over. I didn't know what else to say." As Hua hesitated he added, "I think we have to switch jobs."

"Switch—" Hua tried to think. The change created some problems, but it might work out. His expertise with electronics would make him more valuable inside Green Grove than Cam could ever be. "Can you do the download?"

Cam shrugged. "It's just an app, right? I've done lots of those."

"Okay, but you have to hide it too. Go into settings and make the icon disappear from the display."

"It'll take me longer than it would take you, but if you stall her for a while, I can do it." Hua suspected Cam was relieved he wasn't the bait they'd intended him to be when he added, "Like Em says, we have to be adaptable."

Hua set a glass of champagne in the center of his tray of hors d'oeuvres. "Right. Let's see if we can get her to set that purse down." Approaching Joelle, he asked, "Is there a problem with the service, ma'am?"

As she looked him over, Hua was reminded of the dog Bennett anticipating a treat. "I wanted to meet you," she said coquettishly.

"I am working." He held the tray out. "Please take some champagne."

She took the flute in her free hand. "If your boss asks, you can tell him I'm planning an event and had questions about the company."

"What sort of event are you planning? We offer—"

Her laugh cut off the comment. "The event I'm planning, Lovey, is you and me in a very expensive, very private hotel room. Think room service, a hot tub, and a night of pure enjoyment."

Widening his eyes, Hua replied as the character Cam had meant to portray. "I could not do that."

Her thin brows rose. "What do you mean?"

Putting a hand over his heart Hua said earnestly, "I was raised in an orphanage by six wonderful Catholic nuns. I made vows to God and to myself, and I intend to keep them."

"Vows?" Her tone was disbelieving.

"Chastity until marriage, for one."

"Chastity." The word sounded alien coming from her lips.

He nodded emphatically. "I avoid situations where my virtue might be tested, such as time alone with women. I believe that removing oneself from temptation is the best way to remain pure."

The look on Joelle's face said she intended to rise to the challenge. "That's commendable, Mr. um—"

"Trang." Hua used an identity he'd prepared for emergencies. "Ba Trang."

"How do you occupy your mind without women in your life, Mr. Trang?"

"I am pursuing a degree in history." With the air of being unable to stop himself he added, "The focus of my thesis is Post-tsarist Russia."

Now her expression turned sly. "My brother has a collection of artifacts from that period that's quite impressive."

He pretended surprise. "Is this display open to the public?"

"Oh, no." She chuckled at the idea. "Of course I can visit any time I like."

Now he feigned disappointment. "I often must travel miles and miles on a bus to see one or two pieces. It is expensive and time-consuming, but of course necessary. You are very lucky, madam."

Joelle apparently couldn't resist a convenient double entendre. "I might be able to arrange for you to get lucky, too, Mr. Trang."

***

Cam remained near Joelle and Hua, just far enough away to not seem to be eavesdropping. It was scary to change the plan in the middle of everything, but he was confident he could do Hua's part. With a glance Cam's way to be sure he was ready, Hua sidled toward one of the tall tables set out for guests. He talked as he moved, and Joelle followed unconsciously, her eyes locked on him. When she was next to the table, Hua looked around as if nervous. "I should not be speaking so long to such a beautiful guest. My employers—"

"Tell you what. I'll take my time deciding which of your lovely little treats to try." Joelle smiled as she set her purse down, keeping her champagne flute in hand as she bent to examine the array of crackers, cheeses, and sweets Hua offered. Though he appeared to be focused on Joelle, Hua's body language all but screamed for Cam to hurry.

Cam stepped quietly up behind Joelle. Hua was talking animatedly about his studies, and her attention was on him. He took a step to the side, leading her eye away from the purse. "Try the miniature pecan bites. They are excellent."

With a boldness born of necessity, Cam palmed Joelle's purse with his larger-than-average hand and pulled it across the table top. Removing the phone, he slid the purse back and then adopted the casual pose of someone checking his messages. Within seconds he'd installed an app called Spydie. As it downloaded, Hua spun tales of his childhood and the kindness of the nuns. While Joelle made sympathetic noises, Cam went to Settings and told the new app not to show an icon on the main screen.

Finished, he caught Hua's eye and nodded. "Take one more," Hua urged Joelle. "The lecture will begin soon, and you should not go in there hungry."

Smiling as if he'd said something clever, she bent to look at the tray again. Cam looked around once, opened Joelle's purse, and slid the phone back inside. The whistling he began immediately afterward was probably too much, but she was too busy smiling at Hua to notice. "I'm not kidding about the Soviet artifacts. I can get you in to see them if you're interested."

It was too early in the game to let her think she'd won. "I am sorry, Miss," Hua said, "but I must decline your offer. Now if you will excuse me, the lecture is about to begin." Hua moved away, and Joelle watched him go, apparently appreciative of the rear view. Cam felt a little sorry for Hua. The lady looked like she might run after him and grab him right in front of everybody. Still, they'd got what they wanted. It just hadn't gone the way they'd expected.

***

"The modern phone is a unique sort of Judas," Hua explained to the others when he and Cam returned to the motel. "We can't be without them, yet they can be used against us in many ways. The app Cam put on Joelle's phone will bypass Preston's expensive security, and as long as she carries it, everything they've done to protect themselves from eavesdropping is nullified."

"Don't they know that's a possibility?" Robin asked.

"Tech people are aware of the danger, of course, but they constantly battle their users' demands for convenience. You know of people very high in government who bypass the security measures provided to them because they like things simple and don't think what they do will hurt anything."

"We've certainly heard enough about that," Em said.

"I suspect Monica Covel checks all the phones at Green Grove periodically," Hua told them. "If she looks at Joelle's, she'll find the Spydie app and delete it, and we'll be in trouble. However, Joelle will never notice it, so we're safe if we keep Ms. Covel away from Joelle's phone." Hua's nose crinkled. "People expect tech experts to protect them, yet they do little or nothing to protect themselves."

Worried that was a comment on Hua's efforts to shield members of the gang from discovery, Robin promised herself to be more vigilant about noting and using the safeguards he provided. The problem was she often didn't understand them, so it really was easier to just let him be their watchdog.

There were no revelations from the bugged phone that evening. Joelle spoke to no one when she returned home, and they gave up listening when they heard her preparing for bed. The next morning they took turns waiting by the tablet, wondering when she'd visit her brother.

"Ten o'clock," Em groused as she checked her watch yet again. "That isn't really even morning anymore."

Finally they heard sounds of Joelle getting dressed, leaving her apartment, and riding up in an elevator. After a murmured comment to the personal assistant, a solid door closed behind her. Neil Preston, apparently already at work, greeted his sister. "How was the evening?"

The sound from the phone was better than the pen's had been, but the volume varied due to the speakers' distance from it. Sounds made by Joelle's movements, the A/C, and some kind of office machine competed with the voices. Closing her eyes in order to focus only on her ears, Robin managed to get the gist of the conversation.

"It's too soon to tell," Joelle replied cryptically. "What's the word on the people from TIME?"

"They seem legitimate," Preston replied. "I had Monica recheck the Talman woman's identity."

"Good idea," Joelle said. "Oliva is an optimist, and I don't always trust him to be thorough."

A dry sound followed her comment, and Robin realized it was Preston's laugh. "You don't approve of men who aren't available to you."

"It isn't that." Her tone was petulant. "Monica's like a bulldog when it comes to protecting you."

"Yes, I was lucky to find her, despite her anger issues."

"*I* found her, remember? Belk wasn't fit to be head of security." Joelle shifted her position in the chair, at least that's what it sounded like, and asked, "Are you going to make a deal with this Talman person?"

"I'm looking into it," Preston replied. "Nix is digging up ways to insulate me from blowback if someone discovers the scheme. He already made some good suggestions."

"Such as?"

"We'll pay in cash, so there's no way to trace the money back to us. And if I do meet with the woman, I'll demand verification before I seal the deal." He made a harrumph of self-importance. "I'm a pretty good judge of people."

A tiny pause indicated Joelle might not agree. "Sounds like you've got things under control."

"Bertie will talk with Talman again today. I'll make my decision once he reports in."

A rustle indicated Joelle was readying her departure. "I plan to do a little shopping this afternoon if you don't need me. I met someone last night, and I think I'm going to need a new peignoir."

Preston made a disgusted sound. "Just make sure Monica knows what you're up to and with whom."

"You should come out with me some evening, Neil. It would do you good to have a little fling." Joelle's voice was half teasing, half serious, and Robin thought it was a suggestion she'd made more than once.

His voice dropped ten degrees. "I am not into desperate embraces with quasi-strangers as an emotional outlet."

"No, you'll sit up here in your expensive pile of rocks, counting your money until you die, old and alone."

"But I'm not alone, Joelle. I have you and Bertie and Monica. And if I ever decide I want more people in my life, there are literally thousands of men who'd jump at the chance to come here and laugh at my jokes. If I decide I want female companionship, women will line up outside the gate to be my Bachelorette. As long as I keep making money I can have my pick of them, so I'll never be old and alone."

"That isn't the same as going out and finding someone you're attracted to, Neil. You really should—"

A fist pounded on something. "Do you see how ridiculous it is for you to give me advice on how to live when the *only* reason you can have your boyfriends is my generosity? One of us is successful; the other is pitiful." He paused for a long moment. "Am I wrong, or would you prefer to be on your own?"

There was a pause before she said in a low voice. "You're not wrong."

"Then go do your thing. I have work to do."

When the door had closed and Joelle's footsteps tapped toward the elevator, she muttered something to herself. Robin thought she caught the word "bastard," but she might not have heard it correctly.

Chapter Twelve

Oliva was waiting for Robin this time, and when she approached, he rose and stepped forward to take her hand in both of his. Knowing how much dishonesty lay behind his smile, she had trouble summoning her own. Like her dad, he turned charm on and off at will. Beneath it was nothing but lies.

"Here's what you do, Sweetheart. Sit on the couch and watch TV until I ask if you're sleepy yet. When I say that, answer yes, and I'll tell you to curl up and take a nap. Before you do that, come over like you want to give me a good-night kiss." He showed her a pair of dice. "You're going to have these in your pocket, and I'll take them when you hug me. Don't pay any attention when I do that. Got it?"

She'd wanted to refuse, but she knew what would happen if she did. Opposing even the smallest of her father's orders brought anger without limit. It scared her. It hurt. And sometimes Mom or Chris got hurt because of her.

"Had to bring my daughter," he'd tell the other men apologetically. "Her mom had a family emergency, but the kid won't be any bother, I swear."

Sometimes he played poker, and she had to bring him cards. She could feel his touch, feather light, as he slid his cheats out of her pocket between two fingers. The other men never suspected. Some smiled indulgently at the cute little girl; some ignored her. Still, in each new town, rumors eventually started: Mark Parsons was too lucky, too smooth. Was he dishonest? If not, how did he manage to win so often? If so, what should they do about it? Sometimes he was excluded from games. Sometimes he sensed their suspicions and withdrew. And sometimes there were strong words, threats, and even punches thrown. Then Robin, Chris, and their parents would move, often in the middle of the night so the landlord got cheated too.

But it always started again in the new place. "Smile when you come over to me," Dad would order. "And don't look so nervous. If you keep your cool, there's always a way to win."

Robin thought Bertie Oliva and her father would have been fast friends, at least until one of them cheated the other.

The waiter interrupted her thoughts. "I'll have water and whatever the special is," she said without looking at the menu.

As he moved away Oliva said, "Is everything okay, Ronda?"

Adopting a confiding tone she admitted, "I feel like I'm in over my head."

"You'll be fine." He waved a hand. "How many bidders in the auction?"

"Four, I think. As you can imagine, all this was kept pretty quiet, but four interns were sent 'on assignment' without specifics being discussed. I think the others have the same job I do."

"Do you wonder why four peons were sent to do a million-dollar deal?"

"I'm not stupid," she replied in a defensive tone. "She chose us because we're expendable." His eyes lit up at the feminine pronoun, and Robin smiled to herself. Oliva was collecting clues, trying to figure out who her supposed boss was. "She divided us up so we wouldn't figure it out," she went on. "If word of the br—scheme gets out somehow, she'll insist we cooked it up among ourselves. She'll insist the process of choosing Person of the Year is as pure as Ivory soap."

Oliva nodded approvingly. "You're not completely clueless. Any chance you'd share who 'she' is?"

"None," she said firmly.

"Fair enough, but I warn you, Mr. Preston will require more than your word that this mysterious person is capable of delivering what she promises."

"Once I have a commitment from him, I have something that will answer any questions he might have."

Oliva gave her his thousand-watt smile. Two underlings had clarified their bosses' positions without giving or taking offense.

The waiter set their meals before them, and conversation paused as they assured him there was nothing more they needed at the moment. When he moved away, Robin picked up her fork and speared a bit of salad. "How did you come to work for Preston?"

"Neil found me hawking guided tours in Cuba." When she looked up in surprise, Oliva seemed pleased. "That's right. I'm a kid from the street with no fancy education and zero training in public relations." He smiled at the memory. "I had this patter, an answer for every question, an assurance for every objection. Neil often says he can recognize talent when he sees it."

"That's your talent? Patter?"

"Well, it isn't just the words you say." He tapped his forehead. "It's understanding how people's minds work." Setting down his wrap, Oliva wiped his mouth with the napkin. "It's about knowing what people want to believe, whatever it is you're selling."

"And what do we want to believe about prescription drugs?"

"First, we want to believe they'll make our lives better. That's been part of advertising since day one, and I can imagine some caveman telling his listeners that one berry is far superior to others, but only he knows where it grows." She chuckled appreciatively. "Along with that, people like to think they know what's best for themselves. Do you realize we've seen an 18 percent rise in prescription drug sales since we started advertising to the public in 2002?"

"They weren't advertised before that?"

Oliva gave her a wry look. "The story goes that the drug manufacturers called in a bunch of Madison Avenue admen and asked how they could reach doctors to tell them what was available. One of the ad guys says, 'Why are you limiting yourselves to doctors?'" He raised his hands, palms up. "The light bulb went on, and today, two out of every three patients ask their doctors for a specific medication because they saw an ad for it on TV or in a magazine."

"'Ask your doctor if Product X is right for you.'"

"Exactly." He raised a finger as he cited an example. "Our new cancer medicine offers patients an additional month of life. That might not seem like much to you or me, but they want those thirty days, no matter how miserable they might be to live through."

"Maybe they hope that in that time someone will find a cure."

"You're probably right." He spread his hands. "We advertise 'longer life,' and they run to their doctors and beg for it."

"The doctors go along?"

"Often enough to make it worthwhile. The ones who want payment get some kind of compensation. The rest, hard-working medical people with little time for research, find it hard to keep up with the science." He took on a mock-serious tone. "We at Argent are always willing to instruct them as to the benefits of our products."

"You've changed the business of prescription medicine completely by advertising and promoting medicines."

He nodded. "It works. We spend billions on it each year."

Robin let Ronda show a tiny stab of doubt. "Does anybody care what patients really need?"

A shrug banished such concerns. "Give the people what they believe in. Their insurance pays for it, so who gets hurt?"

"I guess the patient does if the medicine doesn't work."

"Some contend that simply believing in a product is enough to bring results." He toyed with his water glass, making moisture rings on the table. "Like voodoo. It's effective because people believe in it."

She wouldn't have expected such tenuous arguments from someone in the business of treating illness, but then again, one might expect them from a man who worked for Neil Preston. "I remember learning in speech class about a call to action. I guess 'Ask your doctor' is a pretty effective one."

He shrugged. "Why address a problem if you don't give your listeners something to do about it?" After a moment he added, "If we convince one person in ten to act, the product makes money."

Robin was thinking she'd met the P.T. Barnum of her time, a guy who believed there's a sucker born every minute and if he didn't profit from them, someone else would. Just business.

Finishing off his wrap, Oliva returned to the subject of the meeting. "Now, if we agree to participate in your little auction, how might we guarantee that Mr. Preston will come out on top?"

Robin licked her lips. "Here's the thing. The intern that seals the deal will be on the fast track at TIME, and I want that person to be me. I think I know a way to make sure he's the top choice from everyone, not just my boss."

"That's improbable, given how he's been treated by the press in the past."

"That will change if he does what I suggest."

That made him chuckle. "You're offering advice to a man who made more money last year than most Central American countries?"

Robin paused as if reluctant to go on, but when she spoke again, she met Oliva's gaze directly. "Neil Preston is known as a greedy opportunist. He's despised because money is his god and he doesn't care who suffers for it. Now he could be POTY with that approach. He'd represent corporate greed and personal refusal to react to or even recognize the needs of others. I doubt that's how he wants it to go." She paused to sip her water. "The consensus among the editors is that this year's choice should be positive, sort of a ray of hope for the nation after a storm of controversy. In other words, they don't want to focus on a jerk this time around."

Though Robin feared she'd gone too far, Oliva seemed unoffended. "Neil is a genius who saw the potential for pharmaceutical growth early on. We use the system to our advantage. That's no crime."

Robin leaned forward. "Look at the scandals of the past year, with people fired for lying and generally misbehaving in every corner of our society. My bosses want a story that will give people hope and convince them the country isn't going to hell in a handbasket."

"So?" Oliva speared a cottage fry with his fork and dipped it in ketchup.

She raised one finger. "First they want a person who won't be accused of sexual misdeeds. Preston's record there is squeaky clean."

He smiled sardonically. "You won't find many less interested in sex."

Another finger joined the first. "Second, they'd like their choice to be a surprise, which he would be."

"But you said he'd be portrayed negatively. He won't like that."

"What if the leopard changed his spots?" After a pause to let that sink in she added a third finger. "Preston will do something unexpected and change his reputation in the business world."

Oliva set his fork on the table. "I don't follow."

"There's nothing people like better than a scoundrel who discovers he has a heart." Oliva's eyebrow rose, and she added, "The Grinch. Ebenezer Scrooge. Gru from *Despicable Me*."

Oliva leaned back, doubtful. "You want him to donate a kidney or something? Keep in mind you're already hitting us up for a million dollars."

"That's the entry fee, yes. But a large philanthropic gesture could move Preston to the top of the list."

Oliva laughed aloud, and like everything about him, it was charming. "You're kidding, right?"

Robin shook her head. "People are tired of greedy millionaires, and they aren't going to buy a magazine that recognizes someone just for being rich. Preston needs to have a change of heart."

"And how would he demonstrate that?"

She shrugged. "When a company's reputation hits bottom, they usually make some sort of bold move to prove they plan to do better."

"Most fire their CEO." Oliva quirked a brow. "We can't very well do that."

"No. You have to show that Neil Preston has human interests at heart."

Oliva looked thoughtful. "Like opening a charity hospital."

"Not a bad idea," Robin said, "but that takes time. What if he did something immediate, something that touched everyone?" After a moment to let him think about it, she went on, "A couple years back, Tesla released all its patents in the interest of building better electric cars. Now I know that wouldn't go over well with Preston, but think about something like that."

Oliva's expression turned pensive, and she knew the seed she'd planted had immediately borne fruit. "Give me some time to work on this."

"The choice will be made on Tuesday, so you haven't got long."

"If I can get something together, you could come to Green Grove Monday morning and finalize things."

Robin shook her head. "I can't be seen going into Preston's estate."

"No worries. It's pretty remote, and no one there is going to tell."

Doing her best to appear reluctant Robin said, "Can't he meet me at his downtown building or at my hotel?"

"Neil doesn't do things like that." Oliva's tone said there was no room for compromise on that point.

She sighed as if unable to come up with further excuses. "All right. Let's say Monday at nine, unless I hear differently from you. I'll send you some paperwork to look over before then with details and dates. If the agreement is made, Preston and I will both sign. There will also be a nondisclosure document, so he won't be tempted to talk about this."

Oliva raised a hand as if taking an oath. "I can assure you Mr. Preston won't tell any friends what's going on."

Robin guessed that was because Preston didn't have any friends. "If you come up with a philanthropic gesture my boss can use to secure her recommendation to the others on the committee, we'll need specifics that outline the plan and commit to its execution."

"I think we'll be able to surprise and delight your readers."

Clearing her throat, Robin made her last demand. "Of course I'll expect your half-payment at that time. We'd like it—"

"—In cash. Better for both of us. Of course you'll be personally responsible for the money." Though he smiled, there was threat in his tone.

"Of course."

Oliva reached out to shake her hand. "I appreciate your suggestion, Ms. Talman. It shows creativity and cleverness."

But not honesty, Robin thought as she left the restaurant. *No one in Preston's organization has any use for that.*

***

Hua was walking down 13th Street, apparently in a hurry, when he bumped into Joelle Preston leaving her favorite shoe store. "I'm very sorry!"

She grasped his arm. "It's you!"

"Ma'am?" He peered at her as if confused.

"Last night at the lecture. Blue dress, pecan bites?"

Now he appeared embarrassed but bowed politely. "Oh, yes. It is…nice to see you again, Miss."

A great deal of discussion had gone into Hua's appearance for his second meeting with Joelle. Robin suggested a waifish look, so he wore faded cargo pants with a generic t-shirt. On his back he carried what Em called a "geek alert," a battered black backpack. Chris had suggested a religious symbol, so he'd added an embroidered bracelet quoting Philippians 4:13: *I can do all things through Christ.*

"Meeting twice in such a short time? This has to be Kismet, Sweetie." It had actually been through the Spydie app. They'd learned where she was shopping downtown, located her using the phone, and arranged for Hua's second appearance in her life.

Hua affected mild disdain at her comment about Kismet. "I do not believe in the superstitions of the Turks." When she stuck her bottom lip out in a pout he added, "However, it is pleasant to see you again."

Joelle raised the shopping bags she carried. "I bet you've never shopped at Saks. I could buy you something."

"My tastes are simple," Hua said. "I don't need—"

"Do you like electronics? We could go to Best Buy and pick out a tablet."

"Thank you but no. I could never accept such a gift from a woman, even a beautiful one such as you."

"I've got money, Ba, lots of it. I'd like to spend it on you." Her tone made her end goal obvious.

"I appreciate it, really, but no. Thank you."

For a moment Joelle looked angry, and Hua wondered how often she was refused by the men she chose. Probably not often. Either her raw lust or the prospect of significant rewards won most of them over.

"Tell you what," she said when her irritation was under control. "I'm dying for a drink. Why don't you come along?"

Hua tried for just the right mixture of doubt and the desire to be polite. "I suppose I could do that."

Soon they were seated at a table in a café that was air-conditioned to almost polar temperatures. A waiter who sat behind the counter studying from what was obviously a textbook slid it aside to take their orders. He tried to be friendly, but Joelle looked at him as if he were a bug, so he hurried off to get iced tea for Hua and something complicated that started with "latte" for her.

When the waiter was gone, Joelle's eyes turned to Hua, and he fought the urge to duck under the table. "Nice place." He gestured at the trendy, rough-wood décor.

She glanced away for a split second. "I'd buy it for you if you want me to."

Hua treated it as a joke. "That's very kind, but I'm busy with my studies."

The waiter brought their drinks, and Joelle tasted hers. "What is this?" she demanded. "Did I ask for cappuccino?"

"No, ma'am. That's—"

"Do you think I can't tell the difference?" She poked the foam at the top of her drink with a finger. "The layers of espresso and steamed milk should be mixed together. The top should be a light layer of foam. It should be creamier than this, with a more subtle coffee flavor." The waiter blushed as her voice rose. "Do I have to go back there and show you how to make a decent latte?"

"I'm sorry, ma'am." His tone went soft as if to balance hers. "I'll get you another."

"It's pathetic that a person can't get good service." She gestured at the bar. "If you didn't have your nose stuck in a book, you could have paid attention to your job, which you might very well lose. I'm not a person you can screw with." The tirade went on and on, and everyone within earshot seemed to wish they were somewhere else. "I will report you to your boss," Joelle finished. "If the replacement isn't perfect—and I mean perfect—you'll be out of a job by the end of shift."

She picked up the cup before her, and for a moment Hua thought she'd throw it. He apparently feared the same thing, because he took it from her hand. "I'm sorry."

Hua and Joelle sat in silence while the man hurried to the coffee bar. She glared malevolently at him while he made a new latte. Though he didn't turn to look, the awkward set of his shoulders and the flush on his neck revealed that the guy was aware of her stare. When he set the replacement in front of her, Joelle caught his arm, holding him there. "Are you sure you got it right this time?"

Clearing his throat, the waiter said, "Yes, ma'am. I mean, I tried to."

Rolling her eyes, Joelle tipped the cup to her lips. "Better," she said grudgingly. "Enough so that I won't report you this time."

"Thank you. Ma'am." The words sounded strangled, and the man didn't look directly at her as he spoke. "Can I get you anything else?"

"We're fine. Go." Leaning her elbows on the table, she spoke to Hua as if the whole nasty scene had never happened. "You're studying Soviet Russia?"

Letting out a breath, he set her recent behavior aside. "Today, in fact, I am leaving to visit a museum that has several pieces I have not yet seen." He checked his watch. "My bus leaves in an hour."

"You must really love that stuff to go by bus."

Hua nodded. "It is best to see the items in person, so one can walk around them and imagine the people who created and used them."

"But I told you I could show you, oh, forty pieces and guarantee all the time with them you need, as up close as you like."

"I, um—perhaps I misunderstood."

She sipped at her drink. "I think you understood completely." When Hua blushed and lowered his gaze she went on, "Give me a number where I can reach you. I'll set it up for this weekend."

"Is your home on the city transit route?" He smiled shyly. "I have no vehicle at the present time."

Joelle laughed as if he'd said something clever. "Don't worry, Sweetie. I'll send a car to pick you up on Saturday afternoon."

He feigned disappointment. "I don't return from Oklahoma City until Sunday at four-twenty."

The hitch in her plans brought a frown. "Sunday then." She smiled coquettishly. "It's really an intriguing collection. You're going to be amazed."

"Oh, Miss, I—I don't know what to say."

She pushed her phone toward him. "Your number, so I know it's you. Call when you get back."

Minutes later, the Spydie app delivered what the group was waiting to hear. Joelle called Green Grove and spoke to someone on staff. "You know that Malevich painting in the gallery? I want it moved from the showroom to my bedroom by Sunday noon."

"Cool! He's in!" Em crowed.

When he rejoined them, Hua was less than enthusiastic. "Getting inside is only the first step. I'm sure a wired Ethernet has been created to secure their LAN from passive wiretapping, masquerading, man-in-the-middle, and denial-of-service."

Robin glared at him from under her lashes. "Would you repeat that in English?"

"They will have systems that identify unauthorized stations on their local area network and prevent communication from them. Control protocols will manage bridged network and other data through cryptography techniques that authenticate data origin, protect message integrity, and provide replay protection and confidentiality."

"She said English," Em commented.

"I think he's trying to say it will be hard to break into their system."

"Perhaps impossible," Hua agreed. "They will have scanners and such, so I won't be able to carry anything in with me that will allow me to tamper with their devices."

"What will you do?"

He thought about that. "I will make their computers think I belong there."

Chapter Thirteen

Hua and Robin listened as the morning meeting began, and Preston's first comment sent Robin's hopes plummeting. "I've been thinking about this good deed the woman's proposed, and I don't like it. I'll pay them the money, but I refuse to give anything away simply to look like a good guy. What she suggests is more likely to make me seem idiotic, tossing away income that should be mine." There was a pause, and Robin imagined his listeners each hoping someone else would be the first to speak. Preston apparently turned to Oliva. "Bertie, don't you agree? I mean, getting chosen is the main thing, right?"

When Oliva replied, his voice was as smooth as an oil slick. "Do you care what they say about you?"

An ugly snort preceded Preston's reply. "What can they say? I'm the most successful drug manufacturer in the world."

After a pause that indicated he was framing his argument, Oliva spoke again. "Successful, yes. But the media has painted you as an opportunist, and TIME might go with that angle. They could ignore your business acumen and focus on the profits you make from sick, injured, and dying Americans."

Preston's voice turned huffy. "I provide what people need. They pay for it. That's how business works."

"I agree," Oliva said soothingly. "But what if we come up with a splashy stunt that blows away the negative images of you and the company? With one well-conceived stroke, we erase all the negativity of the past year."

A grumpy sound indicated Preston wasn't ready to consider it. Still, he asked after a second, "What kind of stunt?"

Robin imagined the pause that followed meant the PR man was choosing exactly the right words. "People love a villain who has a change of heart, don't they?" When Preston made a second disapproving sound, Oliva hurried on. "We know you aren't a villain, but that's what people have been told. What if we make a gesture that causes America to rethink Argent Chemical in general and specifically its CEO?"

There was a pause as Preston digested that. "Such as?"

"In 2014, Tesla released their patents to advance the electric car industry as a whole. In 2016, NASA released a bunch of patents to stimulate entrepreneurial discovery."

"So?"

"What if we release some patents as a humanitarian gesture? TIME gets to break the story, which will make them happy, and you, Person of the Year Neil Preston, look like Mother Teresa."

"You did it!" Hua turned to Robin, one hand raised, and she slapped it enthusiastically.

Even as they savored the moment Preston said, "You don't really mean we should give up our patents."

"Only a few that aren't going anywhere," Oliva replied. "Anything else would be bad business."

This time the sound Preston made was different. Approving, Robin figured, and why not? Bertie's proposal was slightly crooked, it was decidedly crafty, and it seemed likely to get Argent's CEO his heart's desire. That odd growl was Neil Preston feeling happy.

***

Argent's inner circle held their morning meetings in the third-floor conference room, since Preston became claustrophobic if more than two people entered his office at a time. Even there, the seats on either side of his at the head of the table were left empty to give him space. It sometimes made passing papers back and forth difficult, and of course everyone had to wear gloves, so separating the sheets was a chore, but they were used to it.

Oliva no longer noticed the weirder aspects of Preston's home and office decor, such as the hammer and sickle flags beside the entry doors or the *shashka,* the Circassian sword of old Russia, that hung suspended over the mahogany conference table. Ornately decorated, the sword was reputed to have once belonged to Czar Nicholas, and Preston had been told it was presented to Lenin after the czar's death as a symbol that Russian royalty had come to an end.

Aside from the weapon resting overhead in its jewel-encrusted scabbard, the room was very modern, though stark, the way Oliva imagined Soviet offices would have been. Near Preston's chair was a console that gave him access to everything on the estate: closed-circuit TV, telephones, intercom, and alarm system. The wall Neil faced was completely glass, reinforced and bulletproof. It overlooked the orchard, which helped to keep him calm, unless one of his employees happened to stray into view. Then Preston would tap on the window and make violent shooing motions. Either Monica or Bertie would be required to go outside, track down the careless peasant, and drag him or her upstairs, where Preston would dismiss him on the spot. Giving employees the axe was the only interpersonal exchange Neil truly enjoyed.

Meetings began when Preston arrived. He liked to come in last, when everyone else was there and waiting. The four attendees at the present meeting had been together long enough that they'd settled into predictable roles. Overtly they approved whatever Neil said. If his newest idea was disastrous, no one allowed their facial expressions to reveal it. They often worked together to change his mind, each mentioning some small point so they gradually convinced Neil to reconsider. That didn't really make them allies. They were simply all in the same boat. They knew but would never admit that their boss became a little less reasonable each day.

Oliva knew from the outset of Thursday afternoon's meeting how things would go, but there were traps along the way. He was nervous when Neil seemed likely to reject the patent release, and grateful to Joelle for asking him to explain it. No one in Preston's circle freely exchanged opinions, which meant Oliva had to step carefully and hope someone else would support him. Though he never wanted to be the target of Preston's rage, Bertie felt obligated to lead his boss in positive, even legal, ways when possible.

118

Monica Covel, the security consultant, limited herself to security matters. She had great respect for Preston and Joelle but usually ignored Nixon and showed animosity toward Oliva. Preston seemed amused by her primitive attempts to put the man she sometimes called "The House Spic" in his place. Oliva never rose to her jibes, figuring Preston allowed it to give Monica an outlet for her ever-present anger. It also kept his second banana from becoming too sure of his position.

"All right," Preston said when Bertie had explained the benefits of releasing a few patents with a lot of fanfare. "Discussion?" No one spoke, having already deduced the deal was as good as done. Preston nodded as if they were all enthusiastically on board. "Nix has some suggestions for covering our asses if this doesn't go like Bertie thinks it will."

Baylor Nixon, who sat opposite Oliva, arranged his expensive gray trousers for minimal wrinkling. Beside him on the chair was a matching, pale gray cowboy hat with a discreet eagle feather tucked into its brim. The dark blue of the hat band perfectly matched his bolo tie. "Just doing my job," he said in a rumbling bass. Though he looked like a man of wisdom and integrity, Nixon's mind was more devious than forthright. For all his cowboy manners, he was brilliant at squelching lawsuits against Argent and expert at predicting how far they could stretch claims about a drug before the government stepped in. Bertie could usually count on Nixon to help when it was necessary to talk Preston out of one of his wilder ideas, but in the end he always supported his employer's wishes, no matter how strange.

"We'll move forward with Talman's proposal then," Preston said. "Bertie, get her out here Monday morning."

Covel squirmed in her chair. "Should we let this bunch on the estate?"

"Two people," Oliva said. "Talman and a photographer. Minimal threat."

Her lip curled. "They'll see the layout. They could note our defenses—"

Oliva pursed his lips. "What should we do, Monica, blindfold them?"

As she took breath to make a nasty retort, Preston waved a hand. "Our guards can handle one woman and a photographer. They'll be searched both coming and going." When Covel lapsed into silence, no doubt plotting how to strengthen Green Grove even further before the guests arrived, he went on. "This patent thing will give people a new slant on Argent Chemical."

"Our reputation is at the back end of the cattle drive." Nixon often used terms more suited to Randolph Scott than a modern-day attorney. "We're covered with dust from those hearings and the bad press that came with them."

Neil adjusted his rear in the chair. "Media creates these big flaps about somebody making money, like it's un-American. They forget that profit is what business is all about." A dutiful chorus of agreement followed his remark. "Can anyone see a downside to releasing a few patents?"

It wasn't likely anyone would, since he'd made his wishes clear, but he waited a few seconds anyway. "All right. The next question would be which patents we can give away without losing out. Bertie?"

"I sent Miss Cohee a list and asked her to compile the most recent sales figures, complaints filed, and efficacy studies. She's making copies of her findings for each of us."

"Well, where is she?" Preston pressed a button on the console before him. "Do you have paperwork for us, Mandy?"

A tiny voice answered, "I'm having trouble with the copier. I need a few minutes."

A tense silence fell over the room. When Preston had to wait for those he considered inferiors, his reaction might range from a nasty pout to a full-fledged tantrum. Nixon and Oliva locked gazes briefly. Though not friends in any sense of that word, everyone there shared a dread of Preston's anger. Cohee would probably be fired because of a malfunctioning machine, but the resulting ill will might spread to one or all of them. Preston's tantrums were difficult to tolerate, though luckily they never lasted long. When his anger ebbed and he calmed, everyone was expected to pretend what they'd just witnessed never happened.

"I'll see if I can help Mandy." Though he was sure she only wanted to escape the room, Oliva gave Covel credit for improvisation.

Casting a meaningful glance at Nixon, Oliva said, "One of the drugs on the list is Delicento."

Nixon picked up the thread. "The new allergy medication?"

"Yes. The test results are weak. It really doesn't do much of anything."

Preston snorted a laugh. "So what? We'll be okay with good ad copy and the placebo effect."

"Maybe, but there are indications that it's pretty hard on the lungs of those with chronic breathing problems. If we gave up the patent, we wouldn't have to admit to the side effects. Somebody else can restart the testing, and at some point they'll have to admit to the drawbacks. We'd be in the clear."

Nixon gave a dramatic sigh. "I wish people understood how difficult the pharmaceuticals market is."

His attempt as a distraction was obvious to everyone but Preston. One of the things he found irresistible was lecturing others on what he called the "tough truths" of business. With a little encouragement he might go on for some time, perhaps long enough for Mandy Cohee to fix the copier.

Oliva did his part. "I guess consumers can't handle the truth."

"Exactly!" Neil slapped a hand on the table. "They dislike the quirks and malfunctions of the human body but have no desire to actually work to relieve them. They'd rather believe there's a magic pill, cream, injection, or device that will make every little twinge or irritation go away." He set his elbows on the chair arms, hands folded at his stomach, and grinned like a hungry alligator. "Offer something that sounds good and they'll bite every time."

Preston was on his soapbox now. His listeners, even his sister, arranged their faces to show interest, though they'd all heard it before. "Eighty ads per hour on television. Everybody's a medical expert, or thinks he is." He went on in a dumb-guy voice, "'Hey, doc, I got this pain in my back but I don't like those exercises you recommended. Can't you just shoot me up with something?'"

"We're happy to provide those injections, for a fee," Nixon responded.

"And Bertie's clever ads show a person playing with kids or shopping at a farmers' market to distract from the side effect warnings." It was rare that Joelle acknowledged Oliva's talents, but she was stalling, like everyone else, to avert the looming storm.

"People accept what they see over what they hear," Oliva said agreeably. "That's fact."

Nixon glanced at the door. No Mandy yet. Clearing his throat, he said, "I often wonder why more doctors don't say no when patients ask for a product that isn't right for them."

Preston crossed his arms. "If they don't prescribe something, the patient will go to a physician who's more agreeable."

"More doctors than you might imagine are willing to use the trial and error method." Oliva added. "If the FDA approved a drug, they figure it must be safe."

Preston pointed at Oliva as if he were the star pupil. "And once the prescription gets written, who'll question a refill or six?" He waved a hand like a magician finishing a trick. "Money in the bank for us, probably for years."

Preston looked up as Cohee came in, her face blotchy and her eyes downcast. "It's about time!"

"Sorry to keep you waiting, Mr. Preston." She avoided his eyes. "It's working now."

"Then you are good for something." Preston's tone was mild, but they all knew that was like the first tiny hiss of air before a balloon exploded. "Tell me, Ms. Cohee, exactly what is your job here?"

She looked at Oliva once as if pleading, but he dropped his gaze to his hands. "To—to have paperwork ready when you need it."

"Exactly." He smiled, almost benignly, but Oliva's gut clenched. He liked Mandy Cohee. Eyes down, she moved around the table, placing a packet of papers before each of them. Neil's glare followed. "Your job is to get things ready when I need them. I needed this paperwork ten minutes ago, and what did I get, Mandy? What did I get?"

"I'm sorry. The machine—" She stopped, apparently aware no excuse would be good enough.

"If you'd done proper maintenance on the machine, it wouldn't have malfunctioned. If you'd planned ahead and considered all possibilities, you wouldn't have been caught unprepared."

In a voice that wobbled Cohee said, "You're right, Mr. Preston. It won't happen again."

"No, it won't, because—"

"Preston, we need to get back to what we were doing." It was Joelle.

Oliva cleared his throat. "We're on a deadline. We wouldn't want to slow things down right now."

Taking courage from their urging, Nixon said, "A change in personnel at this juncture is likely to be unfortunate, Neil. We have only days to prepare."

For a moment Preston hovered between anger and desire. Since he wasn't into delayed gratification, Oliva had no idea which would win. Finally he said coldly, "You may go, Mandy."

She backed away, closing the door carefully as she went. When the latch clicked into place, Preston took up the sheet in front of him as if nothing had happened. "Here's our list. We're looking for items that appear impressive but either present problems with approval or have a poor likelihood for being profitable. Those are the ones we're going to dump."

Chapter Fourteen

"How are things on the home turf?" Em asked when she called that evening.

"What is that?" Kai asked in return. "Home is fine but I don't know *turf*."

"It means about the same thing."

"Then why you say it twice?"

Em sniffed impatiently. "Things are okay?"

"Yes. Tom will come home soon, he says."

"That's good. And Bennett?"

"The dog is fine, but I think he does not like being on a diet."

"You put my dog on a diet?"

Kai's tone turned prim. "Just a medium one, so he does not get fat." She changed the subject before Em could complain. "Does your plan go well?"

"I guess. Robin's pretty sure we'll be able to get onto the property."

"You should be careful," Kai warned. "With your hip so bad, you will be caught if escape is necessary."

"I'm not going out there," Em told her. "My job is to distract the lawyer."

"How will you do this?"

Em chuckled. "I'm practicing to be a femme fatale."

"What is a fum fatall?"

"A woman who tempts a man into doing things he shouldn't." At Kai's questioning grunt Em explained, "I contacted him, posing as Marjorie Stanton, and told him that due to his years of kind attention, I'd like to meet him while I'm in Oklahoma. He almost fell over himself arranging it." She sighed. "Now all I have to do is charm the socks off him."

"Oh."

Kai seemed so confused that Em laughed aloud. "I'm practicing batting my eyes and fiddling with my hair."

"Something is wrong with your eyes and your hair?"

"Never mind, dear. We'll talk about it when I get home."

***

Em pulled her rented BMW under the arched portico in front of the lodge and let the valet help her out. Handing him the generous tip he expected she ordered, "Take good care of my baby, Sweet-cheeks."

Nodding agreeably, he got into the car while a second man held the door open, wishing her a wonderful luncheon. She was tempted to say it was likely to be stressful, but he didn't care, no matter how sweetly he smiled.

Today she was not Emily Kane, former FBI agent, but Marjorie Stanton, former movie star. She couldn't recall being more nervous. Though she'd played parts before, she'd never tried to be a person who was well-known, frequently photographed (though not recently), and dubbed "charming" and "glamorous" by the press. Robin had taken her to a salon where her hair and makeup were done in Marjorie's style. She'd had a manicure and a pedicure (over her strong objections). At a high-end resale shop, they'd chosen an outfit Em liked and Robin accepted, though she said it was a little less Hollywood than she'd have liked. When Hua suggested adding a colorful scarf, she'd replied that accessories were his thing, not hers. "I'd garrote myself with the darned thing, like Isadora Duncan and her infamous boa."

As she entered the dining room, Em tried not to lean too heavily on her cane. After all the hoopla of preparation, she felt about as attractive as a woman of her age could feel. "A dishrag with sequins," she muttered as a mirror reflected her new persona. "Hope it's worth the effort."

126

Baylor Nixon wore a tan sport coat over an open-necked brown shirt, khaki pants, and what she guessed were very expensive boots. On the table sat his ten-gallon hat. He rose as the waiter led Em to his table, and she was surprised to see anxiety in his eyes. After years of admiring Marjorie Stanton from afar, the man was nervous about their face-to-face meeting.

In a "What Would Margy Do?" moment, Em opened her arms, embraced him, and did the celebrity air-kiss on either cheek. "It's wonderful to finally meet, Mr. Nixon. After years of letters, I feel I know you."

The grin almost split his face. "Please, Miz Stanton, call me Nix."

"All right, Nix, if you'll call me Margy."

Elbowing the waiter aside, he held her chair for her. "Our Gal Margy."

"I hated that name! I insisted on Marjorie Stanton for billing in my movies, but now that I'm old and decrepit, Margy doesn't seem so bad."

"I don't consider you old, and you're certainly not decrepit." Nixon was already beginning to relax, and his voice changed to a slurred growl. "I think Margy is the perfect name for a purdy little ol' gal like you."

With effort, Em kept her smile in place. *Great. Dinner with a John Wayne wannabe!*

"You've been pretty quiet these last few years."

"I didn't think my fans wanted to see Our Gal hobbling around with a cane." Waving Hollywood away, she went on, "I found other things to keep myself occupied."

"The Marjorie Stanton Foundation." At her look of surprise he added, "I keep up. If I'd been there, I could have helped you make a profit on your money instead of just giving it away."

"What do you mean?"

127

He folded perfectly-manicured hands on the table before him. "I know foundations help one avoid taxes, but there are ways they can be organized that add to your wealth rather than depleting it."

She shook her head. "I have enough money."

His expression turned arch. "No one has enough money, Margy."

Em hoped she was adequately hiding her disgust. To change the subject she asked, "Are you married, Nix?"

He wriggled his brows. "I'm afraid I'm what they call a three-time loser, but honestly, every time I've shed a wife, it felt like winning to me." His smile turned sly. "Why do you ask?"

"Well, I waited to see how we hit it off, but I think we're *sympatico*."

Leaning forward, he drew out a single word. "Verrrrry."

"Well, I have an event coming up, and I'd rather not go alone. I was wondering if you might be willing to accompany me."

"Some sort of public appearance?"

"My 62nd high school class reunion." She made a self-deprecating gesture. "I know it's silly, but they see me as their 'big star' and expect certain things from me." Em laid a hand on Nixon's arm. "You're the perfect plus one: handsome, charming, and intelligent. Will you go with me on Sunday?"

Nixon mimed tipping a hat and exaggerated his drawl. "Ma'am, I'd be truly honored."

***

The District Attorney shook hands with Tom Wyman. "Thanks for your help. Human trafficking cases are hard to prosecute, but your testimony was incontrovertible."

"I'm glad we got them," Tom replied. "Now I need to get home."

"You said you don't live in Georgia anymore?"

"I moved west." Tom smiled. "I'm a big Horace Greeley fan."

Leaving the courthouse, Tom looked for the Uber car he'd arranged. When the driver waved, he boarded and settled in for the ride to the airport. Luckily the guy wasn't a talker, so he could think.

Now that his responsibility to the state of Florida was satisfied, Tom's thoughts turned to KIDNAP's current caper. He wasn't supposed to know how dangerous it was, but he'd followed their communication with Chris and knew that Neil Preston was no choirboy. Other things bothered him too. He wished he'd been able to talk Robin into waiting for him, though he couldn't say how he'd have made things safer or easier. He just wanted to be there.

It wasn't that he didn't trust Robin and the others. They'd operated successfully without him before. Still, he'd missed two capers now, one due to fittings for his new hand and this one due to the trial. He was eager to become a real part of the group—the gang—and make a difference. He'd been a loner growing up in foster care. Then the army had become his family, and he liked the feeling of belonging he'd found there until he got hurt. Now he also liked the idea of Robin's gang, their attempts to make the world a little better. It made no difference to him if no one outside their circle ever knew about it.

In addition to that, Tom wanted to be where Robin was. He wanted to be ready to defend, protect, and support her. He'd never met anyone like Robin, though she insisted if he'd met her BK, "before kidnap," she'd have bored him to death. "I was just an everyday person," she'd said. "You'd never even have noticed me when I handed you copies of your will or escorted you into my boss' office and offered coffee, tea, or soda."

Tom hadn't said it aloud, but he knew that wasn't true. Devin Whoever had noticed her. What had they been to each other? What was he to Robin now? When would he show up again, and what would she do when he did?

Tom looked down at his plane ticket for Kansas City. What would he do when he got home? Tighten up the porch railing and hang out with Kai, Mai, and the dog? He wished he had a ticket for Tulsa, Oklahoma, where he'd be in on the action with the people he cared about.

***

Though Em succeeded in getting Nixon to agree to go with her on Sunday, she was nervous and edgy all afternoon. She forced herself to appear calm, since they all had their worries. Hua's role had expanded, which was stressful. Robin had multiple roles to play and fretted over all of them, as usual. Planning wasn't Cam's forte. Tom was in Florida. Em was determined not to add to the group's problems by admitting she had no idea how she was going to prevent Nixon from attending the meeting at Green Grove Monday morning.

If she disabled the car, Nixon would simply call someone to come and get them. She might fake an illness, but she figured he'd leave her in the hands of medical experts and go back to work. She even thought about seducing him, but there were a dozen arguments against that, all of them embarrassing.

Her most promising idea was to make him sick. She bought a bottle of ipecac tablets on the way back to the hotel, but their lack of predictability worried her. The timing was tricky, as was the dosage, since she didn't want to cause real harm. How sick did Nixon need to be? How could she keep him from warning Preston that something wasn't right? No answers had offered themselves, but she refused to let the others know. When Robin asked how her part was coming along, Em said gruffly, "Got it under control."

As the day slipped away, she became more and more nervous. Was she getting too old for the game? Was her mind losing its sharpness? Why couldn't she function like she had as an FBI whiz kid? Why was she suddenly so unsure, so tentative, so...old? In the past she'd often been the one who knew exactly how to do what was needed. Bennett had called her "Idea Em."

Bennett. Once her supervisor. The source of her dog's name. Her secret love. Though he'd never showed it, Em knew she'd been as special to Bennett as he was to her. Circumstances required they remain merely coworkers, but in her heart, where no one else saw, Bennett belonged to Em. Suddenly she missed him more than she could bear.

Moving quickly to prevent second thoughts from stopping her, Em picked up her phone and entered a number from memory.

"McAdams." Three words and she was back in the Bureau, working beside him, learning from him, wanting to be with him.

Enough of that. "Bennett, it's Em."

"Emily? Is it you?" He went on without waiting for an answer. "Of course I recognize your voice. I just—it's been so long, and I'd begun to think I'd never hear from you again."

"That's what I intended, once upon a time."

"Why, Emily? I thought we were..." His pause said more than words could. "Friends. Good friends."

She tried for a light tone. "Work friendships seldom survive in retirement. With no daily routine to gripe about, no common enemies to defeat or at least deride, things fall apart."

Bennett didn't answer for a while. "I'm not sure that's always true."

Best that we went our separate ways. She didn't say that. "I need advice, Bennett, and you're the only person I can think of both able to give it and discreet enough not to ask why."

"I see." Humor warmed his usually circumspect tone. "Let's hear the question."

"I need to isolate someone for about twenty hours. I don't want to hurt him, and I don't want him to know he's been intentionally sidetracked."

"Hmm. How well are you acquainted?"

"Only slightly. I doubt he'd remain by my side if I had heart palpitations."

"Can you maroon him on an island or a cabin in the mountains?"

"My guess is he wouldn't agree to go that far from his responsibilities, and I can't force him."

Bennett considered, and she imagined one strong hand rubbing at his chin, as he often did when presented with a puzzle. "You're going to have to take a situational approach, Em. Watch for an opportunity and seize it when it arises." When she didn't answer he went on, "Remember when we took down that wannabe Bonnie and Clyde in Minnesota? I was never so scared in my life as when you walked into that restaurant like you had no idea they were robbing the place."

"They'd have shot that old man, sure as sin."

He chuckled. "It certainly stymied them when you started crying and said you'd run over the guy's dog."

She laughed too. "Even stone-cold killers get mushy when a pet dies."

"You see? That was exactly what was needed at that moment. You were always the best at assessing a situation on the fly and coming up with a plan."

"But these days if I don't know what I'm getting into, I doubt myself."

Another pause. "Is this thing you're planning important?"

"Yes."

"Then your need to make it work will overcome your desire to know how it will end."

"You're right," she said. "I just needed to hear you say I can do it. I can't...the people I'm helping now, I don't want them to see me as a liability."

132

"You were the best agent I ever worked with, Em. I have no doubt you still function as well as ever."

She had an irrational and irritating urge to cry. "Thank you, Bennett."

"Um, Emily, I want you to know—I mean, you probably didn't hear—Katherine died."

A stab of grief vied with something else, an emotion she would not acknowledge. "I'm so sorry."

"I never understood people saying it was a blessing that someone died, but honestly, she was so sad the last few years. She lost the power of speech, her eyesight was almost gone, and of course the disease took away all control of her body."

Em's smile was tinged with sadness. As if refusing to give it power, Bennett had never once said aloud the name of the disease that robbed his wife of so much, and now of life itself. "I'm glad she's at peace," she told him. "And I'm sorry you went through so much pain together."

"Thank you."

It seemed there was more they might say, but neither began it. Instead Em said briskly, "Thanks for listening, Bennett. It was good to hear your voice."

"I've missed talking to you."

"Goodbye, old friend."

"Until we meet again, Em."

Chapter Fifteen

Monica Covel was serious about physical fitness. With a daily exercise routine that would wear out most twenty-year-olds, at forty she was strong, lean, and fit. She could bench-press 150 pounds, and her resting heart rate was 55. Even after a run or a vigorous workout, it returned to that point within two minutes.

Her focus on job and fitness level left little time for personal relationships, but Covel didn't mind. She'd never got much of a thrill from friendships or even the few love affairs she'd had. Living the way she wanted was easier, without worrying about what someone else needed or cared about. The internet provided social interaction, mostly watching fools make themselves look more foolish. When she was in the mood for a man, she watched Matt Damon or Dwayne Johnson do manly things on screen. When she tired of them, she shut them off. You can't do that to a lover or a clingy BFF.

Covel's real passion was providing the best possible security for Neil Preston. It wasn't usually difficult, since Preston was as wary of people as she was. Green Grove was like a fortress, and Monica was happy as keeper of the keys. Any improvement to security was hers for the asking, and as a result, her boss was as safe from attack as a person could be in the twenty-first century.

In return for her excellent services, Preston provided Covel with an apartment on the ground floor of his home and the use of a gym completely outfitted with top-of-the-line equipment. She had only to mention that a new fitness machine had come on the market and it appeared. It made her proud to know that Mr. Preston recognized her usefulness and, when required, her ruthlessness as well.

Though she didn't often leave the estate, there was one appointment Covel was not allowed to miss. She'd had a little trouble adjusting to civilian life when she returned from Iraq, and three separate episodes had led to a determination that she needed anger management counseling. It was bull, but a court order is a court order, so once each month she had to drive into Tulsa and attend sessions. In the last few months she'd gone from individual sessions to group meetings, and she hoped to be released completely soon. To achieve that goal, she carefully kept her opinions to herself and said the right words: *co-operation, discussion, calming techniques.* Using terms like those made her therapist nod like a bobble-head doll.

Covel parked the Audi that Preston provided for her use in the clinic parking lot. Traffic had made her tense, and the heat made things worse, but she concentrated on keeping her pulse normal and her expression blank. She tried to enter the sessions with a calm mind, and once there, shut out most of what went on. There were a couple of blacks who felt sorry for themselves every single time, and there was a rag-head the government had brought out after his cover got blown. He'd been tortured for a while, and though his scars were pitiful, he should have expected that from his fellow camel jockeys. She hated being mixed in with people she despised and forced to pretend it was all sweetness and light with the Ay-rabs and the Nigras. She guessed the other real Americans in the group did the same thing she did: play the game in order to get free of the system and its stupid rules.

Covel arrived early, since she liked to choose the chair she wanted and position the blinds to her liking. When she arrived in the second-floor room, a man was there, a new guy. He was in a wheelchair, which he'd parked in the spot she usually took, nearest the door. "Hi," he said cheerfully. "I'm Robert."

"Covel," she said tersely. Closing her eyes for a moment, she recaptured her outward calm, chose a seat on the opposite end of the room, and ignored the interloper. After a while the others began filing in, and only two-and-a-half minutes late by her watch, the counselor arrived and the session began.

Monica was surprised to hear that the new guy, visiting Oklahoma from New York City, had served in the same unit she had in Fallujah, the 173rd Airborne. He hadn't come out of it well, having lost both legs, but he spouted the same garbage the rest did. He'd come to grips with the

135

violence he'd seen. He was finding his way in civilian life. He was getting better.

Yeah, right.

When they left the session, Covel and the man shared an elevator. He was a friendly type, and something she'd said in the session had stuck with him. "When were you in Fallujah?"

"In '03 and again in '05," she said. "Two tours killing criminals and terrorists."

"That's the attitude!" He laughed as if it were a joke, and she let it lie.

When they got outside, he swore softly.

"What's the matter?"

"Nothing. It's fine." Following his gaze, Covel saw what concerned him. A motorcycle sat next to a van parked in a handicap spot, so close there was no way he'd be able to get in.

"What's up with the bike?" she asked.

He made an angry gesture. "You wouldn't believe how often stuff like this happens."

Covel glanced up at the windows above them. The counselor stood looking down, and she saw a chance to score some points. "I can help."

He gave her an appraising look. "How are you going to do that?"

She made her lips form what was for her a smile. "One wheel at a time."

It wasn't that difficult. The bike was one of the smaller models, and she lifted first the back end and then the front, moving each end a few inches several times until she created enough space for him to reach the vehicle. She kind of enjoyed it, since the guy was obviously impressed by her strength.

She opened the door and made a gesture of invitation, and he got in with an agility that revealed plenty of upper-body strength. As he reached for his seatbelt the man asked, "Would you mind stowing the chair? I can set it beside me, but it rides quieter when it's laid flat in the back."

The doctor was no longer at the window, but it was a small request. "Sure." Covel wheeled the chair to the back of the van, collapsed it, and opened the double doors. As she set it inside, she sensed movement behind her. Something stung the base of her neck, strong hands closed on her arms, and she knew nothing for a long time.

***

Devin Ashford sat in his car, trying to understand what he'd just seen. Had it really been an abduction?

Following Robin Parsons to Tulsa, Oklahoma, had been a surreal experience. Robin, an old woman, the big guy, and an Asian man had stopped at a small motel on the outskirts of the city. Booking a room across the courtyard from theirs, he'd watched them come and go, noting their gray van and a car his friends would have called a "grandma-mobile." Later, a third man, this one in a wheelchair, arrived in a taxi and joined them.

She'd told him about a brother who lost his legs overseas. Devin didn't recall the details, but the guy looked enough like Robin to be a relative.

At any point over the last week, Ashford could have called his employer and ended his assignment. Two things held him back. First, the nagging feeling that his employer meant to harm Robin, and second, plain nosiness as to what the odd group was up to. Since he had an expense account and nothing better to do, Ashford had waited to see if he could find out.

There was a lot of coming and going. Sometimes he followed, wearing a knit hat, sunglasses, or a hoodie. He didn't learn much, because all they did was talk to people.

Today, things had turned interesting. He'd followed Robin and the disabled man to a medical office complex. The guy in the wheelchair went inside while Robin waited in the van. Twenty minutes later the big guy showed up on a motorcycle, which he parked very close to the driver's side of the van. Satisfied with its placement, he sat down on the other side of the parking lot, pulled out a phone, and focused on it with the intensity common to gamers.

After about twenty minutes Robin exited the passenger seat, went to the side door, and climbed into the cargo area. Nothing of interest happened for an hour. Devin was almost ready to give up when the building doors opened and people began exiting. The man in the wheelchair came out, talking with a blonde with hard muscles and harder eyes.

When the woman helped the man by moving the bike away from the door, he apparently asked for a final favor. The woman steered the wheelchair to the far side of the van, out of Ashford's view.

Things happened fast after that. The big guy left his seat on the grass and hurried to the van. He was out of sight for only a few seconds before the slider closed and the van left the lot. Getting on the bike, the big man followed.

Frozen by surprise, Ashford almost didn't shake it off in time to follow. By the time he caught up, the van was pulling into a DQ with outside tables. Devin turned into an auto parts store across the street. In a few minutes the big guy came on foot and spoke with the driver. After a brief conference, he went into the DQ and emerged a few minutes later carrying several white sacks and a tray of drinks. Robin got the disabled man's chair out of the back—Where was the blonde?—and the three of them sat at a table. They ended up staying there until after midnight, eating, talking, and generally killing time. About once an hour Robin went to the van and climbed inside for a few minutes.

When they finally left, Ashford again followed, keeping a discreet distance. They pulled into a hospital parking lot, where the Asian man waited near the doors, wearing a white lab coat over a dress shirt and trousers. He pulled a stretcher from the shadows of the building's alcove and wheeled it to the van, which they'd parked some distance from the entry. Robin and the big guy changed into scrubs that the Asian guy handed them. When they were ready, the two men loaded the blonde, who was limp and unconscious, onto the stretcher. Robin spoke to the van driver, who took her hand for a moment, then left. When he was out of sight, the big man pushed the stretcher inside.

Robin, what are you up to?

***

When Cam, Chris, and Robin arrived at Caponetti Memorial Hospital with the unconscious Covel, Hua was doing a terrible job of pretending to smoke a cigarette. As Cam chose a spot well away from the entrance and the security cameras, Hua wheeled a gurney out to meet them. Getting out of the van, Robin asked, "Are we good?"

Hua touched the fake ID badge clipped to his lapel. "I have been all around this place for two days now, speaking to the staff as if I belong." He grinned. "Since all Asians are geniuses who excel in science, no one has questioned that I am a doctor."

Robin smiled tightly as she donned a pale blue, often-washed tunic and clipped her own fake badge in place. Cam hopped modestly into the van to change into the stolen scrubs that had *CMH* stenciled on the front. "What do we do when we get inside?"

"You will pilot the gurney," Hua said. "Robin will walk behind me and appear to be making notes on this." He handed her a clipboard in an aluminum case, adding, "It is HIPAA approved for patient privacy."

As Robin held the gurney still, Hua and Cam hauled Covel out of the van and laid her on it. As they covered her with a sheet and strapped her down, Robin stepped up to the driver's window. "Your part's done, Big Brother. How are you feeling?"

Chris grinned like a teenager. "It's kind of a rush, isn't it?"

139

"It is. But you're going home now. You promised."

"If my wife wasn't due home on leave, I'd insist on staying till the end, but I'll drop the van back at the hotel and be on my way." His face turned serious. "You going to be okay?"

"We're fine. Check the *KIDNAP.org* website, and we'll try to keep you apprised of what's happening."

"It's good to be working together again," Chris said. "Like the old days."

Not like that, Robin thought. *These days I'm scared, but this time around, the person causing it isn't someone who's supposed to protect me.*

Chris seemed to read her thought. "Okay, this is better than the old days. We're fighting to make things better instead of just fighting to survive."

She raised an imaginary glass. "Down with creeps, every one of 'em."

He returned the salute. "Every single one."

The van's back doors closed, and Cam slapped them twice as a signal he was ready. "I'll be waiting to hear from you." With a wave, Chris drove away.

Robin turned to Cam and Hua. "Showtime."

Though Robin expected to be challenged at any moment, wheeling Covel into the building was surprisingly uneventful. Hua had chosen the hospital with the worst reputation for security in the city, and after midnight the chaos of the emergency department was almost beyond belief. Car accidents, gunshot victims, and writhing sufferers of as yet undiagnosed ailments vied for staff attention as they rolled through. The lone security guard was distracted by an argument between a mother and daughter over whether someone named Cleatus was worthy of treatment or whether the doctors should, "Let that sucker die." No one paid any attention to a doctor, nurse, and orderly pushing a gurney across the lobby as if they had every right to be there. They waited in apparent calm for an elevator then rode to the fifth floor. No one seemed curious about where they were taking the patient.

Hua led the way out of the elevator car and passed through double metal doors with a sign that warned: *Infectious diseases: Do Not Enter.* Cam glanced at Robin doubtfully, and she guessed he imagined exotic, colorful germs crawling the walls like clicking spiders in some B movie. He was probably wishing he had a phaser with which to blast them into oblivion. Though she grinned to reassure him, Robin herself was nervous as they stopped at a shelf stocked with protective clothing. Still, the shapeless gown, gloves, and a mask made them less identifiable, and the image of super-viruses streaming down her throat and into her gut receded.

The room Hua had claimed for them was enclosed on three sides by reinforced glass. Shutting the door, he pulled full-length curtains over the glass walls before turning on the overhead light. "Cam, help me put her on the bed. Then we'll step out for a few minutes." When Cam had done as ordered, Hua told Robin, "Dress her in a hospital gown while I give orders for private duty staff only." He left Robin alone with the unconscious woman.

Robin struggled with feelings of pity as she removed Covel's clothes. Possibly no more than a loyal employee, the woman might be an innocent victim in their campaign to bring down Neil Preston. She was almost hating herself for the way they'd treated her until the half-conscious woman muttered, "Did that hurt, Rag-head? The next one will cripple you for life."

***

When Robin came out of the hospital just after 1:00 a.m., she and the Asian man left in their car. Devin had to make a decision: follow them or go into the hospital and find out what had happened to the blonde. If they'd wanted to hurt her, why take her to a hospital? If she was sick, why the long delay in seeking treatment?

Knowing where they were staying, he decided he didn't need to follow Robin. He wanted to talk to the woman they'd left somewhere inside.

Entering the hospital, he stopped for a moment to survey the waiting area. People sat in chairs, holding make-shift compresses to wounds on various body parts. Patients lay on gurneys as worried relatives stood by, comforting them as best they could. A staffer with a cart rolled from person to person, taking down information and offering words of encouragement. A security guard had muscled a drunk into a corner and was trying to convince him to stop cursing at the staff.

No one paid any attention to Devin. He wasn't bloody. He walked upright. He was practically invisible. He began his search for the woman who must now be a patient.

Finding her took a while. The first floor was labeled *Maternity and Pediatrics,* an unlikely place to begin. He looked at the schematic. Up one floor was surgery and ICU. He doubted the patient had been through that in just over an hour. Up another floor were patient rooms. He'd begin there.

Riding the elevator to the third floor, he roamed the halls, checking rooms that had a patient in them but no name in the little card slot outside the door. Nothing. Another floor. Again nothing. On the fifth floor, he stepped out of the stairwell just as a nurse exited double doors separating some rooms at one end of a hallway from the main area. In the gap he glimpsed the big guy, standing in the doorway of a patient room, masked, gloved, and looking uncomfortable. He ran his hands over his chest, as if looking for buttons that weren't there.

The doors between them closed with a hiss of air, and Ashford saw the sign: *Infectious Diseases: See Nurse at Main Desk for Entry Procedures.*

Chapter Sixteen

Luca found the people who'd offered her a job playing nurse more interesting than anyone she'd met in a long time. After Clarabell and Bozo gave her five hundred dollars for practically nothing, she met them as arranged and was taken to a motel on the outskirts of the city. There she was "trained" for her role by an old woman called Loonette, who was cranky, crippled, and corny. Loonette made it clear from the first that she didn't trust their new employee. Once Luca heard her mutter, "No farther than I can toss her, and she's no little thing."

First she'd been ordered to shower and remove her "hardware," various studs and rings. Loonette clicked her tongue at Luca's tats, but Clarabell had bought makeup to cover them as well as a wig to conceal her multi-colored hair. Looking in the bathroom mirror, Luca marveled at how young and innocent she looked. Who was the real Luca, the tough-talking street ho or this sweet-faced girl with sad eyes?

Once she was presentable according to Loonette's standards, the lessons had begun. "You're pretending to be a private duty nurse," the old woman explained. "You need to seem medically competent, so no one thinks you need help. Bubbles will say you're Ethiopian, with rudimentary English skills. Speak as little as possible."

"Okay."

"Your patient is under sedation. I'll teach you how to monitor her vitals and keep track of the drip that keeps her that way. We don't want her hurt, but we sure don't want her to wake up either." Loonette made her watch two videos designed for CNA training. Luca didn't think it would be difficult to read a few gauges every hour or so, but when she said so, Loonette insisted it was important to be watchful. "If there's any sign of respiratory distress or heart irregularity, call for help right away." After a moment she added, "If you have to do that, you'll want to get out of there ASAP."

That was as close as she came to admitting the whole thing was hinky as hell. Luca had wondered aloud if she could get arrested for this, but Loonette pooh-poohed the idea. "Medical people learn to focus on their own business. They have a lot of responsibility, so they don't have time to stick their noses into someone else's cases. Appear competent, and you'll be left alone."

Though she was curious about the escapade, Luca knew she was supposed to take the money and shut up. Balancing her inquisitive mind opposite two thousand dollar signs, she chose money over knowing.

At 6:00 a.m. on Saturday, the least busy time of day on the fifth floor, a guy called Bubbles led Luca into the hospital. She was introduced to the floor nurse as Nurse Afua, who was taking over for the orderly who'd been caring for Patient MC. Luca wasn't surprised to see the "orderly" was the big guy the gang called Bozo.

"Nurse Afua will see to the care of a patient I am monitoring until the seventy-two-hour incubation period for her suspected illness is over." Doctor Minh (Bubbles) warned the staff against speaking about Patient MC to outsiders. "We don't want to create fears of an epidemic if she doesn't actually have the disease I have tentatively diagnosed." Luca was surprised at how easily Bubbles spun a story that made the nurse respond with, "Of course, Doctor." When they were alone, Bubbles explained he'd brought her in just after shift change so the charge nurse would assume the night nurse had done the admission.

"The details are in the computer," Bubbles told Luca with his sweet smile. "It's just that no one actually employed by the hospital put them there."

***

After Hua left with Luca, Em tried to nap for a while, but at six she decided coffee was better than pretending she might at some point drift into slumber. Though their motel wasn't exactly four-star quality, they replenished their not-too-shabby brew in the lobby every few hours. That was good.

Robin and Cam were holed up in his room, discussing all the possible scenarios Monday could bring. Robin had been unusually nervous that morning, and she'd finally told Em about the old boyfriend from Georgia who kept calling her. Watching as Robin talked about Ashford, Em concluded he wasn't someone she loved. Em thought she saw in his reappearance the carefree days before she'd become a criminal. A reminder just before a big caper must have made those days seem idyllic.

The story of Ashford asking her to visit his grandmother came out as a humorous anecdote, but it made Em wonder what the guy was up to. A roll in the hay for old times' sake? A new start on an old romance? Something more sinister? *"Come and meet my grandma,"* said the Big, *Bad Wolf.*

It didn't sit right with Em, and she texted Tom asking him to call her when he was able. He was either back at home or would be soon, so he'd track the guy down and decide if he was a threat to either Robin or the KIDNAP gang.

As luck would have it, when she got back to her door with coffee in one hand and the key card in the other, her phone buzzed. Hurriedly she set the cup on the floor, connected the call, barked, "Hang on a second," and let herself in. Once she'd gone back for the coffee and settled herself on the small couch, she said, "Tom? I'm here." Briefly she told him about Ashford's calls to Robin. "She says you know about him. What do you think?"

"I don't trust him," Wyman said with conviction. "Devin Ashford was let go from his law firm in Cedar for misappropriation of client funds. They apparently couldn't prove it was intentional, so they pretended to believe his story that it was a misunderstanding."

"How did you find this out?"

"I told Mink someone had shown up from Robin's past, and he asked around. Ashford's dismissal was kept quiet because his firm and the legal profession in general didn't need yet another black eye."

Em grunted disgustedly. "So when he told Robin he was moving to South America to take that great opportunity, he'd actually been fired?"

"He did go to Argentina," Tom admitted, "but it was because his license was suspended by the state of Georgia."

"What do you suppose he's doing in Kansas?"

"We can't ignore the possibility he came looking for Robin."

"No," Em said, "we can't, even if she thinks it was some wonderful coincidence. Are you home yet?"

"Just about."

"Then you'd better talk to the grandmother and see what she can tell you." She thought for a moment. "Graystreet Manor Nursing Home, she said, and Grandma's name is Maxine—no, Minnie. Minnie Walter."

***

Tom pressed the red button that allowed him to enter the nursing home without setting off alarms. He felt like a creep going behind Robin's back, but he agreed with Em. They needed to know what Devin Ashford was up to.

Approaching a staffer sorting meds into paper cups he asked, "Where can I find Minnie Walter?"

The woman thought for a second. "Hall 7, fourth room on the left."

"Thanks. Her grandson told me the number, but I forgot what he said."

The woman frowned. "Minnie doesn't have a grandson."

"Devin? Devin Ashford?"

Thin brows formed a squiggle above the aide's doubting gaze. "I don't know any Devin, but I've known Minnie for years. She never married or had kids."

As soon as he was outside, Tom called Em again. "The woman in the nursing facility has no living relatives."

"That rattlesnake-in-the-grass!"

"I looked in on her." Tom went on, "While she can speak, Minnie doesn't have a clue who she's talking to. I suppose Ashford looked till he found a woman who was responsive but not aware enough to ask who he was. If she'd ordered him out, he probably would have claimed it was due to dementia."

"This is all wrong," Em said. "Should we tell the others?"

"Not in the middle of a caper if we can help it," Tom replied. "They need to stay focused."

"True." She thought about it. "Could it be he just wanted an excuse to reconnect with Robin?"

"The fake grandma tells me it's more than that."

Em groaned. "This guy is playing games, and I won't be around to watch for him. I'm supposed to get Nixon out of Tulsa tomorrow and keep him away until after Monday's meeting."

Tom thought for a moment. "Em, you should concentrate on your part. I'll stop Ashford's game, just as soon as I understand the rules."

***

Robin was monitoring the audio on Joelle's phone early Saturday afternoon when Joelle visited her brother's apartment. Preston was apparently having breakfast for lunch, because she heard the jingle of cereal hitting a bowl and milk splashing atop it. Bertie Oliva was already there when Joelle came in, and he was in the middle of reporting a call from Caponetti Memorial Hospital. "They've put her in the isolation ward."

"Who?" Joelle asked.

"Monica Covel has caught some kind of evil bug."

147

Joelle gasped. "That's horrible! Neil, you've got to help her."

Preston made an irritated grunt around a mouthful of cereal. It might have meant he didn't know how. It might have meant he didn't intend to go anywhere near anyone with an "evil bug."

At Joelle's urging, Oliva reported the details provided by Doctor Minh, a specialist in infectious disease. "They think she picked up a fairly rare strain from a guy at her counseling session who just returned from Africa. They rode down in the elevator together, and shortly afterward Monica collapsed. They're looking for the man, who might be Ground Zero for an epidemic, but they haven't located him yet." He ended with a question for his boss. "The doctor says it's fatal for a small segment of the population. What do you want me to do?"

"I suppose you need to go down there and look into it," Preston replied. "Take her some flowers or something, and find out what you can about whatever this sickness is."

"All right."

"Make sure you don't touch her, Bertie. And take extra precautions when you get back here."

"I will." Oliva sounded resigned, and Robin guessed he'd be showering, changing clothes, and scrubbing his hair and nails with disinfectant before being allowed in Preston's presence again.

"If she lives, I don't want her back here until we're certain she's fully recovered," Preston went on. "See that she has somewhere else to go for...let's say two weeks. At least two."

"I'll think of something."

"I expect you to." Preston made a sound Robin guessed was accompanied by a shiver. "Imagine picking up some God-awful germ just by stepping into an elevator. A person has to be really, really careful."

***

148

Tom found the house on Bobby Road depressing, despite the warm welcome his return generated from Kai, Mai, and Bennett the dog. What did Devin Ashford want from Robin? Why had he come to Kansas? Em's call made things worse, since it seemed Ashford hadn't given up on Robin.

Was Tom simply jealous of Ashford, or was the guy a threat? Knowing he had to do something, he called Hua. "I know you're neck-deep in the caper, but can you take a minute and find information for me on a guy named Devin Ashford from Cedar, Georgia? I'd like to know where he is right now."

Hua didn't even ask why. "I will call you back."

The call came as Tom was unpacking the suitcase he'd set in a corner on his return. "Mr. Devin Ashford is presently in Tulsa, staying in the same motel we are." His voice betrayed concern.

"Damn! I was afraid of that."

"Should I be worried about this?"

Tom thought about that for a moment. "I'll take care of Mr. Ashford," he finally replied. "And Hua, don't mention this to Robin, okay? She's got enough to worry about."

Now it was Hua's turn to hesitate. "If you are sure he won't trouble us."

"He won't." Tom ended the call and checked the *KIDNAP.org* website. Each person currently in Tulsa was already committed to a vital task. It was up to Tom to neutralize whatever mischief Ashford had in mind.

He knew the general plan. Em was supposed to take Preston's lawyer on a fake road trip. Hua was going to get onto Preston's estate as the sister's guest and somehow isolate her. They'd hired a woman to monitor the unconscious security woman until Cam and Robin could execute the caper Monday morning. Preston's people would be out of the way, and he would face an accounting of his crimes.

Was he wrong not to warn Robin about Ashford? Would she believe him if he did? Tom feared she'd see his appearance as evidence he didn't trust her judgment. She might think he was motivated by jealousy, which was partly true. Tom didn't like Robin's old boyfriend following her around, but was Ashford a threat to the caper or just an obstacle to Tom's hopes for the future?

Robin wasn't dumb, and she didn't take unnecessary risks. Tom knew better than to ride into Tulsa like a knight on a white horse, declaring he'd come to save her from herself. Still, he could go there and stand on the sidelines, ready to help if needed. A knight-in-waiting. He'd be one of those.

**

Hua dozed in a chair in the out-of-sight corner of Monica Covel's hospital room when his phone pulsed. The text said *Visitor.*

He'd asked the receptionist to let him know if anyone asked for Covel, explaining he wanted to be sure her visitors understood the necessity of special precautions. Now he moved to the bed and pretended to check one of four IV drips that went under the top sheet and then nowhere. Only the fifth was operational, its contents keeping Covel in a peaceful, unconscious state.

The elevator doors opened, and a voice asked for Room 512. A minute or so later, a nurse appeared at the door with a robed, masked Bertie Oliva. "This man is the patient's coworker, Doctor."

"Mr. Oliva? We spoke on the telephone." Hua stood between Covel and the doorway. "Forgive me if I don't shake hands. An unnecessary risk for you."

Oliva took a step back in unconscious reaction. "This disease is deadly?"

The nurse who'd accompanied Oliva peered through the doorway, and Hua guessed there'd been speculation about the mysterious patient. With a cool stare he said, "I will call if we need anything."

When she'd returned to her duties Hua said, "As I told you on the telephone, we believe Ms. Covel was exposed to a strain of the Coxsackievirus that is particularly virulent. In Africa it has shown itself to be very dangerous." He cleared his throat. "The carrier has been found since we spoke. He is dead." Oliva's eyes widened but Hua went on, "Still, the rest of the group seems unaffected. We believe the man must have coughed or sneezed on Ms. Covel. If so, that is unfortunate for her."

"She was exposed to Cox—what?"

"Coxsackievirus. It's fairly harmless in most cases, but this strain is new and as yet we have no effective treatment for it." Adopting the pedantic approach of a scientist Hua explained, "Viruses from this group can cause aseptic meningitis. A patient will often complain of a headache and fever with mild neck stiffness, which Ms. Covel did when brought to my office."

"Did you test her for this Coxsackievirus?"

"Unfortunately, it is not detected in routine culture tests. We can only wait." He glanced at the patient. "I hope I am mistaken, but with the symptoms she exhibited and the death of the other man..." He made a helpless grimace.

"You mean she might not recover?"

Hua pretended to consider. "Since she was actually at a medical clinic when she fell ill, Ms. Covel received help quickly. I put her into an induced coma to protect her brain from damage." He added with a hint of pride, "I have treated such cases in my work with Doctors Without Borders and knew what was needed. Otherwise she might be dead by now."

Wearing scrubs and a serious expression, Luca exited the bathroom with a bag of trash in one hand.

"This is Nurse Afua," Hua said. "She worked for me in Africa last year, and I arranged for her to come to the U.S. to receive training. She is immune to the disease and has experience treating it, so I engaged her as a private duty nurse for Ms. Covel." He paused. "If that is acceptable to you, of course."

"Whatever she needs," Oliva spoke to Luca. "Pleased to meet you, Nurse Afua."

"Allo," Luca said softly.

Hua smiled. "Her English is limited, but I assure you, Afua will take good care of your friend."

"That's great. Can you give me a prognosis?"

"The incubation period is three to five days. Late Monday or early Tuesday we will know if my suspicions are correct. If the disease runs its course while she is sedated, all will be well, and she'll be allowed to go home to complete her recovery."

Oliva shifted his feet. "Mr. Preston, her employer and mine, suggests Ms. Covel take a cruise until—um, to fully recuperate from the disease. He will of course pay all her expenses."

Hua couldn't resist a jab. "Some of the medicine she needs is expensive, and it is not covered by insurance."

"Whatever she needs. Mr. Preston will pay."

"Again she is lucky," Hua said. "Many of my patients must decide between buying the medications they need and purchasing groceries for their families. It is very sad this happens in a developed nation."

Hua was gratified to see Oliva wince. He hoped the man felt at least a small amount of guilt for his part in that state of affairs.

***

When he returned to Green Grove, Oliva did an extended wash-up and changed his clothes before going to Preston's office to make his report.

"How could she be so careless?" Preston said. Picking up a stapler from his desk, he pegged it at the wall. It hit some distance from Oliva's head, which was actually a good sign. When Preston blamed Bertie for something, he actually aimed impromptu missiles at him, and Oliva had to duck like a prairie dog until his boss was out of ammunition. He didn't have to turn to see the new scar on the expensive wood paneling. He made a mental note to have someone fix it before tomorrow.

"How long will she be gone?" Preston demanded. "Two weeks? A month? Should you get started looking for a replacement?"

Oliva sensed Preston was searching for a way to blame him for the problem, which was typical. "We're okay for a while. Monica's got all the procedures in place, and the men know what to do."

"But Belk's in charge!" Preston's voice dripped with contempt. "Aside from being big enough to haul a semi, he's useless!" He rose and stomped around the office, shoving some books to the floor and upsetting a plant with an angry push. "I can't believe Monica left me to deal with this mess!"

Bertie wondered briefly what his boss would say if he suddenly dropped dead. *How thoughtless! Now I need to find a new lackey!* Aloud he said, "I'll talk to Belk and make sure he follows security procedures to the letter."

"I hope they're not written in some difficult format, like cursive." He jabbed a finger at Oliva. "I'm holding you responsible for his conduct."

Because I begged you to hire him? Because I spritzed Monica with deadly saliva? Exactly how is any of this my fault?

To make the moment worse, Lawrence Belk himself tapped at the office door. He appeared nervous, as he always did when he had to speak to Preston. "Sir, there's a guy who's called three times since yesterday, wanting to see you. We told him that was impossible, but this morning he left you a message on my phone."

Preston made a rolling motion with one hand. "Let's hear it."

The recorded voice was smooth and confident. "Mr. Preston, there's a threat to your safety in the next few days. You should be very careful when you leave your estate, especially at night. If you're willing to meet with me, I can tell you more."

"Sounds like a shakedown to me."

"That's what I thought too, sir, but I—"

Preston pointed at Belk's nose. "Are you in charge of security here?"

"Um, temporarily, yes."

"And are you competent in your job?"

"Of course, sir."

Preston's chin rose so he was looking down his nose at Belk. "I have no plans to leave the estate in the near future. Would that indicate that this 'threat' isn't very credible?"

Belk pressed his lips together. "I thought you should know about it, sir."

"Now I do." The chin indicated the door. "Get out of here. Do your job, or I'll find someone who will."

Belk was gone before he got the words out. Despite his dislike for the man, Oliva almost felt sorry for Belk,. Working for Neil was never a treat, and Belk was in no way an adequate replacement for Covel. Prone to tattle on others and often indecisive, he was a frequent target of Preston's anger. Bertie guessed Belk had agonized over the right thing to do and in the end chosen wrongly. The man never knew when to act and when to wait, when to speak and when to stay silent.

For all her weirdness, Covel had a better sense of how to handle Preston. She stroked his ego. She made him feel secure. And she handled problems herself whenever possible. Oliva smiled slightly. Preston and

Belk were in agreement on one thing: they both wanted nothing more than Covel's quick recovery.

Chapter Seventeen

"You've met this Oliva guy," Em said on Saturday afternoon when Robin made her proposal. "If you think it will work, we trust your judgment."

"It's the same thing we always do," Cam added. "Just different."

"I will drive," Hua volunteered. For once no one tried to dissuade him, since they'd need him at the wheel.

"All right," Robin said. "Tonight we smooth our way into Green Grove."

She spoke with Tom later that morning, not to share specifics, because she knew he worried, but because it was good to hear his voice. The trial had resulted in guilty verdicts all around, and when he'd finished telling her about it he asked, "All set for Monday?"

"I think it's under control."

"Em told me about the thing tonight."

"Keeping my fingers crossed." She could have said that her neck was so tight she could hardly turn it to look to the side, or that she felt like a giant hand squeezed her stomach every few seconds.

"Any word from your Georgia friend? Demon?"

"It's Devin, smart aleck, and yes. He's called a couple of times." Devin kept pressing for a time when he could see her again. She couldn't very well admit she was in Tulsa, Oklahoma, planning to commit several serious crimes, so she'd brushed him off with vague claims of busy-ness.

"How long will he be around?" Tom's voice was carefully casual, but she sensed the real question: When is he going to get out of your life?

Did she want to see Devin again? Did she want the chance to discover if their old relationship might be rekindled? It was hard to tell if her pleasant memories focused on the man himself or on the specter of her old life, the Robin Parsons who'd ambled through her days as an upright citizen. Every single moment of her present existence required decisions of utmost importance, decisions that, if wrong, would result in flight, arrest, imprisonment, or even death.

Pharma Con

Was the longing she felt for Devin Ashford or for the days when her most difficult choice was whether to have lunch at Arby's or Chipotle?

***

When the call to Robin ended, Tom sat holding the phone, watching until the count of minutes disappeared and the screen went blank. A battle waged in his mind. On one side of the argument, Robin was a competent woman who dealt with all kinds of complex situations. She'd functioned as leader of the group before he came along. But emotions can divert logic. Feelings, in this case the call of Robin's old love, might easily blind her to possible danger.

Added to that was the call he'd received from Hua, who'd done some investigating on his own. "I had a small eavesdropping device in my knapsack, so I attached it to Mr. Ashford's car," he reported. "He went out to Green Grove and tried to get Neil Preston to meet with him concerning a threat to his safety." He coughed lightly. "Are you certain we don't need to tell Robin about this?"

"For today," Tom replied. "I'll see what I can do and let you know."

He didn't mention to Hua that he was at that moment on I-44, at the outskirts of Tulsa.

***

Luca enjoyed her role as private duty nurse Afua. They'd told her it was a common African name meaning "child born on Friday," and she'd practiced saying it aloud until it sounded natural to her ears.

As directed, she checked the patient's vital signs periodically. When anyone outside the room showed interest, she busied herself with some nurse-like task, keeping her eyes down and her movements brisk. In addition to the promised money, she found the clown gang likeable. Even the old lady hadn't been as bad as she seemed at first. She wanted to help with whatever it was they were trying to do.

When she started feeling hungry around noon, she realized they hadn't told her how she was supposed to get meals. Should she leave the patient alone and go to the hospital cafeteria? Call for pizza delivery in the infectious diseases ward? Her question was answered when "Dr. Minh" arrived with a briefcase. Closing the blinds, Bubbles opened the case to reveal a cardboard carry-out carton. Inside it were four quesadillas with salsa and sour cream packets on the side. "If you do not enjoy Mexican food," he said earnestly, "I can bring something else next time."

"I like pretty much anything in the way of food." Luca gestured at her plump body. "Isn't that obvious?"

Bubbles shook his head and spoke firmly. "You are a very attractive woman, and you must never think of yourself in any other terms." Returning to the briefcase, he took out a Coke. "Is this good too?"

"Very good." Taking it, she popped the top and grinned. "I was afraid I'd have to survive all weekend on stuff from the vending machine down the hall."

Closing the briefcase, he frowned. "We would never do that to you. We are most grateful for your help."

When he was gone, Luca shook her head. She'd never imagined a gang of criminals would be so nice. They didn't know her well, but they didn't seem judgmental about her or her occupation.

All her life people had judged Luca and found her wanting. Her momma had apparently found her worthless, because she'd left her behind when she was still an infant. Daddy had raised her, but when she reached puberty he'd begun wishing aloud for a boy-child who could take care of him. "A man get old, his childs should make his way easier," he'd say. He sent her onto the street to earn a living the only way a female's fit for. She tried, but it was hard. She hated the dirty men, the nasty girls, and the passers-by who looked down their noses at her.

Daddy had died young, but then there was Lettie, her cousin. Lettie was thin and pretty and mean as a snake, but she was all Luca had, so she put up with her cruel comments and sneery eye-rolls. Lettie's friends were no better. In fact, Luca couldn't recall a single person in her life who'd ever asked her if she liked her food or told her she should consider herself attractive. And for sure no one had ever expressed gratitude for her helpfulness. She was just expected to do what people wanted her to.

With the meal question settled, Luca had two remaining problems, the first being boredom. After she'd read the same dumb news stories ten times on her phone, she entertained herself by making up a background story for her patient. Her name was Ivanka. She was a Russian spy, and the clowns, no doubt CIA operatives, had waylaid her so they could send a replacement to some important meeting and recover secret files she'd stolen. It was the plot of several movies she'd seen, but that didn't mean it couldn't be true in real life.

Luca's other problem arrived Saturday night in the form of the shift manager, an RN who was both unfriendly and nosy. When she rapped on the door and gestured for Luca to come into the corridor, she played it cool.

"I understand you're private-duty for this patient."

"Yes, yes," Luca replied. "I am Nurse Afua, but my English, it is not so very nice, understand?"

"And Doctor Minh is her private physician?"

"Yes, yes. He is excellent doctor. Very excellent."

The nurse glared over Luca's shoulder. "What's the matter with her?"

"Um, very sick. Maybe virus in her brain."

"How is she being treated? What medications is she on?"

That was beyond her power of truth-stretching. "My English...You maybe speak to Doctor Minh."

She gestured at the room as a whole. "Who authorized all this?"

159

"Doctor Minh shall return back soon. You speak to him, please."

Though she didn't argue further, the nurse was far from satisfied. From time to time all night she would stop outside the door, forehead creased with doubt. Luca tried to appear busy and efficient, but in her head, she worried. Though she didn't know what the end game was, she hoped Bubbles and his crew had created a plausible background for their scam.

"You'll be done Monday by noon," Loonette had told her. "It's a busy place, and it's the weekend. If we're lucky, everybody will leave you alone."

Glancing sideways at the woman she'd dubbed Nurse Nasty, Luca feared they weren't going to be lucky for much longer.

***

"Luca is doing well," Hua told the others. "Ms. Covel is out of our way."

"The girl's okay," Em admitted. "Backward but not stupid, and she liked the idea of playacting."

"And the staff accepted her?" Robin asked.

"There was a brief period of interest in the case, but I think they have returned to their own concerns."

"Okay," Robin said. "Covel is out of commission, and Hua's got a date with Joelle for tomorrow."

Hua brushed his hair back and frowned. "She said she would call me on Sunday. I hope she follows through."

"She will." Em looked up from the sweater she was knitting, a horrible combination of tan and purple that provided evidence for Robin's belief she was color-blind. "She's got a trap set up for you in her bedroom, remember?"

Hua blushed, and Robin quickly changed the subject. "What's your status with Nixon, Em?"

"We're heading north tomorrow afternoon for Marjorie Stanton's supposed class reunion," she replied. "I'll see he doesn't get back to Tulsa for Monday's meeting."

Robin wanted to ask how that would happen, but something in Em's manner over the last few days said she shouldn't. Em was the most experienced of them all at undercover operations, and she'd earned their trust many times over. If she said she'd keep Nixon away, she would.

"That leaves Oliva," she said. "Is everything ready for our chat with him?"

"According to what I heard from the Spydie app, Oliva is meeting two of Argent's PR men at the downtown office," Hua replied.

"On a Saturday evening?" Em asked doubtfully.

Hua shrugged. "Apparently Preston's people work when he tells them to. It's good, because there should not be many people around when he leaves the building."

"What if Mr. Oliva doesn't react the way we want him to?" Em asked, though they'd been over that topic several times. "If he doesn't know the extent of Preston's crimes, he might bolt."

Robin had worried about that all day. "Oliva could go back and tell Preston about us."

Cam ran a hand through his hair. "That wouldn't be good."

"No," Robin admitted. "If Oliva warns Preston, everything we've done falls apart. We won't get past the front gates, much less up to the third floor."

Em had played devil's advocate in the whole discussion of how to handle Oliva, and she returned to the role. "The guy is Preston's loyal lackey. Why do you think he'll do what you say?"

"I'm not sure," Robin admitted. "I have the sense that he's crooked but not evil, you know?" When the others merely frowned, she tried to explain. "Bertie's a kid from nowhere who gets to live the good life by catering to Preston. I don't think the damage they do has ever really registered with him."

"Because he won't let it." Em's tone turned scornful. "If you think you'll talk a guy like that out of acting in his own self-interest, you're dreaming."

"I know." Robin chewed at a thumbnail before going on. "But we're not trying to rehabilitate him. We're just presenting Mr. Oliva with an alternate view of what his self-interest will be in the near future."

"At least with Spydie letting us listen in, we'll know if he reports the incident to Preston," Hua said.

Em nodded. "And if he does, we fold our tents and steal silently into the desert."

"What desert?" Cam asked. "I thought we were going back to Kansas."

"Figure of speech, Big Guy." Looking at each of them in turn, Em said, "We need to create a perfect storm for Neil Preston to make this caper work, but each of us should have a plan for escape if things go wrong. We'll be separated from each other, unable to communicate, and possibly under duress. Make sure you've got your MacGyver skills sharp and ready."

Cam rubbed his shirt front for a moment then lowered his hands with a conscious effort. "I like MacGyver, Em, but since we're a gang, I think we're more like the A-Team."

Chapter Eighteen

"What have you come up with, Nix?" Preston asked when he entered the conference room. Meetings on Saturday weren't unusual, since Preston lived and breathed business, and the appointment with the people from TIME magazine meant decisions had to be made. They were four this time instead of the usual five, since Preston had seen no reason to invite Lawrence Belk to take Monica Covel's seat.

Nixon took a sheet of paper from his briefcase and slid it to Preston with a gloved hand. He had copies for the others, but Preston liked to see everything first, so they waited as he read silently.

Argent Patents Released for Generic Production

Argent Chemical holds patents for many medicines that heal disease, prolong life, and aid in recovery from injury. Today, in the spirit of the open source movement for the advancement of medicine and the promotion of general welfare, the company is releasing several current patents to allow them to be produced generically.

"We believe that all companies creating and making new medicines would benefit from a common, rapidly-evolving technology platform in which discoveries are shared, not hoarded," said Argent owner and CEO Neil Preston. "It is our belief that applying the open source philosophy to these patents will strengthen rather than diminish Argent's future." Preston went on to say he hopes other developers will follow Argent's lead, making life-saving medicines available to the public. "Argent embraces open sourcing and models a future where companies share their discoveries for the good of all."

While Nixon gave the others their copies, Preston steepled his fingers and set his chin on them. "A very impressive load of crap."

Nixon gave him a tight smile. "Have you decided exactly which patents you'll give up?"

"We have." Oliva held up four fingers. "Two drugs that will never get approved due to side effects, one that doesn't work, and one that works for about ten people in the whole country. We'll make the announcement big news, and—"

Preston broke in. "I get good press for once. TIME sells a ton of magazines."

"How much digging would it take for someone to learn how little we've actually offered?" Joelle asked.

Preston's expression darkened as he turned to Oliva. "Yes. What if some CNN wannabe star researches the releases and sees what we've done?"

"We would handle the situation as we usually do," he answered lightly. "He's a frustrated hack hoping for a Pulitzer. She has mental issues."

Nixon laced his fingers over his flat belly. "And I send notice to his or her employer of the possible legal repercussions of libeling Argent."

Preston shifted in the chair. "So we've got our stuff ready. How will the meeting with TIME go?"

"We have the press release you just read, and Nix is preparing the legal releases for the patents we've chosen. Ms. Talman will have a standard contract from the magazine, and she'll come prepared to guarantee your selection as Person of the Year."

"I've reviewed the contract the lady provided," Nixon said. "You grant the magazine exclusive rights to the announcement in December and provide information for the POTY spread. I am preparing an addendum that says you have the right to edit out anything you feel is damaging to yourself or Argent Chemical."

164

When Preston only nodded, Oliva added, "Ms. Talman wants to interview you once the paperwork is finished."

"Do you really think this will help?" Preston asked. "My reputation has been under attack for a long time."

"There are a lot of people out there who'll get all warm and fuzzy at the thought of a millionaire with a heart of gold," Oliva replied. "People eat that stuff up."

Looking down at the draft Preston asked, "Why do we have to commit to this now? The magazine doesn't announce their choice until December."

Oliva licked his lips. "They won't proceed on faith, Neil."

"Who's supposed to have faith here?" Preston's lips curled. "*I* pay a huge bribe. Then *I* do this big, fat giveaway in order to make them say nice things about me. I'm the one taking chances."

"But look at the positives," Oliva said smoothly. "Changing the public's perception means investigators are likely to back off. Our stock prices will rise, profits will increase, and a host of smart, upcoming scientists will look to Argent as a means of making their life-saving ideas available to the public." Enthusiasm overcame discretion as he added, "You're going to want to give me a raise."

Preston bristled. "Writing to TIME was my idea. If I had a real publicist, I wouldn't have to come up with clever notions by myself."

Oliva immediately backpedaled. "Right. I should have thought of it, because it's genius."

Preston waved impatiently. "Make arrangements for the cash." He raised a finger. "You did specify they only get half now?" When Oliva nodded, he turned to Nixon. "I'll want to see the release paperwork by tomorrow. Email them to me, and once we make any necessary corrections, you can bring hard copies with you Monday morning." He surveyed his coterie. "This little idea of mine is going to get TIME on my side." Pleased with the phrase, he repeated it. "TIME on my side."

"I hope this is worth what it's going to cost you," Nixon commented.

Preston had abandoned his doubts. "Once my picture is on that magazine cover, they can't take it back. Nobody will be able to say I'm not at the top of my field."

Oliva didn't say what came into his mind: *Nobody would dare to.*

***

Devin Ashford sat in a corner booth at Starbucks, taking note of each man who came in. Most went straight to the counter, but he guessed the one he was meeting would scan the crowd to locate him before ordering. Devin's Georgia Bulldogs cap stood out, as he'd been sure it would in Oklahoma.

When a guy wearing a suit entered and stopped to survey the room, Ashford pegged him as the one he'd spoken to on the phone. He met the newcomer's gaze, and after a nod, the other went to the counter and ordered.

When the man came to the table, he didn't offer to shake hands but said tersely, "Lawrence Belk." Setting his coffee down, he pulled out a chair and sat, settling at once into a stillness that was almost eerie. His movements seemed limited to essentials: eyes that seldom blinked, the hand that brought the coffee cup to his lips and back down in automatic fashion. Even his lips hardly moved as he asked, "What is it you want from us?"

Ashford set his forearms on the table. "What's it worth to you?"

Belk's expression, already stony, turned harder. "Extortion, Mr. Ashford?"

He raised his hands in a calming gesture. "Call it a reward. I recently observed some things you need to investigate out of concern for your

166

employer's safety. I'm willing to share what I know for, oh, let's say a thousand dollars."

"You're dreaming," Belk said.

Ashford sipped his espresso. Could those eyes get any colder? "If you want to take chances with Preston's life, it's fine with me."

After consideration Belk said, "I can give you two hundred."

"Three."

"Two-and-a-half." He eyed Ashford before adding, "That's all I brought."

"Let's see it."

Using only one hand, Belk pulled out a wallet, shielding it from the view of the other patrons with his body, and removed five fifty-dollar bills.

"Okay." Ashford leaned back, thumping the table a few times with his thumbs. "I was recently hired to track down a woman I used to date."

"She some kind of assassin?"

"As far as I can tell, she's never hurt anyone."

"Then why are we here?"

"I pretended to run into her by accident. You know, 'Imagine meeting you here!' All surprised."

Belk lost patience. "I'm thrilled you reunited with your lost love. Now how is she a threat to Preston?"

"I sneaked into her car while she was grocery shopping." He stopped. "Do you know the tennis ball trick for unlocking a car door?" The look on Belk's face said it wasn't worth explaining. "Never mind. Anyway, this woman is a list maker. In a little notebook she carries around with her I found notes on Neil Preston of Tulsa, Oklahoma. She researched his business, employees, even the layout of his estate."

Belk seemed unimpressed. "So she's curious. He's a famous man."

"I'm not done. She had something to do with your boss—Covel, is it?—getting put in the hospital."

Belk's brows rose. "What, she sprinkled her with germs to make her sick?"

"Are you sure she's sick?" Ashford folded his hands on the table. "This woman abducted my employer and demanded money for his release. I think she's done it to others."

Still skeptical, Belk asked, "She kidnaps people and they don't tell anybody?"

"My employer couldn't tell the authorities about it because he hasn't exactly got clean hands."

Belk sniffed. "This sounds like some badass comic book superhero somebody dreamed up."

"She has help: an old woman, a big guy, an Asian, and a man in a wheelchair. There could be more."

"Yeah, she probably put an ad on Craigslist: *Kidnapping Help Wanted.*"

Ashford grimaced. "Fine. Don't believe me, but I watched her and the big guy approach Covel in a parking lot. Next thing, your boss is in the hospital with some rare disease, and you're in charge of security." He leaned in again. "I just hope you're up to it, man. Preston won't like it if he finds out you were warned and didn't even offer him the chance to hear my story."

Belk thought about that for some time. Finally he set two hundreds and a fifty on the table and slid them over to Ashford. "We'll look into it." Still holding onto the bills he asked, "What's her name?"

"Robin Parsons. That's not the name she goes by now, but it's the one I knew her by back in Georgia. With your resources and that as a starting point, you should be able to track her down." He slid a piece of paper across the table. "This is the motel where they're staying."

Belk pocketed the note and then leaned toward Ashford, his expression serious. "Here's what you're going to do, man. You will not call or approach Mr. Preston, me, or any of the staff again. We can handle this, and we will. If you're anywhere around, you might get hurt. Get what I'm saying?"

Ashford had to swallow before answering. "Yeah."

Belk rose. "Then I don't expect we'll ever meet again." He left without bothering to look back at Ashford's reaction to the bone-chilling warning.

Chapter Nineteen

Bertie Oliva's phone pulsed as he left Argent's downtown office. Neil, of course. "Where are you?"

It's a wonder he doesn't have GPS on me.

"I met with our PR people and got them started on publicity for December, nothing specific, just "big announcement coming." I'll make sure the patent release gets lots of attention."

Preston's concern was more immediate. "Before you come home, swing by Andy's and pick me up a quart of Snow-monster with Bananas."

"Sure thing, Boss."

Second-in-command at a prominent national firm, Oliva was nonetheless used to being Preston's go-fer. Trusting few people, Neil kept household staff to a minimum, which meant Bertie ended up doing jobs far below his pay grade. Though some would consider it demeaning, Oliva figured if Neil wanted to pay him six figures to pick up his dry cleaning, he was happy to do it.

The advantage to running the boss's errands was that it got him off the estate for a while. When he'd agreed to live at Green Grove, the place had seemed amazing. Though it was weird, it was still a thousand times nicer than anywhere he'd ever lived before. Nowadays he felt like a bird in a gilded cage, and if he was honest, the cage was populated with cuckoos. It was nice to mingle with normal people for a while: swear at bad drivers and blare Cuban music with all the car windows rolled down. The ice cream mission meant he could stay away for at least another hour. As long as he was back in time for dessert, Neil wouldn't complain.

In the parking lot Oliva stopped dead and swore in disgust. Someone had left the remains of his lunch on the lid of his trunk: a plastic cup, a grease-stained food bag, and a cardboard burger container spread out like a picnic meal. He was tempted to sweep the whole mess onto the ground, but the thought of a security camera nearby made him reconsider. In any major city these days, it was wise to assume one's behavior was observed and recorded. He finally spotted a garbage can one lane over, between a pickup truck and a gray van. Muttering unkind things about slobs, he gathered the trash and headed for the bin.

After he'd dumped the trash he started back, but when he passed the van, the slider opened suddenly, causing him to step back. Someone behind him picked Oliva up in a bear-like grip and propelled him toward a yawning, black space inside the van. He tried to use his feet to stop himself, but something, it looked like a cane, rapped his shins sharply, first one, then the other, which caused him to yelp in pain and stop resisting. A final push from the person behind him landed him on the carpeted surface of the cargo area, rear first, then shoulder, and finally his head. The floor was cushioned, so the impact wasn't too painful, but the shock of the impact rendered him helpless for a few seconds. Though his mind screamed *Escape!* he couldn't make his startled body obey.

A figure in black stepped into the van, bent over him, and patted his pockets. Taking his phone, the person stepped back onto the pavement. Struggling to rise, Oliva opened his mouth to call for help, but it was too late. The doors closed, and everything went dark.

In seconds the engine started and the van began to move. With nothing to hold onto, Oliva was tossed from side to side like a marble in a shoebox. He was unhurt, so far, and he tried to calm his frightened mind and reason out what had happened—what was happening. He hadn't been robbed or killed, so that wasn't the plan. This was an abduction. The question was why.

After a ride of about twenty minutes, first with slows, stops, and starts but later with a smoothness that suggested freeway travel, the van stopped. Oliva at first pounded on the walls and called for help, but foam laid over everything made that useless. With mounting dread, he added up the other details around him. Missing interior handles. A padded metal divider that closed him off from the front seats. No windows.

These people had done this before.

Why?

When the engine finally died, Oliva moved to a crouch near the doors, hoping to take his captors by surprise, burst past them, and escape. As he waited, he tried to forget every *Criminal Minds* episode he'd ever seen. Would they have guns? Knives? Tasers? Worse? He was pretty sure that with the amount of adrenaline coursing through his system, he could outrun all but the fleetest of criminals. He'd head for an open space and scream for help.

But there was no open space. When the slider opened again, he was in a garage-like room with two figures in black on either side. Before him sat a lawn chair, brightly lit by a half-dozen trouble lights.

"Exit the van and take a seat." The voice was deep and growly, its tenor altered in some way. Considering his options and finding no alternative, Oliva did as ordered. These people, whoever they were, had planned his capture with great care. All he could do was try to make them happy.

He stepped out of the van onto the bare concrete floor of a ten-by-ten, windowless room. After testing the chair with a hand, he sat in it and looked up at the person who'd spoken.

"What do you want?" When no answer came he said, "I don't know why you're doing this." Though he tried to keep his voice steady, the attempt wasn't completely successful. He was scared. He couldn't think. He couldn't figure out why this was happening. The best he could manage was controlling his bladder, and he wasn't sure how long that would last.

"If you do as we ask," the voice said, "you won't be harmed. When you've told us what we want to know, you'll be set free."

Though it probably wasn't wise to trust the word of kidnappers, Oliva needed at that moment to believe he was going to live through the day. "And what is it you want to know?"

"Everything you can tell us about security procedures at Green Grove."

Suddenly everything made sense. These people planned to rob Neil, and he was supposed to help them. His laugh was almost natural. "I don't know anything about it. Neil and his security chief handle all that."

"You live there. You see what happens."

"I'll help if I can."

He'd given in too easily, and the figure waved impatiently. "Truth is important, Mr. Oliva. We'll know if you're lying."

Damn! What would they do if they caught him making things up? Still, he wasn't about to help these people gain access to the estate. "I'm not up-to-date on alarms and patrols and that sort of thing."

"Before we continue, we'd like to share some things with you." The figure took out a list. "Have you heard of a man named Ralph Baird?"

Frowning, he answered honestly. "No."

"He was a reporter who died recently."

Oliva waited for a connection, but none came.

"How about a woman named Carmen Ostrano?"

"The name sounds familiar, but..." He couldn't place it.

"She worked for Argent Chemical and quit in protest to your testing methods."

"Oh, right. The malcontent."

"Did you know she's dead?"

His frown got deeper. "What happened to her?"

"We'd like to know that ourselves," the voice vibrated with sarcasm. "Then there's William George, Candra Ellis, and Mark Doan, who all died after speaking out about Argent Chemical in some way. Are you getting a picture here, Mr. Oliva?"

"You're crazy!" He tried for a firm tone, but he was shaken. Three of those names had been discussed in the boardroom. He recalled Neil's anger at the lack of loyalty from his employees. He didn't recall if two of them were ever mentioned again, but now he did recall Neil's satisfied grunt when Nixon reported Ostrano's fall from her apartment balcony. "The end of a bothersome woman," he'd commented.

The message was clear. These people thought Neil was killing those who opposed his methods. Could that be true? He wasn't sure. While he didn't see Neil as a killer type, he did become enraged when someone crossed him. He often railed against disloyal employees, lying reporters, and idiots who couldn't accept that business was business and everybody broke the rules.

Should he believe these people? If he even accepted the possibility that they were telling the truth, what did that mean to him? They might be from law enforcement, but he wasn't sure it was legal for police to kidnap someone to question him. They could be relatives of one of the victims, bent on revenge.

"We don't intend to hurt Mr. Preston, if that's what you're thinking." Police or not, the speaker was pretty intuitive. "He's going to lose a little of his wealth, but he won't be harmed."

That relieved Oliva's mind a little. These people weren't cops, at least not cops acting within the law. That meant they were vigilantes who planned to break in and steal from Preston, apparently in reprisal for his crimes. Oliva was in a bad spot, but he was beginning to see a way out. If he told them what he knew, they'd let him go. Once he was free, he could warn Neil, or give Belk a heads up. The guy wasn't top drawer—in fact, he was probably third—but the system itself was good.

"Okay. I'll tell you what I know if you let me go afterward."

"As I said, you won't be harmed if you're truthful."

Oliva decided truthful was good. "Where should I start?"

"How many entry points are there to the estate?"

That was only a matter of driving by and looking, so he figured he was being tested. "Two. Each gate is solid and has a remote vid-cam so the guards can see who's there. The back gate is used for deliveries; Neil doesn't like seeing tradespeople. Guards back there search each truck at the entry, then one of them drives it to the house for unloading or whatever. The driver stays in the shack with the other guard. When he gets his truck back, he leaves."

"Okay. Now tell us about the house."

Oliva took a breath. "Green Grove is three stories, with the center open all the way to a skylight in the roof. The first floor has no windows, the rest are too small for someone to get through."

"Like arrow slits in a castle wall."

"Exactly. On each floor, a walkway leads around the atrium and the rooms are set in a square along it. Neil occupies the whole third floor, with offices on the east side and living quarters on the other. On the roof is a landing pad for a helicopter, which is mostly how he travels nowadays, since he hates traffic."

"Draw a floor plan of the top floor and label the rooms." The speaker handed him a clipboard with a legal pad on it and a fine-tipped marker. Oliva obligingly sketched a large square and then drew in rooms and marked them.

"Okay," the speaker said. "New sheet, middle story."

"Second floor is for housekeeping," Oliva said as he labeled the kitchen, formal dining room, laundry, gym, and several storage areas. "It's also where Neil's pride and joy is displayed, probably the world's largest collection of Soviet artifacts outside Russia."

"We assume that room is very secure."

Was that what they were after? Bertie found the display cold, stark, and dull, but Preston loved his precious Soviet medals, modernist

175

paintings, huge photographs of important moments, and primitive woodcuts. "Alarms on both doors and cameras at either end."

"Okay. Get a new sheet and draw the first floor."

"I hope you get that I'm no artist," Oliva told them as he began. "These two curved staircases go up each side of the atrium. Just past the one on the right is an elevator most of us use." He striped the two stairways and drew a box with an X to indicate the elevator. "Along the outside walls are four apartments." He drew in approximate sizes as he spoke. "Joelle's on the rear east side, and opposite her is an apartment we keep for guests, not that Neil ever has any. At the front my apartment's on the east and Monica Covel's is opposite. She's not there—" Did they know that? Was that why they were planning their crime now?

"What's in the empty apartment?"

He shrugged. "It's set up like a hotel room: bed, TV, fridge and microwave, but the guards use it like a lounge. They eat their meals there or watch TV between patrols. Sometimes a guy will sleep there if he doesn't feel like going home between shifts."

"Exits?"

"Double doors in front and back. Joelle has an exterior entrance off the drive that circles the house. Of course her apartment opens onto the central atrium, as do the other three, but because of the staircases and the plants in the middle, it feels like we're more separated from each other than we are."

"Entry to interior rooms?"

"All the main doors require a passcode for entry. Residents have an app on our phones. The domestics punch in a code that changes every few days."

"Security guards?"

"Six men on duty at all times. The two inside patrol the house, every hour, twenty-four-seven."

"What about local police? Are they called in if there's a problem?"

"Neil prefers our guys. They're paid to do things the way he wants."

"Like keep their mouths shut?"

Oliva shrugged and the voice asked, "What about the technical end?"

He chuckled grimly. "You name it; he's got it. Green Grove is on an LAN that's equipped with sophisticated firewalls and other network safeguards. Non-connected phones or devices are jammed. If you're not right with the system, you get really loud bagpipe music in your ear."

"Alarms?"

"Every window and door, plus the cameras, which are everywhere on the first two floors." He paused. "Well, not everywhere. We get privacy in our apartments, and Joelle insists there not be one outside her doors. There are none on the third floor either, since that's where Preston lives and works."

"He feels safe up there?"

Oliva chuckled. "If there's trouble downstairs, the whole third floor can be closed off, like a giant panic room."

"Steel shutters and doors that slide out of the ceiling?" It was the first time the bigger of his captors spoke, and Oliva heard awe in his voice.

"I've never seen it happen, but I hear it's epic. Besides the lock-down, the decorative grid around the open space becomes electrified so no one can climb up from the floor below."

The smaller kidnapper took over again. "Let's talk about the art display."

Oliva congratulated himself: he'd been correct about the target. "When you exit the elevator, it's on your left. The room's about forty by thirty feet, with stuff on little stands, just like in a museum." He paused as a thought came to him. "I took pictures for the insurance people. They're on my phone."

"Great. I'll find them." Pulling out the phone he'd taken from Oliva, he scrolled through the photos. After a few seconds he asked, "Don't you ever erase anything?"

Oliva shrugged. "I'm not sure how to download photos to somewhere else, so I just keep them."

Eventually he found the pictures. "June 12, 2017." A few seconds later he said, "Is the display the same now as it was then?"

"I think so. Nobody goes in there much, even Neil."

A hand extended the phone so he could see a shot. When Oliva squinted, the kidnapper stepped closer. "What's behind the door on the far end?"

As Oliva frowned at the photo, a scent reached him that made him re-think things. His questioner didn't smell like any man he'd ever encountered. Hiding his surprise he said, "The climate plant, heating and cooling units."

"So there's ductwork in there."

"I guess." He thought a minute. "Yes. I had to get some stuff out of there once, and I remember that."

The person did something Oliva assumed transferred the photos to somewhere else.

"Last question. What's outside the house in the way of security?"

"Regular patrols. Cameras all over." Oliva shook his head. "I can't help you with those because I have no idea where they are."

Finished, she—Oliva was sure now that it was a female, maybe even someone he'd met—said, "There will be an event at the Preston estate in the near future. As I said before, Preston will not be hurt. In fact, no one will. Mr. Preston will lose nothing he doesn't agree to give up."

"I don't get it."

"You don't have to. You only have to keep quiet about what happened here today."

"Sure, sure. I can do that."

Again he'd been too eager, and she pointed a finger at him. "If we're expected at Green Grove, we will share the recording we just made of you telling us about your employer's defenses. One of our group is very clever at editing recordings, and he'll make it sound like you approached us." She stepped back. "At best you'll lose your job. At worst you'll discover for yourself if Neil Preston is capable of murder."

Oliva swallowed hard. "What am I supposed to do when you show up?"

"Nothing, Mr. Oliva. We want you to do nothing."

Amazingly, that was it. The big guy stepped forward and gestured for him to get back into the van. Half an hour later, Oliva was dropped off near his car. The experience, though odd and not particularly pleasant, left him with a lot to think about.

***

After they released Oliva, Cam and Robin went directly to a coffee shop where Hua waited, his fingers drumming nervously on the tabletop. As they listened to the recording, Robin showed him the sketches, which Cam disapproved of. "The rooms look all the same size, and the lines are all wavy."

"The guy was under duress," she replied. "I just wanted him to give us a rough idea of where things are."

"Let me see them." Cam made a new diagram, using Oliva's as a guide and his butter knife as a straight edge. The jumble of hasty lines Oliva had drawn transformed to a clear floor plan with dimensions that seemed likely for a place the size of Green Grove. "It's still not a hundred percent right," Cam said as he worked, "but at least we'll know what's next to what."

179

"I didn't know you were a draftsman, Cam."

He blushed. "I like stuff done right. Dad used to say that was a good thing."

"Your drawing is much better. We don't need these anymore." As they left, Robin dropped the sketches Oliva had made into a waste bin.

When they were gone, an attractive man in a baseball cap and sunglasses rose from a booth in the corner, went to the trash can, and after checking to see it didn't have food on it, fished out the sheets Robin had discarded. Putting them in his pocket, he left the restaurant, whistling as he went.

***

Oliva returned to Green Grove shaken and confused, though he had the presence of mind to pick up the ice cream he'd been ordered to get. The revelations from the figures in black bothered him, but it was somewhat heartening to realize they'd expected him to be surprised. Of Preston's people, they'd chosen him to squeeze, which meant they didn't see him as corrupt, or at least not as corrupt as Neil.

How much trouble was he in? It was shocking to think Preston might be capable of murder, but was that any of his business? Neil tended to compartmentalize, so only he knew everything that went on at Green Grove. If he wanted someone killed, Covel would no doubt be his go-to person. Oliva doubted Nixon would be told, and he guessed the old guy wouldn't want to know anyway. And Joelle? Though Preston used her as a sounding board, she was an emotional mess. Would Neil trust her discretion that far?

What did his own conscience require? He hadn't signed up for murder, but still, he knew which side his bread was buttered on. Was he obligated to try to stop Preston from committing crimes he had no part in? Oliva shook his head, pretty sure he bore no share of guilt.

And what about the upcoming burglary? Upon reflection, he thought the gang's chances of getting into Green Grove were next to none. Once they realized that, they'd probably give up. He'd lose nothing.

If they did succeed, they'd take Neil's valuable bits of history, but again, the scenario ended with Oliva himself losing nothing.

Only one possibility worried him. If the robbers came to Green Grove and got caught, they'd vowed to implicate him. In hindsight, he was appalled that he'd given them what they wanted so easily. Fear and disorientation had done its work, and Oliva concluded that very few people were brave enough to refuse the demands of captors who had them isolated and helpless, despite all those movie heroes who laughed away the possibility of pain and death.

As he rode up in the elevator, Oliva went over his options again and made a decision. It was best to tell Preston right away what he'd been through, while the threat was tentative. He'd spin the part where he cooperated, making it sound as if he did his best to scare off the thieves. Neil would tell Belk to be extra-watchful, and he might even be grateful to Oliva for the warning. He sighed as he got off the elevator. Yes, telling Neil was better than stressing over what might happen for the next week.

But when he handed over the ice cream, Preston flew into a rage. "You bought fat free!" He underlined the words with a finger. "Fat free!"

Oliva shook his head at his mistake. Should he say the lapse was due to recently being kidnapped?

Preston was already on a rant. "How hard is it to get one friggin' quart of ice cream, Bertie? I *hate* fat free. It tastes like piss!"

"I'm really sorry, boss. I—"

There was no sense making excuses, and he was given no chance anyway. "Send someone out for the real stuff, and I'd better have it before time for *Bridezillas!*" He threw the container Oliva had brought against a wall, where it burst and slid to the floor, leaving a creamy trail.

181

On a hunch, Oliva opened Preston's freezer. "There's some Snow-monster in here, boss." The pause that followed his words was fraught with danger, and Oliva realized he'd better offer an excuse for why Preston had missed it earlier. "It got shoved into the back, behind the Rocky Road." And the eight other partial cartons in there.

Suddenly Preston was all smiles. "Great. Hand it over."

Oliva gave him the half-full carton and then bent to clean up the mess Preston had made. When he was sure the eruption had calmed—it usually took only seconds for Neil to forget his tantrums—he asked, "Ever hear of a reporter named Ralph Baird?"

Preston was gerbiling through a drawer in search of something. "What? Who?" After a rattle, clang, and grunt of satisfaction, he turned to get a bowl from the cupboard. "I don't remember him."

"He was researching corruption in the pharmaceutical industry. He got mugged and killed downtown a few months back."

Preston looked at him over his shoulder. "So?"

"It was a lucky break for y—us," he amended. "He was apparently focused on Somatella."

A shrug dismissed concern. "We'd have handled his questions if it became necessary."

Oliva left the apartment without telling Preston what had happened. Why ask for trouble? He'd come up with an explanation for the recording if and when he had to. After all, he was Bertie of the Golden Tongue.

Still, he was glad tomorrow was Sunday and pretty much free of responsibility. He needed time to think about bread, butter, and murder.

Chapter Twenty

Just after Saturday night turned to Sunday morning, Luca went down the hall to call her cousin and check in. Since reception on her cheapie cell phone wasn't great, she needed to be near a window to have any hope of connecting. The call went through, but Lettie didn't answer. Luca left a message saying she was all right and would be home sometime Monday afternoon. Not that Lettie cared much if she never came home, but still.

As she ended the call, she looked up to see Nurse Nasty with her hand on the door handle of Room 512. Luca hurried back, trying not to look upset. "Excuse, please, Miss, but don' go in dere! You maybe get da sickness."

Though somewhat embarrassed to be caught, Nasty was defiant too. "I should check on her."

Luca wanted to deck the old battle-ax, but she forced a sweet tone. "I am trained in this. I can do it." Slipping past the larger woman, she closed the door on Nurse Nasty's scowl.

***

"Do you mind if I drive?" Em had learned over the years to use people's personal traits against them, and she guessed Nix was a person who preferred being in control. Since she made no move to get out of the driver's seat, the question was only a bow to politeness.

He took it well. "Not at all." Turning, he put the Stetson he'd brought along on the back seat of her rented Beemer, choosing a spot where it wasn't likely to slide onto the floor. Of course there'd be a cowboy hat. Thank goodness he didn't have spurs on.

"I want to say again how kind you are to come along to this shindig. It's silly to care at my age what people think, but after my years in Hollywood, my classmates expect me to show up in diamonds, with a handsome man at my side." She waved a hand to show she'd met the expectation of diamonds.

"We'll head 'em off at the pass. Or the punch bowl." He chuckled at his joke, and Em made herself smile appreciatively. Would there be no end to the oater references?

"To be honest, I wasn't considered much of a catch in high school." She quoted Stanton's official biography, which was pure hackneyed Hollywood. Adolescent duds blossomed into bombshells at twenty as if by magic. Em suspected in most cases capped teeth, professional stylists, personal trainers, and strategic surgeries had something to do with it.

"I wasn't one of the popular crowd either," Nixon admitted. "I was a studious type who didn't excel at sports. I was largely ignored." A second later he added with a chuckle, "More than a few old schoolmates have come over the years with their hats in hand, seeking my help."

"And did you help them?"

"Of course!" His chuckle turned to a laugh. "At double my usual fee."

Em turned onto the freeway, and Nixon asked in his corny western accent, "Where exactly are we headin' to, ma'am?"

"Northeast about a hundred miles to a town called Springdale. The picnic ends at six, so we should be back here by nine at the latest."

Glancing at his watch he said, "My client has a rather important meeting in the morning, but as long as I'm back for that, my time is yours."

"Lovely." She made her tone optimistic, though she was trying to figure out how that wouldn't happen. She'd stuffed six ipecac pills into the hem of her sleeve. In theory they'd make Nixon sick enough to cause an overnight hospital stay, but it wasn't a sure bet. Internet comments on ipecac ranged from "very effective in inducing vomiting" to "didn't work for me at all." What if Nixon had a cast-iron stomach to go with his silver tongue and brass ego?

Bennett's advice provided some comfort. "Opportunities will arise," she'd often heard him say in planning sessions. "Seize them and use them. Sometimes it's all you can do."

Nixon had a tendency to brag, which was irritating but also helpful. His long-winded boasts meant Em could spend her time plotting rather than spinning tales of Our Gal Margy. By the time they left the Tulsa city limits, her date was relating the highlights of his supposedly stellar law career. The fact that he'd ended up working for a crook made her less than sympathetic, but she tried to maintain an expression of interest.

"We've got the best record of patent registration in the state," he said at one point, "maybe in the whole Southwest."

Because you cheat! Aloud she said, "That must take a great deal of effort on your part."

"Once you know how the system works, it gets easier."

Em was wondering when she should put the ipecac pills into his drink. Not too soon. She didn't want him feeling better in a few hours.

Maybe she could get him drunk. "Should we stop and get a bottle? The reunion is BYO, but I didn't know what your drink of choice is."

Nixon shook his head. "I don't drink alcohol, but if you want something, go ahead."

Just my luck. A guy who's up for any sin but drunkenness.

"Of course it isn't all a smooth trail ride." Nixon went right back to his brilliant career with Argent. "We've got a patent right now that's problematic from a legal standpoint, a new formula for an anti-inflammatory. Neil bought it at a very good price, but now this piss-ant inspector, excuse my French, ma'am, says extended use might cause permanent tremors."

"How does he know that?"

"That's the thing! One of *our own* scientists reported it." He shook his head with regret over the woman's disloyalty. "Even after she was paid for her work, she kept digging. It's brought us no end of trouble."

Em was tempted to comment on how honesty is a tough friend to have, but the GPS broke in, ordering her to leave the freeway. As she obeyed, she noticed a sheriff's department patrol car sitting at a gas station near the off-ramp. Seizing the opportunity with a resolution Bennett would have applauded, she tromped on the accelerator. Though he grabbed the armrest, Nixon didn't consciously notice. He was too busy explaining how hard it was to work with people whose sense of decency is completely misguided.

Without slowing for the stop sign, Em turned onto the county road and took the BMW past eighty miles per hour. Her companion was still pontificating when a siren sounded behind them. "What's that?"

"Oops! I'm speeding," Em grinned ruefully. "I forgot to reset the cruise when I got off the freeway."

Nixon's smooth manner slipped as he turned to look back. "Damn!"

Em pulled the car onto the side of the road, her heart beating wildly. It was Sunday afternoon. If she could strike just the right note, the opportunity she needed was currently climbing out of his patrol car.

The officer was a middle-aged man with a gut that strained his belt. The permanently unhappy expression on his face made Em want to clap with glee. She'd stumbled upon a deputy who'd no doubt been passed over for promotion more than once. Add dyspepsia from too much fast food and hemorrhoids from long hours on patrol, and, she hoped, a dislike of city people who treated county roads like the Autobahn.

When he'd almost reached the car, Em rolled the window down. "What in the hell did you stop me for?"

Though taken aback, the cop followed protocol. "Ma'am, do you know you were speeding?"

186

"I was not! Just because you've got a trap set up to feed the county coffers, don't count on me playing your little game!"

"Marjorie," Nixon said quietly, "you might want to calm down a little."

"I won't calm down! This guy's on the take, I can tell by looking at him." To the deputy she said, "Are you looking for a little gift, Officer? Am I supposed to slip a hundred in with my license when I hand it over?"

The man's chin jutted. "I clocked you at eighty-two miles per hour in a fifty-five, ma'am. Now may I see that driver's license, please?"

After a moment of pretended confusion, Em switched to a tone of false innocence, "If I was speeding, Officer, it's because my friend here is having chest pains. I need to get him to a hospital as soon as possible." As Nixon grunted in surprise, she focused a glare on the deputy. "You might be contributing to this man's death, you moron!"

Though the cop tried not to roll his eyes, they did move a little. "If you need a hospital, why are you driving away from the nearest one?"

"I got lost." Em kept her tone nasty. "Maybe *you're* perfect, Mr. Small-town Nazi, but some of us make mistakes." She waved at her passenger. "Mr. Nixon here is a prominent Tulsa attorney. He eats peons like you for breakfast and spits out their backbones, and he's going to have your badge by morning!"

"Margy—" Nixon's voice had taken on a hopeless tone.

"Step out of the car, ma'am."

Turning to Nixon, Em gripped his arm and said in a stage whisper, "You've got our picnic supplies stowed securely, right, Babe?" She almost winked as she said it, but that would have been too much.

The deputy leaned in to examine her passenger. "What's the lady talking about, sir? What supplies?"

"What in hell are you doing?" Nixon whispered to Em. Leaning toward the deputy he said, "I have no idea what she means, Officer."

Crawling out of the car, Em raised her arms. "Go ahead! Search! You won't find illegal drugs on *me*."

The deputy's gaze had shifted to Nixon. "I guess that means you've got the 'supplies' she mentioned?"

Nixon's nose rose like he smelled something vile. "I don't take medication, Officer, not even aspirin."

"Then you won't mind letting me have a look. Step out, please, and come around to this side of the car. Keep your hands where I can see them."

The lawyer obeyed with an air of affronted dignity. When the cop patted his jacket pocket, he stopped and looked Nixon in the eye. "What's in there, sir?"

"Nothing. Absolutely nothing."

"Doesn't feel like nothing." Putting a hand in, he took out two capsules. "What are these?"

Nixon took a step back. "They're not mine." He pointed at Em. "She must have put them there."

"Oh, for Pete's sake, Nix, just tell him." Em turned to the cop. "It's not like we planned to sell drugs to the natives. Oxy helps a person relax."

Nixon sputtered some unintelligible phrases before real words came out. "As God is my witness, I have never taken a drug for recreational purposes. I have no idea what this woman is trying to do."

"Well, here's what she *is* doing," the officer answered, "She's getting herself arrested by this small-town Nazi."

"Arrested!" They said it together, but Nixon didn't stop there. "I don't even know this woman very well. I'm not responsible for anything she does or says."

The deputy's growl said he wasn't buying that, and his words confirmed it. "You can come along anyway, Mr. Big-time Lawyer.

We've got adjoining cells where you two can get to know each other better."

Nixon had turned completely against his date by the time they arrived at the jail. In addition to the abuse she'd already heaped on Deputy Spelling, she insulted the sheriff, his receptionist, the building itself, and the deputy's mother. When escorted to a cell she did a flip-flop, offering "a hundred bucks each" if they were allowed to go on their way. The sheriff reminded her that attempted bribery was illegal, and she turned angry again, promising Nixon would rain the legal system's wrath upon them like an Old Testament Moses.

"Listen," Nixon said to the sheriff. "This has gotten out of hand. My companion deserves a citation for speeding, no question. If you intend to hold her for further crimes that's fine, but I should be released. Those pills, whatever they turn out to be, are not mine." He turned to Em. "Margy, please tell them the truth about that."

"I'm not saying one more thing until I see a judge," Em said in a pouty tone. "Nix here says county commissions in BFE always settle out of court so their speed traps don't get publicized."

The sheriff seemed both frustrated and amused by her comments. "You might want to spend some time figuring out a different way to go, ma'am. You're just pokin' the bear every time you open your trap."

Oh, I hope so!

Once they were locked in side-by-side holding cells, Em went quiet. Nixon continued to plead his case with the deputy on guard, insisting the whole matter could be settled amicably. "I absolutely must attend a meeting tomorrow morning at nine," he told the woman.

"I wouldn't count on that," she replied. "On Mondays the judge comes in a little late. They got a pancake special over at Caroline's."

Leery of telling Preston he was enmeshed in a personal scandal, Nixon left a voicemail when allowed his call. "Neil, I can't make the meeting in the morning. I'll explain later." Em listened carefully, though she appeared to be sulking on her bunk. "Ms. Cohee can print the documents from the email I sent you. Have her notarize them as you sign. You'll need a set of each for the magazine, for yourself, and for my office."

When her turn to make a call came, Em told Hua, "I got arrested in Springdale, Oklahoma."

"Oh my."

"Can you arrange it so this all goes away?"

Hua hesitated for a moment, taking in what she'd said and what she needed. "Did they take fingerprints or DNA?"

"The first one."

"All right. I'll see what I can do. You've arranged that Nixon will not bring the documents to the estate?"

"That's correct. There's just this little legal thing to deal with, and then I'll be back home."

"Are you all right?"

"Fine. Give my love to all the kiddies."

Of course she wasn't fine. Fingerprints would reveal she was Emily Kane, retired FBI agent, and they'd snapped her picture too. She could only hope that the wheels of justice ground slowly out in the country, so she had time to figure out what to do about it. Though she wasn't as disdainful of small police departments as she'd pretended, they did often have low staff numbers, which meant she had a chance. She'd seen three people in the office: the sheriff, the arresting deputy, and a receptionist charged with both manning the desk and watching the prisoners. With such a small force and it being the weekend, she hoped they wouldn't send her prints and photo to the national database right away. Hua would remove the information from their computer files. It was up to Em to get the physical documents, herself, and her current alter ego Marjorie Stanton out of the vicinity of Springdale, Oklahoma, ASAP.

Chapter Twenty-one

Hua got a call from Joelle Preston at ten after four on Sunday afternoon. "Are you back in Tulsa, Ba?"

"I have just now arrived at the bus station, Miss." That was true, though he hadn't arrived on a bus.

"Good. I'll send a man to get you. What's your home address?"

He'd considered the problem of where the fictional Ba might live. "Could I be picked up here? That way I will not have to pay for a taxi home."

Joelle chuckled at his apparent thrift. "All right. His name is Belk, and he'll be driving a black Lexus." After a beat she added, "He might be a little grumpy. Just ignore it."

"Grumpy?"

She laughed. "Sometimes Belk forgets he works for me, not just for my brother." When Hua made an indistinct sound, she finished. "Nothing to worry about, love. Belk will do what he's told, and who cares if he likes it?"

Recalling the scene Joelle had made in the café, Hua guessed Lawrence Belk had become his enemy before he ever laid eyes on him. How would that enmity play out? He fingered the red-and-black Hermes scarf he wore, wondering if he should remove it in order to be a little more what a man like Belk might consider acceptable. He liked the scarf, which he'd found at an estate sale. Robin said it was out of character for a self-effacing orphan from Asia, but Hua had argued that beauty is never out of character. She'd let it go, since Robin wasn't one to impose her will on others.

When he arrived an hour later, Lawrence Belk was indeed unhappy. Rolling down the window, he barked, "You Ba?"

Hua nodded.

"Get in."

Tossing his gym bag onto the back seat, Hua got in and closed the door.

Belk seemed to be seething from a combination of things. Since he was currently responsible for security, he probably disapproved of Joelle inviting any guest to the estate. He might figure Hua was looking to take advantage of Joelle. And he no doubt disliked serving as chauffeur for his employer's sister. Whatever his objections, Joelle had overruled them in her belligerent, dismissive manner. Belk had obeyed her order, but he wasn't pleased about it.

Further proof came when Belk twisted in his seat to regard Hua distrustfully. "You been on the bus?" His voice was more suited to a football field than close contact.

"Yes, I went to Oklahoma City for a few days."

"To see posters and stuff." His tone said it was the dumbest reason he could think of for a long bus ride.

"I study history, so I like to see relics of times past."

"Why don't you show me your student ID, Ba?" The tone and familiar form of address added insult to the command. Without hesitation Hua pulled out the false student ID he'd created. Belk studied it closely then sailed it back over the seat like a Frisbee, grinning when Hua failed to catch it. "Here's the thing. If you're lying to Ms. Preston, you're in a world of hurt, get me?"

Hua understood the threat though not the idiom. "She invited me, sir."

"Yeah." Turning forward, he jammed the car into gear. "She does that." His eyes met Hua's in the rear view mirror. "You'll be searched going in and again before you leave, so don't even think about collecting souvenirs while you're there. And if I catch you snooping around the estate, you'll wish you were dead."

Hua's face warmed, but he remained silent.

Before backing out of the parking space Belk added a final threat. "And don't say anything to Joelle about our little talk. I work for Mr. Preston, not her, and part of my job is to watch her boyfriends like a hawk watches a field mouse."

The rest of the ride was silent. Hua pretended to be absorbed in the burner phone he'd brought along, but his mind was busy reaffirming every aspect of his plan. Would things go the way they hoped? What if Joelle decided not to show him the display room after all? What if Belk caught him outside her apartment? What if Robin and Cam didn't get in tomorrow and provide his means of escape? What if...?

Hua bit his upper lip, chiding himself for useless worry. They'd considered all the possible scenarios. Each member of the group knew what to do if plans had to change. Still, it was not knowing *how* things might change that made his jaw keep re-clenching, no matter how many times he made it relax.

After a smooth ride of about twenty minutes, Green Grove appeared before them. First came a ten-foot wall of gray brick topped with semicircles of wrought iron. They appeared decorative, but the spiky swirls would make scaling the wall difficult. Belk turned from the road, stopped at the entry, and barked, "Belk!" into a speaker. In seconds matching iron gates opened for them like graceful hands, and he drove inside. At a building about eight feet by twelve, he stopped the car again and ordered, "Get out and hand over your bag." While one guard rifled through Hua's possessions, another searched him and took his phone. "No outside electronics allowed," he said flatly. "You'll get this back when you leave."

When the guards finished their search, Hua and Belk got back into the car and drove on. Fifty yards down they entered an area of dense pines, creating in Hua a sense he was being separated from the world outside. He suppressed a shiver. If he disappeared in this place, what would his friends do about it? What could they do?

For perhaps a quarter mile there was nothing but trees. After the dense firs came birches and cedars, then cultivated fruit trees, then grapevines and ornamentals. When they left the groves, the view opened on a space about the size of a football field. In its center was the house itself. Square and squat, it had a flat roof, skinny windows, and no exterior decoration that might provide handholds for intruders. All straight lines without a hint of softening, the whole thing was painted a flat, pea-green color. To Hua's mind, Green Grove looked like three garbage truck bins stacked one atop the next.

Driving around to the house's east side, Belk stopped under a small portico that jutted like a plate stuck in a cement wall. Slamming the car into park, he tossed a final threat over his shoulder. "Remember, try anything while you're here and I will personally see that your guts come out your ears."

Before Hua could answer, a set of double doors opened and Joelle stepped out, stopping in the slightly sideways pose one takes when trying to appear thinner. Ignoring Belk's threat, Hua got out and closed the car door. It was time to forget the isolation of this place, the separation from his friends, and the belligerent Belk. He had to focus on Joelle.

"Welcome to my home." She gestured for him to enter, but he stopped as if shy.

"This is all very impressive."

She laughed. "It's horrible, I know. My brother likes the Soviet theory that only function should matter." With a gesture she added, "I think you'll find my corner of Green Grove more aesthetically pleasing."

The apartment she led Hua into was beautiful, with cream-colored walls perfectly complemented by leafy-green patterns on the sofa and draperies. "You have excellent taste, Ms. Preston."

"Please, call me Joelle, Ba."

He bowed slightly. "Joelle."

194

A table sat in the center of the living space. "I thought perhaps you missed dinner on the long bus ride, so I told the cook to make us a little something."

"That is very kind." Hua seized on the delay offered. "I am in fact quite hungry." Going to the table, he uncovered a silver serving dish and feigned the pleasure of a poor student offered a good meal. "Is this beef? It smells delicious." He pulled out a chair for her and she thanked him, her smile full of promise. Hua smiled back, though the promise in his smile was a different kind.

"Have you ever had Billecart-Salmon Brut Champagne?" As Hua served them both from an elegant chafing dish, she poured two glasses of wine from a bottle icing in a stand beside the table.

"I'm sorry, Ms.—"

She raised a warning finger, but her voice was teasing. "Joelle, remember? And even Jesus drank wine."

Hua obligingly sipped at the drink, which tasted like every other wine he'd ever tried. "You're right," he said politely. "It is very good."

"At one-seventy a bottle, it had better be." She seemed disappointed that he wasn't more impressed.

Hua tried harder. "This is your brother's estate? He must be very generous."

Her eyes turned cool. "I do my part."

"Of course." He put just enough disbelief in the words to require an explanation.

"Neil depends on my advice." Joelle set her glass down harder than necessary. "You can ask anyone."

Now he made his tone more doubtful. "I did a little reading, and it seems he's known as a business genius. He is very—"

Joelle interrupted. "Neil has a knack for finding business opportunities."

"And how do you help with that?"

She chuckled. "Wherever I can." She upended her glass and regarded his, still three-quarters full. "Drink your wine, Sweetie. There's plenty more in the bottle." Without asking, she refilled Hua's glass and her own. "You were raised by nuns, you said?"

"Yes. In Laos." He guessed Asians were all one type to her.

"Did they teach you about the birds and the bees?"

He sat straighter in his chair. "Oh, yes. Did you know that there are over 25,000 known species of bees in the world?"

"I didn't mean—"

Taking a forkful of meat, he waved it as he spoke. "Bird species are more difficult to count, since it depends on the classification method, but the number is somewhere between 10,000 and 10,500."

"No, *figurative* birds and bees: attraction between males and females."

"Oh yes, that too is very interesting. Male bees are quite the opposite of male birds, at least in most cases. The male bee, the drone—"

"I'm not talking about things with wings, Ba. I'm talking about men like you and women like me."

"Oh."

"Do you find me attractive?"

"Oh, yes, Ms.—I mean, Joelle. You are quite beautiful."

"And those eyes of yours are so black I could just fall in and swim around."

Setting his fork down, Hua stood. "I believe I misunderstood the purpose of the evening. Though I very much appreciate the invitation, and the meal is delicious, I think I should go now."

With visible effort Joelle reined herself in. Her laugh was only a little false as she said, "I certainly didn't mean to upset you, Sweetie. And you can't leave before you see the display room. I guarantee it will help with your thesis."

Hua pushed his chair under the table. "I would very much like to see it."

Leaving a Peach Melba dessert Cam would have drooled over, Hua followed Joelle out of her apartment. Rumors about Green Grove's interior décor abounded on the internet, and he saw now that it was indeed eccentric.

"Joseph Stalin?" he asked.

"If you saw a photo of our father, you'd understand," Joelle said. "Papa was the spitting image of Uncle Joe, and tough, like him."

Even someone unversed in psychology could see the connection. Doctor Rhee had said Preston could never please his father. A love-hate relationship with Dear Old Dad had translated to the wimpy son admiring the Soviet Man of Steel. After a single glance back at the display, Hua forced himself to focus on the plan and ignore Preston's obvious daddy issues.

He took careful note of the route Joelle took, and he was pleased to see that Oliva had told the truth as to the layout of the place. Leaving her apartment, they crossed the atrium he'd mentioned, which was about twenty feet across. High overhead was the skylight he'd seen on the aerial shots, a metal frame with crossbars. From its center hung a huge chandelier with a tier of lights at each level. On the third floor a metal grid, green, of course, appeared decorative, like vines with lacy leaves. According to Oliva it also served as a barrier to reaching the top floor via the atrium.

At the elevator, Joelle pressed the button for the second floor. Her eyes rested on Hua with an intensity that made a muscle at the back of his neck quiver. "I am so lucky," he said, trying to keep his expression pleasant, "and most grateful to you, Joelle."

"That's good to hear." The heat in her eyes rose like a fire that had just gotten one more log.

The door opened with a soft ding, and she stepped into the corridor and led the way. At a set of double doors, she entered four numbers on a keypad which Hua noted and memorized. "Here we go." She pushed the doors open, allowing Hua to precede her into the room. Motion sensors turned lights on and off as they moved forward.

He didn't have to pretend to be impressed. The display was museum quality, with specialized lighting and security alarms on several of the cases. Probably some of the items had been gained illicitly, but that wasn't his concern right now. Standing reverently before each piece, he played the role of a student, murmuring words like "amazing" and "stunning." Letters from Lenin to his "comrades in arms." Medallions given in recognition of "service to the glorious state." Decorated cups commemorating sports triumphs. And dozens of candid photographs showing men known to history as monsters playing with their grandchildren or drinking with friends.

Though Hua wanted to hurry forward, he had to convince Joelle he was totally absorbed in the collection. He glanced sideways down the row to the storage room door.

A few more steps.

After standing for a respectful period at a case that held a Mauser C96, he turned and pointed. "What is in there?"

"I have no idea. Storage, maybe."

He smiled slyly. "It is a good place to hide from the cameras, yes? Maybe the cleaners take naps in there."

The comment did exactly what he intended. The light in Joelle's eyes amped up as the possibility of a new adventure struck. He guessed she'd seduced men in her bedroom, in hotel rooms, maybe even in her car. But a closet in her brother's art room?

"Let's have a look." Opening the door, she led him inside. "Not much to see." While she eyed the shelves Hua took a glob of KwikiSet, a fast-hardening putty, from the waistband of his jeans and pressed it into the door latch.

When she turned to face him again Joelle said, "Cozy, isn't it?"

"Somewhat claustrophobic, I think."

She stepped toward him. "Don't be nervous, Sweetie. It's not like you're locked in here all alone."

"Ms. Preston—Joelle—I hope I made myself clear when I explained before—"

"Oh, you were clear, but I don't think you realize what you're missing." She touched his face softly. "Ask yourself this, Darling: Why were men and women created if not to enjoy each other's company?"

"I do enjoy your company." Hua stepped back until the door stopped his retreat. "But my vows—"

Joelle's voice took on a teaching tone. "Won't your promise to avoid sex be more valuable once you know what it's like?" Hua remained silent, willing the putty to harden faster. "When people give something up for Lent, they choose things they like, in order to experience the loss. This sex thing should be the same way."

"Ms. Joelle, I think we should return to the—" Hua turned the doorknob and then let his face show consternation. "It is stuck, I think."

"It can't be stuck." Joelle shoved him out of the way and tried to turn the knob. When it didn't turn she rattled it several times, trying to shake the latch free. Next she pushed on the door with her shoulder, gently, then harder and even harder. Finally she swore, quite impressively. None of it worked.

For five full minutes the two of them tried different tactics on the unyielding door. While Hua made a good show of frustration, Joelle wasn't pretending. She was furious.

"Where is your phone?" Hua asked. "We can call for someone to come and let us out."

She shook her head. "I think it's on the end table next to the couch." Actually he'd slid it between the cushions to assure she wouldn't see it and bring it along out of habit. "Where's your phone?"

"Your men took it."

She nodded, aware that was the policy. "Will those who watch the surveillance cameras see that we need help?"

"I had them turn it off to give us some privacy." She tried the door again and kicked it when the effort was useless.

"Then we must find our own way." Looking around the closet as if assessing the possibilities, Hua appeared to notice for the first time an air vent near the ceiling. "Do you think you could crawl through the duct up there and come out in some other room?"

Looking at the space too narrow for her broad shoulders she said, "Are you kidding?"

"If you will offer your back for me to stand on," Hua said innocently, "I think I could do it."

A few minutes later, Hua moved silently through the ductwork of Preston's house, pleased that the first part of his task was complete. Joelle was isolated, so she couldn't interfere with Robin's plan and would be safe from accidental harm. He needed to find his way to her apartment and finish his night's work.

Following the diagram in his head, he made only one wrong turn, which he realized quickly and corrected. The hardest part of the journey was getting from the second floor to the first, which meant traversing a vertical duct. He descended in a controlled slide, bracing himself with feet and hands. Once on the ground floor, he found the shaft that led to the east wing and slid along it, peering through vent slats until he saw Joelle's living room. His bag lay on the floor beside her couch.

His sigh of relief was interrupted by a new concern. How would he make the ten-foot drop to the floor?

Recalling Em's advice, Hua broke the problem into bits, beginning with how to get the vent cover off from the inside. The screws turned easily enough, but he couldn't stop them from dropping one by one to the tile floor. Each time one hit, bounced, and rolled, he flinched. When the cover came loose he almost dropped it too, but he managed to get his fingernails into the slits before it fell. He tossed it gently onto the couch, several feet away, and though he imagined it made a great deal of noise when it bounced off and hit a scatter rug on the floor, no one came to investigate.

He'd solved the first problem, but he was still at ceiling level. He'd come through the ducts head first, and there was no way he could turn his body around in the narrow space. He'd considered his "dismount" in planning and hoped there'd be something beneath the vent, a sturdy table or a soft chair he could drop onto. That hope had been misplaced. Hua looked for something within reach that might slow his fall, a wall sconce or a shelf of some kind. The wall offered no handhold. When he pushed his way out of the vent, he'd free-fall to the floor and land in a sprawl, possibly breaking a bone or two. Then what good would he be to his friends?

Still, it had to be done. As he paused to gather courage for the drop, he noticed a door to his right that he assumed led to Joelle's bedroom. If that door were open, he could grasp it at the top, pull himself from the airshaft, and land on his feet, not his head.

The door was closed.

Reaching down, Hua pried at the nearest corner, but the latch was in place. He tried bumping the door softly with a fist, hoping to spring the catch, but that didn't work either.

Quieting his frustration with a deep sigh, he closed his eyes and let his mind go blank. There had to be a way. When he opened them again, it registered that the handle was a lever, not a knob. If he could reach it and lift, the door would open. Sliding out as far as he dared, he reached down, trying to grasp the hardware. It was too far away. He needed something to lengthen his reach, a rope, a chain...

Letting out a small sound of celebration, Hua untied the scarf from around his neck. It was a crime to knot such fine silk into a noose, but then, crime was his business.

In no time he'd brushed the dust from his clothing and settled on Joelle's sofa, waiting for the household to quiet and for the guard to finish his midnight patrol.

Chapter Twenty-Two

Sunday had gone smoothly for Luca. At noon Bubbles had brought a ton of food, along with a warning. "We will be occupied until late tomorrow morning, so this must last." Along with the KFC meal, he'd included a Subway footlong, a breakfast muffin, and several pieces of fruit.

The afternoon dragged, and Luca napped on and off between episodes of NCIS. The patient slept peacefully, and the novelty of her presence had apparently worn off, since no one even glanced her way as they moved about the ward. Feeling like she'd make it through without a problem, Luca began dreaming about how she'd spend the money. She'd have to give Lettie a lot of it, but there'd be enough for something for herself. A class at the community college, maybe? She thought she might like to try law enforcement, though she'd mostly seen it from the wrong side. Cops looked crisp and competent in their uniforms, and the training would probably help her lose a few pounds. Luca pictured herself graduating the police academy, trim and confident, and getting a real job. She could do it.

Her confidence, at least as far as getting the last $500 went, was premature. At one thirty Monday morning, when she went down the hall to call home again, Nurse Nasty approached the patient's room. Seeing her intent Luca hurried back, reaching the door just ahead of her and slipping inside. "Excuse, please. No one may come in."

Nurse Nasty planted herself in the doorway. "How's your patient?"

Her arch expression made Luca shiver, but she faked confidence. "All things good here."

Nasty's face took on an exaggeratedly puzzled expression. "Know what? I can't find your Doctor Minh in the records before last week, no matter how I spell it. And I can't find a nurse named Afua anywhere in Oklahoma." She raised her chin. "I think somebody's trying to pull a fast one."

Luca retreated into what had been safe territory. "Talk to Doctor Minh. He is in charge."

Nasty looked at her askance. "Where are you from again?"

Now we're playin' geography games? "Sierra Leone, Miss."

"Really. What's the capital of that country?"

Luca played dumb. "What is capital?"

"Forget it. Name one large city in Sierra Leone. Even a middle-sized one."

Luca's knowledge of Africa was limited to Tarzan movies and anecdotes from Trevor Noah. "I don't understand—"

"I'll bet you don't." Nasty took out her cell. "I'm calling security."

Luca's mouth went dry. If she stayed, she'd surely be arrested. Tucked in her bra was the money she'd earned thus far, apparently all she'd get. The tote bag containing her purse and clothing sat beside her chair. Time to go.

As Nasty looked down to find the number, Luca grabbed the tote and swung it at her, sending the phone flying from her hand. Rushing forward, she head-butted the woman in the gut, sending her staggering backward as the breath left her lungs with a whoosh. Pushing past and ducking beneath Nasty's clawing hand, Luca headed down the hall at a dead run.

With little else to occupy her mind for two days, she'd devised an escape route in case things went bad. In a building as large and complicated as a hospital, doors could be monitored, even closed off, but no one could know at a glance who belonged inside and who didn't. Luca planned to use that fact to elude capture, if she could find a few minutes in an unoccupied spot.

Halfway down the first flight of stairs she heard Nasty yell, "Somebody stop that nurse!"

***

For some time, the fifth floor buzzed with activity. Anyone on staff who wasn't actively involved in patient care was sent to look for the fake African nurse. Police were called, and their number added to the searchers. Though they were determined the woman wouldn't escape the building, it seemed after a thorough search that she had. Theories as to how that might have happened were varied and often colorful. She'd ridden out in a laundry hamper. She'd disguised herself as a man. She'd gone up on the roof and made a death-defying leap to the medical building next door. No matter the theory, the fact was that no one saw Afua after her mad dash down the hallway.

The patient in Room 512 was examined by a real physician, who discovered the reason for her unconscious state. Within minutes of being disconnected from the IV, Covel stirred and looked around. "Where am I?"

"You're in the hospital," the young doctor replied. "The problem is, I can't figure out why."

***

Hua was frustrated to hear voices outside Joelle's apartment, when he'd planned to start upstairs. Two men stood talking for some time, and from the recordings he'd heard, he thought one of them was Bernie Oliva.

"Working late?" a voice asked.

"Ran into a snarl on tomorrow's meeting," Oliva responded. "Nixon can't make it, so I'm playing backup."

"Bet the boss was happy about that," the other man, apparently a security guard, remarked.

"Um, no. I'd say happy was the one thing he wasn't."

That ended the conversation, and Hua heard the elevator bell chime. Which of them had gone upstairs? How long would he remain? He decided he'd better wait until after the one o'clock patrol.

Hua was pretty certain he was safe in the apartment. At some point Joelle would realize he wasn't coming back for her. She'd pound on the door and yell for release, but since the cameras were video only, no one would hear. She'd curse his name repeatedly, no doubt, but since Ba wasn't really his name, her curses would be as useless as her cries for help.

At 1:20 a.m., it appeared the household had settled in for the night. Unzipping his duffel bag, Hua removed the clothing, took out the bag's false bottom, and unrolled a sheet of black plastic. The sheet was a little over ten feet square, and he'd dulled its shine with a matte coating. He opened the compact umbrella he'd brought and laid the tarp atop it, matching stick-on Velcro bits to hold it in place. When the tarp was secured, Hua crawled under it and stood up, holding the umbrella handle in the usual way. The tarp fell to the floor, covering him completely.

The contraption, though cumbersome, would fool Preston's infrared cameras by keeping Hua's body heat inside. In the dark hallways, the dull, black shape would go undetected on CCTV screens as well, unless someone was actually looking for a walking tent. If he went at a slow and steady pace, Hua doubted a bored guard with twenty screens to watch would notice the small anomaly his passing made.

Oliva had told them Joelle refused to have a camera pointed directly at her door, which meant no one would see it open and close. Leaning into the atrium, Hua listened carefully for the sound of footsteps.

Nothing.

Most of the cameras were set to pan, which was a help. When he reached the stairway door, Hua waited out of range until the lens was pointed away from him, then slid through the fire door, catching it to be sure it didn't slam. The stairs were problematic, since there were safety lights at the sides of every other riser. Pulling his skirts inward like a Victorian lady, Hua stayed in the center as he ascended. He stepped carefully to maintain sure footing. While a black shadow moving across a screen might be interpreted as a camera glitch, the sound of a toe stubbing would bring instant, unwanted attention.

Reaching the third floor, Hua removed his shield in the stairwell and laid it in a corner. There were no cameras here because, like his sister, Preston demanded privacy. For a moment Hua savored the irony of a criminal's paranoia providing his nemesis freedom to move about his home undetected.

Cautiously Hua opened the door and peeped out. As with the other floors, the stairway door opened onto the atrium, He took a moment to look at the metal grate up close, reminded of screens he'd seen in pictures of mosques, which, though beautiful, signaled strict and unchangeable separation.

To his left, double doors led to Preston's apartment where, according to Oliva, at this time of night he'd be sleeping with the television on. On his immediate right was a door marked *Roof* and, peering through a reinforced glass window, Hua saw stairs leading upward. The door had a lock like the others, but he was almost sure Joelle's code would open them all. Farther down, four doors led to various points on the business side of the space. First he came to double doors with *Conference* written on a frosted-glass pane. Next was a single door that read *Administrative Office*. After that was a solid oak door with a metal plaque that read *Neil G. Preston*. The last door said *B. Oliva*, though the letters were much smaller. That door was open, and Hua saw an elbow resting on the desk inside the second. Oliva was still at work.

Setting each foot carefully to avoid making a sound, Hua tried the door of the administrative office. It was open, and he guessed Oliva had either used the copier there or intended to. Going inside, Hua pulled the chair out from the desk as a precaution. If Oliva left his office, Hua would slide into the kneehole and hide.

Though Hua knew a young woman named Mandy Cohee worked there, her name wasn't anywhere in the room. Nor did he sense she felt at home there, since the place was empty of personal touches. Every file cabinet was locked. Every drawer in the desk was too. Attuned to any sign of Oliva getting up from his chair, Hua booted the computer on the desk. He was pleased when the screen filled with icons and no request for a password, but he soon saw why. The files were for normal, day-to-day business such as electric bills and correspondence with suppliers. When he clicked on *Documents,* a few folders opened, none of them worth investigating. Ms. Cohee was not privy to the real workings of Argent Chemical.

Where were the files on the patent releases? Hua looked longingly at Oliva's office door, where light spilled into the hallway. It was a good bet he had access to everything. His fingers fairly itched to get at Oliva's computer, and he wrung his hands like a frustrated magician.

He couldn't stay where he was. There'd be another patrol soon, and the tent he'd left in the stairwell would be discovered. He had to go back downstairs, wait in Joelle's apartment, and come back in an hour. It wasn't a great option, since he'd run the risk of running into either Oliva or a guard.

He tried to send Oliva a mental command: *Go to bed. Rest up for tomorrow's meeting.*

Oliva coughed and shuffled papers, but he didn't leave his desk.

Reluctantly, Hua rose and put the chair back at the desk. As he moved to the door, he had a flash of genius. Removing the toner cartridge from the copier, he hid it under some papers in the wastebasket. Oliva would be unable to print the documents he was working on because, in Hua's experience, only one person in any office knew how to deal with toner. He was betting that person was Mandy Cohee.

Putting his tent back on, Hua glided down the stairs like a nervous ghost. On the ground floor, he waited until he was sure there was no one in the atrium before returning to Joelle's apartment. It was just as he'd left it, and he set his tent aside gently so it was ready for the next trip. He paced the living room, frustrated that he hadn't considered the possibility someone would work late on the night before an important undertaking. Though he could still go back upstairs, it would be more dangerous a second time. A second pass by the cameras made it more likely someone would notice and wonder what that shadow was.

At 2:15 a.m., the elevator chimed. Shortly afterward, a door closed. Oliva was apparently back in his apartment, but the guard was still on his two o'clock rounds. How long did it take to check the whole house? Hua was so antsy he made endless circles around the room.

Pacing was good, it turned out, because on about the twentieth pass, his restless gaze fell on something pink protruding from under the couch. Investigating, he found a laptop, slid there to be out of the way when not in use. He recalled Joelle's boast that she advised Preston on everything. Might she have access to the documents prepared for tomorrow?

He retrieved the laptop, frowning when his fingers encountered something sticky on its lid. When he opened the cover, Hua chortled with joy. The screen lit immediately, which meant it was probably left on all the time. Settling himself in a corner of the sofa, he scanned the page that popped up, a site selling purses. Deleting that page, he got a similar one, this time focused on dresses. Behind that was a shoe page and then ads for river cruises in Europe. Joelle seldom closed a page or an app. The navigation bar had tab after tab open, with everything from shopping sites to news items. On the bottom Hua found six open files that looked promising, and he clicked through them until he saw what he wanted. The top line said, *Patent Releases.*

First he got a paper towel and cleaned the spill off the laptop case. Then, rubbing his hands together lightly, he went to work.

***

Luca spent several hours in an empty examination room on the ground floor. She changed into her own clothes, tossing the scrubs into a laundry bin in the corner. She stuffed the wig she'd worn as Afua into the trash. Though she hated giving up her tote bag, she feared it was recognizable, so she flattened it, adding it to the metal trash can then wadding some paper towels and tossing them on top to hide it from view. That done, she climbed inside the base of the exam table and tried to nap on the clean sheets stacked there. Once she heard the door open, and someone walked slowly around the room. She imagined a security guard peering into the corners and behind the curtain. She prayed he wouldn't think of opening the metal doors and, in this case, her prayers were answered.

It was hard to tell how long she lay there, but when it seemed like the activity outside the room picked up, she crawled out and straightened herself as best she could. Setting her purse strap on one shoulder, she checked her reflection in an aluminum canister on the work table. She was as unlike Nurse Afua as she could make herself without makeup. She'd make up for the lack with some home-girl swagger. Showtime.

Opening the door a crack, she waited until a dark-skinned woman in ragged jeans and a faded t-shirt came by. Stepping out, she said sheepishly, "Oops! Wrong room."

The woman smiled. "Hospitals are just big mazes, you ask me." As they walked on together, chatting idly, a police officer passed them with hardly a glance. At the end of the corridor, Luca left her companion and followed the arrows that led to the Emergency Room. Figuring it was the best place in a hospital to sit unnoticed, she took a seat between a worried-looking older woman and a young man who appeared to be asleep. Turning to the woman Luca asked, "You waiting for somebody?"

As she'd hoped, the question launched a detailed story about the woman's ten-year-old son, who'd woken in the night with troubling symptoms. Luca nodded encouragingly, asking questions each time her new acquaintance ran out of things to say. When searchers circled the room or stopped in the doorway to frown over the crowd, they saw only what appeared to be weary family members talking quietly as they waited to hear the news, good or bad, about their loved ones.

***

Robin lay on the bed, eyes closed but mind bubbling. She hadn't slept and had to content herself with resting her body while her mind tossed one possibility for disaster after another to the forefront.

What if Hua couldn't do what he'd gone to Green Grove to do?

What if Oliva told Preston about being abducted and there was a force of hired goons waiting for them when they arrived?

What if Em couldn't keep Nixon from returning to Tulsa and he brought the documents he'd prepared to the meeting?

What if?

What if?

What if?

The minute hand on the clock seemed weighted with stones. She got up, drank some water, and went back to the bed. Her phone lay on the night stand, and she picked it up. She wanted to talk to someone. No. She wanted to talk to Tom. But it was the wee hours of the morning, and he was probably still tired from his Florida trip. And what would she say, anyway? *I'm scared? Please talk me out of being a wimp?* Only she could accomplish that. Still, it would be nice to hear his voice.

When the ringtone sounded, she almost dropped the phone. The screen lit, and *Tom* came up. How did he know?

"Hello?"

"You're awake."

She huffed a dry laugh. "As in, not gone to sleep yet."

"I was afraid of that."

"I'll be fine."

"You will, but it would be better if you got some rest before your big day."

"Tell that to my whirling brain. Are things okay at home?"

"Good, except Bennett seems to expect me to do something about his diet."

"Bennett's on a diet?"

"Kai says he's getting fat. He stares at me with big doggie eyes, waiting for an intervention."

"When Kai's on a mission? Not a good idea."

"That's what I told him."

She felt better. A little conversation, a few thoughts of home...and Tom's voice. "If all goes well, we'll be back in Kansas late Monday night."

Later it registered that his response was odd. "If all goes well, I'll be here."

Chapter Twenty-Three

At 6:00 a.m., the active search for Nurse Afua seemed to be over. Cops and security guards shook their heads. They'd done what they could. Luca watched as a man in a suit bustled around, ordering guards and officers to various posts. At that point the woman Luca had been talking to was called in to see her son. As she hurried off, Luca sent wishes for a good result.

Was it safe to leave the hospital now? Sooner or later someone would wonder which patient she was waiting for. On the other hand, the security people were looking for a lone woman. Even with her changed looks, she'd be stopped and scrutinized.

Then the tired young man beside her stirred and rose. Luca looked up to see a woman coming toward him, wearing a rueful smile and a blinding-white cast on one wrist. "It's a clean break," she told the man. "The doctor doesn't think I'll need surgery."

Rising, Luca picked up her purse. "What happened?" she asked.

Again she served as eager listener while the couple joined to tell the story. "I was trying to change a light bulb—"

"I was so scared when I heard Dana fall—"

As they walked toward the door, Luca stayed with them, and the three left together, the couple still answering Luca's questions. The man at the door looked them over but didn't interrupt Dana's account of her treatment.

"What's all the excitement?" Dana asked once they were outside.

"I don't know," her husband replied. "They came through a few times like they were looking for somebody but never said who or why."

"You never know what kind of crazies you'll see in that place," Dana said. Struck by a thought, the husband turned to Luca. "Who were you waiting for?"

"I brought my neighbor in with chest pains," she replied smoothly. "She texted a minute ago to say she's being admitted, so I'm supposed to get some things from her apartment."

"I hope she's okay," Dana said.

"I think she gonna be." Wishing the couple well, Luca left them at their car and headed for the bus stop.

It was after eight when she got home. The boys were parked in front of the TV, their faces blank. Lettie sat at the window, smoking and looking down at the street.

"I'm back."

"I seen." She exhaled upward, sending a plume toward the seventh floor. "I thought you said you'd be back this afternoon."

She'd told Lettie only that she had a weekend job that paid well. "Things fell apart. I had to get out."

Lettie's dark eyes turned to her. "Does that mean you di'n't get paid?" She chuffed derisively. "I tol' you it was some kinda scam."

Luca took nine hundred-dollar bills from her bra and held them out. "This will help with the rent."

Lettie snatched the money from her hand as if Luca might reconsider. "That's good! Get us ahead a little."

She felt a rush of pleasure at Lettie's approval. "There would have been more," she told her, "but some nosy old woman screwed it up."

"And you ran." A sniff hinted she could have done better. Stuffing the money in the pocket of her jeans, Lettie went back to staring out the window.

Luca was allowed to live at her cousin's without the landlord's knowledge and with the understanding that she had to pay her own way. That meant kicking in half of everything, though what she got for it was a saggy couch and two dollar-store bins stacked in a corner for her things.

Lettie's boys occupied the apartment with gusto, and Luca's repeated attempts to keep them from rifling through her clothes had never been successful. She often came home to find the contents of her tubs spilled onto the floor and the boys wearing items that caught their fancy: the tube top covered with gold sequins, the mini-skirt with bangles at the hem, or one of her many outlandish hats. The outfits were chosen deliberately. Luca had learned early that if you weren't the prettiest or the skinniest girl on the street, you had to be the most noticeable.

For once her stuff was undisturbed, so she turned to finding something to eat. Though she was expected to buy her own food, the boys took groceries from her shelf whenever they felt like it. Stepping onto her booster stool, she checked her larder and found only a granola bar and some crackers. Unwrapping the bar, she sat down at the kitchen table and took a bite. She chewed slowly, making it last, but the image of the muffin Bubbles had bought for her came to mind, making the bar a poor substitute.

Home and safe, Luca thought about the people who'd hired her to be Nurse Afua. As she ate her meager meal, she recalled how Bubbles had asked earnestly if she liked what he brought. The young woman, Clarabell, had treated her like a real person, the old woman, Loony or something like that, had been okay, and Bozo, the big guy, had called her "ma'am" and opened the car door for her, though he seemed afraid to look directly at her.

"I got places to be," Lettie said without turning from the window. "Can you stay here until James comes to pick the boys up?"

"Sure." Another expectation was that Luca would watch the kids whenever Lettie asked. She didn't mind, though their mother always undid any lessons she tried to instill in them about decent meals and proper behavior.

"Let 'em eat what they want and do what they want," Lettie would say. "You gotta have fun when you're young, cuz bein' an adult sure ain't a barrel of laughs." Her definition of fun was letting the boys bang on the walls with saucepans and practice their ABCs on the floors with nail polish. Luca suspected her cousin's tolerance came from laziness more than regard for her children's happiness. "They sposed to repaint and re-carpet when we leave anyhow," she'd say from her seat at the window. "Don't worry about it."

Those words, delivered in a completely different tone, came into Luca's mind. The old woman had explained that the patient's sedation was harmless. "We need her to miss work for a few days, but don't worry about it. She'll be fine come Monday."

What would happen to Bubbles and Clarabell now that the hospital was aware of their scheme? It occurred to Luca that the least she could do was call the emergency number they'd given her and alert them to the danger. Opening her bag, she sorted through once and then again. Her phone wasn't there. She looked up. Lettie had gone, taking her phone with her.

Fighting panic, Luca tried to recall where she'd had the phone last. She'd gone down the hallway to call Lettie and turned to see Nurse Nasty hovering by the hospital room door. She must have set the phone down somewhere instead of returning it to her purse.

Several concerns hit at once: The phone was the only thing of value she owned, so she was poorer than she'd been an hour ago. If the police found it in the room, she'd be easily identifiable as the fake nurse. And she had no way now to warn her new friends. They were on their own.

***

Dressed as Ronda Talman, Robin sat in the passenger seat with Cam's camera bag at her feet when he stopped at the gated entry to the estate and offered their fake IDs to the guard. "Step out of the car, folks. Once we check you out, we'll give you a ride in." He gestured at a golf cart sitting nearby.

Robin glanced at Cam. "We'd prefer to drive, in case we need something from the car."

He didn't look up from his examination of her carryall. "Only residents' vehicles allowed on the grounds."

The plan had been for Hua to leave the estate in the trunk, which Cam would leave unlatched. Would he figure out where the car was, and could he make his way to the gate without being seen?

The guard passed a wand over each of them and searched Cam's camera bag thoroughly, taking everything out and flashing a light inside the bag itself. Robin berated herself for not asking Oliva about transport on Preston's turf. What else had she failed to discover, and what other surprises awaited them inside? Upset with herself, she didn't hear the guard ask for her purse until he repeated himself. Handing it over, she tried for a confident smile. There was one good thing: Hua was better able to make adjustments on the fly than Cam would have been. If she and Cam had to change the plan, at least he'd have her there to tell him what to do.

Once they and their belongings had passed inspection, Robin took the seat beside the driver while Cam dangled his long legs off the back of the cart, holding the camera bag on his lap. The brick wall that surrounded the estate made it seem somewhat prisonlike, and though trees, shrubs, and plants softened the view, it felt they were entering a separate world. Cam, who loved vegetation of any kind, began identifying species he knew: a climbing bush was Hall's Honeysuckle, and he wondered aloud if a flowering plant on a trellis was some kind of clematis. "These are nice trees," he told the driver as they passed from sunshine to shaded, quiet darkness in the pines. "Somebody takes good care of them."

"I guess so." The driver sounded as if he'd never noticed them before.

When they left the pines and entered the orchard, Cam waved at three workers bent at some task around an apple tree. They looked back at him, faces blank under their straw hats. "Guess you don't get much company here."

217

"You guys were lucky to get in." The man's tone said he didn't approve.

"It's really pretty. You should let people drive through to see all your plants and stuff." Robin wondered how he could think of botany when the caper already had a kink in it, but Cam lived in the moment. As for herself, she promised her roiling mind and churning stomach, *You can relax at*—she glanced at her watch—*ten thirty, eleven at the latest. At that point you can faint or throw up, whatever you need to, but it cannot happen until then.* Oddly, she sensed a quieting of her symptoms as her old training kicked in.

"You can do this, Rob," Dad would say when she objected to being his shill, his shield, or his lure. "Mom and Chris are counting on you to pull your weight. You don't want us to have to move again, do you?

"No. I really like my teacher this year."

"Then you have to do what I tell you."

"I don't like lying to people."

"It isn't lying. It's a story. People love a story, especially when a pretty little girl tells it."

"But I feel sick when I say things that aren't true."

"You can be sick later." His hand had tightened on her shoulder. "Right now you have a job to do, so get over there and do what I tell you."

The rows of fruit trees ended, and they passed into rows of grapevines connected to each other in a catch wire system, posts connected by wires spaced to support both plant and fruit. Beyond that was the house, which Robin had thought homely when she saw the aerial photograph. That impression was confirmed. It looked like a WWII bunker, actually three of them stacked atop each other. Straight lines.

Sharp edges. Skinny windows on the ground floor, larger ones higher up, all trimmed with the same green as the walls, so they seemed like blank eyes. Green Grove? "House of Floral Foam" would have been more apt.

Lawrence Belk waited under a portico supported by square-hewn beams. Robin took a deep breath. Everything she said and did from now on mattered.

"Ms. Talman?"

"Yes." She gestured at Cam. "This is Phil. He'll be taking pictures."

Belk regarded Cam with a frown, possibly unused to people who met him at eye level. "Mr. Preston will say when and how many," he finally said.

"Of course." Robin followed him inside, so nervous she had to concentrate on putting her feet in the right places. She stepped up four stucco steps and entered the double doors. Stepping inside the house confirmed what she'd suspected for some time: Neil Preston was nuts.

Green Grove might have been a set for a production of Dr. Strangelove. Bare walls rose around a central space with a large, red star set into slate tiles. Doors on the left and right Robin knew led into apartments for the residents of Green Grove other than Preston himself. Their footsteps echoed in the empty chamber, bounced off granite walls hung with pictures of Stalin: Stalin in a white military coat, Stalin with Lenin's silhouette behind him, Stalin lifting a beautiful child who held flowers and a Soviet flag. There was nothing to absorb sound, nothing to soften the sense of stark hardness of the place.

"I would guess your boss admires Joseph Stalin," she said in a casual tone.

"I hear he was pretty tough," Belk responded. He pointed to one of the portraits. "I always feel like the eyes in that one follow when I walk through."

With typical candor Cam said, "I wouldn't want to live here. It's spooky." Belk gave a shrug that relegated "spooky" to somewhere behind "healthy paycheck" in his personal concerns.

As they waited for the elevator car, Robin noted that the back side of the house mirrored the front, with apartments on either side. Oliva hadn't lied to them, at least not yet.

With a soft chime, the doors opened and they entered the elevator. Belk punched a code in and pressed three, and the familiar feeling of gravity-versus-thrust hit her stomach. What was usually a slightly odd sensation made her feel sick, and she put a hand to her gut, hoping she didn't lose her breakfast on the ride up.

They'd known from the first that Neil Preston was eccentric. They'd had hints that his home was different from the usual millionaire's mansion with gold-plated faucets and Jackson Pollack on the walls. But seeing evidence of Preston's weirdness amplified her fears. How far did his fascination with Stalin go? Was there a spot at Green Grove where unwelcome guests might be forgotten until they starved or went mad?

Though bad décor wasn't a sign of evil, Robin sensed they were all in danger. Already their plan needed adjustment, and she had no way to let Hua know. She'd never felt so blind, so out-of-control, at the beginning of a caper. Why hadn't she spent more time in preparation? What further surprises awaited them in this place? Her brain screamed, *Leave now. Run!*

Stop it, Robin. When she was most afraid, her father's voice came into her head, unbidden and mostly unwelcome. She hated him and his cheating ways, but along with the wrongs he'd taught her were lessons on dealing with fear and doubt. *Most things you fear never happen. If they do, worry didn't change it. If they don't, you wasted time you could have spent enjoying life.*

Mark Parsons had never been righteous, but sometimes he'd been right. There was no way Robin could enjoy the next hour or so, but it was counterproductive at this point to fret about what might go wrong. As they entered the ornately decorated elevator, her stronger half said aloud, "I can't wait to meet Mr. Preston in person."

Chapter Twenty-Four

The more Luca thought about her missing phone, the loss of her contact information, pictures, and means of communicating with the world, the more it bothered her. No police officer had appeared at her door. What if by some miracle they hadn't found it yet? The phone might have been covered by a sheet or pushed aside while they worked on the patient. It could have fallen to the floor and been kicked under the bed. Listing the possibilities and waiting for her doom to arrive almost drove her crazy.

She felt guilty about Clarabell and the others too. She'd let them down after they trusted her to keep people like Nurse Nasty out of their business.

When there was no sign of the police after Lettie's ex picked up the kids, Luca began plotting ways to retrieve the phone. She took a quick shower in Lettie's clunky stall, washing away the concealer that hid her body art. She applied the makeup that made her Luca, adding false eyelashes and long, dangly earrings. Changing into turquoise leggings and a zebra-print top, she put on a lavender wig and the biggest pair of sunglasses she could find. Standing before the slightly wavy mirror tacked to Lettie's bedroom door, she gave herself a sassy smile. "You don't look like no African nurse now, sugar!"

As she got on the first of two buses that would get her to Caponetti Memorial Hospital, she told herself she'd be fine. She could always back away if things didn't look right.

No one paid any attention as she entered the hospital, though she noted extra security people still stood by the doors. The clerk at the reception desk was on the phone, and the guard seemed concerned with a spot on his arm. Doing her best to look innocent, Luca approached the elevator. As she waited for the doors to open, fear battled courage. The staff on the fifth floor had seen her many times over two days. What if someone up there recognized her despite her different look?

She had to do it. If they hadn't yet found the phone, she'd get it and get out in just a few minutes. Of course those few minutes would be filled with absolute terror.

As she stood there arguing with herself, a man approached and said softly, "Excuse me. Are you Luca?"

***

Tom Wyman noticed the woman at the elevator precisely because she seemed eager to avoid notice. Though she wore a casual expression, her spine was rigid with tension and her feet shuffled constantly as she waited for the elevator. She seemed ready to bolt at any moment.

The stir he saw when he entered the hospital had told him something was wrong. Police officers stood in the corridors, and a general sense of unease rippled through the building as the staff went about their duties. He'd taken a seat on a plastic chair and observed for a while, but after a few minutes he concluded that though the atmosphere was tense, there didn't seem to be an active situation. The cops and security people frowned suspiciously at anyone who exited, but their scrutiny brought no result. That meant they knew something was wrong but hadn't caught the people responsible, at least not all of them.

As he sat wondering what to do next, Tom noticed a woman with body art that rang a bell. "Robin handed this woman a wad of cash and said, 'Come and work for us,'" Em had sputtered a few nights earlier. "There's a starfish tattoo on her neck, for criminey's sake. Spongebob's gal-pal!" Apparently Em thought marine images inked on the skin demonstrated a person's inherent dishonesty.

Later, when Luca was on the job, Em had admitted she seemed capable. "Hua thinks she's great, so what do I know?" The comment about the starfish tattoo had stuck with him, and he spoke to her by name.

Taking Luca aside, Tom described Robin, Cam, Em, and Hua and revealed that he knew what she'd been asked to do. He even mentioned the money she was still owed, in case that was her motive for sticking around after the caper went sour. Though doubtful at first, he saw the change in Luca's eyes when she began to believe he was a legitimate member of the group. Once he had her on his side, he asked her what had happened.

Luca's account was clear and concise. Though she didn't seem to have done anything wrong, she was upset at not being able to fulfill the obligation she'd taken on. "I got out like they told me to," she finished, "but I left my phone up there. I got no way to tell them what happened."

"Do you think the police have it?"

"They ain't come after me yet. I thought maybe it got overlooked in all the excitement." She glanced at the elevator. "I planned to sneak up there and see if I could get it back."

"How about you let me do that?" As he spoke Tom texted, *C awake Get out*, to both Cam's and Robin's phones. They'd probably gone dark by now, since the caper was underway, but if by some miracle his text reached them, they'd make up some sort of excuse and leave Green Grove. That done, he said to Luca, "Tell me the room number. Then wait here while I see what I can do."

As he exited the elevator on the fifth floor, Tom kept his eyes lowered. While he wasn't generally someone people noticed, he'd been told, by Robin among others, that his direct gaze was sharp and a little unsettling. There was a sign-in sheet at the quarantine doors, but he didn't know if that was the usual practice or something new since the discovery of Covel's fake admission. He signed a false name, and in the space marked *Patient Seen*, copied the name and room number of a man who'd had three different visitors in the last twenty-four hours. Putting on the mask, gown, and gloves, he tried not to meet anyone's eyes. Just another guy visiting a sick relative.

Finding 512 wasn't difficult, since a loud female voice drew his attention. "You cannot keep me here! I'm not a patient, and I don't need treatment!"

Softer voices answered in calming tones. In response the woman shouted, "Then get somebody up here who can! I am leaving. I want my phone. I want my clothes. I want a taxi. If you don't get me out of here A-SAP, my employer is going to bury you in lawsuits!"

What a surprise. A Preston employee threatening legal action in order to get her way.

An aide pushed a wheelchair past Tom, looking stressed. A nurse explained in low tones that tests were needed before Covel could be released. When she objected the nurse persisted, asking, "What if those people did something to you while you were unconscious?"

Apparently that concerned the pseudo-patient, though it didn't soften her attitude. "All right, but move your ass. I need to go."

Tom turned away, using his peripheral vision to observe as she was helped into the chair and wheeled down the hallway. When the elevator doors closed on Covel and her escort, he waited to see where it stopped. First floor. In the meantime, Room 512 stood empty.

Taking his phone from his pocket, Wyman called the number Luca had provided. In seconds a ringtone sounded, but he was surprised to hear the music play behind him, not from the room. Turning, he saw the phone lying on a windowsill at the end of the corridor. Face down, its white cover blended with the marble sill, but the call he'd made caused a glow that made it easy to spot. He moved toward the phone, but just before he reached it a CNA came out of a patient room, picked it up, and peered at the screen.

"Excuse me," Tom said as he reached her. "That's mine."

She looked at the phone and then at him. The tone sounded again. "Your phone plays Young Thug?"

"I set it down when a nurse came to ask some questions about my wife." Having memorized the number, he rattled it off. "It's a good thing I got that call, or I'd have walked away without it."

She held the phone in both hands, her expression doubtful. "You don't look like the type."

He made a casual shrug as he took the phone from her and dropped it into his pocket. "The things we do for love, right?"

Having accomplished the first part of his goal, Tom went to find Monica Covel and learn what she'd told the police. On-duty officers had no doubt already interviewed her, but detectives were sure to show up at the report of her odd abduction. A person smuggled into a hospital and kept sedated for days was bound to create waves in both police and media circles.

Tom walked quickly down several hallways, aware that Luca was waiting nervously for his return. About two-thirds of the way down one corridor, he spotted a grumpy-looking Covel slouched in a wheelchair in a room full of large pieces of equipment whose purpose he couldn't conceive. She was alone but probably not for long, so he stopped in the doorway and said in his best tough-guy tone, "You're awake."

Hard eyes turned to him. "Who are you?"

"That doesn't matter. I came to tell you to keep your mouth shut."

She tried to rise from the chair, but her arms couldn't yet support her and she fell back into the seat with a plop. "What is all this?" she demanded. "Why am I here?"

"Don't say anything, understand?"

"Who are you? Who sent you here?" Her voice rose. "Who did this?"

He gave her an enigmatic smile. "Ask the staff who came to see you on Saturday, to make sure you were safely in La-la Land."

He'd gauged Covel's paranoia perfectly. Her eyes searched the room as if Ninja assassins lay in wait behind the machines. "What were you supposed to do when I woke up? Who do you tell?"

Flashing his nastiest smile, Tom backed away. Covel would now ask herself who at Green Grove wanted her out of the way. She'd probably clam up when the police questioned her and plot her own revenge. With that, the hospital's procedural delays, and the time needed for her physical recovery, he might get to the estate before she could sound a warning. It helped that Luca said Hua had dumped her clothes, wallet, and phone in the hospital Lost and Found. Any delay was a good delay.

When he handed Luca the phone, she took it joyfully. "We have to go," he said. "Covel can barely sit up, but she'll get out of here as soon as she can."

Taking his arm, Luca exited the hospital with him, smiling into his eyes as if she were his girlfriend. Once they passed the man on duty she asked, "Her getting out is gonna mess up Clarabell's plan, right?"

Tom nodded, leading the way to the parking ramp and his car. "I sent a text, but they're probably past aborting the mission."

Climbing into the back seat, he opened the case lying there. Luca, who seemed in no hurry to leave, watched in fascination as he took off his prosthetic hand and replaced it with the metal hook. "Are Clarabell and them robbing that woman's place?" she asked when he finished.

"Not exactly." Her face revealed an obvious struggle between her sense of right and something else. It seemed like more than a desire for money. "It's good to stop bad people if you can, right?"

"I guess."

"Well, that's what we do. We find rich people who don't do what's right, and we try to make them change their ways. The plan for this morning, well, it's gone cockeyed, and that's bad."

"Your friends are in danger?"

"I'm afraid so." He got out of the back and into the driver's seat. When he started the engine, Luca hurried around to the passenger side and got in. "I don't have the rest of your payment, Luca. We'll get it to you somehow, but I have to get going."

"You going to try and help them, right?" Her tone said she wasn't accepting non-answers.

"I probably won't get in, but I have to try."

"What are you gonna do?"

He shrugged. "Make some sort of ruckus, I guess. They'll know how to take advantage of a distraction."

Luca thought about that for a moment. "Then take me along. I'm pretty good at making a ruckus."

***

The Honorable Judge Edgar Miller took the bench at 9:15 a.m., satisfied after a pancake breakfast and three cups of excellent coffee. Turning to his bailiff he asked, "What have we got today, Brad?"

"Up first is a guy that refused a court-appointed attorney," Brad replied. "Says he's a lawyer."

The accused was a dignified-looking man in his late seventies, slightly rumpled from a night in the sheriff's holding cell. "Your Honor," he said, stepping forward. "My name is Baylor Nixon. May I simply tell you what happened yesterday?"

In an expansive mood enhanced by generous amounts of real maple syrup, His Honor agreed.

The accused put on a dignified courtroom demeanor, strutting a little with his head bowed in thought before he began. "I have for years been an admirer of Marjorie Stanton, the actress."

"From the fifties?" His Honor was just forty-one, but he did enjoy the classic movie channels.

"That's the one. She recently contacted me to say she'd be visiting Tulsa and, because I've been a fan for so long, she wanted to meet me. We had dinner together, during which she invited me to escort her to a class reunion near Springdale." Here Nixon sighed. "Miss Stanton turned out to be a much different person than I imagined. When stopped in a completely legal manner by one of your local officers, she became abusive and argumentative. Apparently fearing the consequences of driving under the influence, she planted some pills in my pocket, causing me to be arrested along with her."

Miller turned to the prosecutor. "What do you know about this, Dave?"

"Well, the pills aren't oxy, and the woman isn't Marjorie Stanton. The real one's at home in Malibu."

"Who is she then?"

"Scam-artist, maybe. Bell's sending her prints in, but it'll take a while."

The judge turned back to the accused. "This woman lied to you, sir."

Nixon bowed his head. "And foolishly, Your Honor, I believed her."

"I'd like to meet this woman," Miller said. "Is she coming before me today?"

"Yes, sir," the bailiff said. "They brought her over with Mr. Nixon, but she had stomach issues."

"Issues?"

"Threw up in the hallway. Connors is with her in the ladies' room."

"Well, go out and see if she's able to appear." As he turned to go Miller added, "Only if she's done puking. I don't need to see that in my courtroom."

A few minutes later the bailiff returned, his calm demeanor gone. "She escaped, Judge!"

"Escaped?" Nixon and the judge spoke in unison.

A female deputy entered, stopping at the back of the room as if reluctant to approach. "She said she was better," she began apologetically. "We started out of the restroom, but she stopped in the doorway and said she'd lost her dental plate, said it must have fallen in the toilet while she was heaving." The woman's tone turned defensive as she added, "She showed me this big gap in her teeth." With a sigh she went on. "When I turned back to look, she ran out and locked me in."

"I heard the commotion," the first deputy said, "but it took a minute to figure out that it was Janie in the ladies' room, hollering for help. The old b—" He remembered his dignity. "The suspect wedged her cane under the handle and made it into a doorstop." In an attempt to excuse his coworker's mistake he added, "Judge, she seemed like she was all crippled up, and she's eighty if she's a day. You'd never think she'd try to escape."

"What's the status?"

The deputy checked his phone. "We've got everybody available out looking for her, but she's gone. Must have had an accomplice waiting outside."

***

As she squatted in the back seat of the judge's car (the *JDGEM-9* license plate gave it away), Em felt grateful that people in small towns were so careless about locking their doors. With the vehicle's tinted windows, she was safe for a while. Her hip hurt like the devil, and her gut still roiled from the ipecac, but she was free.

Em gave her stomach time to settle and the searchers time to give up on the immediate area. Though she wasn't fast on her feet and every cop in the area was on alert, she couldn't leave the information the Springdale PD had gathered about her behind. She watched as both the town's patrol cars left, no doubt on the hunt for her. With at least one officer required in court, she figured only one was left manning the sheriff's office at the other end of the building.

Leaving the car, Em walked to the office door, apparently in no hurry and hiding her limp as best she could. She peeped in the window and saw a man at the reception desk. There was no other movement, so she entered and closed the door behind her. When he looked up in surprise she

230

slumped against a wall and said, "I'm turning myself in. I thought I could run, but I just can't."

The deputy was young, which was good, because the young tend to underestimate the old. He seemed relaxed, almost smug, as he rose and came toward her. "That's a smart move, ma'am," he said. "It's best to face up to—"

Em started swaying. "I don't feel so good."

"Take it easy. I'll—" His words were cut off as Em grabbed the hand he'd stretched toward her and gave it a twist that spun him around. "Hey! Ow!"

Applying upward force with one hand, she used the other to take his gun from its holster. "Be quiet, boy. I don't want to hurt you, but if I have to, I can break you into pieces." Frog-walking him to his chair, she ordered, "Sit."

He obeyed, rubbing the shoulder she'd stressed and glaring at her. "You won't get away."

"Watch me." Taking his cuffs, Em secured his right hand and then closed the other cuff around a file cabinet handle some distance from the phone. Taking a pair of gloves from a box on his desk she put them on and began her search. It was right on top, a folder marked *M. Stanton*.

"Won't do you no good to take that," the man said. "I already sent copies to the FBI and every county in this state."

Em regarded him for a moment. "You're not a very good liar, kid. You need to practice." She slid the folder into the back waistband of her underpants. Next she found the envelope containing personal items they'd taken from her and stuffed that down her pants front. Going to the desktop computer, she located the files where her photograph and other information were stored, deleted them, dumped the trash, and cleared the history. If they had a guy like Hua on staff they might be able to get it back, but how many guys like Hua could there be in the world?

Finished, Em wiped down all the places she'd touched without gloves, as she'd done in her cell that morning. Leaving the office, she got back in the judge's car. This time she got into the hatch, where he wouldn't see her when he drove away at the end of his workday. Once the judge went into his house, she'd steal away, borrow a phone, and call someone to come for her. While she waited, a nap didn't sound bad. The cargo bed wasn't great, but it had been years since she slept on anything as uncomfortable as the cot in the jail. Drifting off, Em imagined her nice, soft bed back in Kansas and promised herself she'd stay there for twenty-four hours straight when they got home.

Chapter Twenty-Five

Monica Covel was furious—more furious, to be precise—by the time she was released from the hospital. Once it was determined she suffered no ill effects from her long sleep except some weakness the doctor said would disappear in a few hours, she had to wait while they located her things. Her bellowed epithets eventually resulted in someone checking Lost and Found. Everything was there, tied neatly in a plastic grocery bag. An aide helped her dress, but when she was ready to go, two police detectives arrived to interview her.

Covel was in no mood to chat. "I need to get to work," she said when the older one introduced himself. "I'm Neil Preston's head of security, and I need to be at Green Grove now."

"We understand, Ms. Covel, but we have questions."

"Look. I don't know what happened. I don't remember anything after I left anger management on Friday."

"Anger management? Then you've had issues in the past?"

She thought the guy knew more than he admitted about that. He was Mexican, which irritated her, but she needed to get this over with. "I'll come to your precinct tomorrow, and we'll talk. Right now I need to get back."

"Do you need a police presence out there, Ms. Covel?"

"No." She'd be fired for sure if she brought the Local Leos into whatever's going on. "Mr. Preston will be worried, and I want him to see that I'm all right."

"But why did someone sedate you and keep you here all weekend?"

Losing the tiny amount of control she'd been holding onto, Covel lashed out. "That's what you need to find out, Chico." As the detective's eyes went darker, she slung her purse over her shoulder. "Do your job, and I'll go home and do mine."

As she waited for a cab, Covel called Joelle. Though not friends, Monica and Joelle were allies, and she could count on Joelle to tell her the truth. When Joelle didn't pick up, Covel's dread deepened. What was going on at Green Grove? When the cab pulled up, she climbed in and ordered, "Take Creek Turnpike south. I'll direct you from there, and I'll give you ten dollars for every minute less than twenty it takes to get there."

***

Using Joelle's computer, Hua had finished his most important task, making changes to the patent release documents. His second job required study, and he spent several hours perusing the estate's closed-circuit TV system. Once he understood how it worked, he began making changes. By the time Robin and Cam arrived at the front gate, he'd altered the system so that while the cameras monitored activity as usual, they no longer recorded it. As long as the guards failed to notice the absence of the tiny red light on their instrument panel, there'd be no visual record of KIDNAP's visit to Green Grove.

As Hua finished the task, he saw Cam and Robin arrive at the front gate. They went through the same search he had, though it was a little less aggressive. When they got into a golf cart with one of the guards, Hua felt a stab of dread. They hadn't realized they wouldn't be allowed to drive to the house, though now he recalled Oliva saying something about truck drivers having to wait at the back gate. Preston's secret fears must include being whisked away in the back of a vehicle which, Hua thought with a tiny smile, wasn't completely unheard of.

Having the car that far away made his escape more difficult, and he adjusted his mental time frame. Navigating to the schematic that showed camera placement on the grounds, he charted a path to the front gate that avoided the wall and the road, where most of the cameras were located. In the orchard he might run into groundskeepers, but according to Oliva, there was little communication between them and the residents. If he greeted them cheerfully, they might take him for a guest out for a morning walk. Hua twisted his shoulders to relax them. He had his Plan B. He should be okay.

As far as Hua knew, Plan A was still in place for everyone else. Nixon hadn't shown up. Joelle was out of the way, as was Monica Covel. Oliva had been warned to stay out of things. That meant Cam and Robin would meet with Preston without backup. If their luck held, the Kidnap Gang would leave Green Grove with a half million dollars and Preston's signature on documents that would disrupt his business for a long time. Preston and his cronies would take action to repair what Hua had done, but it would take time. Preston's bottom line would suffer, as it should.

Hua made a schedule in his head. Robin's meeting with Preston was sure to last an hour. Since he calculated it would take him about fifteen minutes to reach the car, he could remain where he was until nine-thirty. That meant he had twenty minutes to snoop through Joelle's computer a little more.

Those minutes were eye-opening, and soon Hua was emailing himself whole files that indicated Joelle was no innocent bystander. She was in it up to her neck, aware of the bribes, threats, and conniving Preston did to steal patents from their developers and push them through the testing phase.

Five minutes before he needed to close the laptop and begin wiping away traces of his presence, he noticed that Joelle's Yahoo account contained ninety-two draft emails. Drafts were a convenient form of communication for criminals, since multiple people could access an email account and read the unsent messages without them ever being sent and therefore recorded.

Hua clicked on the folder, and that was when things took on a whole different aspect.

***

After a short elevator ride, Robin and Cam stepped onto the third floor of Neil Preston's home. They were met by a young woman whose white face said her day was not going well.

235

"Hey, there, Miss Cohee," Belk said, his voice turning silky. "I hear Nixon failed to show up this morning. Bet that made a lot of hoopla."

Her eyes flashed a warning. "Mondays are often stressful."

"Well, Mr. Preston's guests are right on time." He leaned toward her, lowering his voice. "That should put him in a better mood, right?"

She didn't back away, though her posture hinted she really wanted to. "Thank you, Mr. Belk. I'll show them to the conference room so you can get back to work."

"And I'll see you later." Belk's tone was full of promise, but she didn't answer. Maintaining eye contact, he stepped back into the elevator and pressed a button. Cohee seemed relieved when the doors closed on him, and she turned to Robin and Cam with a more natural smile. "We'll be meeting down there."

As they went, Robin made a quick assessment of Preston's newest PA. Tall and more skinny than slender, Cohee wore her dark hair in a modernized bun, low on her neck with bangs swept to one side. The look of a mannish white shirt was softened by a pink skirt that buttoned down the front topped with a wide, matching belt. Navy heels and a chunky necklace in shades of blue and pink almost completed the outfit. Glancing into the office she'd come out of, Robin saw a navy blazer hung over a chair that would add a more formal tone when required.

"Have you worked for Mr. Preston long?" Robin knew exactly how long, six and a half months, but she asked the question as an icebreaker.

Cohee shook her head. "I'm still learning the ropes." She stopped in the doorway. "Please sit where I've indicated, and I'll let Mr. Preston know you're here."

As visitors to a multi-million dollar operation with a proposal that would provide its owner something he wanted badly, they might have expected to be offered coffee or perhaps water. That didn't happen, and Robin guessed it wasn't Cohee's fault.

The room continued the theme from below, starkly gray furnished only with a long ebony table set with four straight chairs on each side and a state-of-the-art desk chair at the head. Preston's place at the table had a telephone console with a dozen buttons. She guessed he could control everything that happened in the room and possibly on the estate from that console.

On her right Robin noticed a number pad near the door frame. A light at its top glowed green, signaling that things were okay, she hoped. On the wall opposite Neil's chair was a large TV screen with floor-to-ceiling bookshelves on either side of it. The exterior wall across from her was all window, somewhat surprising given Neil's paranoia. Then she noticed it had a slightly bronze tint. Bulletproof glass.

The room's decoration consisted of a half-dozen swords. A rather odd-looking one was suspended over the table by two chain brackets. A set with sharply curved blades hung over the bookcases. Another set, longer and straighter, were crossed over the doorway, and the last was in a glass case on the wall opposite the window. Stepping closer, she read the plaque below it: *The Sword of Stalingrad, Presented to Stalin by Winston Churchill, 1943.*

Robin took a seat at the table where a placard printed in bold Times New Roman font said *Talman*. Cam sat where another said *Photographer*. Silently they waited, Robin doubly uncomfortable. First, after only a few minutes, the straight, unpadded chair felt like a medieval torture device, and second, she couldn't banish the thought that coming to Green Grove had been a mistake. *We're in Preston's territory, where he has all the power.*

When the door opened she jumped, but it was only Bertie Oliva. Setting a black valise down in the corner near the doorway, he greeted "Ronda" warmly and shook Cam's hand. As they took their seats he held Robin's gaze for a few seconds, which made her even more nervous than before. Was he comparing her height and frame to the person who'd questioned him in a dark storage unit from behind a mask? His eyes revealed nothing, and he said, "It's going to be a good day, Ms. Talman."

"Everything is ready?"

"We've had some minor problems, but we managed to overcome them." His charming smile flashed. "There are a few more hoops to jump through. First, Mr. Preston wants advance copies of the articles, so we can correct any errors and make suggestions for improvement. I took the liberty of adding that to the contract you sent over."

He'll want to add a little propaganda. Aloud Robin said, "Our editor will arrange to speak with Mr. Preston by telephone over the next few months. And before we publish anything, he'll be given the material to preview: copy, photographs, the entire layout."

Oliva nodded. "Then I think we can proceed."

She made herself smile, though under the table one leg jiggled like a jackhammer. "Great."

Oliva pressed a button on a console. "We're ready for you."

The door opened and Neil Preston stepped into the room. Forcing back visions of Monica Covel arriving downstairs with a dozen armed police officers, Robin stood, and Cam followed suit.

"Mr. Preston, so nice to meet you." She knew better than to offer to shake hands. They'd stopped at a restroom downstairs and taken turns scrubbing like O.R. doctors in order to be allowed into the Great Man's presence.

Physically, Neil Preston was unimpressive. His frame was spindly under his expensive clothing, and his posture radiated tension. His bulgy eyes never stopped moving, and he seemed unable to meet Robin's gaze for longer than a few seconds. His nose and chin looked sharp enough to slice her if she got too close, and his hair! Why would a man who could afford the best stylists go around looking like he barbered himself with gardening shears?

His voice was deep and a little raspy. "So this is the little lady who says she can put me on the cover of TIME."

Strike one: Talking about me like I'm not in the room. Strike two: Calling me "little lady" when I'm two inches taller than he'll ever be.

Robin forced herself to smile. "We can make it happen, Mr. Preston."

Oliva was still focused on her, his expression unreadable, and Robin's pulse jumped yet another notch. Was he listening to her syntax, comparing her speech cadence and vocabulary with that of the person who'd abducted him? Had he noted Cam's wide shoulders and strong arms and connected them with the man who'd tossed him into the van like a corn-hole bag?

Whatever Oliva was thinking, Preston was focused on the award. "I need a guarantee your offer is real before we proceed."

"You do realize I can't just call my boss and ask her to confirm she'll take a million-dollar bribe."

Preston grimaced. "Yet you expect me to hand you half that much on faith. That won't happen."

"Have you ever heard TIME's managing editor speak?"

"Judith Kupenski?" Preston seemed impressed to learn the proposal came from the very top. "I've, um, spoken with her on the phone." As he flushed Robin guessed he'd called, disguising his voice, to recommend himself for Person of the Year. He adjusted his necktie. "I'd know her voice if I heard it."

"I recorded our conversation." Robin made a rueful grin. "I wasn't sure she'd back me if you decided to make trouble." Taking a thumb drive from her jacket pocket, she handed it to Oliva. "I didn't get all of it, because I didn't realize right away what she was asking me to do." Oliva put the portable drive into his laptop and clicked the only file, a WAV recording. It had begun as an actual conversation Robin had with

Kupenski, though it was on a completely different subject than TIME's Person of the Year. A cat lover, Ms. Kupenski had been looking for an Abyssinian to replace one of hers that died. Posing as a cat breeder, Robin had called to say she had a kitten for sale. Recording the conversation, Hua had spliced new questions from Robin in place of their discussion of the cat.

Oliva clicked on the file, his expression almost amused. He knew something was up, and Robin waited for him to act. Was he waiting for the right moment to expose them? What would happen if he did?

Hua had argued with this part of the plan, claiming everyone knows how easily recordings can be altered. "Mr. Preston will reject your "evidence," he'd maintained.

Em had taken the opposite view. "That jerk wants this so badly it hurts. He'll try to hold back, but he'll want to believe." As usual, Em's judgment seemed spot on.

If Nixon had been here, or Covel or Joelle, one or all of them might have pointed out that audio tape is unreliable unless verified by experts. Oliva said nothing.

As Preston leaned toward the laptop in order to hear better, Robin's voice came first. "—want me to offer Mr. Preston the chance to be Person of the Year in return for a financial consideration?"

The reply came in Kupenski's notably husky voice. "I'm very excited about the possibility." Her next response had been to Robin's warning that the cat had a tendency to claw furniture and fight with other animals. "To be honest, he sounds like a tough case," Kupenski said. "Under the right circumstances, do you think he'd change his ways?"

"I can make it clear that's what we expect."

"All right then. Let's see if things work out with him."

"Ms. Kupenski, you want me to accept money from Mr. Preston in exchange for this?" What she'd really asked was whether she wanted the cat spayed.

"I do, and make it as soon as possible. I'd like to have things wrapped up by next Tuesday if possible."

The segment ended. "Is that good enough for you?"

Preston tried to appear cool. "Bertie mentioned that others were offered the same deal. Who are they and what's their status?"

She didn't dare look at Oliva, though his gaze felt like a cold wind off a wintery lake. "I checked last night. Two of them turned the offer down outright, one can't get the money together, and the last is dickering for a lower price."

"Then if you and I come to an agreement right now, I'd be in?"

"Yes, Mr. Preston." She appeared to give her next comment some thought. "However, there's still the question of how you'll appear in the layout. Have you considered the humanitarian gesture Mr. Oliva and I discussed? That would make all the difference in the tone of the spread."

"We've come up with something I think will impress you." Preston did the preening thing again, adjusting his tie and wriggling his shoulders under his steel-gray jacket. "To coincide with your announcement that I'm POTY, Argent will release several very important patents." He stopped to explain—she thought *patronize* was a better term since he leaned forward as if to force her to focus on his words. "That means anyone can manufacture and distribute the drugs named. The cost of each one will decrease significantly, but we care about people and we want them to have access to medicines that will improve their lives." He sat back in his chair, smiling in a way he probably thought was attractive, and waited for her reaction.

Robin replied in a gushing tone. "That's very impressive, Mr. Preston. I'm thrilled to be able to return to my bosses and tell them our POTY will make such a wonderful gesture of caring to benefit the nation." She smiled, "And of course it will be a great incentive for people to buy the magazine, since TIME will have all the relevant details."

"The idea is pure genius," Preston replied, "but I'm known for my intelligence. You should put something in the article about how many great ideas I've had over the years. Bertie will make you a list, and I can talk with Judith about them whenever she wants."

Oliva nodded when his name was mentioned, and Robin saw humor light his eyes. Was his amusement aimed at his boss, who claimed credit for an idea that wasn't his at all, or at her, because he knew what she was up to?

Preston folded his hands on the tabletop. "I had my lawyer draw up the patent release documents." He stopped. "Bertie, you've looked them over?"

"As of 1:00 a.m. this morning, they're good to go. I asked Ms. Cohee to make us all copies."

"Right." Preston turned back to Robin. "I'll sign the releases today, so the magazine is assured of my good intentions."

"Great. That will give us a start on the layout."

"Make it positive, Missy!" Preston said coldly. "Not this fake, negative crap that's gone around for months now."

"If you're releasing the rights to medicines people need, that will certainly help Argent's image," Robin said, "and yours as well."

"Well, that's what we're doing. Thousands of people, maybe hundreds of thousands, will feel better because of my gesture. Of course, I'm giving up a lot of revenue, but it's more important to help people than it is to make a profit. I always say that, don't I Bertie?"

"Always." Oliva's tone was sardonic, but Preston failed to notice. "So here we go. I'm going to give up all the profits on these medicines for the good of everyone. And who knows? We might do this again in a year, because people matter. Right, Bertie?"

"They do." Oliva's gaze flickered to Robin as he passed a folder to Preston. "You'll sign each document at the bottom, and Mandy will notarize it." He signaled to Cohee, who hovered by the door, now wearing the blazer that completed her outfit. She stepped into the office, notary seal in hand.

Preston picked up a pen, but instead of using it, clicked the point in and out as he perused the first page. "Nixon should be here to interpret the legalese for us."

"Where exactly is he?" Oliva asked, and again his glance flickered to Robin. She tried to freeze her face in an expression of innocent interest.

"I'm not sure. He left a message, but it was vague." Preston turned petulant and he kicked the table, making the others jump in surprise. "His absence at this juncture is completely unacceptable!"

Oliva spoke quickly, obviously hoping to head off a tantrum. "I went over the whole document very thoroughly last night, Mr. Preston. It's exactly as we discussed, and Nixon included all the safeguards you required."

"Still, a man has to be careful." To Robin's horror, Preston began reading the release, sliding a finger down the page to mark his place. They'd assumed he'd trust Nixon's work, but the lawyer's absence apparently made him extra cautious. Robin's lips felt like stretched rubber bands. If he read the whole thing, he'd find the part Hua had changed, and it would all be over.

Beside her, Cam ran his hands over his shirt-front. When he caught himself, he put one under each thigh to keep them still, but the look he shot Robin said he realized they were in trouble.

Preston finished reading the first page, mostly boiler-plate language that identified Argent and listed its various operations. Setting the page aside, he went on to the second.

Desperate for a distraction Robin asked, "Is it okay if my associate takes photos while you read?"

Preston replied without looking up. "I'll want to choose which ones you use in the spread."

"No problem." Robin nodded to Cam, who managed to do a fair portrayal of a photographer, standing at different spots in the room, peering at the lights, and taking shot after shot. Whether by accident or design, he began humming as he worked. Robin approved, since Cam's version of "Bohemian Rhapsody" was definitely distracting.

Preston didn't seem to notice. He turned to page three.

Oliva watched Robin, his dark eyes unreadable. She met his gaze, asking a tacit question. *Whose side are you on?*

After a second Oliva said, "Neil, you need to get Belk in here."

Robin's breath caught in her chest, like a balloon expanding toward imminent explosion.

Preston looked up from the papers. "Why?"

"I'm thinking a group shot, you with your inner circle." Oliva turned to Robin. "You'll want photos of the honoree alone, of course, but a few with his people standing behind him will give a sense of solidarity."

She didn't know what Oliva was up to, but Preston was no longer reading. "Great idea," she said, trying to make her voice sound normal. "The successful businessman with his trusted associates."

"I should be solo on page one, and then with my team on page two." Preston looked at Ms. Cohee, who'd remained by the door like an uninvited guest. "Where's Joelle?"

Oliva glanced at his watch. "It's only 9:30, sir."

"Just rolling out of bed then. Mandy, go down and knock on her door."

Oliva stood. "Mandy has to witness your signatures. I'll go."

Preston nodded. "Tell my sister I'm giving her the chance to be pictured in a national magazine. She might even hurry for that." He looked around, his brow darkening again. "I can't believe Nixon isn't here. He's a corny old bastard, but he does add *gravitas* to the group."

"Tell you what," Oliva said. "Let's plan on a group shot in, say, half an hour." He turned to Robin. "You said you have questions for Mr. Preston for the article."

The knot in her chest loosened a little. "I can do the interview while you round people up for the photo."

Preston leaned back in his chair. "This is working out very well."

"It will be great," Oliva assured him. "Mandy, show Mr. Preston where to sign." Cohee moved to the table, and Robin stifled her surprise when, as Cohee blocked Preston's view for a moment, Oliva scooped up the black valise he'd brought in earlier. As he closed the door he shot her a glance she couldn't interpret. Warning? Congratulation? Derision? With Oliva it was hard to tell.

When the latch clicked softly into place, Robin considered what to do next. She didn't think for a moment Oliva was leaving to arrange a photo shoot. Still, his interruption had sidetracked Preston, who began signing and dating in the spots indicated. As ordered, Cam set a small vid-cam on the table and pressed the record button: evidence that Preston had signed the release willingly. As the camera did its work, Preston signed, sliding the copies to Cohee, who notarized each set. "You can go now, Mandy," Preston said offhandedly when they were finished. "I'll call if I need you." Without a word she left the room.

Preston pushed a copy of the release down the table to Robin, who folded it carefully and slid it into her jeans pocket. It was a relief to have it done, and she wished they could leave, but they had to go through the motions of interviewing Preston. It was stressful to sit there wondering if Oliva was rounding up security in order to have them arrested, beaten, or killed. While she didn't trust the man, she found it hard to believe he'd tell on them, first because they could prove he'd betrayed Green Grove's secrets and second because she couldn't see him condoning murder. He'd tricked Preston into signing the release without reading it. That was good, but he'd taken the bag Robin guessed contained the half million cash payment, which was bad. Still, he hadn't betrayed Ronda Talman as a fraud. She trusted him, but only a little.

Taking up her pad and pen she said, "Mr. Preston, can you tell me a little about your childhood?"

"My parents were great people," Preston began. "They were really proud of me because I was such a good student. I was the best student; you can ask anyone. And in college I did even better. My dad used to say how proud of me he was, and my mother! It was embarrassing sometimes because she told everybody what a genius her son was growing up to be."

"Hold up the papers so I can get a picture," Cam interrupted. Preston obeyed, grinning up at Cam, who took a photo of Argent's CEO releasing every single one of Argent's patents, both devices and medications, "for the good of the nation's health."

As Cam took a second and then a third shot Preston said happily, "Yup, my parents knew from the first how smart I'd turn out to be. I just wish they'd lived to see how big a genius their son really is."

Chapter Twenty-Six

Malcolm Wells ("Call me Mac") was the newest employee among the guards at Green Grove. He liked the job pretty well, though he'd been warned not to take it for granted. "It seems easy," one of the other men told him, "but if you screw up, Preston comes down on you like Darth Vader in a bad mood. There ain't no second chances with him."

Since it was Davis's turn to walk the perimeter, Mac was alone in the guard shack when a car pulled up outside. The monitor revealed a sedan with an attractive though loudly-dressed woman in the driver's seat. She had several body piercings and wore earrings the size of dinner plates. Not the usual Green Grove visitor—not that they had many at all.

"Can I help you?"

"Please tell the woman of the house that Ms. Allison DeNeuve would like a word with her about women's issues in the upcoming election."

Taking in the visitor's earrings, which were the size of Maxwell House can lids, he replied, "She isn't interested."

The woman's dark eyes turned a shade darker. "Are you authorized to make decisions for her, or are you making a typically male assumption that you know what's best for a woman?"

"I'm authorized to monitor this gate, lady, and that means—"

Her face came closer to the monitor and her voice crackled through the speaker. "*Lady*? First you decide who your employer might want to see and now you call me *lady*? Let me assure you, you aren't dealing with a *lady*! I am a woman, and I have the right to be treated with respect! I don't need you man-splaining what it means to be a flunky security guard at the gate of some rich guy's estate!" She muttered to herself a little, the words *lady* and *that means* prominent in her criticism.

Mac was disconcerted. How had a simple refusal to grant entry suddenly become a major incident in the annals of feminism? "Look, M—" What did these women want to be called? "Ms., I'm not trying to insult you. I just know Ms. Preston does not see people who don't have an appointment." Certainly not before noon, but he was wise enough not to say that out loud.

"How do you know that? Have you asked her?"

"Well, I didn't personally, but my supervisor—"

"Who is a man, am I right? Another man making decisions for a woman."

"She don't decide. It's Mr. Preston who says who'll be let in here."

"So this woman's husband says who she can and can't see?"

"He ain't her husband. He's her brother."

"And that makes it better how? The woman is confined by a male sibling? That's positively Old Testament!"

"She ain't a prisoner. She comes and goes whenever she wants."

"But she isn't allowed to have visitors." The woman's earrings swung like gyroscopes. "This is why I am running for county commissioner, to see that women are represented in government and respected in its applications."

"You're running for office?"

Now her eyes flashed hot and angry. "You think I shouldn't? Is that because I'm female or maybe because I don't fit your vision of civil service? I know I'm not old *or* white *or* male, Bubba. You don't have to point it out."

Mac was having trouble keeping up. How did a simple "You can't come in here" make him into an example of toxic masculinity? "I didn't say she can't have visitors. I said she doesn't want to."

Her expression turned even more disdainful. "How am I supposed to know that's true? Because some man in a monkey suit says it is?"

Mac sighed. "Listen. I don't have to argue with you. This is private property, so just back out onto the road and go on your way."

"Oh, I'll back out of here all right. But I'm not going on my way. I'm going to call the sheriff's office and have them come out here and do a wellness check on Ms. Prescott."

"Preston."

"Whoever. I want to see for myself that you all aren't keeping her a prisoner in her own home."

Mac's gaze bounced around the guard shack, looking for inspiration. He couldn't let this woman in. That was a given. He couldn't call Ms. Preston and ask her to confirm his authority to deny entrance to the estate. And he damned sure couldn't let this woman call the cops on his boss.

"What if I ask Ms. Preston to call you this afternoon, when she isn't busy?"

The woman thought about that. "I'd want you to take her a note I will write. I don't trust you to convey how serious I am about this."

"Okay. Write the note and I'll get it to her."

The woman started fishing around in her car, came up with a scrap of paper and a pen, and got out of the car. Leaning against the trunk lid, she began writing, stopping every few seconds to think. Mac opened the gate just enough to let himself out. When he got to the car, she was looking over what she'd written, her brow furrowed. After a few seconds she handed him the note.

"I'll expect her to call me today."

"I'll make sure you're contacted." *By someone who'll say she's Joelle Preston,* he added silently. His sister, maybe, or one of the guys' wives. No way was he going to bother the prickly Ms. Preston with this woman's concerns.

***

As soon as the gate cracked open, Tom, who was crouched at the passenger-side fender, moved toward it. While the guard was focused on

Luca and her note, he slipped through. He half expected a second guard in the shack, but it was empty at the moment. Probably on patrol.

Finding a convenient clump of azaleas, Tom sat down to wait until both guards returned and went inside. Once that happened, Tom figured he'd have an hour to move about the grounds in relative safety. The fatal flaw in any security system is predictability. People like routine, but routine offers opportunities for evading surveillance.

His first thoughts were appreciation for Luca's acting job. She'd provided the diversion he needed, and she'd showed a natural talent for playing a role. He was inside because Luca was quick-witted and definitely not shy.

Now it was up to him, but Tom hadn't come to Tulsa prepared for a clandestine operation. A quick check of the *KIDNAP.org* website gave him the general layout of the estate as they knew it, and he recognized Cam's square printing. There was lots of security, both human and technological. Tom read Plan A, which seemed sound, but he had no idea if the others knew it was time to put Plan B into effect. He shifted uneasily in his leafy bower. Playing it by ear wasn't his favorite method of operation, but Monica Covel's imminent arrival meant it was required.

Luca had offered her version of a defensive weapon: a can of Hi-Lites Hair Spray (Golden Lioness) she carried in her purse. "Point it at somebody's eyes if you get caught," she'd urged. "It burns like crazy." Carrying the mini-canister in his hand, he left his hiding place and began moving toward the house. When he came to a camera mounted in a tree and whirring gently from side to side, he thought of another use for Luca's gift.

***

Pleased that her distraction had allowed Tom to get inside, Luca considered ways to extend the ruse. She tried flirting a little with the guy whose shirt said *Mac*, but he kept glancing backward as if nervous about being away from his post. Finally he said, "You need to go now. I got things to do." He turned, punched a code into the gate panel, and disappeared inside.

Getting into the car, Luca backed away from the gate. Tom had instructed her to wait on a side road just out of sight of the estate's back gate. "My phone won't work in there," he'd said. "Give me an hour and then call the police. Tell them you heard shots fired or saw smoke, whatever will get them out here."

"I'll think of something," she assured him. Now all Luca could do was wait, and that was hard. She wanted to help, but since she had no idea what was going on, waiting was all she could do.

***

Hua used Joelle's laptop to check the monitors every few minutes to keep track of what was going on around the estate. He was surprised to see Luca pull up to the front gate in a rental car at 9:33 a.m. Even more surprising, Tom Wyman stole onto the grounds while Luca distracted the guard with lots of shouting and arm-waving. If Luca and Tom were here, something had gone wrong, and it probably concerned Monica Covel.

That meant moving to Plan C, which called for each of them to leave the estate by any route possible and reconnoiter at a nearby crossroad. A good thing for Hua was that in perusing Joelle's files, he'd discovered a means of escape he guessed was unknown to most. He could leave Green Grove whenever he chose, but he was reluctant to go without Cam and Robin. Picking up his bag, he wiped down the room to erase his prints, checked the hallway, and then slid out into the atrium.

***

Baylor Nixon was released from police custody just after ten. When his phone was returned to him, the first thing he did was call his office in Tulsa and order his clerk to send someone to fetch him. While he waited, Nixon went to the diner Judge Miller had recommended and ordered eggs, bacon, grits, and hash browns. Though the judge praised the pancakes to the skies, Nixon had never developed a liking for fried flour.

As the waitress filled his coffee cup a third time, Nixon stared out the window and tried to put recent events into a coherent frame. Margy wasn't Margy. What he'd experienced had been a plot to get him...what? Into legal trouble? No, he'd explained away the charges fairly easily.

To get him away from Tulsa. That had to be it. The fake Margy had prevented him from attending the meeting between Preston and the TIME magazine people. Why? What would have happened if he'd been there? He listed things mentally. He'd have brought copies of the patent release documents. He'd have been there to explain anything Preston had doubts about. Someone wanted him to be unable to do one or both of those things. But who cared about a few almost worthless patents?

Unless that wasn't what Preston had been given to sign.

Grabbing his phone, Nixon called Neil's private number. The call went directly to voicemail. No doubt he was unwilling to interrupt his long-awaited interview. Gritting his teeth, he called the main number for Green Grove. Mandy Cohee answered, "Argent Chemical, Neil Preston's office."

"Ms. Cohee, it's Baylor Nixon. I need to speak with Mr. Preston."

"He's in a meeting."

"What I have to tell him may have to do with that meeting."

There was a pause. "He said he didn't want to be disturbed."

"Mandy, I'm his lawyer. I have urgent legal advice."

Another pause. "He doesn't like it when I don't follow orders."

"I must speak with him. Now!" Bits and pieces had come together in his head. Monica Covel's sudden, odd illness. The offer of an honor Neil wanted badly enough to ignore his own safety protocols. The invitation out of the blue that had lured Nixon away from Tulsa. His heart beat in his chest. "There's something going on there, Mandy, and I have to stop it."

The last pause was the longest of all, and Nixon gripped the phone as if it were a lifeline. Finally he heard a deep sigh. "We're supposed to go in for a group photo soon," she said. "When he calls me in for that, I'll hand him a note asking him to call you right away."

"That isn't—"

"I need this job, Mr. Nixon."

Her tone told him it was useless to argue. The poor girl was so terrified of upsetting Preston that everything was a compromise. "Do that, Miss Cohee. I'll wait for his call."

Almost as soon as he set the phone down, it rang. The caller was unknown, so he let it go to voicemail, but some sense that the call had purpose made him check the message left. Anger tightened his mouth at the sound of her voice, and he hit the callback button. "Who are you really, Miss Margy?"

"Doesn't matter. Neil Preston is as crooked as a barrel of fishhooks, and you've been enabling him for years."

"I don't have to—"

"No, you don't, and we think you should stop. For all your Southern drawl and your cowboy manners, *Nix,* you're as guilty as Preston is, and when they get him for murder, you're going down with him."

"Murder!" The truth of it struck his heart like a shard of glass, but he sputtered, "Don't be ridiculous."

"Don't pretend you don't know about the dead whistleblowers." She sounded tired.

He sniffed. "I know there have been some accidental deaths, but—"

"We're both too old for this!" she snapped. "Those people were killed, and Preston's responsible."

"Oh, God." The truth sank from his heart to his gut, and he thought his breakfast would reappear in a rush. It had been convenient when the scientist fell from her balcony. It had been even more so when the troublesome reporter died in a mugging. He'd never questioned what happened to them or to the others, even in his own mind. Instead he'd protected Preston's interests, so closely tied to his own.

Margy, or rather Not-Margy, went on. "It's time to cut ties with Preston."

"What have you done to him?"

"Me? I was in a cell next to you all night, remember? But you need to decide where your future lies."

"Why are you telling me this?"

She hesitated before answering. "I wasn't sure you knew about the killing, and your reaction just now convinced me you didn't know Preston ordered those deaths." After a moment she added, "Still, your kind of lawyering stinks."

He retreated to the last resort of legal scoundrels. "Everyone deserves competent legal representation."

"But a great deal of money buys a great deal of looking the other way, doesn't it?" She snorted derisively. "Here's what I suggest in the strongest possible terms. Retire from legal practice immediately. Today. Create some nebulous but worrisome physical symptoms that make it necessary."

"What? I'm fit as a—"

"Don't you dare say it!" She interrupted. "Get out of Preston's business or go down with him. Those are your options."

He was silent for a few moments before asking, "If I retire, I'll be left out of any, um, legal problems?"

He heard a smile enter her voice. "That's doable, Counselor, but there's a fee attached to the service."

Chapter Twenty-Seven

The guard at the front gate called Belk twice while he was trying to take his morning break. First Mac reported a woman who'd come to see Joelle and got nasty when he wouldn't let her in. He seemed pleased with himself when he said he'd gotten rid of her. The second time Mac called, he had two concerns. Some of the outdoor cameras had gone blurry, and he thought someone should check them. The other question involved a man sitting in a parked car in a grove of trees about a quarter mile from the gate. "He wasn't there before that reporter came," Mac said. "You think he's waiting for her?"

"I'll take care of it." Setting down the bagel he'd smeared with cream cheese, Belk massaged his acidy stomach. "We gotta make a plan," he said aloud, though there was no one else in the room.

First he needed to decide whether to tell Mr. Preston any of it. Belk figured he'd be wrong no matter what he did, since he wasn't the boss's fair-haired Monica Covel. But there had been those phone calls warning of danger, so he needed to be vigilant. Taking action on his own initiative would make him look competent too. He didn't think Preston knew everything Covel did to keep him safe. He just trusted her to get it done.

Going over Mac's concerns, he tried to decide which things needed action. The woman was gone, so he could forget her for now. The cameras could be checked during the next patrol. That left the guy waiting outside the wall. After some thought, Belk decided the guy was probably connected to Joelle's little boy toy. If he was up to no good, the guy outside the wall was probably an accomplice.

Taking out his radio, Belk contacted the guards on outdoor duty. "I think Joelle's date from last night might be up to something. Make sure he isn't out there tossing Mr. Preston's artwork over the wall."

"You think she picked up a bad one?" Mo asked. "Gee, I hope she's okay."

That brought a sudden, horrifying image of Joelle sprawled across her bed, beaten senseless or even murdered. Though he could barely stand the woman, Belk knew who'd get the blame if that happened. To calm a rising sense of panic he reminded himself the guy had checked out on their people search. "I'm sure she's okay, but I'll check on her anyway."

He ended the call, angry and scared. What if he'd missed something? With sudden vehemence, Belk cursed Covel for getting sick and leaving him with decisions he didn't want to make.

First he'd see that Joelle was all right. She wouldn't be happy to be bothered before ten, but he had to do it. At her door he knocked softly. "Ms. Preston? It's Lawrence Belk."

There was no answer. Now what?

He knocked again, a little louder. "Ms. Preston? I'm going to come in and see if you're okay."

Though he had the code for her door, Belk had never even considered using it before this. *Please God, don't let her be all sliced up.* With trembling fingers he entered the four-digit code and peered inside.

***

Hua was leaving the apartment when he heard footsteps in the hallway and hurried back inside. When the sound stopped outside Joelle's door, he turned in near panic, looking for a hiding spot. After a second it occurred to him that hiding wasn't enough. If someone had come looking for Joelle, that person needed to leave thinking she was here, safe and sound.

A light knock sounded on the door. "Ms. Preston?"

Hua scanned the apartment again. Only one possibility. Going to the large bathroom off the master bedroom, he turned the *H* shower knob as far as it would go, causing a noisy rush of water. Thanks to an efficient heating system, a cloud of steam immediately began to collect in the stall. Hua turned on the cold tap, but only a little.

Another knock. "Ms. Preston? It's Lawrence Belk."

Quickly and quietly, Hua stripped off his clothes and tossed them into a wicker hamper. Stepping into the shower, he closed the frosted-glass door and turned his back. A towel hung on a hook, and he put it on to cover his dark hair.

"Ms. Preston? I'm going to come in to see if you're okay."

At the last moment Hua recalled how much shorter he was than Joelle. As the lock whirred softly, responding to Belk's passcode, he reached out of the stall and grabbed a plastic box that sat on the vanity. The front said HAIRSETPRO, which told him nothing about what was inside. It didn't matter. Setting the box on the shower stall floor, he stepped onto it. Raised eight inches he was taller—not tall enough to be Joelle, but close.

The entry door opened and closed. Hua didn't dare turn to see who was there, but his back muscles rippled with dread as almost scalding water cascaded over him. Grabbing one of an array of choices for cleansing, he lathered his shoulders liberally.

Who was out there? With the frosted stall door, the clouds of steam, and the foamy soap, would he be able to tell the person in the stall was olive-skinned, not pale? Would he notice Hua's frame was narrower than the statuesque Joelle?

In a few seconds a voice at the bathroom door said tentatively, "Ms. Preston?"

Hua did something he'd seen in one of Cam's old movies. With his back to the frosted-glass shower door, he crossed his arms and put his hands on his own back.

When a shift of light told him the bathroom door had opened, he gave a high-pitched yelp and dropped his hands.

"Ms. Preston? Is everything okay in here?"

In answer Hua launched a bottle of conditioner over the stall door.

"I'm sorry!" Belk said. "I didn't mean to bother you, but there's been some trouble, and you didn't answer your phone. I got worried."

Now Hua made a questioning sound and slid one of his hands onto his back again, making it appear to be a caress.

"Um, like I said, I was worried, but as long as you're okay…I'll just go."

Hua's response was an angry "Humpf!" With a final apology, Belk backed out of the doorway. Soon the outer door closed behind him, and Hua exited the shower, his legs a lobster red. Though steam was a great disguise, the temperature required to produce it wasn't meant for human skin.

Dressing quickly, he considered what to do next. If Belk found Joelle he'd soon be back, so Hua couldn't stay where he was. If he went out her exterior door, cameras would pick him up almost immediately. If he took the secret exit he'd leave the grounds entirely and might not be able to re-enter. It would help if he knew more about the "trouble" Belk had alluded to. If his friends had been caught, he would stay and try to help them. That meant he had to go into the house and assess the situation.

Opening the door cautiously, he checked the area. There was no one. Shouldering his gym bag, he stepped out, listened for a moment, and then began a cautious circle, staying out of the range of the cameras mounted overhead.

When he was halfway around the open space, a hand closed on his arm and a voice said, "You need to come with me."

***

While Neil Preston went on at length about his accomplishments, Robin pretended to take notes. Much of what he said was outright lies; the rest wasn't anything a normal person would boast about. Knowing what she did about Preston, terms like "clever deals" and "opportunities seized," translated to "cheating." He talked on with only the slightest

258

encouragement, and she guessed he'd waited his whole life for someone to believe he really was as great as he imagined himself to be.

At least his self-indulgent babble gave her time to think. She had the document, and Preston had signed it. Once they were gone from Tulsa, Chris would take over, revealing the deal with plenty of publicity. Preston and his crew could try to control the damage, but anything they did would only create questions as to why they'd made the deal and then tried to quash it. The half million she'd expected was probably gone, but Robin decided it would be worth the effort if Neil Preston had to start over.

As she continued the interview, the proverbial pins and needles made sitting there almost unbearable. Oliva hadn't reappeared, but no one called her out as an imposter either. After what seemed like a day and a half, the console near Preston's elbow buzzed. He pressed a button and she heard Belk's distinctive voice. "We got some weird stuff going on, sir."

A line appeared between Preston's brows. "I pay you very well, Mr. Belk. Do I have to do your job too?"

"No, sir. But I thought you should know we might have an intruder."

"And how did someone get in?"

"Well." Belk paused, and Robin imagined him swallowing hard before continuing. "Ms. Preston had a…guest last night, and now there's a guy waiting outside in a car. I don't want to interfere if he's there to pick the guy up when they're, um, done visiting, but Ms. Preston was, um, busy so I couldn't ask."

Now Preston's eyes rolled like a teenager asked to load the dishwasher. "Why don't you ask the man in the car what he's doing here?"

He cleared his throat. "All right, but there's another thing. Some of the outside cameras have gone real fuzzy, like there's a film on them."

Preston's face turned pink. "Go see what's wrong, you imbecile!"

Robin glanced at Cam, whose face had gone tight. Knowing what he was thinking, she struggled to find a comment that would calm her partner without alarming Preston.

She wasn't fast enough. Setting his still camera next to the vid-cam, Cam rose and left the conference room with ungraceful haste, slamming the door behind him.

Preston half rose from his chair and turned to regard the heavy door. "Where's he going?"

Robin thought fast. "He probably wants to make sure our car is locked. We have a lot of valuable equipment in there."

"That's no excuse for tearing out of here like a madman."

Feeling the blush that telling a lie always brought on, she struggled to maintain a causal appearance. "He suffers from PTSD. It makes him act funny sometimes."

Preston examined her closely, his brows closing together. As the sound of Cam's steps faded, he pressed a button on the control panel. Immediately things began whirring, clunking, and beeping all around them. The room darkened as shutters closed over the window, but soft lights came on to counter the dimness. The door Cam had exited made metallic clunks as bolts slid into place. Looking toward the sound, Robin noticed the two-button panel next to the door now showed a red light.

She turned to Preston. "What did you do?"

He seemed pleased at her discomfort. "I've closed this whole floor off. You and I are locked in until my men assure me that all is secure below. Even they can't get in until I allow it." Looking down his skinny nose at her, he warned, "And you can't leave."

Though Robin felt as if she'd been locked in a cage with a cobra, she held onto her innocent persona. "I didn't intend to leave, Mr. Preston. We haven't finished our interview." He seemed confused by her calm acceptance, but Robin went on, "Shall we talk about your collection of Stalin mementos?"

***

Belk took a golf cart to the gate and entered the shack. "Did you find anyone on the grounds?"

"No," Albertson reported, "but that car's still out there. Guy's definitely waiting for somebody." He pointed to a spot on a monitor where a slice of the front bumper of a cream-colored car showed.

Belk leaned toward the monitors. "What the hell is wrong with the camera on the second floor?"

Mac leaned over his shoulder. "Geez. Looks like somebody turned it." Albertson pointed to another screen. "The next one down is turned too. Let's see how that happened." His hand hovered over the playback button. "Hey! The cameras aren't recording! What the—" He pulled in a breath. "Somebody's screwing with our equipment."

"Joelle's little friend." Tapping the cream-colored car on the screen, Belk said, "He's here to rob us, and that guy's out there waiting to pick up the stuff."

Albertson called the house, spoke briefly, and reported, "Bishop says the big guy who came in with that reporter is messing with the cameras. He's running around the house smacking them so they go cockeyed."

"Well, stop him!"

"They're trying. Bishop thought they had him, but he disappeared."

"Guys that big don't vanish into thin air," Belk said.

"They're still looking. In the meantime, Preston has gone on lockdown."

"What?" Belk rubbed his forehead, where a horrible ache was building. *Why, Covel? Why'd you get sick this week of all the weeks in the year?* With a huff of decision he said, "We'll call in the rest of the guys, everybody who can get here, and do a thorough search of the estate." Glancing toward the house, he said, "We need to show Mr. Preston we can handle this."

Albertson gave him a look. "No cops?"

"Are you gonna tell him we need outside help to deal with a couple thieves?"

Albertson shook his head. "I guess not." He turned back to the computer. "I'll turn recording back on for the cameras that still work."

Belk raised a hand. "Don't." When Al looked puzzled he said, "We might not want what's going to happen here today saved for posterity."

Albertson glanced at the house. "Is Ms. Preston okay?"

Belk shrugged. "Yeah. I went and checked on her."

"And the boyfriend?"

"I'm pretty sure he was in the shower with her."

"Pretty sure? He could be tossing stolen stuff over the wall right now for his buddy to pick up."

Belk made an angry gesture. "What was I supposed to do? A head count?"

Albertson frowned. "If we got robbers, why wouldn't they have made their move in the night?"

With a sleazy grin Belk replied, "Maybe a certain hot and bothered cougar messed up their plan."

Albertson grinned too. "Joelle's more than the guy expected."

Belk gestured at the blurry outdoor monitors. "They're in panic mode. They messed with the cameras so they can get to the wall without being seen."

Rubbing his chin Albertson mused, "It isn't a bad plan."

"Except we're going to catch them." Belk stood with sudden decisiveness. "Mac, start calling the off-duty guards in. Al and me will go have a chat with the guy in the car."

Albertson pointed to the monitor, indicating the empty space between the gate and the suspicious car. "He'll see us coming."

"No, he won't. I know a secret that's gonna let us come at him from a totally different direction. A big old surprise."

Chapter Twenty-Eight

Leaving Preston's conference room, Cam bypassed the elevator and took the stairs to the second floor. There he paused and tried to decide what to do. If the guards were looking for an intruder, it had to be Hua, which meant something had gone wrong. Robin could handle Preston for a few minutes. The vague plan in Cam's mind was to find Hua and boost him over the wall, then return to Preston's office to get Robin.

Suddenly strange, ominous noises sounded overhead. Cam hurried back up the stairs and approached the stairway door. Just as his hand reached it, a firm click told him multiple locks had engaged. He tried the door anyway, but it was no use. Preston had initiated the protective shields Oliva described. Robin was trapped inside with him, and no one, presumably even his own people, could get to them.

The sound of hurried feet came from the ground floor, and he guessed the guards were searching the premises. Cam tried to think. If he found Hua, they'd figure out together how to rescue Robin. He began knocking on doors.

"Bubbles? Bubbles?"

While guards called out to each other below, he circled the entire second floor. Some rooms were empty; other times a worker opened the door a few inches and peered out at him fearfully. When that happened he said, "Sorry, wrong door," and went on. No one tried to stop him, but he didn't find any sign of Hua either.

That called for a new plan. Since he was pretty sure Hua wasn't on the second floor, it would be good if the guards wasted a bunch of time searching there. If he could lure the guards upstairs, Hua would have a chance to get away. All Cam had to do was lead them on a chase and not get caught.

Cam had experience evading pursuers, though not in the real world. His games often required a choice between concealment and distraction in order to escape Jihadists, Ninjas, and aliens. Hiding was well suited to a man of small stature, like Hua, and Cam guessed he was holed up somewhere on the first floor. The opposite was best for Cam. He would become a moving target, stirring up as much confusion as possible. When they finally cornered him, he'd claim he'd been trying to help them find the intruder.

Since confusion was essential, Cam began by attacking the surveillance. A camera panning left and right was within arm's reach. When it swung away from him, Cam grabbed it and bent the frame, wedging the lens against the wall. Farther down he smacked another camera with an open hand, turning its lens to the floor. As he passed the elevator he pressed the call button, waited for the doors to open, and hit the alarm, wincing when a loud, irritating buzz resulted. *Good. They'll think there's a dozen of us, all over the place.*

The next camera was too high for him to reach, so he picked up a chair and smashed it, dissolving the lens into a maze of cracks. In response to the crash, a maid peered out of a room, screamed when she saw him, and dived back inside. A fire alarm pull a few steps farther down added another loud noise and spurts of water from overhead sprinklers. Imagining lights on the monitors flashing red in four, five, even six different locations, Cam hoped Hua would use the chaos to escape.

His actions were noted, of course, and there was pursuit. Two men pounded up the stairs, but Cam ducked into a room where several domestics drew away from him in fear.

One of the braver women called out, "He's in the kitchen!"

Charging past them, Cam exited through a formal dining room and emerged again in the circular inner hallway. Seeing a camera, he bent its frame sideways, leaving the lens facing the wall. How many cameras were there? He'd disabled six so far, but where was Hua? He needed to get upstairs and get Robin, and then—

He didn't know. They'd think of something.

It was time to leave the second floor. Two staircases descended, one sweeping along the wall to his right and another bending out of sight across the atrium's central space. He took the near one, almost tumbling down in his haste. A camera mounted over the front doors panned the area. Taking an umbrella set in a nearby stand, Cam jammed the handle into the brace, stopping it in a useless position.

That was when they almost caught him. The heavy front door opened and a guard entered. When he saw Cam, he fumbled at his belt for his weapon, but he hadn't practiced the move often enough to be proficient. Cam turned to see a second man hurrying down the staircase toward him. Though not in uniform, he was apparently willing to help the bad guys. Cam started across the atrium, toward the exit. His chance of escaping his pursuers was better outdoors, where the trees would hide him.

Past the atrium were three sets of double doors. Those directly ahead led outside, but his plan for escaping through them died when through the window he saw a golf cart pulling up with another security man at the wheel. He couldn't leave the house, but where could he go? On his left was Oliva's apartment. On his right was the studio kept for guests. The doors to both had locks with entry codes. He was trapped.

Hushed voices behind him indicated the two men at the front were constructing a plan. Should he charge the back door and try to get past the approaching newcomer? Or should he turn and—

The door on Cam's left opened a crack, and a hand waved him forward. With no time to think, he dived through, and the door closed behind him.

The world seemed to slow for a moment as Cam took in what was happening. The space he'd stepped into was the opposite of the space he'd left. Cool, light, and tastefully decorated, the apartment felt like a summer day after a long winter. The apartment's occupant was visible through the open bedroom doorway, tossing items into a small suitcase with dignified haste. Hua stood behind the door, his face lit with pleasure at the sight of his friend.

Almost immediately someone knocked. "Mr. Oliva, it's security. There's an intruder in the house."

Pulling on his sleeve, Hua led Cam into the bathroom, where he closed the door enough to conceal them. "Mr. Oliva will cover for us," he told Cam softly. "In exchange he asks that we help him leave the estate as soon as possible."

***

Devin Ashford had ignored the advice he was given to back away from Robin Parsons and ignore her activities. Instead he continued to watch her, careful to remain at a distance in case Belk made good on this threats. On Monday morning he followed Robin and the big guy out of Tulsa to Neil Preston's estate. When they turned in at the gate, Ashford continued past, did a U-ey up the road, and parked his rental in a grove of spindly trees. If he was correct, the visit was the payoff they'd been working toward over the last week.

Ashford saw immediately that the wall presented an impenetrable barrier, at least for a guy dressed in a suit. There was no way to get inside, and the warning he'd received from Belk made it dangerous to even consider trying. Still, he was curious about what would happen. Did Robin plan to leave with Preston bound and gagged and stashed in the trunk of her car? Would the big guy put a gun to Preston's head and demand money in exchange for his life? All Devin could do was wait and see.

At first he'd been only mildly interested in the crimes Robin committed. Hired to find her and report her whereabouts, he'd enjoyed the chase and the reunion with her. But when he realized Robin was planning another of her extortion crimes, he decided there had to be a way for him to profit from it. That had led him to follow her to Tulsa. His attempts to warn Preston hadn't worked, but today was the score she'd been planning. At the first opportunity, Devin intended to catch Robin alone and shake her down for a chunk of the money. She'd have to pay, since he knew enough to get her arrested in at least three states.

Waiting outside the estate, with his back against the door and his head against the window, Devin twisted his legs to the most comfortable position he could arrange and wondered how much his silence was worth. A hundred thousand? Two?

Suddenly the car door opened, sending him tumbling. His shoulder jolted painfully against the ground, but there wasn't time to even say "Ow!" before a hand grabbed his shirt and a voice shouted, "What are you doing here?"

He looked up to see a large, uniformed man with beefy fists and a face to match standing over him. A second man, thinner, homelier, and also dressed in the uniform of Preston's security force, peered over the first one's shoulder. "Speak up, buddy," the big man said, "or we'll help you remember how to answer a question."

Ashford struggled to come up with a story. "I'm waiting for someone."

The big man dragged him to his feet by his shirt-front and put his face close to his. "Who would that be?"

Ashford struggled for a plausible story. "A woman went th-through the g-gate a while ago. Her boyfriend h-hired me to find out if she's sleeping with the b-big guy she's with."

As he stuttered out the lie, the second man had gone around to the other side of the car and opened the door. His grunt boded ill, and he held up the sketch Ashford had fished out of the trash can after Robin threw it away. "He's got a drawing of the inside of the manor in here."

Before he could think of another lie, a fist to Ashford's gut knocked every bit of wind from his lungs. While he struggled to breathe, the beating began in earnest. It wasn't long before he wished he'd never heard of Robin Parsons.

"Listen!" he gasped. "I c-can—I can t-tell you—"

They paid no attention. Both men were getting their daily workout by stomping his ass.

Later, as he lay barely conscious on the ground, he heard the big man say, "Help me get him in the back seat, then have Miguel drive the car to the airport. He can leave it in long-term parking and take a cab back here." Bending to speak directly into Ashford's ear he said, "Forget you ever heard of this place, bud. You will not live through a second visit."

"You're gonna let him go?" the other guy asked doubtfully.

"He's just their ride." Through a fast-closing eye, Ashford watched the guy wipe his blood from his hands with a handkerchief. "With him gone, the rest are stuck out here, so it's just a matter of us tracking 'em down."

***

Robin found it increasingly difficult to feign interest in Preston's self-indulgent anecdotes. Her mind kept wandering off, wondering where Hua was and what Cam was doing. It got worse when Belk called a second time. This time Preston took up the receiver, glancing distrustfully at Robin. In a voice that caused Preston to hold the phone away from his ear, Belk crowed, "We got one of 'em, Mr. Preston."

Robin's insides clenched, and she forced her shoulders to stop creeping toward her ears. Chris had been right. These were not people who called the police when they were threatened. Which of her crew was hurt—or dead? *My fault. It's all my fault.*

"One of them?" Preston asked. "How many are there?"

"I don't know."

"The guy we caught is the driver—well, he was. We took care of him, but now the guy that came with the reporter is running around wrecking things."

Preston shot her a look. "She says he has some post-war issues."

Belk's grunt signaled disbelief. "Whatever he's up to, we'll stop him."

"One would hope so." Ending the call, Preston got up, and with a completely unnatural attempt to appear natural, took hold of the sword hanging over the table. Pulling it from its scabbard, he brandished it clumsily.

"What's going on?" he demanded. "What's your real purpose here?"

"Mr. Preston, I don't know what you're—"

He raised the sword overhead, using both hands. "I will defend myself."

It might have been ridiculous, being threatened by a pipsqueak who held his improvised weapon like a meat cleaver. Still, he was serious, and if he started swinging, there was no place in the room for her to get out of his range.

Having no defense, Robin went on offense. "Okay, here's the truth. I'm not from TIME magazine, and you'll never be anybody's Person of the Year. I'm here to stop your crimes and your"—she fumbled for a word—"meanness!"

Preston's response was surprisingly calm. "A noble cause, but I don't see how you'll accomplish it. You can't leave and, as we speak, my men are hunting down your confederates. Whatever your scheme was, it has failed." He leaned against the door, setting the sword on the floor like a cane. "While we wait, I'd be fascinated to hear what you thought you were going to accomplish."

Robin's mind raced through the possible scenarios. Hua would find a way to summon the police if he could, but they might not reach her in time. If Preston was going to kill her, she had nothing to lose by telling him everything. Once he understood his crimes would be exposed no matter what he did to her, he might let them live.

It was more difficult to summon the facts and figures than she'd hoped. Usually she had a list of points she wanted to make. Now she had to recall what she'd read about Preston over the last weeks in order to use it against him. Usually she was a mechanized voice in a dark room, a faceless accuser. Now she kept picturing Belk disposing of her lifeless body in some unmarked grave on estate property. Usually she was supported by Cam's solid strength. Now she was alone, on Preston's turf, exposed to his arrogant, malevolent gaze while his men hunted down her friends.

She had to hide her fears, because a single doubtful expression or a discernable shake in her voice would work against her. If Preston suspected she was lying, or if she seemed unsure that what she said would happen, he'd have her taken to some lonely place and murdered. Could she find the confidence to brazen this out? Could she save her team? Herself?

As if he spoke in her ear, she heard her father whisper, *Play the hand out, kid. You can't win if you fold.*

As much as she hated to admit it, he was right. Cam was tough. Hua was inventive. It was her job to keep the con going, as she'd seen her father do. *Even if the hand you're holding doesn't look like a winner, it might take the pot if your bluff is good.*

"The only award you're eligible for is Pig of the Year," she said, making her tone taunting. "You got rich by taking advantage of sick people."

Preston sniffed. "You're some sort of confidence artist and *you* criticize *me*? What exactly do you contribute to the world, madam?"

She ignored the attempt at diversion. "You planned to buy national recognition. You even planned to cheat on the price of the bribe."

He shrugged. "I guarantee you won't be telling anyone that."

It felt as if her blood temperature dropped ten degrees. "You can kill me," she said, trying to keep her voice steady, "but it won't change anything."

Preston looked at her as if she'd gone off the deep end. "Kill you?" He shook his head. "Lady, I'm going to sue you and every single person who had a hand in this. I will take everything you've got and then make you issue a public apology for impugning my reputation." His bottom lip jutted, making him look like a bratty three-year-old. "I can do it, and believe me, I will."

Preston is about as angry as a person can be, and his first thought is to file a lawsuit?

That can't be right.

"You kill people who threaten to reveal your illegal practices."

He looked shocked. "I do no such thing."

There was a long silence.

"Then you're not going to kill me?"

He shook his head as if she were a child. "Lady, I intend to sue you until you *wish* you were dead."

Chapter Twenty-Nine

Tom Wyman crouched among the apple trees, peering at Preston's house and battling frustration. Robin was somewhere inside, facing danger, and he was outside, unable to get to her. As he'd made his way from the front gate inward, the place had gone on alert. Alarms had sounded, and men rushed back and forth, shouting, "Did you find him?" Once he'd had to crawl into the undergrowth as a searcher passed, and he emerged with bark in his hair, prickers in his clothing, and scratches on his hands and neck. Tom didn't think they knew he was on site, but they were definitely looking for someone.

In time the alarms quieted, but the search went on. They hadn't caught their quarry, at least not all of them. He still had time.

As he pondered how to get to the house unnoticed, a golf cart whirred up the road. Driven by a security guard, its passenger was a tight-faced Monica Covel. Though her posture was as erect as always, she held onto the upright for balance. Still woozy—a tiny advantage for the good guys.

Tom circled through the trees, following their progress as they approached the back of the house, where the cart stopped and Covel got out. Though pale and wobbly, she surveyed the grounds with intense anger in her eyes. "You haven't found any sign of them?"

"They ain't in the house." Tom recognized the driver: Lawrence Belk. He followed Covel onto the porch like a dog begging his owner to forgive his misdeeds. "We've been all over it."

"Everywhere?"

"Well, we didn't search the apartments. Joelle's in hers; I saw her. Oliva says he hasn't seen anybody."

"And you accepted his word on that?"

The man's head drooped. "I didn't think he'd lie."

"Would you lie if someone had a gun to your back?" She put up a hand to stop him from saying more. "Search the grounds. Every inch." She paused. "You said Joelle had a man in last night?"

"Um, I went to her place and she was in the shower. I think maybe he was, you know, in there with her, but she threw something at me." Apparently reacting to Covel's expression he added, "I couldn't very well ask her if she was alone!"

"But you're sure he hasn't left the estate."

"We found a guy waiting in a car outside the wall. Me and Al taught him a little lesson."

"Is he dead?"

He looked surprised. "No. We sent one of the gardeners to drive him back to the city. Trust me, he ain't coming back here." Even across the space that divided them, Tom could feel Covel's disapproval, and Belk apparently felt it too. "They can't get off the estate," he said defensively, "and even if they do, they got no wheels. We just gotta look until we find them."

"Yes. Do that."

"What are you going to do?"

"First I need to make sure the Prestons are safe."

"I told you, Mr. Preston's on lockdown with the reporter. I don't know if she's part of this or not, but—"

"Oh, she's part of it," Covel interrupted. "These people went to great lengths to get to Neil."

Belk gave a nervous laugh. "Then I bet she was surprised when he closed everything down. She ain't getting out of there."

"That's good." Covel seemed reluctant to admit to a positive side. "It gives us leverage on the others." She climbed out of the cart. "After I check on Joelle, I'll search the house myself."

"I told you, we—"

"I know what you said. We'll talk later about how you handled this." She paused as a thought struck her. "Give me your gun."

"What?"

"Your gun. Mine's locked in my car somewhere in Tulsa." Reluctantly Belk handed over his pistol, which she stuck in the back of her waistband. Obviously irritated, Covel went to the door and entered the code. Her frustration level rose when it didn't work and Belk had to enter the current one. Crouching in the vegetation, Tom wished he were close enough to see which buttons were pressed to gain entry.

***

Hua listened as Bertie Oliva calmly lied to the guards, telling them he'd seen no one since leaving the third floor. Accepting this, the two men went off to look elsewhere for their quarry.

When they were gone, Cam and Hua came out of the bathroom to find Oliva had gone back to packing, his movements hurried but by no means panicked. As they stood waiting to find out what happened next, Oliva said, "Are you the one who tossed me into that van?"

Cam was never a good liar, and there was no need now anyway. "We do stuff that seems bad sometimes, but we don't do it to *be* bad, you know?"

Oliva took a moment to process that before he turned to Hua. "What did you do to the security cameras?"

"They are no longer recording what happens on the estate."

"So if I leave Green Grove, there'll be no record of how I went or when."

"You want us to let you walk away." Hua shook his head. "No."

Cam's brows made a *V* over his eyes. "People die of cancer or something when guys like you jack up prices and lie about stuff."

"You're right." Oliva seemed sorry. "I grew up with nothing, you know? One of a thousand kids hustling to eat at least once a day. Along comes Neil Preston, and suddenly I can have everything."

275

That justified nothing in Hua's view. "You thought only of yourself."

Oliva stared out the window. "As God is my witness, guys, I didn't know people were being murdered. I would never go along with that."

"What is your proposal, Mr. Oliva?"

He looked them in turn, his gaze telegraphing sincerity. "I help you escape. In exchange, you forget you ever met me."

Cam shook his head emphatically. "We can't leave. We have to help R—our friend get away."

Oliva's scowl said he didn't like that idea. "Preston's put his emergency procedures into effect, so the third floor is one big panic room. The elevator won't go up there, the stairway door is triple bolted, the windows are shuttered, and the metal grating around the atrium is electrified. She can't get out, and you can't get to her."

"He'd better not hurt her." Cam's hands traveled over his shirt like meandering mice.

"I don't think he will," Hua said. When Cam looked to Hua in surprise, he added, "I can't explain right now, but Robin is probably safe with Mr. Preston."

Oliva agreed. "Even if there's been some, um, killing, Neil isn't going to murder your friend in his own house. After I help you get out, you can send the police in to rescue her."

Cam was still reluctant. "Are you sure there's no way to get to them?"

"Neil has a generator up there. He's got heat, A/C, lighting, an independent water supply, and food to last a couple of weeks. Your girl is staying put."

"With a killer for company." Cam chewed on a fingernail. "What are we going to do, Bubbles?"

"As I said—" Hua stopped, glancing at Oliva. How much did he know?

Oliva made a calming gesture. "Neil won't even touch another person, guys. He might have ordered murder, but there's no way he'd do it himself."

Cam's lower lip jutted. "You better hope he doesn't make an exception."

A noise in the corridor made them all start. Oliva ordered, "Get out of sight."

Retreating to the bathroom again, they listened as he opened the door. "Monica! You're looking much better than the last time I saw you. And Joelle. You look, um, tired."

Two female voices spoke at once, one low and angry, the other higher and almost hysterical. There was a hiss from Covel, and Joelle stopped babbling. "I'm sure you know we have intruders on the grounds." Covel's voice was cold.

"Yes. Neil's closed himself in upstairs, so I came back here to wait for instructions. Have you regained control of the situation yet?" His voice held the slightest tinge of criticism.

"Belk caught one of them. He beat the crap out of him and then let him go." Her tone revealed disdain for Belk's action, but it turned to warning as she went on. "You let these people on the estate, Oliva. If I find out you had anything to do with it, you'll be sorry."

Listening from behind the bathroom door, Hua wondered if Tom had been the unfortunate victim of the beating. Another person in need of rescue?

Oliva remained calm in the face of Covel's threat. "Someone told me the man they're looking for came at Joelle's invitation, not mine." His voice took on a tone of innocent inquiry. "What if he was already on the third floor when Neil initiated lockdown?"

"Oh, God," Joelle said. "We have to see if he's okay."

Covel glared at Oliva, still suspicious. "I have more questions for Bertie."

"But we need to—"

"Joelle." Covel spoke distinctly, as if to a two-year-old. "Do you know the code for the private door?"

When Joelle answered, her voice was less agitated. "No, but it's in my address book."

"Okay. Go look it up. I'll be along in a minute." Apparently Joelle agreed to that, because the next thing Hua heard was Covel speaking to Oliva. "I need to search your apartment."

"Why? I said I haven't seen anyone."

"Then you won't mind if I take a look."

Oliva made several objections, obviously delaying the search but unable to refuse it. Hua turned to Cam and said in the calmest voice he could manage, "Take off your clothes and get into the bed." He expected an argument, or at least some hesitation, but Cam obeyed without hesitation. "When she comes in, act sleepy and confused. Let Oliva do the explaining."

As Cam unbuttoned his shirt Hua looked around, noting the betraying presence of bags: his own, a satchel that had to be Oliva's, and the suitcase they'd watched him pack. All three lay in plain sight. Closing Oliva's case, Hua set it at the back of the closet. Unless she opened it, Covel wouldn't know it was packed and ready. Crawling into the main room, he reached around the couch, got the other two bags, and dragged them into the bedroom. His own he unzipped and set in a corner like an overnight guest might and tossed Cam's shirt atop it. The second bag he set at the head of the bed and concealed it behind some of the half-dozen pillows there. Standing back, Hua looked at the room. Nothing screamed that there were secrets there, except him and Cam.

Covel's rising tone brought him to the next concern: where he might hide. Oliva's bedroom didn't provide many possibilities for concealment. Under the bed, but everyone looked there. In the closet, but that was even more obvious. Except...

"Cam," he whispered, "can you boost me up onto that shelf?"

Cam now wore only his favorite underwear, which proclaimed he was a John Deere fan. He'd hung his jeans over a chair and tossed his shoes and socks into the corner with the gym bag. In the other room Oliva objected and Covel insisted. Again without hesitating, Cam made a stirrup of his hands. Hua stepped into it and Cam lifted him up. The deep, high shelf was stocked with linens, which he shoved to one end. Climbing onto the shelf, he lay along it, praying it would hold his weight.

It did. Cam piled towels and bedsheets in front of Hua until he was hidden from sight. Stepping back, he held up a thumb to signal success. Quickly he got into the bed, pulled the covers up, and feigned sleep.

They were only seconds ahead of Covel, who gave up arguing and simply pushed past Oliva. "If you're not doing anything wrong, I'll be out of here in—" She stopped as she entered the bedroom and saw Cam. "What's this?"

There was a long pause, and Hua imagined Oliva adjusting his story to fit the scenario. Like the practiced liar he was, he came through beautifully. "Joelle isn't the only one at Green Grove who likes to bring a friend home from time to time."

Hua had a slit of vision that looked over Covel's shoulder. The size of Oliva's bed—was there something bigger than a king?—made Cam look smaller than usual, closer to normal-size.

"You! Wake up!"

He did a commendable job of appearing to rouse from sleep. "What?"

"How long has he been here?" she demanded.

"He spent the weekend," Oliva replied. "I planned to take him back to the city after this morning's meeting." He managed to sound chagrined, adding, "Who knew it would turn into a three-ring circus?"

"How did you get him in?"

A casual shrug dismissed that. "I'm good to your guys. They like me, so they don't search my car anymore."

Hua imagined Covel's anger at learning her orders were not always followed to the letter. "How do I know he's not part of this?"

Hua held his breath, but again Oliva's talent came through. "We have video if you're interested."

Though he couldn't see the look on Covel's face, her shoulders twitched and her voice turned frosty. "Mr. Preston will hear about this."

"Then I guess we'll find out which of us he deems more valuable."

It was the perfect taunt, and Covel reacted exactly the way they wanted her to. "I don't have time for this right now. Stay here, both of you. Keep the door closed and wait for Mr. Preston's all-clear."

When she was gone, Hua slid down from his perch. Watching Cam get dressed again, Oliva commented, "You guys have definitely upset things."

"It sounded like they have a way to get into Preston's panic area," Hua said. "How?"

"I don't know, but Joelle went into her apartment."

"There must be a way upstairs you don't know about."

He nodded. "Given Neil's paranoia, that figures."

"We must follow them."

Oliva put up a hand. "Are you kidding? I'm leaving Green Grove before somebody decides I can't. You should come with me."

"We can't leave our friends here."

Oliva's frown said he thought they were insane. "Once we're away, you can use my phone and call the cops." Going into the bedroom, he got the bag he'd packed out of the closet. "Bad things are going to happen here, and I don't plan to be within a twenty-mile radius when they do."

Chapter Thirty

"I don't get it." Robin heard the confusion in her own voice. "People who try to take down Argent Chemical have been killed. If it isn't you, then—"

Before she could finish, a voice behind her said, "My brother sees the law as the proper tool for revenge. I take a different view."

"Joelle." Robin turned to see an open space that had been a bookcase until now. A very angry, very disheveled Joelle stood framed in it, and behind her was Monica Covel. Though she leaned against the door frame for support, the gun she held in her hand pointed steadily at Robin's chest.

Preston stared at his sister in surprise. "What happened to you?"

Joelle's face was a mess, red with anger and streaked with makeup. Her clothing was wrinkled and dusty, and she wore no shoes. "Ask her," she snapped. "She sent a guy to distract me, and he locked me in a storage closet. I called and banged half the night, but no one heard me."

"Where was this?"

"In the display room. I must have fallen asleep at some point, because I didn't hear the guards when they searched this morning." She turned to her hero. "It was Monica who found me."

Preston turned to Covel. "I thought you had some horrible disease."

Covel jabbed a thumb at Robin. "Part of her plan to get to you, though I haven't figured out why."

"Ms. Talman seems to be some sort of vigilante." Preston raised his hands in mock horror. "I think I was supposed to be scared straight."

"We have enough evidence to ruin you," Robin tried for a confident tone, though her chest felt like someone had filled it with Jell-O. "No matter what you do to me, my friends will tell what they know."

"We've faced questions before," Preston said. "My team is good at diversion and obfuscation."

"I have a feeling your team is dissolving." Robin had to convince them it was useless to kill her. "Where's Nixon? Will he stand by you when he learns about the murders? And how about Oliva? Are you aware he took the money bag when he left to arrange the photo? He's probably at the airport by now."

Preston's eyes widened. "Monica?"

"I'll get him." In a flash she was gone.

Robin told herself it was a victory. She was down to two opponents, one of them unwilling, possibly unable, to touch another person. Of course he had the sword. He wouldn't have to make physical contact with that in hand.

Time to divide and conquer—I hope.

"Mr. Preston, do you approve of your sister killing people?"

Joelle answered for him. "Preston's genius is business, but he knows there are those who can't be sued into silence. I did my part to help out."

"So she's correct?" Preston asked. "People have been murdered?"

Joelle took a step toward her brother. "That reporter refused Oliva's bribe. That scientist wouldn't shut up even after Nixon threatened to take her to court. They had to be silenced."

Robin was only half listening as she surveyed the room for some means of escape. It took a second for her to realize that the blinking red light on Cam's video camera meant it was still recording. As Joelle explained herself to her brother, Robin surreptitiously turned the lens toward her. Even if she didn't live through this, there'd be evidence of what Joelle had done.

Preston was trying to absorb what he'd learned. "You killed people?"

"Of course *I* didn't. Monica did. Just like she'll take care of these people. Once we catch them, we'll make sure the staff sees them leave. That way nothing can be connected to Green Grove."

"You mean we're going to kill them too?"

Was Preston shocked? Horrified?

"A car accident, probably." Joelle was unmoved by the prospect. "In for a penny, in for a pound, Neil."

Preston stared at his sister, obviously uncertain, but Joelle turned to Robin. "Your plan isn't working out so well, is it?"

Robin spoke directly to Preston. "Murder. Is that what you wanted to happen, Mr. Preston?"

Joelle answered for him. "Neil does what it takes to be successful." Holding his gaze she added, "Monica and I have his back, and he knows that."

A voice came through the intercom. "Mr. Preston, we caught one of the intruders. Ms. Covel's going to question him."

Joelle spoke first. "Is it my guest from last night or Mr. Preston's visitor?"

"Neither, ma'am. This one's got a hook for a hand."

Turning to Robin she demanded, "How many of you are there, anyway?"

Trying to hide her distress Robin said, "It won't do you any good to hurt him. We'll just keep coming."

"That remains to be seen." With a smile that revealed how clever she thought herself, Joelle took a gun from the back of her waistband.

Though no expert, Robin knew an antique when she saw one. The gun had a pearl handle and a rotating cylinder that she thought meant it was a six-shooter. Etching on the barrel made it look more like Grandma's company silverware than a weapon.

"Is that Father's Smith and Wesson?" Neil asked.

"He gave it to me when I was sixteen, in case I ever needed protection."

He looked uncomfortable. "Um, can you handle it?"

"Of course," she said breezily. "He showed me how to load it, and I shot it lots of times."

"Lots?"

"At least four."

He seemed doubtful. "Recently?"

She gave him a look. "Stop fussing, Neil! I'm quite capable of hitting a target at close range, and you've got your sword for backup. We'll take her downstairs and send for her car. Monica will handle the rest."

***

Unable to think of any other way to get into the house, Tom decided to let himself be captured. While it wasn't the smartest move it was the fastest, and the only one sure to work. The more interlopers the guards had to watch over, the more diluted their resources were. Inside he might get an opportunity to help Robin, Hua, or Cam escape. Helping all three would be nice.

With that in mind, he made a purposefully clumsy attempt to cross the open space between the orchard and the house. When seen, he made an equally clumsy attempt to elude his pursuers. Soon rough hands grabbed him, and multiple fists welcomed him to captivity.

"Wait!" said a voice. "We need to find out what he knows." He turned to see Belk standing on the porch. "Who are you?"

Tom replied lightly, though he struggled to get the words out. "Just a tourist who came for Preston's indictment party."

"Bring him." He was dragged inside, taken through two sets of doors, and thrown in the general direction of a chair. They searched his pockets, took his phone, and in a move that felt surprisingly embarrassing, unstrapped his prosthesis and tossed it on the table. Detached, the hook looked like dead metal, and Tom felt almost the same sense of loss he'd felt when he awoke in Afghanistan and saw that he was missing a flesh-and-blood hand. The hook was ugly without him, and he felt ugly without it.

He was in what looked like a motel room, an impersonal, all-in-one area with a bathroom set into one corner. He sat in a desk chair along one wall, and next to him was a TV on a long credenza. On the opposite end of it was a coffee setup on a tray, and next to that was a mini-fridge with a microwave atop it. A card table and four folding chairs in another corner didn't seem to belong. Tom guessed the guards had turned an unused guest room into their lounge.

The men who'd caught him left, but Belk leaned his rear against the door. "Wanna tell me what you're doing here?"

"I'll wait and speak to whoever's really in charge. Don't want to have to repeat myself."

Belk shrugged. "Either way, you ain't going to like what comes after." When Tom didn't answer he added, "You can't get out of here, so don't waste your energy." With that he left.

When the door closed, Tom heard muted beeps. Stepping forward, he tried the handle. It didn't open. "That's for sure against fire codes," he muttered. Another crime laid at Preston's door, but hardly the worst of them.

He made a sweep of the room, opening cabinets and pulling out drawers. No weapons. Nothing that could be made into a weapon. He surveyed the coffee pot briefly. Maybe he could heat up some water and toss it at the next person who came through the door. *Lame idea.*

On the credenza lay the things they'd taken from him. He'd left his identification in the car, so they had no name for him, not even a false one. The pocketknife he'd carried since high school was a wreck. One of his captors had demonstrated their power over him by systematically breaking off each blade and tossing it into the woods. Aside from that, there was only Luca's can of hair spray and his prosthetic arm.

Should he put it back on? It was hard not to, but he decided it was better to appear helpless.

His gaze fell on the microwave. Now there was a possibility. On the internet he'd seen people zap items that shouldn't be heated that way. Though he'd thought it was dumb then, now it might be helpful.

How long did it take to nuke an aerosol can to the point that it blew up? Tom hoped it was less time than it would take for Preston's people to kill him.

Hurriedly he put his plan, such as it was, into action. Setting the can of hair spray in a mug, he filled the mug with water and set it at the center of the microwave. Turning the timer to ten minutes, he pressed START. The thing hummed to life, and the turntable inside spun at a slow, steady pace.

He judged seven minutes had passed when the door opened and Monica Covel came in, now wearing a holstered gun on her hip. Her frown deepened as she recognized Tom. "We meet again." She stood with her back against the door, her toned body promising it wouldn't be easy to get past her. Hearing the hum of the microwave she asked, "Making lunch?"

"Tea," he replied. "Want a cup?" Remaining casual, he stood and moved to the side, guessing, or at least hoping, the oven would explode outward.

When it blows. If it blows.

Glancing through the appliance window, Covel saw the outline of the mug inside. The counter was down to 1:53, but she made an impatient gesture "Let's start with your name."

"Richard Kimball."

She'd apparently never seen *The Fugitive*, so his feeble attempt at a joke fell flat. "Okay, Dick, what's going on here?"

Tom had decided he might get himself and the others out of Green Grove with their lives if he confessed to a crime Covel and Preston could understand. "We planned to help ourselves to your boss's collection of Soviet art, but things went wrong."

A nod said that had been her working theory. "You took me out of it then got your man in by using Joelle's unfortunate habit of picking up strangers."

He raised his brows as if to say, "Why not?"

"It wasn't a terrible plan," Covel said, "but I'm back now. The terrible part is what's going to happen to the whole bunch of you."

At that point the can inside the microwave reached its limit. With a muted bang it exploded, blowing the door off and sending hot water and steam out in a rush. Covel wasn't close enough to get the full effect, but she gasped as scalding drops hit her face. Instinctively she reached up to wipe them away. She should have gone for the gun.

With his right hand Tom picked up his prosthesis and struck the side of Covel's head with it. She fell like an imploding building, straight down. Tom moved quickly to the door, holding his own hand, as it were, ready to smack the next person who entered.

No one did.

Covel groaned behind him, and Tom turned from reattaching his prosthesis to assess her condition. Her eyelids fluttered, and she turned her head from side to side as if searching for help. He considered whacking her a second time but remembered Robin's abhorrence of actually hurting targets. Yanking the rope out of the window blinds, he rolled Covel onto her stomach and tied her arms behind her back, using the figure eight knot he found easiest to make these days. He secured her legs with the other end of the rope, making it impossible for her to do anything but writhe like an earthworm. By the time he finished, she was beginning to get control of her brain again. Taking a washcloth from the bathroom, he stuffed it into her mouth and fastened it in place with a rubber band he took from the guards' deck of cards.

The whole time he expected someone to interrupt, but that didn't happen. Preston's men must have gone back to searching, which was somewhat encouraging. They hadn't captured the others, at least not all of them. To gain a few more minutes, he hauled the dazed Covel into the bathroom and closed the door. If her men looked in, they might assume she'd taken Tom somewhere else.

Confident in her power, Covel had left the door unlocked. Opening it a crack, Tom listened, hoping there was no one in the atrium. To his surprise, Hua came tiptoeing past like a teenager returning after curfew.

"In here!" Tom called softly. Hua stopped with a jolt, recognized him, and veered quickly into the room. "I'm pleased to see you, Homey."

Tom opened the bathroom door so Hua could see Covel. "One down. Now what's going on?"

"Clarabell is locked with Mr. Preston. I think Joelle is there too."

"Where's Cam?"

"He left with Oliva, who offered escape if we promise not to pursue him."

"How'd you get Cam to go without you and Robin?"

"Someone had to fetch the police." Hua smiled. "I argued that I am better able to hide than someone the size of a Chiefs linebacker."

"That's true." Tom rubbed his neck. "Then help is on the way?"

"If it arrives in time." Hua's expression was grave. "It isn't Preston, but his sister who is the real danger here."

"Joelle is the one behind the murders?"

"Yes, though her accomplice does the actual killing." Hua glanced upward. "It is hard to say how Joelle will react when Covel does not return."

"How many of them are there?"

"Mr. Belk has called for reinforcements, but at this point we face him and six men. One is stationed at each gate, so there are five searching for us."

"What about the staff?"

"Belk ordered them all to go into the kitchen and stay there until this is over." Hua's expression turned grave. "I believe they don't want witnesses."

Tom's jaw felt rock hard. "We have to act fast."

"Yes," Hua agreed. "It is good that you are here, since my idea for neutralizing the remaining guards will work much better with two people."

Tom was in place a few minutes later when a guard came through the atrium below him. As the man approached the door, Hua burst from behind a pillar and headed up the front stairway.

"Mac!" the man called over his shoulder. "The little guy went upstairs!"

In seconds Mac joined his coworker and there was a whispered conference. Separating, they each ascended a staircase. The second floor was still and quiet. They met at the railing and looked around, trying to decide where their quarry might have gone.

"There!" Mac pointed at the door to the display room, just swinging closed. Hurrying forward, he punched in the code and led the way inside. As soon as the men moved farther into the room, Tom left his hiding place, stepped quietly forward, and caught the door before it closed completely.

Lights were on all along the room, revealing that someone had passed through ahead of the two guards. Tom watched them make their way slowly along, one taking a few steps forward while the other stood ready to fire. Closing the door, he put his ear to it and listened. After several minutes one man ordered, "Mac, go back out the way we came in then come around to the rear exit. I'll give you a minute to get into place and then push him that way. When he comes out that door, grab him."

A few seconds later Tom stepped back from the door as the handle rattled. "I can't open it!" Soon there was another rattle farther down the hallway and Mac's companion shouted, "Call for somebody to bring a crowbar, and tell them to move their asses!"

Meeting Hua in the hallway Tom said, "That KwikiSet is incredible! In seconds it's like iron."

"It is lucky I brought extra," Hua said. "One never knows when he will need more than one helping."

"Somebody will come along to release them soon."

"Yes," Hua said. "We must be ready."

***

As Tom took a stand just inside the wide doorway of the formal dining room, which they'd propped open with Hua's shoes, Hua stood halfway between the two staircases, working to calm his breathing and relax his muscles. *Deep breaths. Drop the shoulders. Relax the jaw and tongue.*

Hearing steps on the stairs he waited, every muscle tense. On one side, an unfamiliar man came up the staircase. Handling him was Tom's job. When he saw his opponent, who carried a Taser in one hand and a pry-bar in the other, Hua was both pleased and terrified. Belk's piggy eyes sized him up warily, ready to fend off an attack. That was okay, because Hua didn't intend to attack. Lawrence Belk's dislike of him would be Hua's ally in the fight, that and a sense of overconfidence bullies like Belk always seemed to possess.

Moving into the open, Hua stopped as if surprised. Belk's eyes lit with anticipation, and he quickened his pace. As he reached the top of the stairs, a crash sounded behind him. Both Belk and the other man turned toward the sound, but Belk's gaze returned to Hua. "Find out what that was," he ordered. "I've got this one."

Step one: Divide and conquer. Hua stood still, eyes alert, weight resting on the balls of his feet. Belk's weapon gave Hua some advantages. Most Tasers allowed only one shot, and the range was about fifteen feet. Law enforcement officers could buy Tasers with up to three shots and double the range, so Hua had to hope Green Grove's security didn't include police-grade equipment.

When Belk stopped at the top of the stairs, Hua managed a confident grin. "We meet again."

"You won't be so smiley when I catch you." Fingers tightening on the Taser, Belk took a step toward Hua. It was tempting to use his superior speed and dart away, daring Belk to chase him. But with Robin trapped upstairs, they had no time for hide-and-seek. Hua had to deal with his adversary now.

Belk took a step closer, raised the weapon, and fired. Hua saw—or thought he saw—the darts coming toward him. He flinched, but at 180 feet per second, that meant nothing. The barbs hit him squarely on the chest.

A second later they fell impotently to the ground.

Belk's brows rose in surprise as Hua drew a metal serving tray from under his shirt. "I borrowed this from your dining room. I will put it back."

"You little—" Belk tossed the Taser aside. "I'll catch you myself and wring your scrawny neck!"

"Think you can do that, fat man? You look out of shape to me."

"I got lots more men coming in. You're out of options, boy."

Running to the railing, Hua hopped onto it, teetered wildly for a moment, and then launched himself toward the huge chandelier. Reaching out for a hold, any hold, he managed to catch a firm grip with his right hand. The other encountered something sharp: a screw perhaps, and he gasped as it tore into his palm. He let go, fumbled for a new handhold, and found one as the chandelier swung away, pushed by his weight. Ignoring the pain, Hua climbed onto the metal ring and pulled himself to a standing position.

"Hey!" Belk roared. After a second he added, "Dolman, get out here."

Dolman didn't answer, presumably because Tom had rendered him incapable of reply.

The force of Hua's jump caused the light to arc away from center, and he used his body to extend the swing to the widest arc possible. Watching, Belk smiled. Like a pendulum, the chandelier would return, and Hua would be carried back to his enemy. Belk had only to reach out and grab the chandelier when it came close enough.

The first swing didn't reach the railing, though Belk made a grab when Hua's path brought him near. Hua pumped like a child on a swing, encouraging a wider arc. As he returned toward Belk a second time he picked up speed. Hua gripped the chain with both hands, ignoring the blood that made his left slippery. He came closer this time, and Belk touched the light bar, though he wasn't fast enough to grasp it.

"Once more, boy!" he panted, and Hua pumped again. The chandelier's arc widened, and he heard the tier below clunk against something. He couldn't look down to see what it was, but the vibration stung his hands. The next swing had to be the last.

As Hua swung forward again, Belk's face lit with anticipation. Hua's hand throbbed, and he adjusted his grip, getting ready. As he neared, Belk reached for him. Just before Belk made contact, Hua let go of the chain and let his body drop through the circle of bulbs. Catching the metal frame to stop his fall, he stretched out his legs and kicked Belk squarely in the chest. Belk fell backward, gasping, and his head knocked loudly on the floor.

One more swing and Hua was able to propel himself over the railing. As he dropped, Tom hurried forward to steady him so he didn't fall flat on his face. "Are you okay?"

Hua looked down at the cut on his hand. "Nothing that won't heal."

Tom went to Belk, who still struggled to breathe, and spoke to him directly. "It's nice of you to bring handcuffs." Taking Belk's set from his belt, he asked Hua, "Where can we put these two to keep them out of our hair?"

Hua looked around. "We can no longer get into the display room, but perhaps the gym door has the same code." It did. They dragged Belk and the other man into the sauna and blocked the door with a stair-climber.

"They'll holler their heads off as soon as we're gone," Tom observed.

"Then let's find Clarabell and get out of here."

Chapter Thirty-One

Robin watched Neil Preston absorb the fact that his sister was a murderer several times over. If he had a spark of humanity, he'd be horrified. He might insist Joelle let Robin go. He might even suggest she turn herself in to the police. Instead he asked, "How do these people know what you did?"

Joelle shrugged. "They can't *know* anything. There's no evidence tying us to the deaths."

"But now the estate is crawling with strangers."

"Monica will deal with them."

Robin tried not to glance at the vid-cam on the desk, still recording away. The red light was encouraging, but at any moment either Neil or Joelle might notice, and that would be the end of its usefulness. How could she save the recording?

You can't even save yourself!

Again her father's voice sounded in her head. *Pay attention, Robbie. When a situation gets weird, most people don't, so you'll have the upper hand.*

Obeying his imagined command, Robin tried to make herself observe the situation without emotion. Preston and Joelle were confused, unsure what to do. That would make their reactions slow. They might even work against each other. She also noticed that Joelle, unused to firearms, held the gun at arm's length, like some movie hero. Her arm had begun to tire in that abnormal position, and the barrel dipped, aiming more toward the floor than at Robin.

It wasn't much of an advantage, but it beat standing mouse-meek while they shot her dead.

Robin grabbed her notebook from the table and spun it sideways at Joelle, like a boomerang. Surprise did what accuracy didn't. Joelle ducked aside with a squeal of protest. The gun went off, but the shot went wide. Hurrying around the table, Robin slipped behind Neil, slid a hand under his suit coat, and grabbed his belt at center back. With her other hand she reached around and grabbed his necktie. Twisting it to the back, she pulled until he made a choking sound. "Drop the gun, Joelle."

After a moment's thought she replied, "No."

"I said drop it!"

"And I said no. When Neil passes out, I'll shoot you."

Preston made a sound of protest, but he was having a hard time staying upright. Robin couldn't fathom Joelle's calm assessment of her brother's peril, but she had to admit she was correct. Without Preston as a shield, she'd be an easy target. She had to get out.

She maneuvered Preston backward, toward the door. Joelle saw her intention, but there was nothing she could do about it. Feeling the handle at her back, Robin let go of Preston's belt just long enough to turn it. Then, putting a foot on her captive's backside, she let go of his tie and shoved as hard as she could. Preston stumbled forward, blocking Joelle's shot. Robin backed out the door and slammed it closed. Two bullets hit the wood with a dull thud. At least Preston's wealth was beneficial in one way, she thought as she tipped the bench beside the door on end and wedged it under the handle. With cheaper wood she'd be bleeding all over his Mediterranean tile by now.

What now?

She was in the hallway that circled the atrium, but she was stuck there. The stairway door was locked, the grid was electrified, and the elevator was disabled. Joelle and Neil were already rattling at the conference room door. The bench she'd used as a brace would eventually fall away, and they'd come after her. She had nowhere to go.

"Hey!"

Robin turned, ready to duck another bullet. Peering from her office doorway was Mandy Cohee.

"In here!"

296

Robin hurried toward her, slipping into Mandy's office just as the bench made a scraping noise that signaled movement along the tile floor. A second later it fell to the side, and a few seconds after that, a latch clicked. Robin heard Joelle order, "Stay here, Neil." She guessed Preston was only too willing to stay put and avoid danger, and the conference room door slammed shut.

As steps sounded on the tiles, Cohee went to the doorway and peered out. Robin pressed her back against the wall, picturing Joelle, gun in hand, menacing the young PA. Would Cohee stand up to her? She had no reason to stick her neck out for the fake Ronda Talman.

"What's happening, Ms. Preston?" Cohee asked.

"We have intruders. Stay in your office until we decide it's safe to leave."

Cohee shivered. "Intruders? Staying here is fine with me."

"The reporter who came this morning. Have you seen her?"

"Not since Mr. Preston sent me out of the meeting."

Stepping back toward the conference room Joelle called out, "Neil! What's the code for your office door?" Preston mumbled some numbers, and her tapping steps receded.

Cohee stepped back inside and spoke softly to Robin. "Hide under the desk. She's bound to look in here when she doesn't find you."

Robin did as suggested, folding herself small so her feet didn't show. Cohee sat at the desk, hiding her from sight. A slit in the front panel allowed a view of the doorway, and in a few minutes she saw Joelle, at least the ten inches from neck to waist. As Robin squeezed herself even smaller, Cohee began stapling sheets of paper together on the desktop above her head.

"There's no one in Preston's office or Oliva's either," Joelle reported. "I went through the connecting door."

Robin held her breath as Joelle walked around the secretary's office. When she'd made a complete circuit of the room Cohee asked, "Could she have gone into Mr. Preston's apartment?"

The feet disappeared, and seconds later Joelle called, "Neil! Is your apartment code the same as the other?" He made an affirmative answer, and Joelle reappeared at the PA's door. In a voice incongruous with the pistol she held, she said, "Mandy, these people came here to kill my brother, and I will not let that happen. I hope you understand."

"Desperate measures, right?"

"Yes." There was a pause, and Robin imagined Joelle looking at the young woman suspiciously. "You should go down to the conference room and keep Mr. Preston company. He's a little stressed right now."

"Of course."

"Once you're there, stay put." Then she was gone.

Mandy's face appeared at the desk. "You should probably come with me."

"What about Preston?"

"I think we can handle him together."

"Ms. Cohee, I don't want to get you in trouble or even hurt."

"I've been listening in on the intercom since we went on lockdown, so I know what's happening here." She smiled ruefully. "If she kills you, do you think they'll let me live to tell anyone?"

"I'm sorry. We didn't mean for you to get dragged into this."

"I should have quit a long time ago." She looked out into the hallway. "Joelle's going into the apartment. Be ready when I get him to open the door."

Following Mandy to the conference room, Robin set her back against the wall next to the door.

Mandy rapped lightly on the door. "Mr. Preston? Your sister wants me to come in there with you so we'll both be safe."

Silence. What if Preston refused to let her in?

To Robin's relief, the door opened a slit.

"It's nice to see a familiar face, Ms. Cohee. Come in."

With all her strength Robin pushed on the door, sending him back a few steps. Before he could call out, she closed all three of them inside and pressed the electronic latch until green went red.

"Mandy!" Preston's voice vibrated with outrage.

The PA raised a square metal paperweight she'd picked up somewhere. "Shut up or I'll smack you!" Preston's mouth gaped, but she ordered, "Sit down and put your hands flat on the table."

He obeyed, his face ashen. Robin was almost as cowed as Preston. Apparently Mandy had a lot of built-up hostility toward her boss.

Noticing the bookcase that had become a door, she asked, "What's that?"

"A secret staircase. That's how Joelle got up here."

Cohee glared at Preston. "You're as paranoid as you are greedy."

"Where is my sister?" Preston mewed. "I want to see Joelle."

Instead of answering, Cohee turned to Robin. "We don't have a lot of time. What should we do?"

Taking the video camera from the table, Robin handed it to her. "Take this. Get in your car and leave the estate like you've been sent on an errand. As soon as you can, call the police."

"What about you?"

"I have friends here. We'll be okay once we find each other."

Preston pulled himself together in a final attempt at intimidation. "You've put yourself in an unfortunate position, Mandy. You won't just lose your job for this. I'll take every penny you have in the bank as well."

"If you can manage that from a prison cell, go for it." Turning to Robin she said, "What should I tell the police about you?"

Robin smiled. "As little as possible?"

A tilt of her head indicated she was thinking things through. "You came here to stop their crimes?"

"We did."

Mandy thought about that for a moment. "I'll try to give you some time."

A voice behind them said, "I don't think that works for me." Joelle stood in the entry to the secret passage. Once again her nasty, shiny gun was aimed at Robin's middle.

Immediately recovering his courage Preston crowed, "Did you think there'd be only one escape route? The passage has exits from my bedroom and my office as well as this room."

For a moment Robin wished excessive pride could actually choke a person.

Joelle gestured toward the doorway with the gun. "We need to find Monica and get this situation under control. Neil, go down first so they can't run. I'll follow and keep them in line."

"But it might not be safe down there, Jo. Shouldn't I stay here?"

"We're going to leave the estate entirely," she replied. "We'll go out the tunnel and wait outside until things are settled." He didn't like that, but she added, "I think the police are on their way."

"The police!"

"We'll come up with a cover story," she said soothingly. "Still, I think it's best if we aren't home when they start sticking their noses into our business."

"You're right." He went to the false door then turned. "Be sure to close this behind you. No sense letting others know the secret if we don't have to."

Joelle looked at Robin and Mandy. "It isn't like these two are going to tell anyone what they've seen. Now go."

With Joelle close behind, Robin and Mandy followed Preston through the exit into a narrow passageway lit by security lights along the floor and above each of the doors that presumably led to the rooms Preston had mentioned. Midway along the passage was a metal spiral staircase enclosed in wire mesh.

At the head of the stairs, Preston turned back to be sure Joelle did as he'd ordered. Seizing the opportunity Robin whispered to Mandy, "Run! Take the first door you come to!"

She obeyed without hesitation. Joelle turned, swore, and fired at the PA's retreating form, but Cohee disappeared. The door slammed behind her.

"Watch that one!" Joelle ordered. "And hold onto her so she doesn't bolt." Preston looked like he'd been asked to eat an earthworm. "Do it!" Joelle repeated, "Or I'll shoot her right now and you'll have to drag her dead body down two flights of stairs."

Reluctantly Preston took hold of Robin's arm, his touch so feeble she almost laughed aloud. As soon as Joelle turned away, she'd break his hold and run...Where? If she went down the passageway she'd still be stuck on the third floor. If she went down the stairs she'd be an easy target for Joelle's bullets.

The staircase went up as well as down. Ascending would make it harder for Joelle to shoot her, since the stairs themselves would act as shields. While she wasn't sure what she'd do once she got to the roof, it was better than meekly going to her death. Tearing her arm from Neil's puny grip, Robin started up. By the time Joelle realized her brother had failed her, she was only a pair of feet pounding above them.

***

"We have to get to Robin," Tom said for the third time as they stood looking up at the metal barrier surrounding the top floor. "Could you get on the chandelier again and climb up there? Maybe if you swing hard enough you could smash through the mesh."

"It is electrified," Hua said. "There's a passageway in Joelle's apartment, but we don't have the code for the secret door or know where the door is."

Tom stared upward a moment longer, hating the grid, hating the height, hating the Prestons. Robin was up there, in danger and afraid. He had to do something. He had to—

Shaking himself free of indecision, he hurried after Hua, who was already entering the code that would let him into Joelle Preston's apartment.

They stepped inside cautiously, but the place was empty. Tom noticed the open vent overhead and the screws that had once held the cover in place on the floor. Hua stood for a moment, looking at the place with an analytical air. "There has to be something I didn't see earlier," he said. "A passageway to serve as an escape route."

"Preston's certainly paranoid enough to want one of those."

"But how does one access it?" Hua was speaking mostly to himself. "This wall is most likely, I think. Easy to disguise a few extra feet of width." He approached the back wall of Joelle's bedroom. "Ah!"

"What?" Tom demanded. "'Ah!' means what?"

"A bookshelf," Hua replied. "You must trust me when I say that Joelle Preston is not an avid reader. Why does she have a bookcase in her boudoir?"

302

Once Hua pointed that out, Tom saw that the bookcase was the perfect size and shape for a door. Stepping forward, he began pulling books from the shelves, revealing on the second from the top yet another entry code mechanism. "How do we open it?"

Hua shook his head. "I will have to search her computer for the code. There is no other—"

A sound from behind the bookcase alerted them, and they stepped back as the hidden door opened and a young woman peered out cautiously.

Hua stepped forward and made a polite bow. "Ms. Cohee, I presume."

She appeared ready to bolt, but Tom moved to block her escape. She turned back, possibly considering returning to the passageway, but Hua took a firm grip on the bookcase-slash-door.

Seeing no escape, Cohee asked, "Who are you?"

"The reporter," Tom demanded. "Do you know where she is?"

Her lips formed a straight line. "Why do you want to know?"

"She's a friend, and we know she's in trouble."

Cohee looked relieved. "She sent me to call the police. I didn't know whether it was faster to come through here or continue through the passage. It looks like it goes on for a long way."

"Probably to the wall and under it," Hua guessed.

"Is she up there with Preston?" Tom asked.

"And Joelle. She has a gun, and—" Tears threatened as she tried to go on. "You have to get up there and help her!"

***

Robin hurried up the narrow spiral in a crouch, keeping her hands close to her body to be the smallest target possible. At the top of the steps was a tiny room with no door. At first she almost screamed in frustration, but

303

recalling the false bookcase, she pushed first on one wall, then the next. The third rotated like a turnstile, sending her stumbling into a second, larger room with a four-by-four trapdoor. Through a Plexiglas window she saw below it a staircase: the official roof exit. Only those in on the secret would realize there was a second staircase to the roof. Robin tried to open the trapdoor, but like so much of Green Grove, access was electronically secured. Her only option was going onto the rooftop.

Stepping into the harsh sunlight, she stopped to look for a fire ladder or similar means of descent. There was nothing. Edged by a low wall, the roof of Green Grove stretched flat before her, most of it to her left. At the center was the skylight, covered with a grayish coating that diffused the light and softened the glare of the Tulsa sun. Beyond it was a section marked with a huge painted X: the helipad landing spot. On her right were two metal units, one squat and wide, the other taller but narrower. Other than that there was nothing. No place to run. Very few places to hide.

Steps sounded behind her, and Robin turned back to the shed that enclosed the stairway. She had to jam the door with something, but there was nothing nearby. Pulling off a sandal, she hooked the heel strap over the doorknob and the toe strap over a metal screw that protruded from the side of the frame. It wouldn't stop them for long.

She considered the three structures as hiding places. The stairway shed backed up to the wall, so she couldn't go around it to evade her pursuers. She could hide behind the air conditioning unit or whatever the other housing was, but if they went around opposite sides she'd be caught between them like the monkey in the middle.

A metallic clang sounded at the top of the stairs, and she heard Joelle admonishing Neil to stay behind her until she told him otherwise. Her voice was authoritative; his reply was resentful, like a child told not to misbehave.

The Prestons were on their home turf. They each had a weapon, and she had nowhere to go. What hope did she have of escaping them?

The gun was her biggest concern, but Tom's post-breakfast talk with Kai came to mind. Joelle was a gun amateur; her handling of the weapon thus far had revealed that. Counting in her head, Robin figured she'd fired five shots: one by accident, two at her, and two at Mandy Cohee. If the gun was in fact an old-fashioned six-shooter, Joelle had only one shot left. Had she thought to bring along extra bullets? Even then, reloading would take time, assuming she remembered how it was done.

A crash signaled the destruction of Robin's sandal. The door banged against the frame, and a moment of silence followed. She imagined Joelle peering out cautiously, gun in hand, searching the roof for her quarry.

If Robin could get her to empty the gun, her odds of escaping got better.

The next question was the scary one. Could Joelle hit a moving target?

Before a possible affirmative answer stole her courage, Robin kicked off her remaining shoe, left her hiding place, and zig-zagged her way to the other housing cowl, about thirty feet away. It seemed a lifetime as she waited for the sound of the shot and the feeling of a bullet piercing her body. There was nothing. Joelle had to be aware that her ammunition was limited.

From the shed Preston's cautious voice came. "Jo?"

"Neil!" she ordered. "Come out here and help me."

"I can't—" he began, but she interrupted.

"It's your fault she got away. It's your fault she's even here. Do as I say."

There was a long pause. "Bertie brought her in, not me, and your 'boyfriend' is part of this too."

Joelle backtracked. "All right. I screwed up. Bertie screwed up. Now we have to fix it." She went on in a wheedling tone. "You need to flush her out from behind that metal thing."

"I don't want to."

Her temporary calm evaporated. "Oh, for God's sake, Neil. She isn't going to hurt you, because I'm going to shoot her. Now do it!"

Crouched like a threatened cat, Robin waited for Preston to make his decision. Would he take the step that made him as guilty of murder as his sister? She hoped he would say, "Joelle, we can't do this."

Instead he said, "Make sure you don't hit me."

She made a disgusted snort. "I'm not going to shoot you, Neil!"

Robin didn't hear anything for a few seconds, and the tension in her spine increased to an unbearable degree. How close was he? Which side would he come from? Could she overpower him somehow and get away?

And while you're fighting him, she'll walk up and shoot you in the back.

Finally the slightest brush of a shoe on the roof surface told her where Preston was. Breaking from cover she ran in the opposite direction. In her peripheral vision she glimpsed Joelle, standing with feet apart and arm raised, following Robin's path. When she fired, there was a *ping!* off to the right. Then a searing pain hit Robin's calf, and her leg buckled. Though she stumbled and fell to her knees, stopping was not an option. She rolled to her feet and hobbled behind the stairway shed, the closest cover.

Several metallic clicks told her Joelle was indeed out of bullets. Despite that bit of good news, Robin's left leg felt like it was on fire. She spared a second to look. The injury looked more like a burn than a bullet wound. Joelle's aim had been off, but so had Robin's luck. The bullet had ricocheted, and the resulting graze felt like a hot poker on her skin.

"Where is she?" Preston demanded.

"Behind the shed."

Robin stood, willing herself to ignore the pain. The corrugated metal walls of the shed, warmed by the morning sun, were almost too hot to touch. To her left was a sheer drop to the concrete courtyard. On the other side, probably only ten or fifteen feet away, were Joelle and Neil.

What now?

Preston joined Joelle, and she heard them whispering. Though shooting her was no longer an option, Neil had his sword. All they had to do was force her to the edge and push.

Exhausted and terrified, Robin would not give in to despair. There had to be a way, but she couldn't go around the shed. She could run away from them, but that would gain only a few more minutes of life. What she had to do was get them away from the stairway door so that she could get inside the shed.

She bit at her top lip. Since she couldn't go right, left, or back, she had to go over. If she climbed on top of the stairway shed, she could launch herself over their heads and hit the ground running. She guessed they both would chase her across the helipad, leaving the stairway unguarded. Once she'd led them far enough away, she'd turn and start a deadly game. Her frazzled mind conjured an image of the Prestons holding hands and chanting, "Red Rover, Red Rover. Let Robin come over!"

Her wounded leg would be a detriment, but neither Joelle nor Neil seemed the least bit athletic. Younger, faster, and more desperate than they, she would win the game or die trying. Before she could number the many ways her plan could fail, Robin put it into action. Bracing one foot on the half-wall, she grasped the roof gable and hoisted herself up.

"What was that?" Neil asked softly.

"Stay here," Joelle replied. "Do *not* let her get by you."

"What are you going to do?"

"I'm going to have a look."

Robin had reached the roof, and she tried not to look to her left at the expanse of nothing there. She also forced herself not to imagine the roof caving under her weight. With agonizing slowness, she brought her feet around to the other side. The metal was hot, and she winced each time her skin touched a new spot. Sucking air through gritted teeth, she moved to a point where she could peer down and see what the Prestons were up to.

Joelle was tiptoeing around the corner of the shed, and in a very short time, she'd see that Robin wasn't where they thought she was. Directly below she spotted Neil leaning around the corner, watching his sister's progress. It was the best chance she'd get. Setting her feet carefully, Robin braced herself for as long a jump as possible. She had to sail over Neil and hit the ground running, before he could turn and grab hold of her.

Rising to a crouch, Robin launched herself from the roof. She had a momentary glimpse of Neil's surprised face as he looked up and saw her. An instant later she heard Joelle screech, "Where is she?"

"Over here!"

"Well, get her!"

Neil hesitated just a second too long. By the time he overcame his reluctance, Robin had rolled to her feet and sped away.

"You idiot!" Joelle screamed. "She went right past you."

His reply was petulant, but Robin couldn't make out the words. She was too busy running.

"Stay to the right!" Joelle shouted. "I'll stay left."

It was hard for Robin not to glance over her shoulder. Judging by the grunts and panting, Neil obeyed his sister's command. She guessed they'd swing farther and farther apart in order to trap her between them when she ran out of roof. That point was close. Time to see if she was going to live or die.

In a move that sent stabs of pain through the singed soles of her feet and her injured leg, Robin stopped abruptly, turned a hundred-eighty degrees, and took off again. Joelle and Neil were far enough apart that she was able to run directly between them, and she glimpsed the surprised looks on their faces. Before either could stop their forward impetus and make the turn, Robin was racing toward the staircase they'd abandoned to pursue her.

She reached the shed, threw open the door, and tumbled through. Turning quickly, she shot the deadbolt, locking Neil and Joelle out. Seconds later two bodies crashed against the door. Joelle pounded at the metal for a few seconds before she turned on her brother. "Why didn't you guard the door, like I said?"

"You said to grab her. I tried—"

"I said, 'Don't let her get by you.'"

"We were fine until you started *killing* people!"

"You were being investigated by the goddam United States Congress, Neil! Is that doing 'fine' in your book? Those people were a threat. I had to do something!"

"You should have stuck to your shopping trips and boy-toys," he snarled. "You haven't got the skills to understand business, but I—"

"I know—you're a frigging *genius*!" Anger boiled beneath Joelle's every word. "If not for my actions, you'd be in jail by now."

"And look where your actions brought us!" A sharp *thunk!* on the door made Robin jump, and she realized he'd struck the door frame with the sword. "I've put up with you for far too long." His voice was bitter. "I should have tossed you out on the street and let you make your own way."

"*You* put up with *me*?" Now her voice rose to a shriek. "After the hours I spend listening to you brag on yourself, soothing your enormous ego?"

"That's it!" Preston shouted. "I'm done with you. You're going down for murder, you and Monica both. I'll claim I had no idea what you were doing, which is completely true."

Though Robin didn't see what happened next, for weeks afterward, images formed in her mind at night when she tried to sleep. In her anger, Joelle must have pushed Neil. He must have staggered backward, teetering and flailing for balance. Grasping for anything in reach, he'd found his sister's arm or shirt or hair—something. There must have been a moment when they both realized they couldn't maintain their footing. They must have looked into each other's eyes, disbelieving, as they went over the edge.

When the silence was too much to bear, Robin ventured out. The air over the roof wobbled with heat, but nothing else moved. Stepping cautiously to the roof edge, she looked over. Preston lay sprawled on the concrete walkway below. Joelle lay atop him. Both were completely still.

In the distance, three sheriff's cars pulled up at the gates of Green Grove. When she turned and saw Tom Wyman standing behind her, she was hardly surprised at all.

"Come on, Rob," Tom said softly. "We have to go."

"There are bad guys downstairs. And they took our car."

Tom smiled. "We found a private way to leave Green Grove, and there's a car waiting for us outside. I think you'll be surprised to see who's driving."

Chapter Thirty-Two

They moved to a new motel. Using the *Kidnap.org* website, Hua let Cam know where they were, and within an hour he showed up.

"Oliva did as he promised," Hua said when Cam arrived. "He let you call the police in."

Cam frowned. "I'm not sure he's a good guy though."

"What do you mean?"

"He had me hide in the trunk of his car when we left the estate." He turned to Hua. "You saw him pack one suitcase."

"I did."

"He put two bags in. He looked at me kinda funny, like he wondered if I noticed."

Robin hid a smile. Cam didn't always pay attention, but he was getting better. "What did you do?"

"I know it isn't nice to snoop, but I checked it out anyway. The bag was full of money."

"It was the half million meant for Ronda Talman," Robin said.

Hua shook his head. "So Oliva wasn't really helping us. He was only benefitting himself."

Tom chuckled dryly. "So much for reforming a con man."

Cam frowned. "Then maybe I did the right thing."

They waited a few seconds then Robin prompted, "What was that, Cam?"

"Well, I was kind of mad at him. He let me use his phone like he promised, but he wouldn't take me back so I could help you guys." Cam scrubbed a hand through his hair, making it stand up at the crown. "While I was in the trunk I switched things around. I put the money in Hua's gym bag, so Oliva has his car jack wrapped in Hua's extra t-shirt."

Hua hugged his partner. "Cam, you are awesome! Completely awesome!"

Cam looked pleased. "I didn't believe all that stuff he said about his bad childhood making him into a criminal. You had a worse time than him, and you don't steal people's money."

"Actually, I do," Hua corrected, "but only with the best of intentions."

Cam went to fetch Em, who called from a rest area after catching a ride with a friendly truck driver. While he was gone, Hua offered to return to their original motel to retrieve their belongings.

"I doubt anyone's watching," Robin said, "but be careful anyway."

"He could dress like a woman," Luca said. They'd almost forgotten her, sitting in a corner, looking confused but not disapproving. "In fact, we could go together. Nobody will pay any attention to a couple of women."

"Perfect!" Robin said. "Hua can take you home when you've finished." She gave Luca a hug. "We can't thank you enough for your help."

Luca gave her a look. "Sugar, I ain't even sure what I did."

"Look here," Hua ordered, and they crowded around to look at his phone. In case some couldn't see, he read the news bulletin aloud.

"In a tragic accident, CEO and owner of Argent Chemical Company Neil Preston died in a fall from the roof of his estate. His sister Joelle, who also fell in an apparent attempt to save her brother, is alive but listed in critical condition. Unconfirmed sources tell us that Preston had recently decided to release all of Argent's current patents to the public for the good of the nation. It is unclear whether his intention had been legally executed, but if so, prices for many medicines and assistive devices will lower dramatically over the next few months."

"They'll reverse it somehow," Robin said.

"Who will?" Tom asked. "If she lives, Joelle's going to jail, as is Monica Covel. Oliva is MIA, and if Em did her part, Baylor Nixon will back away from anything Argent-related."

"Then it will depend on who controls the estate."

"I'm sure Nixon is listed as executor."

"Em says she made it clear his retirement is required. We'll contact him one more time."

Tom chuckled. "You're going to make Nixon turn the job down."

"Yes. He can name another person to take his place."

"Who do we trust to handle the company and Preston's estate honestly?"

"How about Preston's loyal, efficient personal assistant, Amanda Cohee?"

***

Em returned to her friends and her new hotel room a little depressed. They hadn't meant for Neil Preston to die, and it hadn't been their fault, not really. But he was dead, and things they'd done had led to it. Em wasn't one to question Karma, and Preston was guilty of everything except actual murder. For sick people without affordable medicine, he was at the very least a factor in their suffering and eventual death.

Why did she feel so bad then? Why wouldn't her mind let it go? For once even Robin seemed less affected than Em, who kept circling back over their actions. They'd formed a plan. They'd executed it. The result was a man's death and a woman's horrible, crippling injury. It was reported that Joelle would never walk again. Who were they to say anyone deserved that?

She opened the door to her motel room with the magnetic key and entered, shoulders slumped and head hung low. That was why at first she saw only shoes. A man sat in a chair in the corner, and it took her a moment, even when her gaze reached his face, to realize who it was.

"Bennett?"

"Are you surprised, Emily?"

The question made her chuckle. "Shocked would be a better word."

"When we spoke last week, it sounded like you needed a friend."

A friend? In another life they'd have been lovers, but by the time they met, too much stood between them: The job. His disabled wife. His sense of duty. Her pride.

"How did you find me?"

He made a small gesture, just a flick of the fingers. "I still have some tricks at my disposal."

She thought of Hua, who so carefully covered their tracks and guarded their identities. He was probably no match for the FBI, if that august organization ever turned all its resources to finding them. Though Bennett had probably used the Bureau to hunt her down, Em didn't worry he'd betray them. He wasn't that kind of man.

That led to a new question. "Why?"

He smiled. "The things you left out interested me." He paused. "I assume you have it worked out?"

"Yes," she replied. "My part went well."

"But other parts didn't?"

She shook her head. "I can't discuss it, Bennett. There are others involved, and I can't violate the trust they've placed in me."

He nodded. "I understand."

"Did you come all the way from California just to see if I was okay?"

"Yes. Well, partly." His gaze met hers. "I also wondered if we might spend some time together." He seemed shy as he said it, a trait she'd never seen in him before. "We're old, Em, and we might not have much time left on this earth. I'd like to spend my remaining days with you."

Pharma Con

***

Devin Ashford woke once or twice before he really came to. He had a vague impression of hospital people looking at him, doing things to him, and talking about him. They seemed to agree he'd recover, but one remark penetrated his consciousness. "Somebody really did a number on this guy."

At first the "number" wouldn't come to memory, but as his mind began to function again, Ashford recalled the two men who'd hauled him from his car and beaten him like the experts they were. It took more time to remember where he'd been and what the circumstances were. He'd followed someone—Robin—to an estate. Nate, no, Neil Preston's place. He'd concealed his car in some trees. And then two goons had found him, accused him of things he didn't understand, and pounded him senseless.

That was as much as he could pull together.

The sound of footsteps made him open his eyes. A man stood at his bedside. It took a minute, but he pulled a name from his memory. "Belk?"

The gray-eyed man shook his head. "Belk is the guy who put you here."

"But—"

"I tried to save you a bunch of trouble, man, but you didn't listen."

"Who are you?"

"Let's just say I work for justice."

"Justice like the Justice Department?"

The man pulled out a badge wallet and put it close enough to Ashford's face for him to read: *John Clein, Federal Bureau of Investigation.* "Now listen, don't talk, and for damn sure don't ask questions. You're here because you couldn't leave a certain woman alone. You stuck your nose into her business, which complicated things for us in ways that could be considered obstruction."

"Robin works with you?"

"I'm telling you to leave it alone."

Ashford tried to put together what he knew for sure and what he could guess at. He'd apparently blundered into an FBI sting operation, and the G-men were unhappy with him. "Why are you here?"

The man's brow rose slightly. "It's a courtesy call, you might say. You're going to recover in a day or two and be released from the hospital. You'll find that your employer back in Georgia is in legal trouble again. This time he'll get a much longer prison sentence."

"Oh." There was a world of disappointment in that single syllable.

"If you go back to Cedar, you'll be mired in his problems. If you go back to Kansas, you'll be stepping on our toes. Here in Oklahoma, the police could have questions about your involvement in the events at Green Grove, at least they will if I pass the information on to them."

Ashford's gaze darted around the room. "I can help you guys. I can testify against Belk, and then go into Witness Protection—"

"We've got him for crimes a lot worse than whaling on you, so forget about moving to a farm in Minnesota." When Ashford had absorbed that, he went on. "You're a nosy snoop, Ashford, but you don't actually know anything about what happened on Monday."

"So what can I do to get out of this mess?"

Clein folded his arms, and for the first time Ashford noticed he had a prosthetic hand. How had he missed that before?

"You spent some time in South America," Clein said. "Have you still got contacts down there?"

"Well, yeah, but—"

"It might be a good idea to go back. We'll provide a ticket and enough cash to get you settled."

After a second he said, "How much are we talking?"

"Ten thousand."

"Twenty would be better."

That was dismissed with a shrug. "You can take your chances here in the States if that's what you want."

Ashford heaved a sigh that made his cracked ribs feel like they might burst through his chest wall. "If I get on a plane the Bureau leaves me alone?"

"Mr. Ashford, I will personally escort you to the airport and see you safely on your way."

***

Robin waited in the hallway outside Ashford's room. She'd filled the time by calling home to check in with Kai, who proclaimed things there were "Hokay, but a little bit boring. When you coming home?"

"On our way soon."

"Tom is all right?"

"Yes."

"And you?"

"I'm fine." She was wearing flip-flops because her feet were too tender for real shoes, but generally it was true.

"Em is hokay?" Kai's tone was odd, almost pleading. "Her hip is so bad."

It struck Robin that Kai, for all her cool exterior, was afraid. She'd lost so much: home, family and friends, and any sense of personal security. Robin, Tom, and the others were the replacement for what she'd lost. Tom, a knight in shining armor who'd rescued her. Robin, who provided for Kai and her sister. Em, who treated them like daughters. And Cam and Hua, like older brothers who showed them how to adapt to their new surroundings.

"Kai, we're all safe and sound. Honestly."

"Good, because if someone hurt you or Tom or anyone, I would kill them and make them sorry."

Note for list: try to help Kai get over wanting to kill people she doesn't like.

Looking up, she saw Tom coming toward her, a grin indicating he was pleased at the results of his meeting with Devin Ashford.

"I'll call you tonight," she told Kai. Pocketing the phone she asked, "Does that smile mean he went for it?"

"All the way."

As they exited the building together, her good mood dissipated. On the sidewalk she turned, her face a mask of regret. "I'm sorry, Tom. I could have got us all killed. If you hadn't pretended to be Belk and turned Devin in a different direction—"

"Robin."

"Don't try to tell me it's okay. I should have put on a blank look that first day in the grocery store and insisted he had the wrong person."

"He knew better."

"Maybe. But everything I said gave him a clue. When I said I was busy last week, he guessed we were on a caper. He knows what each one of us looks like. How can we ever feel safe again?"

Tom didn't attempt to allay that fear, because it was too real to ignore. "Maybe we'll get lucky and he'll go to jail in Argentina."

"He should. Following me to Tulsa proves he's a creep!"

He grinned at the vehemence of her words. "While I agree with your assessment, there's no law against lying to a woman you're attracted to or following her to Oklahoma."

"Right. But I'll never let my emotions get the better of my brain again."

"You're human, Robin. We all are."

She waved that away. "I missed my old life. Not all of it, but parts of it, you know?"

"I get that." After a pause he added, "It's hard to accept that no matter how much you'd like to, things will never go back to the way they were before."

She thought he spoke as much about himself as of her. War was something a person didn't simply forget, especially when he carried the reminders every day. "We'll just have to find things to enjoy in the present," she said, making her tone cheerful. "The past can't hurt if we leave it behind."

Tom said nothing, but she could almost hear his thought: *The past is never really behind you.*

***

Later in the day Devin Ashford had a second visitor, a Tulsa police detective. After introducing himself and showing his badge he said, "Mr. Ashford, your doctor reported your admission because he concluded your injuries are the result of a beating. Can you tell me what happened?"

Ashford was vague. "I'm not sure. I must have cut a guy off in traffic, because when I stopped at a light, two men came up to the car and dragged me out. They started screaming at me in some foreign language while they hit me and kicked me."

"They were foreign?"

"Arabs, I think. Probably terrorists."

The detective's face revealed faint irritation. People who lied about their injuries had once claimed "two black guys" accosted and beat them. These days it was "two Arabs." Either way, the detective saw through his story. *The guy got into something that ended badly: dating the wrong girl, angering the wrong prostitute, cheating the wrong drug dealer. He came out on the short end of the deal, but he isn't about to tell the truth to the cops.*

319

The detective took out a notebook and pen. "Describe the two attackers as best you can, Mr. Ashford. We'll see what we can find out."

Chapter Thirty-Three

Cam stowed the bags in the van, and he and Hua got into back. Robin offered to let Tom drive, but he said, "You take the first shift. Once we're out of Oklahoma, I'll spell you."

Em would ride with Bennett (*The person, not the dog*, Robin reminded herself) and once they got back to Kansas, Em planned to pack up her things and move with him to California.

"I'll visit," she'd said when breaking the news. "But not in wintertime."

For once it was Cam who found the right thing to say. "We'll miss you, Em. You're kinda like our mentor."

She shook her head as if to warn off any sentimentality. "I'll be a phone call away if you need me. You know that."

"We do," Robin said. She'd liked Bennett immediately, though he was a bit stiff: ramrod posture, steely eyes, and no-nonsense demeanor. But then, she recalled counting those same traits against Tom Wyman when they first met, and she'd been wrong. He was no martinet, and Bennett probably wasn't either, at least around those he cared about.

Bennett held the car door for Em and then went around to the driver's side. As he pulled out of the motel parking lot, Robin watched them go, aware that KIDNAP had just undergone a major shift. Em was gone, but she deserved the happiness Robin had seen in her eyes. She, Tom, Cam, and Hua would go on together. They'd be okay.

Still watching the retreating car, Robin caught a glimpse of a familiar figure coming toward them. She was hurrying as best she could with platform heels, a mini-skirt, and a bulging JC Penney shopping bag in each hand.

"Luca?"

"Hey." She was out of breath and a little embarrassed. "I was hoping y'all wasn't gone yet, 'cause I was wondering if you might have room for somebody like me in your gang." When they all stared at her, unable to think what to say, she said, "What? You can't use a girl that's ready to do whatever?"

Robin glanced at Tom, who was trying not to smile. Cam looked lost, but Hua nodded.

"Actually, Luca, I think we all agree you'd be perfect for our group. Hop in the back seat, and we'll tell you about it on the way."

Notes

Dear Reader,

If you enjoy my books, please write a review, tell a friend, or pass the book on to someone else who loves to read. It's the nicest thing a fan can do for an author, and we're grateful for the help.

Peg

ABOUT THE AUTHOR

Peg Herring reads, writes, and loves mysteries. As an educator she once set the school stage on fire. As a driver she's been so lost that she passed through the same town in Pennsylvania three times in one day. Family and friends have lost count of how many times she's locked herself out of her house. As the award-winning author of several mysteries series and standalone books, it's much safer if she sits in her office and writes, either as herself or as her younger, hipper alter ego, Maggie Pill.
Visit http://pegherring.com for Strong Women, Great Stories

Books by Peg Herring

The Simon & Elizabeth Mysteries *(Tudor Era Historical)*

Her Highness' First Murder
Poison, Your Grace
The Lady Flirts with Death
Her Majesty's Mischief
***

The Loser Mysteries *(Contemporary Mystery/Suspense)*

Killing Silence
Killing Memories
Killing Despair
***

Peg Herring is also Maggie Pill (although Maggie's much younger and cooler).

http://maggiepill.maggiepillmysteries.com

www.ingramcontent.com/pod-product-compliance
Lightning Source LLC
Chambersburg PA
CBHW051236260626
47162CB00002B/468